THE LAND OF T
VOLUME

C000227111

Flesh *and* Blood

Emyr Humphreys was born in the Welsh seaside resort of Prestatyn and educated at the University College of Wales, Aberystwyth, where he began to develop his lifelong interest in Welsh literature, language and politics. He has worked as a teacher in London, as a radio and television drama producer, and as a lecturer in drama at the University of Wales, Bangor.

A highly acclaimed novelist, Emyr Humphreys has won the Somerset Maugham Award and the Hawthornden Prize. He has published books of poetry, and his *Collected Poems* appeared in 1999. He is a productive and greatly respected television dramatist and has produced works of non-fiction in both English and Welsh, one of which, *The Taliesin Tradition*, won a Welsh Arts Council Prize.

THE LAND OF THE LIVING
VOLUME ONE

Flesh
and
Blood

EMYR HUMPHREYS

UNIVERSITY OF WALES PRESS • CARDIFF • 1999

British Library Cataloguing-in-Publication Data.
A catalogue record for this book is available from the British Library.

ISBN 0–7083–1512–7

First published in Great Britain by Hodder & Stoughton Ltd., 1974
Reprinted by Hodder & Stoughton Ltd., 1978
Second edition published by Sphere Books Ltd., 1986
Reprinted by Sphere Books Ltd., 1986, 1990

Published with the financial support of the Arts Council of Wales

Cover design by Olwen Fowler, The Beacon Studio

Typeset at University of Wales Press
Printed in Great Britain by Dinefwr Press, Llandybïe

I

Mair

The Land of the Living

Diffygiaswn pe na chredaswn weled daioni yr Arglwydd yn nhir y rhai byw. *

The seven volumes of this series observe a mainly chronological order. It reads as follows:

* Author's note:

This is the penultimate verse of Psalm 27: '*I had fainted* unless I had believed to see the goodness of the Lord in the land of the living.' It was the word '*diffygiaswn*' that attracted me, and I took it to mean that the poet would give up without the hope of a meaningful destiny for his people. I am aware that the word has been omitted in more recent translations: but it remains apposite to a sequence of stories drawn from the life of a society under siege.

The remaining titles in this series will be reprinted in 1999 and 2000.

Book One

1

SHADOWS OF SAPLINGS AND LANKY YOUNG TREES FLITTED OVER THE sunlit railway carriage as the squat engine laboured up the single line. The seats were not upholstered but the afternoon sun warmed the varnished wood and gave the interior dignity and spaciousness. The complete journey on this branch line which provided only one type of open carriage was scheduled to take thirty-five minutes. The passengers were not segregated into classes but the ceremonial sunlight fixed them in their seats as though they had always been intended for them. They were all neatly dressed. One bearded gentleman, seated in isolation, wore a silk hat and a smart frock-coat. His gloved hands rested on the silver knob of his walking stick. The authority of his stillness must have influenced the behaviour of the other passengers in the scattered places they occupied. His imposing presence and the bright exposure of light combined to make them all stiff and self-conscious: without any rules being issued or a single word spoken, all the passengers, as the train drew them along the narrow line, seemed intent on preserving a high standard of behaviour not only to satisfy each other or the important-looking stranger but most of all to comply with the image of themselves they desired the world around them to accept. When a small boy, sweatily encumbered by his thick best suit, broke out of the control of his anxious grandmother and stamped noisily down the whole length of the carriage, he could have been charging down the aisle in church.

He revelled openly in alarming his grandmother. He rocked his plump body and stamped his feet to show that he knew about her fear that too much movement would upset the delicate balance of their carriage on the narrow gauge. It was his special privilege to shatter the silence, to disrupt the accepted pattern, and he stretched his arms to inspect with a new-found approval the thick material of his Sunday suit. He was reconciled to wearing it on a week-day. The princely cut helped after all to draw attention to his agreeable appearance. He smiled at everybody with equal benevolence. His tongue hung out as he considered further moves to display his innate gifts for conspicuous daring and agility. His small fists closed

3

and he began to bang an imaginary drum, supplying a token sound from his own wet lips in between winning smiles.

A hard hand suddenly fastened on his shoulder. A man's pale clean-shaven face came close to his. A rasping whisper transformed the little boy's behaviour: he froze into sudden fear. Only his eyes moved in his head to look down and see the man's left leg thrust out in front of him and ending in a threatening shining surgical boot. Alongside the stern man sat a woman with a two-year-old girl asleep on her lap. The woman's eyes were still red and bloodshot after prolonged weeping. Her empty stare alarmed the little boy still further. He saw that the hands which supported the relaxed form of the sleeping child were hidden in thin black cotton gloves. Her good-looking regular features were prematurely worn. In spite of the warmth of the enclosed carriage she kept her gloves on to conceal the condition of her enlarged hands.

'You must not wake this little girl.'

The man's thin lips were stretched with the effort of whispering benevolently but nothing could soften the menacing rasp in his voice.

'She's lost her Mam. This little girl has buried her mother. So you don't want to wake her, do you?'

The little girl's dry teeth were sunk into the corner of a piece of white shawl which she had been sucking. Her golden curls were damp on her domed forehead. She clutched the fragment of shawl with both hands but her sleep seemed peaceful enough.

'Well now, sonny. That's your nain over there, isn't it?'

He leaned away to give the frightened boy an uninterrupted view of his grandmother. The weight of the old woman's black clothes appeared to make it impossible for her to move from her seat, but her small white hands were fluttering about like distressed birds in a cage.

'What is your name?'

'Frankie.'

Frankie stared hard at the gold medal that dangled importantly from the watch-chain drawn high across the man's chest.

'Well now, Frankie. Just walk back very softly to your nain. That's all I ask you to do.'

The boy began to walk obediently on tiptoe but as he moved all the bounce drained away from his sturdy legs. He tottered back to his corner like a boxer at the end of a punishing bout and there his grandmother used her voluminous skirts to pen him in. She mouthed a formula of silent gratitude to the pale-faced man whose features shone in her direction in an awkward pose that was maintained in anticipation of her gesture. He nodded with stiff grace and his sharp nose came round in a slow circle as he took in as much as he could of the other travellers before leaning back and adjusting the heavy boot that anchored his body to the peculiar position it occupied in the seat. Folding his arms, he shifted his head closer to his wife's so that she could hear what he wanted to mutter. The weight of the sleeping child made it difficult for her to move.

'That's Pulford,' he said.

Her cracked lips came apart as she emerged sufficiently from her daze of sorrow to take in his confident pronouncement.

'Edwin Pulford. You've heard me talk about Pulford.'

Dutifully she struggled to remember. She screwed up her sore eyes against the light.

'He sacked me. From Gwaith Marian. Just for speaking up. On behalf of the others. I told you about it. Don't you remember?'

Whether she remembered or not, she appeased him with a brief nod.

'I was on the night shift so I was able to go with the choir. To the New Brighton Eisteddfod. Not that it made any difference. We didn't win. When I got back the men had given in. Pulford said he'd have them back on the old rates so long as they promised not to join the Union. They were all back. Given in like a pack of cards. Two of us went to see him. About the Union business. He sacked us on the spot. Just like that.'

He snapped his fingers silently so as not to wake the little girl. He turned his head to glance quickly at the traveller in the silk hat in case, by some accoustic freak, he had heard his name being uttered. If he had heard, it had done nothing to disturb his statuesque stillness. He was staring at the different trees which grew out of the rocky slope with a haughty indifference that made

5

the pale-faced man paler still with suppressed resentment. He tightened his jaw to maintain control. The little girl began to stir uneasily in his wife's lap. It was essential not to wake her up. She would be so bewildered and distressed by her strange surroundings. She would burst out crying. She would howl. They would be held responsible. They would be seen in an unfavourable light. His wife eased herself into a more comfortable shape so that the sleeping child could lie in the softest contour her body could make. He disciplined himself to remain still and silent and satisfy himself by thinking about the past with a sardonic smile. Only when he was certain the child was safely asleep again did he allow himself to mutter further reflections.

'He knows perfectly well who I am.'

He wanted her to appreciate more fully the potential drama of the situation, but her attention was still concentrated on the well-being of the sleeping child.

'He sacked us by name. "I'm having them all back," he said, "except Lias Buckley and Lucas Parry."'

He pointed at his own chest as he spoke the last name and stared at his wife resentfully. If only she would listen a shade more attentively he would be able to evaluate the situation more shrewdly: even prepare himself with a sequence of effective phrases for the inevitable encounter.

'"They can all come back, *except* Lias Buckley and Lucas Parry."' He shook his head. The more he considered it, the more the recollected words appalled him. 'I'm not condemning the men,' he said. 'They betrayed us. They let us down, but I'm not condemning them. They all had families to support. Nearly all of them. Lias Buckley and I were young with no responsibilities. I told them what I thought of them at the time. But that was ten years ago. They were weak. Unreliable. Unfaithful. But I knew it was my business as a Christian to forgive them.'

He nudged his wife. She cushioned the child from the impact and smiled to show that she concurred fully with his sentiments. His own anxiety seemed assuaged by the phrases he had achieved. When he muttered again, 'He must know me. He knows perfectly well who I am,' it was in a much calmer tone. He was able to stare indulgently at the view and to extract his heavy watch from his waistcoat pocket and estimate the approximate time of their arrival like any other responsible traveller who had paid the appropriate fares and was entitled to expect prompt and efficient service. As he replaced the watch, however, he could not resist a half-turn of the upper part of his body to steal one more glance at the traveller in a silk hat.

'Oh it's Pulford all right. Beard a bit different. Flecked with the snow of time. But I'd recognise him anywhere.'

The train steamed under the long shadow of the superstructure where noisy machinery crushed the limestone from the open quarry on the mountainside. Lucas Parry closed his lips tightly and his wife, Esther, bent over the little girl on her lap as if to protect her as much as possible from the noise around them. She relaxed gratefully when the train had puffed on to arrive at the comparative quiet of a terminus almost surrounded by large comforting trees. The neat stone buildings were fringed with carefully tended flower-beds and even the warehouse looked rural. Beyond the white ticket-barrier there was a large open space where waggons and other vehicles could turn easily before carrying goods or passengers to their ultimate destination.

'Well we'll see, won't we?' Lucas Parry seemed to be muttering nervously to himself. 'In the sight of the Lord, I'm as good a man as he is. That's what we have to remember. Be firm. Be courteous. Be prepared.'

He pulled down the luggage as he spoke, his voice drowned by the squeal of the wheels as the train ground to a final halt. Esther became intent on an attempt to descend from the carriage without disturbing the little girl in her arms. On the platform the old lady in black again lost control of her grandson. This time Lucas Parry was too preoccupied with arranging his baggage to be of any help to her. In any case he was hampered by his heavy boot. The small boy snatched his hand easily out of her weak grip and pulled off his sailor cap to wave it in the air and race, whooping, towards the shandry which had been sent to meet them. Esther Parry waited at the barrier for her husband to extract their tickets from the depth of his waistcoat pocket. His penetrating voice took on a note of irritation.

7

'You'll have to put her down,' he said. 'You can't carry her up the hill to begin with. She's not a babe in arms.'

Esther kept her voice very low.

'I would like her to wake up in her own time,' she said. 'In the peace of the countryside. You know what I mean, Lucas.'

'It's two and a half miles,' he said. 'You'll have to put her down sooner or later.'

Outside the station the traveller in a silk hat was already seated in an open carriage. The black horse in the shafts was beautifully groomed. The polished harness glittered in the afternoon sunlight. The traveller had unbent sufficiently to talk in a relaxed and jovial fashion to his coachman who was beaming patiently under his walrus moustache. Esther passed the carriage with her head bowed still carrying the child. She was leaning forward protectively, but moving at such a speed she could have been abducting a child by stealth and even hoping to pass out of sight unnoticed. She was followed by her husband encumbered with a large suitcase, a basket tied up with rope and two brown-paper parcels. His burdens accentuated his limp and his whole person tilted from one side to the other with each step he took.

When the carriage overtook Esther on the hill, the traveller seemed to be enjoying the drive already. Nevertheless he asked the smiling coachman to stop.

'It's a steep hill.'

He spoke pleasantly enough in English, looking down at Esther from his comfortable seat.

'Where are you bound for? Can I offer you a help on the way? Would you like a lift?'

Esther smiled hesitantly: a smile intended to show that she understood and that she was grateful for a gracious offer. But the backward glance she took betrayed that she would not presume to speak until her limping and encumbered husband had drawn near enough to accept or reject the offer. The child whimpered peevishly in her sleep and Esther lifted her higher so that the small head slumped on her right shoulder.

'Is the little girl not well?'

Seated alone in the handsome open carriage, the manners of the large elegant man were as smooth as his silk hat. Esther frowned. She was confused. She seemed to be struggling to recall the details of the unfavourable comments her husband had made about this stranger, who was lifting his hat now to mop his brow and his balding regal head with a large cream-coloured handkerchief. He was waiting, smiling patiently, for an answer to his question.

'Her mother was my sister.'

A piece of common knowledge there could be no possible reason for not uttering in his language. She put out the statement quietly enough. He was interested and openly benevolent.

'We buried her yesterday in Llanbeblig churchyard.'

He held on silently to his silk hat and he appeared to be saluting her simple courage and dignity in misfortune. He bowed his head gravely to Lucas Parry who had now reached the side of his wife and was looking up, panting slightly and eager to be recognised.

'How very sad about this little girl.'

The gentleman shook his head sympathetically and then replaced his silk hat. Lucas Parry placed a heavy hand on the back of the sleeping child.

'She has no idea,' he said. 'She does not feel it. She is already in the protective arms of a second mother.'

The coachman and the gentleman were giving him close attention. Lucas Parry was taking a convenient occasion to publish certain facts and to state their intentions.

'Esther and Grace were twin sisters. Such is the working of Providence. I have no doubt at all that this little thing has been delivered unto us as our responsibility. And we are taking it on with willing hearts.'

The coachman pressed in his chin to show his approval.

'What is the little girl's name?'

Lucas seemed to take the gentle tone of the gentleman's enquiry as an instant tribute to the moral authority of his position.

'It was Amy Price,' he said. 'But from henceforth it will be Amy Parry.'

'Let me offer you a lift. I don't know how far you are going but we'd be very pleased to take you as far as the West Lodge.'

The coachman was smiling again behind his straggling

9

moustache to show further approval. Esther was looking hopeful but her husband had raised his hand like a policeman stopping traffic.

'We shall not be needing a lift. Thank you.'

He spoke so loudly, little Amy stirred in Esther's arms. She opened her eyes sleepily and whimpered.

'We have a way of our own.' Lucas waved his hand and sounded almost lordly. 'A narrow path. Very beautiful and leafy. But too narrow and inaccessible for this vehicle, I fear.'

'As you wish.'

The gentleman leaned back in his comfortable leather seat. He seemed put off by the bold rasp in Lucas Parry's voice. He had made his benevolent gesture and he was under no obligation to press his invitation. The coachman flicked his whip and allowed the black horse to resume his patient ascent of the hill. Amy began to stir fretfully in her aunt's arms. Esther frowned hard as she tried to make out what the child needed.

'He knew perfectly well who I was.'

Lucas squared his shoulders resolutely. He watched the open carriage climbing the hill as though it was bearing away an unworthy adversary who had declined to take up his challenge. Esther imagined she had discovered what was causing Amy to moan and whimper. With one hand she felt for the fragment of white shawl in the open bag that hung on her arm. She offered the corner in the direction of the little girl's mouth.

'Put her down Esther, for goodness' sake. She's got to learn to use her own two legs you know. You won't be able to carry her all the way through life. You may as well face that.'

Gently Esther set the little girl down on the road. Amy's face began to crumple up. Her mouth grew slack and she let the piece of shawl fall on to the dusty surface of the metalled road. Esther snatched it up quickly, anxious to keep it clean: a talisman that had to be preserved in order to protect her from unknown hazards and extremities. Amy wouldn't move. She clutched the material of her aunt's skirt like the victim of a shipwreck. Lucas made an effort to be patient and Esther touched the back of his hand briefly so that he could look at her and see that she was grateful to him.

'There's time enough to teach her,' he said. 'All the time in the world.'

He resolved not to mind how slowly they moved. The afternoon was pleasantly warm. Amy responded well to their leisurely pace. She was attracted to a neat heap of dried horse dung in the middle of the road. Esther snatched at campion and stitchwort growing in the damp banks under the untrimmed hedge. Amy sat down by the dung. Lucas was prepared to stand and watch her with patriarchal benevolence.

'It was a cold job,' he said.

Esther bent down and tried to attract Amy's attention by making patterns of the wild flower blooms against the thin black glove on her hand.

'Digging out the white stuff. Cold but not dangerous. You can do it on your knees or lying on your side. Everyone said he was a first-class mining engineer. Maybe he was. I wasn't there long enough to notice.'

Amy's interest was diverted. She took possession of the flowers. Esther picked her up by the armpits and swung her from side to side as she stepped carefully across the wide patch of wet mud across the opening to the leafy lane. Amy clutched her campion and stitchwort. Esther set her down and crossed the mud to give her husband a helping hand with his load.

'I'd be all right for doing it now.'

'Doing what, Lucas?'

'Working on my knees and on my side. Digging out the white stuff.'

'Don't you be silly,' Esther rebuked him fondly. 'You're well out of it. Mines indeed. They're not healthy. You want time to study now, Lucas. That's the important thing.'

The little girl could wander ahead safely now. Great beams of sunlight filtered between the beech trees. She was absorbed by the new green world she was being allowed to explore. From the slope above them came the smell of wild garlic. Esther took the heavy suitcase and Lucas limped behind her with the rest of the baggage.

'I think it was Williams Treffynnon who said it. "A man with a good woman behind him is worth a troop of men on their own."'

11

The compliment made Esther blush. Amy was taking a close interest in the closed petals of a patch of pimpernel. There was a small stream to cross by stepping-stones. The stones stood out white and dry above the lazy midsummer trickle of water.

'I'm glad you are a man of principle, Lucas. I really am.'

'Well I try to be. Let's put it like that.' He smiled and his broken discoloured teeth came into full view.

'And the way you've taken on this little girl. Grace's little girl. I'll never forget it.' Her large sad eyes began to fill with tears.

'We'll do our best for her.'

He spoke briskly like a man determined to control his emotions.

'Bring her up in the fear of the Lord. As a child should be brought up. The best possible upbringing. "The fear of the Lord is the beginning of wisdom." '

'It won't interfere with your studies, Lucas. I promise that.'

Lucas was looking down benevolently at the child playing on the ground.

'I'll build her a doll's house,' he said. 'Nothing elaborate. But something she can call her own. I'll try and do that.'

He knew that she was looking at him with undisguised admiration, her sad eyes set deep in her pale handsome face.

'We'll do our best for her. I think the Lord has given her to us as a special blessing.'

Tears began to flow silently down Esther's cheeks.

'Now come on,' he said. 'We can't dawdle about in the woods all day. Come on. Come on.'

With a fresh access of energy, Lucas picked up all the pieces of luggage and forged ahead. He looked more encumbered than a one-man-band but he wanted to show his wife that all the extra effort cost him nothing. He burst out singing in his sharp powerful tenor voice. Amy looked up into the trees to see where the noise was coming from. The tune was Luther's hymn. Esther bent down to pick up the little child. She hurried after her husband, singing herself, rather breathlessly. Amy was delighted with all the sound and the movement. She gurgled happily in Esther's arms looking down at the ground as it rose and fell below her and kicking her strong little legs against Esther's stomach. She waved her arms about when she saw startled rabbits exposed on the path rushing off for cover into damp undergrowth that was not their normal habitat.

Lucas had arrived at a wooden stile. He sat on the top bar to take a brief rest. His arms were folded and he looked reflective. Amy was wriggling in Esther's arms wanting to be set down again.

'You don't forget a thing like that in a hurry.' His voice was solemn.

'What, Lucas?'

Amy wanted to crawl off the path among the elephantine leaves attracted by bright yellow blooms of the marsh marigolds. Esther picked Amy up and set her down at Lucas's feet.

' "You're a trouble-maker, Parry!" That's what he said.'

He looked down at Amy who had trotted forward to finger the shining toe-cap of his surgical boot. He tried to reach down and pat her on the head.

'She's a bright little button.'

Esther nodded happily. She was eager that her husband should begin to develop an affection for the child.

'I think she's taken to you, Lucas. I really do.'

'She's intelligent,' Lucas said. 'It's easy to see that.'

'I think she'll be easy.' Esther searched for the best words to draw attention to the merits of the child. 'She's got a sweet disposition.'

Esther knelt down so that Amy could press into the soft protection of her body. She brushed her lips against the little girl's round cheek and looked up at her husband sitting on the stile. Her eyes were wide and bright. She spoke softly.

'What shall we teach her to call us, Lucas?'

He listened with judicial impartiality to the note of supplication. A horse-fly settled on the back of his right hand. The sting made him look down. Deliberately he raised his other hand and brought it down to crush the offending fly. He flicked the corpse away with the side of a finger.

'Amy Parry,' he said. 'We decided that. Not Amy Price. So that we should not be reminded daily of Hefin Price. Of the man who deserted Grace. We decided that, didn't we?'

Lucas stared at the child intently. Amy turned her head and buried her face in Esther's breast.

13

'Life does not contain a more important problem.'

'What do you mean, Lucas? I don't follow you.'

The woman's arm tightened lovingly around the little body. Lucas was too lost in meditative thought to answer her question.

'What she calls us, do you mean?'

Esther was still hopeful of a simple answer.

'God's grace fills up and transforms the fallen man. Does it work in the blood or does it work in the breath?' He stared eagerly at his wife.

'Is she her father's daughter because of her father's blood? Or will she be ours because of our bringing her up? Nature or nurture. It's a delicate matter.'

'It's bringing up of course. I'm sure of that.'

Her sudden understanding and instant confidence amazed him.

'What shall she call us?'

'Should it ever be anything more or less than the truth?'

She saw his mind was made up and she lowered her head as she listened to the reasons.

'Uncle and aunt is what we are in fact. And in law if it comes to that. She's not my flesh and blood. And she's not yours. Think. Among other children. How unpleasant it would be for her to find out from others that we are not her real father and mother.'

Esther kept her head down to hide her face as she listened to him talking.

'And he could return. I'm not saying he will or ever would. But he might. If it were only to claim his gold watch. You can never tell with a man like that. He wouldn't be afraid of causing trouble. Or of hurting people's feelings.'

Esther raised her head. She seemed to be comparing the reliable figure of her own husband, sitting on the stile and resting his weak leg, with the man who deserted her dying sister.

'He went away to sing with the Carl Rosa. That was his excuse. He may be in America. But he could come back. So let us take refuge in the truth.'

Esther frowned as she tried to follow his argument. She looked eager to be convinced. Amy began to whine and mutter into her blouse.

14

'Hush, little Amy.' Esther spoke very softly. 'Hush now. Your uncle is talking.'

Lucas nodded approvingly. It was what he wanted to be called. By gravity Amy sank out of Esther's embrace to squat on the ground. She saw a snail lurking in the dark damp earth under the stile. She lowered her head to the ground so that she could observe it more closely. Above her the warmth of understanding communication between her aunt and uncle stretched like a protective canopy.

' "It's my ambition to be a preacher, Mr Pulford," I said. "And preachers are not trouble-makers. Preachers bring peace. Not trouble." '

'Did you put it like that, Lucas?'

'Indeed I did. It cost me something. I was so young you see. I didn't want to speak at all. The men asked me to. I knew I was risking it. It's easy to get a bad name.'

'Of course it is.' Esther spoke fervently.

'I think he must have recognised me.'

'Of course he did.'

'Time doesn't wipe away everything. That's why he wanted to help us on our way. It was his conscience you see. His conscience stirred when he saw me.'

'Of course it did.'

They smiled at each other. Conscience was a force in the universe that was on their side. Lucas shrugged his shoulders inside his jacket as if to show a weight had been lifted from them.

2

'IT WAS A GREAT WATCH-TOWER. IN ITS TIME!'

Lucas Parry had achieved the highest possible standing position on the ruined tower. He looked down to call out enthusiastically to his companion. For safety he wedged his heavy boot into a weathered hole in the massive wall. His jacket was open and it fluttered in the breeze as he pointed north-east. Below him the new minister held on to his black hat and peered over the edge of the ivy-covered parapet to observe whatever Lucas chose to show him. He was a dark young man who needed to shave twice a day to preserve his smart appearance. His small mouth appeared fixed in an enigmatic smile and his eyes were restless with the predatory nervousness of a magpie. He was wearing a new suit complete with black spats and he was concerned to keep it all spotless and undamaged. He tired of holding on to his hat and took it off. The breeze snatched at his luxurious black hair and, because his hairline was receding prematurely, for a moment it looked like a wig that would lift off and blow away. Above their heads, young gulls in their first year of plumage floated easily on currents of air, testing the shape of the warm wind before making the flight from the top of the hill to the open sea.

'Liverpool is over there!' Lucas pointed dramatically: but the pale outline of land and the horizon were washed together in a vague anonymous September haze. 'To think of me landing there at sixteen years of age without hardly a word of English.'

Lucas was so overwhelmed with the fresh recollection of his predicament that he failed to notice the young minister's pitying smile.

'They spoke too quick, you see, and it didn't sound a bit like the English of Davies the School. I don't know where I would have been but for the chapel, I can tell you that much. I would have been lost. Physically as well as spiritually. I learnt the first and the last lesson in Liverpool. There's no hope for a Welshman in this world without his chapel.'

He stared at the young minister until he had been awarded a perfunctory nod.

'And that was where I met your brother, poor Lias. In Trinity Road. We were like David and Jonathan. I can remember us standing on the street corner by the Exchange in the middle of the uncivilised Irish, begging for work. We worked side by side for three months in the cotton. And then in a foundry right behind Hudson's Dry Soap. The smell was awful. It used to make your brother Lias sick. And the Irishmen were like savages. Talk about the dregs of humanity, Mr Buckley. I'll never forget it. Is it too draughty for you up here?'

16

'It's not warm, is it?'

'I've been rambling on . . .'

Descending in apologetic haste, Lucas slipped on some loose rubble. He saved himself by grabbing at an ivy bush but his heavy boot pushed small stones and loose mortar over Mr Buckley's new clothes. The young minister was unable to suppress a howl of anguish. Lucas offered to brush off the dirt. Mr Buckley looked at the large outstretched hands and shook his head.

'It's all right,' he said agitatedly. 'There's no harm done.'

'Esther will take care of it.'

Buckley waved him on and Lucas stumped cautiously down the stone stairway, his left hand pressing against the wall.

'Never seen anyone like her for taking care of clothes. Fanatically clean. That's what I'd call her. Always has been. Doesn't spare herself. And she knows her Bible. She's had a hard life you know. Many afflictions. But she has borne them all with a courage founded in deep faith. And more than a mother to that little child.'

They moved down the southern slope of the hill towards a surface of greensward where Amy was playing by herself. The little girl was intent on creating the outline of a little house with the white stones she carried from an exposed ridge of crumbling limestone. She was lost in her private domesticity and did not notice the two men approaching. She had a rag doll which she spoke to as she moved it about from time to time from one room to the other. Lucas pointed with pride at a basket that lay on the closely cropped grass beyond where Amy was playing. The basket was filled with a heap of rich blackberries.

'The poor man's vineyard,' Lucas said. 'Look at her working. Just look at her.'

Esther Parry had penetrated a great mass of brambles beyond an unsightly patch of burnt gorse. Her battered straw hat bobbed up and down as she trampled on more stems and branches to get closer to black clusters that glittered temptingly in the sunlight, out of her reach. She had a crooked stick which she used adroitly to bring the branches closer so that she could pick them rapidly with her purple-stained fingers.

'We love this spot. It's like a great garden you know in its own

17

strange way. Never cultivated since time began I should think. Still in its own riotous way a perfect garden. That's what I always think.'

He had found somewhere to sit where he could observe his family and talk to the young minister. It was warm and sheltered. He pulled away creeping bramble stems and showed the minister where he could sit on the warm rock without damaging his clothes. When the minister sat down he studied the world Lucas wanted him to appreciate a little apprehensively. Varieties of moss, wild thyme and wild strawberries grew in the fissures of the weather-eroded rock. Wherever there was soil there were domed ant-heaps. Lucas poked his finger in a crack of the rock to show him where small herbs grew. There seemed to be spiders everywhere. They worked their webs over the dwarf ferns. Not far away an untidy copse of hazel and thorn displayed small green nuts and red berries tangled together.

'Herbs,' Lucas was saying. 'And food!' He sounded triumphant with moral certainty. 'For animals and men. And we know all about them. Even fern tips for the pig barrel.' He smiled and made generous gestures with his arms. 'The fruits of the earth that the Lord has provided for his poor people to enjoy. The free man's harvest. That's what I call it. It's easy for mountain men to believe, Mr Buckley. To believe and to be free. I'm not a poet and I never will be. But I feel these things. If you are free and if you believe, then you belong to the Chosen People. That's what I think.'

The young man cleared his throat cautiously.

'We mustn't think too highly of ourselves.'

Lucas leaned away to look at the young man and show his open appreciation of his wisdom.

'You are just like your brother. That could have been Lias talking. Exactly the same.'

He marvelled at the significant resemblance.

'Did you ever hear him pray?'

'I might have done.' The young minister spoke judiciously. 'He left home when I was six. He was twelve years older than I. That's a big difference. I wouldn't remember if I had.'

'I owe him a deep debt. I was a rough lad. He showed me the way. We were very close, you know. I was with him the night he started spitting blood.'

18

The minister winced. Lucas pushed his heavy boot against the green side of a soft anthill. It lifted slowly like a lid over a dark private world of disorientated insects scattering in sudden panic.

'We were in the same bed. He used to have nightmares. He would sit bolt upright in bed with his eyes wide open and the sweat pouring off him. I never realised how ill he was, poor fellow.'

They observed a respectful silence in memory of Mr Buckley's brother. A grasshopper clicked away not far from their feet. The warm wind carried Amy's childish voice in their direction. She was reproving her doll sternly for some imagined misdemeanour.

'I tell you how I see the world when I come up the Foel, Mr Buckley. You may think this is childish. I see the world as a great cradle. And this good air about us like God's loving breath as he leans over the cradle to look at us.'

Mr Buckley's face was shadowed with fastidious but unvoiced objections. Lucas Parry shut his eyes and lifted his face to the sun.

'It is as clear to me as the rays of the living sun, brother. I breathe in the love of God. God's breath. I have the Spirit inside me. The Spirit tells me that my Saviour has bought my worthless life with his Precious Blood. I want to spend all my waking hours spreading the Good News. And yet my denomination doesn't want my services.'

The sudden change of tone failed to take the minister by surprise.

'That's not completely fair, Mr Parry.'

'I'm too old they say. And yet I have seen men my age passed quickly through the mill and into the ministry. They can do it when they like, Mr Buckley. I know that for a fact.'

'Let's try and be fair . . .'

The young minister pressed his pale hands together judiciously. In turn Lucas pressed his lips together in a visible effort to impose a disciplined humility upon himself. He inclined his left ear delicately towards his companion to show that he would hold it there to pick up the slightest signals of criticism and examine them in his own mind with rigid objectivity.

'Education is vital in the modern world. A minister can't go out into the modern world unless he is properly armed with the weapons of education.'

Lucas bowed his head. He looked doubtful and yet unable to muster an effective counter-argument.

'We've got to accept this I'm afraid. Whether we like it or not.'

Mr Buckley crossed his legs carefully and leaned forward in the manner of a college tutor conducting a tutorial in the open air.

'Let's look at the problem from the point of view of the Connexion. Look at the theological colleges. Every single one of them. They are full to overflowing. Now what else can the authorities do except make the entrance exams stiffer? They have no alternative. And the same applies to the District Meeting. If there is a wide choice of candidates the chairman must cross-examine relentlessly. I'm not saying the system is perfect. But it works. Let's put it no higher than that.'

Lucas stretched out his jaw. 'You don't think I'm jealous?' The minister laughed at the manifest absurdity of the idea. 'Good heavens, no.'

Lucas was staring at Mr Buckley's new suit as if it were visible evidence of the advantages which he and Lias Buckley had never been allowed to enjoy.

'You've been through it all,' Lucas said. 'Matriculation. The Oral Exam. The Synod. The July Examinations. And you've got a university degree.'

Mr Buckley smiled modestly.

'We were born too soon, Lias and I.' There was dark conviction in Lucas Parry's voice. 'The paths of learning were not open to us. Your brother used to feel it you know. Especially towards the end. But he never grew bitter. The seeds of prayer were in his breast. He was wonderful on his knees. There was nobody to touch him in the whole Circuit. Nobody under forty anyway, I'm quite sure of that.'

'I'm not sure that that is the way we should look at prayer.'

Mr Buckley made the rebuke as lightly as he could. He adjusted the distance between his stiff shirt cuffs and the sleeves of his jacket.

'He put everything he had into it.' Lucas was determined to defend the reputation of his dead friend.

'Oh I'm not denying that for one moment,' Mr Buckley said. 'In any case I'm not in a position to do so. My point was that praying is not to be thought of in terms of competition.'

20

Lucas looked genuinely puzzled. 'I don't follow,' he said. 'In examinations you have first and second and so on. Someone always comes out on top.'

Mr Buckley smiled pityingly. 'Ah yes,' he said. 'But that's rather different.'

'In what way? I don't see it can be all that different. Examinations they use to keep people like me out. We are not good enough. Not had enough education . . . That's what they say. But I can tell you this. I knew chunks of John Wesley's sermon on Justification of Faith off by heart. And he didn't ask me a thing about it.'

'Forgive me if I speak frankly . . .'

Lucas stared fascinatedly at the white hand the minister had held out.

'You are a lay-preacher.'

'On probation,' Lucas said. 'On approval.'

The humiliating reservations stuck in his throat, but he was determined to utter them.

'A man my age. And promising young boys are given every support. Moved on. Moved up. Taken under the Superintendent's wing. And I am kept down. I am kept back. I ask myself why. Can you blame me?'

'We must be fair . . .'

Lucas had made his protest. Once more he inclined his ear to listen in patient humility to the young man's honeyed tones and practised exposition.

'Lay-preachers are the backbone of our system. The Connexion has always held them in the highest regard. And quite rightly so. These selfless men put themselves at the service of the Superintendent and the Circuit and render their full and unfettered service to the Plan. And all this unpaid. It is in many ways the chief glory of our system. But it requires a very special calibre of Christian manhood . . .'

'And I'm not suitable.' Lucas could not prevent himself making a blunt interruption in his rasping voice.

'You've moved about, Mr Parry. It's not always helpful.'

Lucas grinned unexpectedly. The minister had not seen any joke. Lucas had to explain.

21

'Funny to hear a Wesleyan minister disapproving of moving about.'

Mr Buckley was not especially amused. 'Your spiritual pilgrimage has been a little erratic, Mr Parry.'

'What do you mean by that?' Lucas was back on the defensive.

'You have been a member of a Calvinistic Methodist church for example . . .'

'My wife's chapel!' Lucas protested vigorously. 'From respect for her and for her family. Good gracious, I hope the Connexion would never hold that against me . . .'

'Far from it,' Mr Buckley said firmly. 'I am only trying to indicate what I mean by moving about. In the nature of things it can't be helpful.'

'Coke-Hughes was against me.' Lucas could not prevent himself becoming agitated. 'And I can tell you exactly why. It's to do with my disability.' He pointed at his surgical boot. 'It was my first boot after my accident in the quarry. It never fitted properly. It used to squeak with every move I made. But I was determined not to miss my chapel service. And as it happened I took the collection without thinking about the boot. The squeaking was awful. And some of the children started to giggle. He was furious. He said I destroyed the devotional atmosphere.'

'I can't believe that the Reverend Coke-Hughes . . .' Mr Buckley hesitated in order to shape what he had to say into a considered, tactful and elegant judgement.

'I wouldn't have believed it myself,' Lucas Parry said. 'But he was staying with us in chapel house. He asked to have his supper in his room.'

'Well, obviously . . .' Mr Buckley spread out his hands palm upwards as though he were displaying a wide variety of reasonable explanations.

'And it was damp you see. The wallpaper was tumbling off the wall next to the chapel. And he blamed us for not keeping the chapel house in good condition. I told him damp had always been a problem in Siloam. But he didn't take any notice. He said the paraffin lamps were smelling in the chapel. And I said, "Look Mr Coke-Hughes, it takes me nearly all day Friday to clean and fill the lamps and trim the wicks et cetera." And do you know what he said to me? He said, "You ought to do it twice a week." '

Lucas paused to give Mr Buckley an opportunity to appreciate to the full the Superintendent's harsh and unsympathetic attitude.

'I was obliged to defend myself,' Lucas said. 'To defend my reputation as a conscientious workman. I was obliged to. And do you know what he said to me?'

He waited as if it was necessary for Mr Buckley to brace his imagination in order to absorb the shocking impact of his next astonishing revelation.

' "You are restless with Socialism, Parry!" That's what he said. To tell the truth I was bowled over by the injustice of the accusation. And if there's one thing that upsets me, it's injustice. "Look, Mr Coke-Hughes," I said, "I'm a working man and I've never pretended to be anything else. I owe you respect and I hope I have always shown it, but you cannot accuse me of socialistic tendencies. I've given addresses to week-night classes on the four perils of socialistic thought and I can give you my headings now," I said.'

Lucas counted on his fingers to give dramatic emphasis to what he was saying.

'The four dangers of Socialism. One. An attempt to make a party of the working people and turn them against the better-off on the basis of envy and greed. Two. To make monetary reward, hard cash, the only condition of self-improvement and elevation of character. Three. To dwell on the suffering of society instead of its sinfulness. Fourthly and lastly, but most importantly, the perpetual elevation of the Rights of Man and the increasingly shameful neglect of the Rights of God!'

Mr Buckley had raised his eyebrows and was showing signs of qualified appreciation.

'I had it at my fingertips,' Lucas said. 'One, two, three, four. Just like that. I don't want to sound immodest, but it's one of my best addresses. I've given it in a lot of week-night meetings.' A cloud of gloom settled back on his pale face. 'But I'm afraid it did me more harm than good,' he said. 'I never had any support for my candidature from Mr Coke-Hughes, as long as he was here. None.'

'Tact,' Mr Buckley said carefully. 'Tact is very important.'

'To be absolutely honest with you – and I'm talking now to the brother of my best friend rather than my minister – I was very glad when his term of office came to an end. He's a hard man is Mr Coke-Hughes.'

'Yes. But let's be fair. A just man.'

'A just man and a hard man.'

As a token of appreciation for the minister's show of understanding Lucas made the concession. Amy was calling. Abruptly she had lost interest in her imaginary house. Her arms hung helplessly at her sides as she called out in desperation.

'Wees! I want to wees.'

The minister looked away as if to indicate it was absolutely no affair of his. Amy's cry became more urgent.

'Esther!'

Lucas cupped his hands around his mouth so that the breeze would not snatch away the cutting edge of his voice.

'Esther!'

She turned at once, able to hear him from the depth of the bramble bush as she had not been able to hear Amy's cries. Lucas stood up and waved his message with his arms.

'The child! Attend to the needs of the child!'

With some difficulty Esther extricated herself from her advanced position inside the brambles. She ignored the pricks of the thorns and the stems which clung to her skirts and the hessian apron she was wearing. She dropped her stick and put down the basket of blackberries with more care before she ran up the hill to where Amy stood waiting for attention.

3

IT WAS HOT INSIDE THE CHAPEL. THE PEWS WERE OCCUPIED BY WHOLE families who had come to chapel prepared to face bad weather. Their clothing would protect them on the journey home. The wind had been rising all through the evening service. Impetuous gusts raced around the stout square walls searching for a gap in the defences. But Siloam was built solidly of stone quarried from the same hillside on which it stood. In spite of its exposed position above the road which led down to the sheltered centre of the village, the chapel was nailed safely to the hillside. The congregation sat drowsy with comfort and security. At the back of the chapel, in its own corner, an old iron stove maintained its distant roar and its chimney threatened to turn from black to dull red. Iron railings three foot high surrounded the stove so that the heat machine rumbled as harmlessly as a savage animal inside a cage. The tall chapel windows were decently draped in drawn blinds of a faded green colour, but not the decorative circles of glass above them. These, like portholes in a diving bell, gave an awesome glimpse of the black hostile night. But they were so high up it was easy to ignore them.

Inside the warmth of the chapel the well-trimmed lamps burned steadily, refusing to flare or flicker, and the smell of paraffin was so reassuring it took on something of the power of incense. In the pulpit Mr Buckley was immaculately dressed. He could have been a perfect model for an ecclesiastical tailor who also catered for non-conformist ministers. His voice was not as effective as his appearance and from time to time he had to clear his throat. But the whole congregation was on his side and sympathised with him in his struggle against the opposition of the elements.

Amy sat close to her aunt in a short pew. Her eyes were closed and she was perfectly behaved. Nothing more was required of her. But above her head, the clatter of a loose ventilator lid was giving her aunt cause for anxiety. The noise had no effect on Amy, but it was distracting the minister. Esther closed her eyes prayerfully but the wind refused to die down. The piece of clapping iron was part of her responsibility as caretaker of the chapel. When the minister looked at the ventilator, she blushed and went hot and cold inside her neat grey coat. She was known as a woman who took trouble never to draw attention to herself. She looked appealingly at her husband Lucas for guidance. But he sat in the deacon's pew, with his back to the congregation, his arms folded and his whole demeanour an example of concentration on the concluding argument of the sermon. Mr Buckley brought his pale hands together just below his chin. The ventilator continued to clatter. Esther steered the sleepy Amy to sit on her other side. She reached her right hand up the wall which was wet with condensation. It was too far up. The handle shaped like a small mailed fist was well out of her reach even if she stood up. The minister's pale hands were trembling slightly above his starched shirt cuffs. He seemed to be gathering his strength for a peroration that would overcome all opposition when a door at the back of the chapel flew open.

In the doorway a stoutly built man in his early sixties held out his hand to show it was empty because the unruly wind had blown the door knob out of it. He beamed and nodded at Mr Buckley, as if begging him to take no notice but to continue with his peroration. Mothers prevented their children from turning around. The newcomer's long overcoat was open. He stepped inside on tip-toe and turned his back on the preacher to deal with the door with the tact and skill of an expert at closing doors quietly. He remembered just in time that he was wearing a small tweed cap on his head. He retreated hurriedly into the shadow of the entrance to sweep it off. He reappeared with unsteady alacrity and resumed his efforts at closing the door. The task proved more difficult than he had anticipated. The marauding wind had won a second point of entry. The late arrival began to drift down the aisle to a vacant space in the pew at right angles to where Esther and Amy were sitting. Before he had taken four steps the door blew open again and he had to hurry back to close it. He leaned his back against it and lifted his hand to assure the preacher he would not allow it to blow open again as long as the sermon lasted.

The draught of cold air, the clatter of the ventilator lid, the squeaking of the last arrival's boots, the wind outside the door had broken the atmosphere of mesmerised attention. All Mr Buckley could do was speed up. His voice grew a little strident as he rushed on determined not to abbreviate his sermon. Breathless but triumphant he brought it to an end by closing the large pulpit Bible with a resounding thud that roused Amy from her stupor and made her look around her to make sure where she was. The heavy wheezing of the organ as the bellows filled with air made her yawn.

Gently Esther lifted the little girl's hand to cover her open mouth. She made Amy stand neatly on her feet and hold on to the left corner of the open hymn-book they were sharing. Obediently they watched Lucas as he stood up to face the congregation, ready to play his part as appointed leader of the singing. Esther saw at once that her husband was unnerved by the sight of his father standing against the door at the back of the chapel. His jaw sagged and his face went pale. The organist had to sustain the opening chord while Lucas Parry recovered himself.

As soon as the singing began, Lucas's father gave the door a good slam. When he was satisfied that it was shut, he strode confidently to the standing space around the iron railings. There he raised his right hand to cover his right ear, turned sideways and beat time with his head and foot before joining in the singing at the beginning of the second verse. At once his resonant baritone established itself. It seemed more closely related to the wind outside than the congregational chorus. Amy tugged excitedly at Esther's coat, so that she could speak into her ear. Esther bent down.

'That's Taid!'

Amy was roused. She wanted to scramble up on the seat so that she could look back and see the man she called her grandfather.

'Auntie! I can hear him. It's Taid singing.'

Esther pursed her lips and nodded very slowly and wisely to calm the little girl down. Meanwhile the powerful voice dominated the singing. With a graceful and melodious insistence it took over the lead from the organ and precentor and under the warm spell of the popular hymn and the pleasurable sound, the congregation went with it. Mr Buckley descended the pulpit steps. Lucas turned to look at him with some appeal on his face for support, but Mr Buckley had withdrawn into a state of reverent sagacity. When he closed the pulpit Bible his main task of the evening had been completed. Any decision concerning the repetition of the last verse was not his: it was left by preacher, organist, and congregation to the precentor. Lucas closed his gilt-edged hymn book. This was the normal sign that he would not be urging them on to a repeat. But before the organist could press the first chord of the 'Amen' the

27

most powerful voice in the chapel had soared on into the repeat. In the shadow of the pulpit Mr Buckley slid his thin fingers inside each other, cracked his knuckles and looked down at his spats with a modest smile: a man resigned to accepting the extra surge of song as a tribute to the eloquence of his message. Lucas's father's rusty eyebrows rose, trembled and fell as he slurred out a luxurious Amen.

The congregation sat down. Richard Parry continued to stand. He took hold of the iron railings as a support. His face glowed with benevolence as the children were called on to troop forward from their family pews and enter the deacon's pew, like a small crush of passengers waiting to board a mahogany raft moored under the pulpit and surrounded by a polished communion rail. He was looking out for Amy and waiting for a chance to wave to her, but she was completely hidden by the taller children around her. He decided to be patient. His attitude was as jaunty and as jolly as a squire visiting a feast at the village hall for which he has paid out of his own pocket. Jones Tŷ-hen, the senior deacon, was sorting the children out according to size. There was barely enough room for them all. He pushed them about with his horny hands on their shoulders. He could have been arranging sheep in a pen to their best advantage before the arrival of the judges.

Esther, alone in her pew, was tapped on the shoulder by a woman behind her. She leaned back to accept a surreptitiously offered Mint Imperial of the kind known locally as the Wesleyan sweet. In case Lucas should see her, she did not put it in her mouth but buried it in the handkerchief she clutched nervously in her left hand. Jones Tŷ-hen had steered Amy and two other small ones to the very front of the ranks of children. When their turn came, the minister could lift them on the deacon's seat so that they would no longer be concealed by the communion rail. At last all the shuffling subsided. Jones Tŷ-hen gave the minister a brief nod. The minister stood up and made his way to the front in order to lift Amy first on the seat. In position, she looked down apprehensively on either side to judge how far she would have to fall. As soon as she gained her confidence, she raised her hand to the familiar figure standing by the chapel stove.

'Can I hear your little verse, then, Amy?'

The minister spoke in a deliberate gentle voice that Amy did not hear. She was too absorbed in her desire to communicate with the man by the stove who was beaming at her so fondly and stroking his stubbly beard.

'Look Taid,' she said. 'I'm standing on the big seat.'

Women in the congregation made forgiving doting noises. Richard Parry gave Amy a quick encouraging wave. He had begun to chew tobacco. The older boys in the deacon's pew were already watching his jaws with wide-eyed fascination. He was noted for the accuracy of his spitting. They waited for the moment when he would turn his head sideways and spit tobacco juice with unerring aim into the ashbin hole. Esther was blushing. She raised a fist that held a sweet wrapped in a handkerchief to urge Amy to launch herself into rhythmic recitation. Amy stared back at her blankly. The warm agreeable scene with which she was encompassed would not break up if her mouth remained open but silent: it would last for ever if she contained herself in her own stillness like the subject of a trance. The whole place on the hillside seemed to be within the power of her open mouth, like a bubble of saliva. If she spoke, her lips would destroy a perfect moment – even the place itself. The muscles of her face remained rigid while her unblinking eyes stared at the congregation. Her uncle leaned sideways from his centre seat in the pew and whispered fiercely in her right ear. Amy was galvanised into action. In one breath she exhaled the verse she had learnt.

> 'I bend my neck to take the yoke
> And love the words that Jesus spoke
> I consecrate my life and days
> To walk his way and sing his praise.'

The minister set Amy down on the floor as near to her uncle as he could. She was a responsibility he was glad to be rid of and he had no intention of asking her to repeat the lines more slowly as he often did with the smaller children. He concentrated on the orderly and dutiful recitations of the other children and Lucas held Amy

29

firmly and bent his head close to hers to draw her interest to excellent unobtrusive performances. Before the end the minister seized on one line of a text to make a brief homily on the virtue of truthfulness to the children. The service came to its sedate conclusion. Only once was the sizzling of Richard Parry's spit heard above the wind outside in a brief pause between Mr Buckley's devoutly spoken benediction and the last lingering Amen.

The small children were the first to raise their heads. The deacons took longer to emerge from their postures of devotion. Amy was eager, as soon as the wooden gate had been opened, to gallop down the chapel and join her jolly Taid near the stove. He was waiting there for her, all smiles and swaying slightly. But no one was in a hurry to move.

The night outside was not inviting. While hymn-books were collected and denominational publications were tucked away from the weather in inside pockets, there was subdued communication with neighbours to enjoy. The women smiled at each other as they buttoned their gloves, the men and the boys dipped down to the racks under the pews for hats and caps and scarves and, in the back, the younger men began sly jokes about Richard Parry who gave them a friendly nod and didn't seem to mind.

In the deacon's pew, Jones Tŷ-hen leaned over to ask Lucas about his class-list. To reach into his inside pocket, Lucas let go of Amy. At once she eluded his grasp and skipped out of the deacon's pew. But Esther had her eye on her. She slid swiftly to the end of her pew, reached out and captured the little girl as she was running past. Amy tried to wriggle free. Her aunt whispered urgently in her ear.

'Now Amy,' she said. 'You just keep still like a good little girl. Behave yourself. Remember this is the house of God so don't go making silly noises. You can see Taid in a minute. When we get in the house. Keep still, Amy. Be patient. Do you hear? You must learn to be patient.'

People were standing up and exchanging greetings. Some already stood in the aisles. Conversations were begun in subdued tones. There was a general movement towards the porch where everyone felt entitled to talk in louder tones and even to laugh aloud if they felt like it. The space there was limited. Young men were crouching in the dark corners lighting their carbide bicycle lamps out of the draught. There were general complaints about the weather and Richard Parry's voice could be heard above all others. In the confined space he was staring happily into the long melancholy features of a man he seemed to know well enough to address in the second person singular.

'Half a guinea, old fellow. On the penillion. And that's not something you just bawl out you know. It's an art, Guto bach. It's an art.'

Amy became excited and started pulling hard at Esther's arm. Esther was engaged in polite conversation with the woman who had given her a Mint Imperial. She was anxious to show gratitude for a sign of friendship from a woman whose family had been members of Siloam from the year it was built. She shook Amy's arm. Then she lifted her up so that she should not feel suffocated by the press of people around them. Esther looked back at the deacon's pew but Lucas was still absorbed in his conversation with Jones Tŷ-hen, about the membership of the class-lists. The minister was making gestures of fatigue as he spoke to another deacon. Soon they would all retire to the vestry for a brief meeting about Circuit business. There was no chance of making a quick escape to the chapel house the back way now.

'And I was second on the englyn digrif, brother. Think of that. And I was good enough to be equal first in my opinion. I got five shillings for that.'

Esther's embarrassment grew as she listened. In the dimly lit porch she could see clearly enough the surly face of the man Richard Parry was talking to. In a little community so anxious to be amiable, this was a formidable figure. Richard Parry was courting trouble with his childish boasts. This man had an awesome reputation as a skilled stockbreeder with a sharp tongue. Esther pushed forward but she was encumbered with Amy in her arms and she could not reach her father-in-law.

'I can smell what you spent it on.'

So many people were listening. Guto's voice was gruff and disagreeable.

31

'My clock stopped.' Richard Parry was intent on making excuses for being late. 'The clock I won in the Llanrwst Semi-National. It stopped.'

'You must have breathed on it.'

Guto was not displeased when he heard an appreciative snigger from some young men behind him. His thin mouth showed the suspicion of a grin.

'Don't be so discourteous, Griffith Owen.'

Richard Parry shifted back to a more formal address giving Guto his registered name.

'I've come a long way to hear my little granddaughter saying her verse. I come here as a guest from a sister-church to hear the little one. And I'm justified. There's a talent there. It's worth starting as early as possible. To get the confidence. And there's singing in her too. The old family gift. The old nature. The old style. Finding its way out.'

Esther saw her father-in-law making a flourishing gesture to represent some mysterious force of nature.

'No relation at all to you, Richard Parry.'

Guto spoke with all the weight of an authority on stockbreeding. He pulled a sou'-wester firmly down over his long head and tied the tapes under his raised chin. His lowered eyelids looked particularly supercilious.

'No relation at all. You're in my way you know. I've got a long road ahead of me.'

The brief trial was over and sentence duly passed. But Richard Parry stood in his way.

'I'm her grandfather. Everybody knows that. You heard that little girl call me Taid right across the chapel. In front of everybody.'

'Words.' Guto's weathered face was fixed in permanent disapproval. 'That's your trouble, Richard Parry. Drunk on words. Not to mention anything else.'

He elbowed past the older man to reach the outer door. The cold rain was sweeping into the porch, visible in the weak light that fell from the outside lantern set above the door. From the paved area outside there were four slate steps that led down to the chapel gate. They glistened dangerously in the feeble light: steps to be

32

negotiated with care at the best of times. As Guto the stockbreeder prepared to launch himself into the night, Richard Parry clapped a heavy hand on his shoulder.

'I'll have respect from you,' he said. 'And if it's a fight you want, I'll take you on.'

'Go home, you old fool. You couldn't fight a lame hen.'

Esther turned to ask the woman who had given her a Mint Imperial to hold Amy. She wanted to get to Richard Parry and restrain him. But before she could reach him, her father-in-law had leapt with surprising agility on to the stockbreeder's back. He gripped Guto's neck in his forearm. They staggered about above the steps, a grotesque shape in the dim light.

'Taid!'

Esther tried to catch hold of him.

'Stop it will you. Think where you are. Do you want to shame us all?'

Richard Parry paid no attention to her. He had Guto's head back and he was hissing into his ear.

'Words is it? Here are some words for you. Listen to these.'

He sank his teeth into Guto's left ear. The stockman let out a roar of pain and rage.

'You savage . . . You bottle-sucker . . .'

Richard bit harder. Guto roared again and swung around furiously to rid himself of the dangerous load on his back. Esther was knocked over. She crawled out of the way. Her fall seemed to break the spell of inactive horror that had gripped the people in the porch. In high-pitched indignant tones, several women called for action and reluctantly the men began to move. But they were too late to prevent the two contestants sprawling down the steps. In one heavily clothed bundle they rolled against the wrought-iron gate which burst open at the impact. They landed together in a gutter that was already threatening to become a torrent bed. When the woman who had been holding Amy put her down in order to go to Esther's aid, Amy began to howl with fear. Long skirts smelling of camphor and heavy coats were swirling about her, pressing in from every side. Caught up in the confusion, other children began to cry. Outside in the darkness the deep voice of Guto the stockbreeder

33

could be heard in the middle of the road describing Richard Parry as a dog with rabies who ought to be shot. The minister was called for and the deacons. Esther scrambled to her feet, unhurt. She would not stand still while two women tried to brush her skirt. She pushed her way back into the porch to find Amy and pick her up. She searched about in her pockets for her small handkerchief to dry her eyes and wipe her nose. The child was utterly bewildered. She gave her hurried comfort. At the inside doors of the chapel a way was made for the minister, closely followed by Jones Tŷ-hen, Lucas and the other deacons. More space was given them as the representatives of church order. Lucas found Esther's elbow and squeezed it. He whispered close to her face.

'Take the child into the house.'

Esther stared at him. He could not see that her skirt was wet. She was uncertain how to obey him.

'Take her.'

The minister was standing on the edge of the porch, turning up the collar of his jacket, concerned for his clothes. He peered nervously into the rain at the figures and shapes moving about on the steps, muttering to those nearest him that he could see very little. Away in the darkness Guto the stockman was shouting against the wind.

'He's a monster! He should be excommunicated! No man has a right to enter the house of the Lord under the influence of strong drink!'

'Excuse me, Mr Buckley.'

Esther, holding a snivelling Amy tightly in her arms, edged past the minister who was too preoccupied to move out of her way. She stepped very carefully among the people outside. As she made her way through the gate, two young farm-workers were shining their carbide lamps straight into Richard Parry's face as he lay in the gutter. His beard was wet and there was blood on his face and on his bald head. The young men were alarmed by his stillness. His eyes were wide open and there was blood around his mouth. From the security of Esther's arms, Amy leaned back to stare at the sight with dull wonder as a child on a first visit to the circus looks at the clown and waits to know whether to laugh or cry.

34

'Do you think he's dead or something, Albert?'

The beam of light swung around in the rain as one of the young farm hands turned to ask his companion the frightened question. Esther moved closer so that she could attract the calmer man's attention with a nudge of her elbow.

'Can you shine your light to the small gate, please,' she said. 'I want to take this little girl in and get the place ready.'

'Yes. Yes, of course. I'll come with you.'

The lamp light led the way through the small gate and up the path to the back door of the chapel house. Esther turned the heavy key which had been left in the lock and pushed the door open. Albert stood in the doorway flashing his light into the kitchen, but Esther did not really need it any more. She set Amy down in the high-backed wooden chair. She removed the round lid on the iron range with a bent poker and put the kettle on. She poked the fire so that the flames shot up comfortably. Amy watched the shadows leaping about harmlessly on the ceiling. Esther's hand descended accurately on the box of matches on the high mantelshelf. Albert asked if it was all right now for him to leave them. Esther thanked him and asked him if he would mind shutting the back door. With expert speed she removed the glass mantle of the lamp that hung over the kitchen table. Reassured by the comfortable familiarity of her surroundings, Amy began to ask questions.

'Auntie,' she said. 'Who was naughty in the chapel porch?'

'Men,' Esther said. 'Silly men.'

Without taking off her overcoat, Esther lit a candlestick in its blue enamel stand and took it into the lean-to pantry behind the kitchen. She ladled drinking water out of a large earthenware pot with a wooden lid into a saucepan which she brought back to set on the range next to the kettle.

'Plenty of hot water . . .'

She was muttering to herself.

'He'll have to stay here. There's nothing else for it.'

'Who'll have to stay here, Auntie?'

Esther looked at Amy as though she had not realised she was listening.

'Why don't you go upstairs like a good little girl and take your hat and coat off? Then you can come down and help your Auntie make the supper – all right?'

Reluctantly Amy came down from the armchair. A small light flickered on the window-sill at the top of the stairs. Amy lingered at the bottom. She came back into the kitchen doorway. Esther had placed a tray on a corner of the table. She was setting out a meal of cold meat for one. Amy held on to the brass door knob and swung her legs about.

'What's the matter?'

Esther had so much to do, she could barely pause to ask the question.

'I'm afraid. You come upstairs with me.'

'Indeed I won't.'

Esther disappeared into the pantry. She re-emerged with a dish of butter and a jug of milk.

'Can't you see I've got so much to do? There's nothing to be afraid of.'

'I can hear the naughty men,' Amy said. 'They're fighting.'

Esther stood still to listen. There was a noise on the path outside. She recognised her husband's voice and Richard Parry groaning and protesting.

'Go upstairs,' Esther said. 'Go upstairs and get into bed. Take the light from the landing. I'll come up with your supper as soon as I can. Go along, Amy.'

Amy moved from the door, but only as far as the bottom of the stairs. When the back door opened, she slunk back to see her Uncle Lucas helping his father, Richard Parry, into the house. Behind them on the garden path, Albert and his friend stood shining their bicycle lamps at the door and at each other. Richard was recovering rapidly. He raised an arm to greet his daughter-in-law.

'Esther fach,' he said. 'I'm as wet as a spaniel. And I'll stink like a wet dog too when I'm drying out. Did you ever see such an unfortunate accident?'

He groaned momentarily as Lucas set him down in the high-backed wooden chair near the fire. He pulled a face and rubbed his wet beard with the back of his hand. He lifted a hand in gratitude to the men outside.

'All praise to them,' he said. 'They rose to the occasion. I'd like to ask them one question before they go. What did John Wesley and the Duke of Wellington have in common?'

The men outside shifted about sheepishly. Lucas thanked them both and closed the back door. He took the roller-towel down and thrust it at his father.

'Here,' he said. 'Start drying yourself with that.'

'Lucas,' Esther said, her hand near her mouth. 'Do you think we ought to ask one of those young men to go for the doctor?'

'Doctor and the Devil!' Richard Parry said. 'No thank you . . . They're not putting their knives into me if I can help it.' He held his fist in the air so that they could both see it. 'Ten years ago I would have felled him with one blow. I remember when I used to follow the Fairs, there was a fellow in Conwy. Just like Guto Owen to look at too, now I come to think of it . . . I floored him with one smack . . .'

'Father!'

Lucas pressed both hands against his head. 'Do you want to drag us all down to your level?'

Richard Parry was offended by the bitterness in his son's voice. He tried to stand up, but the pain in his back made him give a sudden yelp.

'I'm going home,' he said.

'You can't go home.' Lucas struggled to stifle the impatience in his voice. 'You've hurt your back . . .'

'A touch of lumbago.'

'You can't walk three miles on a night like this. It's out of the question. You'll spend the night here.'

'What about the minister?'

'He'll stay at Tŷ-hen. They are quite keen to have him.'

Lucas looked sadly at the supper tray Esther had been preparing.

'We won't see him tonight, Esther. You can let the fire in the front room go out.'

Esther looked at her husband sympathetically, aware of his keen disappointment. He was foregoing the pleasures of elevated conversation with an educated man and the relaxation of a friendly chat about Connexional matters in front of the parlour fire.

'I didn't think all that much of his sermon.'

Richard Parry was searching his waistcoat pocket for his little ivory tobacco box. Lucas watched him with open distaste as he tugged out a plug of shag and popped it in his mouth.

'I reckon he learns them off by heart. It's a sort of sausage isn't it? A meat and crumbs mixture packed in a thin skin. A bit of Eglwys Bach. A bit of Hugh Jones. A sprinkling of this and that. But mostly second-hand. Luke-warm stuff. He's a bit of a dilly-doh, isn't he?'

Richard Parry was so absorbed in the niceties of his own method of analysis that he ignored the fact that Lucas was white with indignation.

'Who are you to judge?' The question sounded strangulated.

'Well I have a right to my opinion. I'm a full member of Moriah. I've bought the first volume of *Hanes Wesleyaeth Gymreig* and I'm down for the next.'

'He's an educated man, father. He's a B.A.'

Richard chewed thoughtfully and spat with effortless accuracy into the fire.

'Education, father. You have never begun to understand the importance of education.'

'Wren's piss.' Richard Parry spoke with dogmatic emphasis. 'Turning good Welshmen into English dummies. That's your schools system for you. I wish sometimes I'd gone to America with my brother Bob. Do you know what he said to my mother the night before he left? "Mam," he said. "I don't want to leave you, Mam. But I don't want to spend my life as a slave of the English crown." And off he went, taking his bag of tools with him. To North Dakota. But it's all English there now, they tell me. Old Bob won't like that.' He chuckled to himself as he thought of his older brother. 'Now he was a reader. Knocked spots off me. And the best carpenter in the district. But I was the best for singing and fighting. And the englyn too, strangely enough.'

He turned in his chair with some difficulty to point at the plates on the dresser.

'I could strike a note, you know, that could make those plates jump and rattle.'

Lucas turned despairingly to Esther. She went into the pantry and he followed her there.

'He was going to put my name forward,' he said urgently. 'We were going to discuss it tonight.'

'It will be all right, Lucas. You mustn't worry.'

She bent her head under the low ceiling to extract a large loaf from the bread pot. Richard Parry was shouting in the kitchen.

'Where's that little girl, then? I've come all this way to see her. Where is she, for heaven's sake?'

Lucas looked up to heaven in open despair and bent his knees to avoid bumping his head.

'What chance have I got?' he said. 'What chance at all?'

4

ESTHER HURRIED ALONG THE WARM PAVEMENT WITH SUCH URGENT speed that Amy had to trot, from time to time, to keep up with her aunt. Prematurely grey curls escaped from the dish-shaped hat on Esther's head that was penetrated by two long hatpins. Quite unintentionally the curls softened the lines that unremitting hard labour was engraving on her anaemic handsome face. Esther was wearing a black armband on her grey jacket. Trotting along, Amy managed to study the rhythm with which her aunt's boots shot out of her long grey skirt and relate it to the action of her own busy feet until the exercise made her aware that the unusually extended effort was making her tired. She made an unsuccessful attempt to clutch at her aunt's arm and slow her down. She was shaken off and rebuked.

'Now then, Amy Parry,' her aunt said. 'You can see I'm carrying all these things.'

She carried a tin in a black bag and a tart on a plate ineffectively concealed from passers-by by brown paper crumpled and untidy after their long journey. The tart had to be carried with some care but there was a determined frown on her face which suggested that while she was concentrating hard on preserving the tart in perfect condition she would not allow small burdens to impede the speed of her progress.

'I've told you once and I'll tell you again,' Esther said. 'It's a long and expensive journey. We don't want to waste a second.'

She turned abruptly from the High Street just as they reached the shops. Amy groaned with disappointment but she was obliged to follow her aunt.

'I want to see the castle, Auntie,' Amy said. 'Are we going to see the castle?'

Esther was in too much of a hurry to reply. She seemed to be concentrating on short cuts that would allow her to avoid main thoroughfares and any chance encounter with old acquaintances who might require her to give an account of herself and her present circumstances. Up a long narrow street Amy caught a brief glimpse of a great white and blue motor bus moving in noisy majesty towards its parking position alongside the fountain in the centre of the town square.

'I saw the motor, Auntie! I saw the motor.'

Esther balanced the tart with the hand that carried the black bag to free her left hand to give Amy an unexpected push. Amy looked surprised and startled.

'Now come on,' Esther said in a softer voice. 'We haven't any time to waste. Nain is expecting us.'

They passed under the arch of an ancient gateway and turned to climb a narrow street with a row of houses built against the old town wall. Amy was intrigued by a yellow baker's handcart with its shafts resting in the cobbled gutter. She loitered to examine it and Esther had to urge her on. Near the top of the street the houses grew slightly larger but still stood in the shadow of the wall. The pavement narrowed. Esther knocked at a thickly painted brown door, paused for a second and then opened it. Amy stepped back, reluctant to enter such a dark interior. She turned around to gaze longingly at the bright sunlight on the other side of the street. There was a dirty boy working in a tinman's repair shop next to an exposed lean-to bicycle shed that Amy expressed a sudden urge to visit.

'Is that the tinman's, Auntie? Can I go and see the tinman?'

'No, of course you can't. We've come to visit your nain. Put your hat straight, Amy.'

Immediately to the left of the door Esther had just opened, a wooden staircase wound its constricted way to another floor that was hidden in stygian darkness. Esther still stood expectantly on the narrow pavement. Amy was about to speak when she suddenly saw in the interior at a level six inches lower than the street, her grandmother standing in the kitchen doorway. Her hands folded in front of her black apron and her sallow face glimmering in the dim light as still as a painted face under the varnish of an old portrait. Her unexpectedly dark hair was parted in the middle and drawn back tightly to a severe bun on the nape of her neck. She was as quiet as a ghost. She made no move, as if unwilling to expose herself to the brightness outside her front door. She did not invite her visitors inside. Her eyes were still making a mental note of the parcels Esther was carrying: a high-priestess assessing the moral and material worth of offerings on their way to the shrine. At last a brief movement of her head implied that Esther should have compelled Amy as part of her proper training to share the load.

'Children can be very cruel.'

Her grandmother's voice was remote, monotonous and unforgiving. Amy blinked innocently. She touched Esther's skirt and looked up as if to show she expected a stout defence against any accusations about to be made. But her grandmother was talking about someone else.

'There was no need for him to go at all.'

Esther's dish hat flopped sympathetically. Amy listened to her grandmother's low voice with reverent curiosity. She could have been memorising every word she heard.

'He went against my wishes. He went because I wanted him not to go. I find it hard to forget that.'

The still unwavering stare announced that she had long experience in being called upon to try to forget and even forgive. Esther, too, had done something against her wishes. She had borne children and now she bore the wounds they chose to inflict upon

41

her. Amy's left knee began to tremble independently as though she were forcing her legs to resist a temptation to skip and jump.

'William . . . Poor William . . .'

Esther muttered her brother's name. She was ready to weep.

'You'd better come inside,' her mother said. 'We don't want people seeing you standing in the street outside your mother's house.'

Esther stepped forward eagerly. She was met in the confined corridor by her mother who stretched out a cold hand to open the door of the front parlour. Her formality was unobtrusive but unyielding. The room was crammed with furniture. It was as clean and as cold as a small mausoleum. The round table in the centre was covered with a chenille cloth. Every chair had a white crocheted antimacassar on the back. The black iron mantelpiece was dominated by a pair of stuffed owls under tall glass domes. Esther laid her offerings carefully on the table.

'I've brought you a gooseberry tart,' she said. 'I know you like my gooseberry tarts. We've had ever such a heavy crop in the garden this year.'

The spotless white lace curtains subdued the bright summer light. Amy's grandmother pointed silently to the sofa under the window. Esther and Amy took their seats obediently. Solemnly, she closed the door. Even this simple act seemed an assertion of power. She moved to stand by the mantelpiece, between the two owls.

' "I'm going to join the soldiers," he said. Just like that. Not a thought for his mother and what he owed her.'

'William.'

The tears accumulated in Esther's eyes. Her mother watched her as though she was about to give her permission to sob.

'Poor William.'

Esther sounded as if she was choking. Amy slid her hand along the cold surface of the horsehair sofa until her fingertips touched her aunt's clothes.

'And Lucas's brother Hugh. He is missing too. Missing believed killed. That means they're dead. Young boys dressed like soldiers. Sent away to be killed. And for what, I ask myself. For what?'

'He had to go,' her mother said. 'I couldn't stop him. Your father

42

wouldn't have stopped him either if he'd been alive. Nobody could.'

She stopped to listen to Esther weeping quietly. Amy noticed her grandmother's goitre. It rose and fell in her neck like the only part of her rigid body allowed to move freely and express her grief. Esther's subdued sobs became melancholy music in a religious observance that obliged Amy to remain respectfully still.

' "I'm going to enlist," he said. Just like that.'

With her head turned away at an angle Amy paid close attention to her grandmother from the corner of her eyes. There was so much that was strange that she wanted to question, but she knew well enough she had been sentenced to stillness and silence for the duration of the visit.

'What he said to your uncle. That hurt me. I heard him say it. "What are you joining the soldiers for? What's the army got to do with you?" your uncle said. "It's better than serving soup in Hole-in-the-Wall," he said. That's what he said to your uncle. "Serving soup." That's what he calls our keeping a café. That's what he thinks of all the hard work I put into that place. And your father when he was alive. It's not good enough for him. He looks down on it.'

'Mam,' Esther said. 'William's killed. He's dead.'

'You don't have to tell me. I know. He went against my wishes. I've had to sell the business.'

Esther bit her lip and struggled to find words to express more sympathy.

'I'm sorry, Mam,' she said.

'I've got a photograph of him dressed as a soldier. That's all I've got.'

Amy watched the goitre rising and falling rapidly in her grandmother's neck.

'I spoilt him I suppose. And this is my reward.'

The dish hat trembled violently as Esther shook her head.

'Why does God allow it? That's what I can't understand. Why does He let it go on. And it will go on, won't it? Where's the end of it? I can't help asking, Mam.'

Amy could see her aunt waiting eagerly for an answer. Her grandmother had the authority to speak. She sat by the empty

43

fireplace, her back still rigid with self-discipline, stroking the back of one cold hand with the fingers of the other.

'Why,' Esther said, desperately. 'I ask myself, why?'

'It's not for us to question.'

After the pronouncement she drew a deep silence like a sheet over the little room. There was nothing more to be said. Even the goitre subsided. Amy watched it closely. When her grandmother caught her staring, she tried to pretend she was watching the left hand owl in its glass case. She studied first one owl and then the other. Across the street a boy was whistling cheerfully and there was the sound of a hammer on thin metal. Amy became restless. She pushed her hand against her aunt to let her know that she would like some attention.

'Auntie.'

When she spoke at last it was like a quiet squeak.

'What is it?'

Amy wanted to put her request as quietly as she could. The effect was a sulky mutter.

'Can we go and see the castle now?'

'Haven't you taught that girl anything?'

Esther accepted the rebuke. She lifted her left hand and squeezed Amy's shoulder.

'She's a fidget. Can't sit still for one minute. You must teach her, Esther. To observe decent silence. Remember her mother's nature. Bend her will or she'll bend yours.'

She seemed to find her last sentence deeply consoling. She listened to it reverberate in the small crowded parlour in a way that invited her daughter to partake of rare drops of wisdom that could only be distilled from a lifetime's experience. Amy stared desperately at the owls. Their indifference seemed even worse than her grandmother's disapproval. She slid down the couch until her knees were almost close enough to touch the tassels of the tablecloth. Her grandmother cleared her throat and her goitre became active again.

'And how is Lucas Parry?'

The question was carefully put. Lucas's name was uttered and the atmosphere became secular enough for Amy to relax and sink quietly to the floor without being noticed or reproved: but the manner in which the name was spoken implied a cautious neutral attitude, a reluctance to infuse the name with any degree of warmth or give it an unqualified stamp of approval. Out of sight, Amy began to treat the tassels of the tablecloth like bells, tapping them against each other with a soft touch of one index finger or the other.

'He's being wronged.' Esther spoke up loyally.

'Who isn't?' Her mother was reserving her position with her own brand of fortifying scepticism. Esther looked pale and afraid, but she pressed on.

'He gets no support from the Superintendent of the Circuit. In spite of all the good work he does, he gets no proper recognition. He's very hurt about it. He's being treated as a stop-gap lay-preacher in war time. And we get next to nothing for being chapel caretakers. It's not right. It's really not right. And the minister is no support at all. He just doesn't give him any support at all.'

'Wesleyans.'

Her mother made no attempt to conceal her Calvinist contempt for an alien and inferior order.

'They have their rules, Mam.'

'So he's not even a proper lay-preacher. So much for all the talk of becoming a minister. All he is, when it comes down to it, is a chapel caretaker with a bad leg.'

Esther began to tremble. There was such a look of misery on her face that Amy reached up from the floor and touched her knee.

'The truth hurts. I know it does. It's like physic. We have to swallow it even when we can't bear it. And he's got a drunken father too, hasn't he? A drunken fighter who used to follow the Fairs. He kept that very quiet, didn't he?'

Esther's fingers worked in her lap as she struggled to keep back her tears.

'You mustn't think because I speak the truth, I don't want to help you. You are the only daughter I've got left.'

Esther seemed to contemplate flinging herself down on her knees in front of her mother and taking her cold hands in her own hot grasp. Her hat trembled on top of her loosening hair.

45

'Oh Mam. We would so much like to move. I am not saying Lucas wants to leave the chapel, but we would so much like to be more independent. There's a little smallholding coming vacant in September. On the side of the hill, Swyn-y-Mynydd it's called. It's such a pretty place.'

'How many acres?'

'I'm not sure, Mam. Fifteen I think. It's not so much the land. Although there is a grazing right on the mountain, Lucas says. It's the cottage really. Of course the land would be useful. And there's a big garden. Lucas says he could build a greenhouse there.'

'What's the rent?'

'Well that's it, Mam. We were wondering, for the first year, to start us off, if you could lend us . . .'

'What is the rent?'

'Twenty pounds a year. I know it sounds a lot. But I'll be getting seven and six a week for cleaning the schools.'

'What schools?'

'The elementary. It's a church school but it's the village school as well, if you know what I mean. I'm going to be the cleaner.'

'And you get the chapel house rent free. With most of your coal. And paraffin. That's what I would describe as a little gold mine.'

Esther bowed her head. Her mother's arguments were so brutally conclusive.

'Nobody in their senses would want to move from there. At least you get that much for the privilege of being a Wesleyan, my girl.'

She gave the beginnings of a frosty smile, but Esther was not receptive.

'I get so worried about him. The theological colleges are full. He's a clever man. He's a good man. But what chance has he got?'

'The same chance as anybody else. And when they bring in this conscription thing, he won't get sent for, will he? So you're lucky really, Esther. You've got a lot to be thankful for. You won't see him coming home wrapped in khaki like a parcel ready to be sent to the Front to be killed.'

Esther was completely subdued. Amy's playing was so quiet it did nothing to break the spell of melancholy resignation that her grandmother had cast over her aunt. The dream of freedom in the

46

smallholding in the hills was shattered. Her mother's relentless realism left them nothing except making the best of the existing yoke. Esther's head was inclined forward and when someone knocked at the door her eyes moved nervously like the eyes of a deer disturbed while drinking at the edge of a dark sorrowful pool.

'Shall I go?'

She was still eager to please her mother.

'If you like.'

The small service was accepted on the clear understanding that no gratitude or favours would be expected in return. With a graceful economy of movement, Esther negotiated the narrow space between her mother's chair and the table. She entered the familiar darkness of the small corridor and opened the front door. She held up a hand to protect her eyes against the bright light outside.

'Hello, Esther.'

She was being greeted with friendly condescension by a woman about her own age. She saw teeth being generously displayed in a long face and a fine complexion greatly cared for. The visitor wore gloves and carried a parasol and took obvious satisfaction in her own refinement. A frilly white blouse was gathered high under her pointed chin. The wrist of her free hand was pressed against the back of her waist and it seemed an elegant pose she had noticed in society and was now choosing to cultivate.

'Connie,' Esther said.

She pressed her thumb down on the worn lever of the latch and kept it down while she thought of something she could say.

'Are you home then?'

Connie glanced down gracefully to make sure she could change her pose without stumbling into the gutter.

'I've brought the rent,' she said. 'Since I'm home. And visit my aunt. Did she get my letter of condolence?'

She spoke loudly enough to be heard indoors.

'Ask her in.'

Esther's mother issued her direction without moving from her seat in the small parlour. She spoke quietly but with complete authority.

47

'It's Connie Clayton . . .'

By now Esther's feeble announcement was superfluous. Connie entered looking confident of a welcome. When she did appear in the parlour, she was given Esther's seat and Esther remained standing at her mother's side to show her readiness to serve.

'How nice to see you.'

They listened to Connie with a keen yet detached interest. She was in gentleman's service and seemed to have acquired new modes of talking.

'I was heart-broken about William. Those horrible horrible Germans. I wish I could kill them all. That's what I said to uncle and I meant it.'

She took her aunt's silence to represent grief beyond words. She observed a token silence and then set about the business of cheering up the bereaved.

'Uncle sends you all the best, Auntie! "Give my regards to my dear old sister," he said. He's so quaint, honestly. And he's not so well, either. I don't know whether he's putting it on a bit. He might just be. I've been offered a very good position at Cranforth Royal, and he doesn't like the idea of me moving so very far away. Hampshire is a lovely county of course. The trees.'

Something in her aunt's stony silence discouraged her from giving more details of the beauties of Hampshire or of the latest developments in her exciting career in the big houses. She noted the untidy parcels on the table and turned her head to avoid staring at them. She saw Amy sitting on the floor.

'My goodness. Whom do we have here? It's not poor Gracie's little girl is it? It's not Amy! My goodness how you've grown. Isn't she a sweet little thing? She's going to be beautiful, isn't she? Just like her poor mother.'

Connie's efforts to be agreeable and charming were making no headway with her aunt. Another opportunity to warm the cold of the room with a little cheerful conversation was not taken up.

'Did you say you'd brought the rent?'

'Yes indeed I have, Auntie. I was hoping to have a word with you about that. Just a word if I may. In private.'

Esther gazed at her cousin with grudging admiration. Connie

48

had contrived to be businesslike without losing any of her poise. It had to be something she had picked up by living with the aristocracy. Her mother had jerked her head. She was being told to take herself and the child elsewhere while private business was being transacted. Whatever Connie wanted, she was to be given a serious official hearing.

'Come along, Amy.'

Amy hurried to Esther's side, pleased at the prospect of being allowed out. They stepped down into a kitchen which was spotlessly clean but even gloomier than the parlour in spite of the low fire burning in the grate. In the back there was a yard not more than a few feet wide and steep slate steps laid solidly against the old town wall. Amy scrambled up, delighted with the chance to visit the tiny water closet to the left of the top of the steps. Without bothering to close the door, which had a heart-shaped hole carved out of its centre, she prepared for the rare pleasure of sitting above the decorated blue porcelain bowl on the warm wood of the much scrubbed seat. There were further pleasures to come. When she had pulled up her drawers she tugged at the heavy chain and watched the dark rain-water cascade into the bowl. She leaned against the seat to admire the blue foliage that spread out of the pair of Grecian urns under their freshly washed glaze. Amy hopped out of the closet to join her aunt. Esther stood on the parapet enjoying the sunlight and leaning against the dark iron bar that surmounted the old wall. On the gravelled promenade below, two nursemaids pushed large perambulators. A group of old men sat on the sea wall sunning themselves and watching a light boat occupied by two sun-tanned boys gliding landwards on the tide. Esther was gazing with unconcealed nostalgia at the straits and flat island across the water.

'Can you see the lighthouse? We went there for our Sunday School trip. On the little steamer. It was lovely.'

Amy wanted to stand on the wall.

'Now keep still,' Esther said. 'Look at those boys. They've been fishing.'

'Hold me, Auntie. I want to see the castle.'

Bravely Amy stood on the wall while her aunt held on tightly to her waist. Only the highest towers of the castle were in view. The rest was hidden by the crowded roof-tops of the old town.

'Can we go there now, Auntie? Can we go and wave at the prisoners?'

'The jail isn't there any more.'

'But you said you used to wave at the prisoners.'

'Yes, we did. From the castle tower. When I was a little girl. But the jail isn't there any more.'

'Are they all set free? All the prisoners?'

Esther smiled and shook her head.

'Is there a king in the castle, Auntie? Can you have a castle without a king?'

'Youoo-oo!'

Connie Clayton was standing in the narrow yard below them. Amy could see her summer hat through the branches of a straggling pear tree.

'Can I come up?'

It was a coy request for an invitation. Esther said nothing but Amy nodded her head vigorously. Connie still hesitated.

'Is it clean up there?' she said. 'I don't want to dirty my dress.'

Amy watched her ascent of the slate stairs with great interest. They were so steep and uneven, it was difficult for Connie to preserve the kind of refined and graceful movement she was concerned to display.

'Oh dear,' she said, when she reached the parapet. 'What an awkward climb. But what a glorious view.'

She fingered her cameo brooch and made gestures of admiration.

' "Sunset and evening star,

And one clear call for me . . ." That's what it always reminds me of . . .'

' "And may there be no moaning of the bar

When I put out to sea . . ." That's English poetry, Amy. Famous English poetry. Written by Alfred Lord Tennyson. My favourite poet.'

She gave Esther an encouraging smile, but Esther looked resolved never to share her cousin's enthusiasm for a foreign author.

'Does she read English yet?' Connie asked the question very politely. 'The sooner the better, you know. It's such an advantage. How is Lucas Parry?'

'He's very well, all things considered.'

Esther blushed and turned her head away to watch the two boys in their boat.

'Does he have a job now or is he studying? He wanted to be a minister, didn't he?'

'He is at home at the moment,' Esther said.

'Out of work?'

'Not really.'

'Why doesn't he go and make munitions? Shotton is not all that far away from you, is it? He could come home weekends.'

Connie held her head to one side to emphasise that she was being helpful.

'They get very good pay I hear. And it helps the war effort.'

'Lucas is a lay-preacher,' Esther said. 'It wouldn't be the right work for him.'

'Oh I don't know . . .'

Esther snatched Amy down from her perch on the wall. Some form of action helped to conceal her feelings. Connie tried to be tactful.

'Poor Auntie,' she said. 'She's so upset. She doesn't understand at all.'

'Understand what?'

'Poor William's sacrifice. He felt the call of duty. The call of king and country. We don't want the boys to go of course. My beau is out there. I've got his picture. Would you like to see it?'

She extracted two postcards from an envelope in her handbag. One was an oval print of a group of seven cavalrymen outside their bell-tent in a summer camp. The other was a carefully posed studio portrait of a young footman in his livery.

'That's James,' Connie Clayton said. 'Third from the left. Just look what he's scribbled on the back. In blue pencil if you please.'

Under the printed line *This space may be used for communication* a pencil message was written in an unsteady hand, *Just a little reminder from an old sweat goin' on all right guess who?*

'Isn't he awful?' Connie said. 'He never signed it. And this is him

51

in livery. He wears uniform ever so well you see. He's used to it. He came to see us all at Baron Hall when he was on leave. He looked ever so spick and span. I wanted to cry when it was time for him to go. "Don't fret upon it, Miss Connie," he said. "It's bad on the men but it's worse on the horses." That's how he is, always joking. He's such a good sport. Always cheers you up. And we need to be cheered up in these dark days. I'm going over to Penrhyn Castle tomorrow afternoon. Would you like to come with me, Amy?'

The word 'castle' made Amy nod enthusiastically.

'Mrs Jones is the cook-housekeeper there. She's an old friend you see. Very responsible position. In charge of twenty indoor servants. There's always a place for me there she says if ever I want to move nearer home. I may be glad of the chance one day I know, but I want to see the world while I'm young. "It's soon enough to be old-fashioned when you're old," James always says.'

With a sense of the drama in her life, she turned to face the sea. She lifted her head to breathe in the salt air deeply.

'We've been so narrow,' she said. 'It's no use being narrow. Remember all that fuss about the regatta? A harmless thing like that. The people of this town can be very narrow you know.'

Esther seized on the chance to disagree.

'I've always found them very reliable,' she said.

'Oh I'm not denying that,' Connie said airily. 'Reliability is one thing, narrowness is another. Some people are just set against any kind of change.'

Esther's face flushed. 'We have to go down. We can't stay up here all afternoon.'

She spoke quite crossly to Amy. Connie placed a friendly hand on Amy's shoulder.

'Would you like to see an ostrich?' Her mouth was stretched wide with a particularly inviting smile. 'We have one in the park at Baron Hall. Would you like to come and see it?'

'Oh yes, I would.' Amy became excited. 'I've never seen an ostrich.' Connie kneeled down to look into the little girl's eyes.

'Your mother was my best friend. My very best friend. You can come and stay with me and you'll see the ostrich.'

Amy was enthusiastic.

'She'll do no such thing!'

Connie's presence blocked the way to the slate steps, but Esther looked capable of pushing her aside.

'It's not your house is it? I don't see how you can invite her. It's wrong to raise children's hopes.'

'Mrs Wicken-Lewis has told me I can have a close relative at any time, only to give her proper notice. At any time, she said.'

'You said you were leaving.'

Connie seized the chance of going into detail.

'Mrs Wicken-Lewis is an Honourable. She and Lady Cranforth are very great friends. She recommended me. Her eldest son Major William is as good as engaged to Lady Anne. Lady Anne Cranforth that is.'

Esther could no longer contain her righteous anger. She pushed Amy behind her.

'In my opinion it's time the whole lot of them were drowned in a bucket of cold water.'

Connie's fine complexion grew instantly paler.

'Parasites! That's what they all are. Living off the backs of working people. I don't know what pride you have I'm sure, Connie Clayton, slaving for that lot. I'd rather be poor than a slave. I know that much.' Esther felt the declaration was worth repeating. 'I'd rather be poor than be a slave. I know that much.'

'Really . . .' The attack had come so unexpectedly and Connie was lost for words. 'Really . . . well I never. I don't see that I have to stand here to be insulted.'

'I'm not talking about you,' Esther said. 'I'm talking about the people you work for.'

'The best people,' Connie said. 'And you can't talk about them like that. The aristocracy in fact. That's what they are. How can you be so disrespectful, Esther Parry?'

'Wastrels,' Esther said. 'The dregs of humanity. That's what I'd call them. Never done a day's work in their lives. Betting. Drinking. Chasing women. Like that awful old King Edward. Rogues and vagabonds, the lot of them.'

'Esther.' Connie was genuinely shocked. 'You're talking about Royalty. The King-Emperor!'

'King-Adulterer more like.'

Connie put her gloved hand against her open mouth. 'Oh Esther. That's terrible. You could be arrested for saying that.'

'Could I?'

Esther was cool now and prepared to enjoy the fruits of her little victory.

'It's treason. What you're saying. It's real treason that is.'

'Well I'd better get down from here before I get arrested,' Esther said. 'That is if you don't mind getting out of my way.'

Connie pressed herself against the iron bar as if not to be contaminated by contact with Esther as she passed by.

'It's disloyal. The things you are saying are disloyal. Disloyal to the crown.'

'It's you that's disloyal.' Esther paused on the slate steps to look up at her cousin. 'Turning your back on your own people. Turning your back on the chapel. Speaking your own language as if you had a mouth full of marbles. Don't you talk to me about being disloyal.'

Amy had reached the bottom of the slate steps.

'Auntie.' She whispered fiercely. 'I want to see the ostrich.'

'Well you can't and that's the end of it.'

She pushed Amy in front of her as they re-entered the dark house. The grandmother was seated by the fire, waiting for a kettle to boil.

'If you reach the things, Esther, we'll have a cup of tea and some of your gooseberry tart,' she said. 'Is that Connie still there?'

Esther raised a warning finger. Just outside Connie was pulling furiously at the bolt on a small entry door that wasn't easily opened.

'What have you said to her?'

Amy tried to creep out of range of her grandmother's stern eye. The atmosphere all around her made her frightened and uneasy.

'I only said what needed saying.'

Both women kept still to listen to the noise outside. Connie was slamming the entry door on the outside and failing to get it on the latch. She succeeded on the fourth try. Esther started laughing.

'There's nothing to laugh about. Go and bolt the entry door. Lift it. It's quite easy if you use your sense.'

Her grandmother lifted an arm in stern command and Amy fled to do her bidding.

'One door is enough to guard when I'm alone in the house.'

Esther was flushed and happy with her small triumph. She chatted gaily as she prepared tea. Her mother listened as though listening was in itself a gracious act of reward.

'You know what they call her in Snowdon Street? The Queen of Spain. Some flunkey or other sent her a postcard from the South of France. It was a picture of the Queen of Spain. He wrote on the back that it looked like her. And she was daft enough to show it to Jane Hughes next door. There's something very foolish about her.'

Her mother smiled grimly.

'Not so foolish. I'll have to get Williams the carpenter to put new floorboards in the front parlour of number twelve. And Connie says I've got to pay because I'm the landlord. Her uncle would never have had enough gumption to say that. She's got more sense than you've got, Esther Parry. You or your sister!'

'Poor Gracie.'

'She'll marry a husband who can keep her.'

Her mother was relentless. Esther lowered her head. Her brief pleasure was over and she looked ready to cry.

'Marrying a man who runs away to join a fancy choir.' There was bitterness and contempt in the old woman's voice. 'He must have been in a hurry. To leave his precious gold watch and chain behind him. And what about you? What have you married?'

The implied insult was unmistakable. But her habit of obedience was so strong, the only protest Esther could make had to be directed against Connie Clayton.

'Nobody would have her,' she said. 'She's as ugly as sin for all her finery.'

'Don't you be too sure. If she turned up in this town one day with a rich husband, I wouldn't be the one to be surprised.'

5

A MY WALKED DAINTILY DOWN THE LANE. HER BOOTS WERE HIGHLY polished and she had to avoid the muddy water in the potholes on the way. Her golden ringlets hung down as she bent her head to observe the blueish drops of milk that seeped between the domed lid and the smooth rim of the enamelled can she was carrying. She appeared deeply conscious of her responsibility. The can had been entrusted to her. It contained a very generous pint of milk. It was her business to see that the load arrived at its destination intact and unspoilt.

A hot sun was rapidly dispersing the clouds that remained after the heavy rain during the night. Dandelions grew in profusion in the grass verge. The high hedge above her head was a sweet-smelling refuge for the nesting birds. Amy clutched the wire handle of the can so tightly it stuck to the hot fold of the palm of her right hand. Her lips were pressed together with concentrated effort. She stood very still in order to transfer the can from her right hand to her left without spilling a drop on the clean pinafore that reached well below her knees. She moved forward again, taking her bearings, without raising her head, from the appearance of the edge of the lane. When a crude boulder used as a mounting stone came into view, she knew she had reached the end of the lane. Out on the main road she was able to step on to a rough pavement. The surface was uneven and she still had to watch her step as she balanced the milk can. Above her, to her right, dressed stone of the retaining wall of the school garden was already warm in the sudden heat of the sun. All over the expanse of wall a pleasing pattern was made by the pointed mortar.

'Little girl!'

The voice seemed to come out of the sky above. It was deep and authoritative and also female. Squinting into the hazy light, Amy saw first the white marking down the face of a patient horse in his light harness. Above it and beyond it she saw the image of a woman in a large diaphanous hat seated in a governess cart, swathed in daffodil colours. A second squint identified bright ear-rings and ropes of pearls resting like military decorations across a broad chest. The lady was dressed with great femininity but her shoulders had masculine mass. She was so big her age was difficult to determine. An application of face powder if anything made her look older. She held a smart leather whip mounted with silver in her right hand. It was poised threateningly in the still warm air.

'Little girl! Where are you taking that milk?'

The whip oscillated like the wooden lips of a ventriloquist's doll.

'Schoolhouse. It's for the teacher.'

Amy screwed up her eyes against the sun and then looked down again prepared to continue her slow progress towards the school gates.

'Little girl! I'm still talking to you. Don't you understand English?'

The raised voice obliged her to stop and prove she was a well-trained child. The sun was no longer directly in her eyes. She could stand still as long as she was asked to, holding the milk-can, and presenting a pleasing picture of pretty and obedient innocence.

'What is your name?'

Amy blinked hard to stop herself staring at the unfamiliar powder on the lady's face.

'I said what is your name?'

'Amy.'

'Amy what?'

'Amy Parry.'

'I am Miss Vanstrack.'

Amy raised the milk-can an inch or two to indicate that it was so full, it prevented her making a curtsey.

'That is an old Dutch name. Van not Von. It's not German at all. So don't you let people say it's German. Do you understand, Amy?'

'Yes, Miss.'

Amy nodded and her golden ringlets shimmered cheerfully in the morning sunlight.

'The Vanstracks are pure English. It used to be two words but now its one. Pure, pure English. Liverpool merchants for three generations. Now that's what you say, Amy, if anybody asks you. The Vanstracks are British to the core.'

'Yes, Miss.'

'Don't say, Miss. Say Miss Vanstrack.'

'Yes, Miss.'

Her willing obedience drew out her native obtrusive 's'.

'Would you like to do me a little service?'

Miss Vanstrack was leaning out with her elbow on the wooden mudguard. Amy glanced at the springs to make sure the cart would not tip over.

'It's perfectly simple. I just want to check something.'

She spoke very briskly and lifted her whip to point at the school buildings. Under a long verandah there were two heavy doors made to match, fitting into twin Victorian gothic arches edged with bathstone. The school door was wide open. The schoolhouse door was shut.

'Find out if the Rector is in there.'

Miss Vanstrack gave a haughty smile that lifted the right nostril of her powdered fleshy nose. Then she shook with gay laughter that made the cart springs creak. Amy was confused. She lifted her head to catch the comforting sound of children playing in the centre of the village. The large playground alongside the school was silent and deserted. It sounded like a game that called for numbers, a hunt perhaps or a paper-chase in which anyone could join. Amy looked down at her feet and wriggled her toes inside her boots.

'Shall I ask my Auntie? She's cleaning the school.'

Miss Vanstrack leaned over the mudguard and beckoned Amy closer so that she could smile at her conspiratorially.

'I think he could be in the house,' she said. 'Hiding. A certain person who shall be nameless said he'd gone to St Asaph to see the lord bishop. Now to be absolutely frank about it I don't believe her.'

Amy lifted a hand to shade her eyes. She was puzzled but ready to be helpful and win the important lady's approval.

'Now see here.' Miss Vanstrack was rummaging in the bottom of a leather shopping bag for her purse. She held out a piece of silver. Amy looked bashful. 'Take it,' she said. 'It's the king's shilling. You can buy an awful lot of sweets with it. I can see you are a bright little girl. A very bright little girl indeed. You and I can help each other. Did you say your name was Amy?'

'Yes, Miss.'

'Now isn't that strange? My best friend at school was called Amy. Amy Silk. I used to think it was such a lovely name. Her uncle was Captain Silk of the *Teutonic*. You've heard of the *Teutonic*?'

Amy shook her head regretfully.

'Never mind,' Miss Vanstrack said. 'I trust you. All you have to do is put two and two together. And report back to me. Do you understand?'

'Yes, Miss.'

'Miss Van-strack.'

Miss Vanstrack bent over the wheel to mouth the syllables. Amy frowned to show that she was making a particular effort to learn the unfamiliar surname.

'Use your intelligence. Put two and two together,' Miss Vanstrack said. 'Simple justice. That's all I'm asking.'

With the shilling in one palm and the wire handle of the milk-can in the other, Amy carefully ascended the steps from the road level to the wide drive that led to the school buildings. The lawns on either side of the drive had been roughly cut. The warm damp morning had brought out a fresh carpet of daisies and dandelions. Trimmed yew trees stood at intervals up the drive and between them there were patches of Spanish gorse and white heather overwhelmed with working bees. Amy kept to the middle of the stony drive. From the interior of the school, through the open door, came a clang of metal echoing like a mythological black-smith's forge in time of war. Esther Parry was hauling the desks about on their iron frames and the noise reverberated in the high rafters of the school's main hall. Amy squeezed up her eyes as though the sound distressed her. She paused for a moment and the noise stopped, only to be followed by a sound which made her shrink and shiver inside her dress: with unabating vigour her aunt was now scrubbing the bare wooden floor. The grey water was being worked backwards and forwards by the tough brush in a remorseless tide and the sweat running down her aunt's face and back would be a foam of the same distasteful colour.

She fixed her eyes on the ground and proceeded neatly along the path that led around to the back of the schoolhouse. She did not see the Rector squatting behind the ivy-covered rampart between the path and the front lawn until she almost trod on his straw boater. With unforced childish wisdom, she focused her stare on an ink smudge on his narrow clerical collar. Periwinkles grew among the ivy behind him. The Rector had broken one off. He lowered his fine-boned nose into the pale petals. His black crinkly hair was cut short and parted in the middle. He had not shaved and the dark stubble contrasted strongly with his pale delicate complexion.

'No smell,' he murmured softly through his even false teeth. He held out the flower so that Amy could smell it, but she did not move.

'Odourless,' he said. 'Like water and fresh air.'

She could not tell whether he was making a statement or a joke.

'Botany. I'm giving myself a botany lesson.'

The Rector spoke very softly. They were invisible from the road but his voice could still carry within reach of Miss Vanstrack's hearing.

'March on,' the Rector whispered in a comic croak. He nodded in the direction of the neat path that went around the house between laurel bushes and an herbaceous border. His predicament was such a source of amusement to him that he had difficulty in subduing the flow of giggling comment that forced its way to his thin lips like bubbles working up through still water. Crouching forward, he picked up his straw boater and clapped it down on Amy's head.

'There you are,' he said. 'A tin hat. Pack up your troubles, Miss Atkins.'

He crawled behind Amy on all fours until he felt he could stand upright and be concealed from the road by the tall laurel bushes. With the shilling deep in the palm of her hand, she took off the boater and held it out to the Rector who shrank back into the laurel bush. He took the hat but did not put it on his head. Two of his fly buttons were undone. He used the hat as a screen while he did them up with grubby fingers. Amy looked down modestly and she saw that his boots were only laced halfway up.

'Pity we couldn't have a picnic,' he said. 'Since you've brought the milk.'

He snorted through his delicate nostrils and raised an arm to try and part branches of the laurel bush to get a view of the road. Miss Vanstrack was not visible, but he heard the horse stamping its foot and the rattle of the harness.

'Do you think she'll go away in a minute?'

Amy bit her lip. He was not encouraged by her visible dilemma.

'She's after me day and night,' he said. 'It's verging on persecution. I was just going across the road to look at the traps on the edge of the Top Wood and there she was like an Assyrian coming down like a wolf on the fold . . . And so I was trapped instead of the rabbit . . .'

He sniggered cheerfully, openly pleased with his own fancies.

'Where are you going with that?' He pointed at the milk-can.

'To the schoolhouse of course,' he answered himself and raised a warning finger and tapped it against his lips.

'Now you wait a minute,' he said. 'I'll get through first. It's not too safe in there either. The world is full of rapacious women. I'd be safer at the Front, and that's a fact. I'll get through. As soon as you see me safely past the back door come along quickly and knock it. Then I can get across to the back playground, behind the outhouses, over the wall, through the wood and on to the mountain and freedom. It's a long way round I know but believe me, Miss Atkins, it will get me home in the end. Wait until I've gone around the corner. Right? We shall pass this way, but once . . .'

The Rector held himself back as if he were on the verge of making a risqué remark. He straightened his boater over his eyes, wiped his hands on the seat of his clerical grey trousers and prepared to walk quickly past the schoolhouse back door. Before he could reach it, the door opened and a fat woman with carpet slippers on her feet shambled out to shake a large tablecloth on the green mound where a few pullets were allowed to graze. They scattered in fright when she shook the white cloth but quickly returned in search of the crumbs.

'Rector!'

The woman turned her head and looked up to display wrinkles like fissures in her double chin.

'How very nice! You've come to visit us. On a Saturday morning.

61

How nice and homely. Take us as you find us. I'll just call my Morfydd. Upstairs I expect. You know what girls are like. College or no college.'

'Ah good morning, Mrs Owen! Isn't it a beautiful morning?'

The Rector was trying to project an Oxford manner at its most amiable and detached, but Mrs Owen was already back in the house calling her daughter urgently.

'Oh damn.'

The Rector thrust his hands in his pockets and kicked his heels helplessly.

'Miss M. A. Owen,' he muttered. 'But alas not Miss Owen M.A.'

Amy was still standing patiently on the path. Gloomily the Rector beckoned her forward. He paced about outside the door and did not go in the house. Amy waited to hand the milk can over to Mrs Owen, the schoolmistress's mother, who kept house for her.

'Little Amy.'

Mrs Owen's voice trembled with a display of benevolence as she bent to receive the can.

'And you haven't spilled a drop, have you?'

She removed the lid and looked pleased at the level of the milk.

'Are you going to sing for us today, Amy dear? Have you heard Amy sing, Rector? She's quite a little nightingale. Aren't you coming inside? Morfydd will be down directly. I'll make you a cup of tea.'

She disappeared into the scullery to pour the milk into a jug and rinse the milk-can under a cold-water tap. Her daughter appeared silently from the interior of the house. She was a thin refined woman with large protruding brown eyes and spots on her face which she covered with a white arsenic powder. She had been smoking a cigarette upstairs and the faint smell still clung to the folds of her smock.

'I see Miss V is in the road.'

She spoke as softly as she could but her mother heard her.

'What's that you say, my pet? Miss V in the road?'

She was wiping the milk-can with a damp cloth before handing it back to Amy.

'Miss V . . . the Hun you mean. Vans Tract? I'll see her off the premises. I'd like to go upstairs you know and take a pot shot at her.'

Mrs Owen aimed an imaginary gun.

'Mother!'

The schoolmistress gave a fastidious frown indicating the little girl who was standing patiently in the doorway.

'I could do it, you know. I've got your father's gun. And his bowler hat. Fire a shot across her bows. That would get her moving.'

'Hush, mother. Don't talk like that.'

'Hush! How can I hush? It makes my blood boil just to look at her. I've got my brave boy out there. My own boy. The finest son a mother ever had and I just can't bear to see the likes of her riding about like the Kaiser's mare and spying on our sacred homes.'

'Mother, you mustn't talk like that. Miss Vanstrack is English. Liverpool English.'

'English!'

Mrs Owen seemed to like the word only a degree less than German.

'They've bought Meifod Hall.'

'Upstarts,' Mrs Owen said. 'Trying to buy their way into high positions. And they think they can do it when nobody's looking. Where would they be without our illustrious fellow-countryman? Rector, I'm a good churchwoman although my mother was a Calvin. But I always thought the Lord had a purpose in rising up such restless cohorts of non-conformity in Wales. To think a little bread-and-butter Baptist has become the leader of the British Empire and the Prime Minister of Europe!'

Mrs Owen's eyes shone with mystical pride.

'You get so carried away, mother.'

Miss Owen moved closer to the door to see how the Rector was responding to her mother's emotional outburst. He had raised his boater to scratch his head. His eyes were screwed up tight as he wrestled with his thoughts. He bent his knees in turn and straightened out his long legs, to show he too was prepared to scrutinise mentally the mysterious undercurrents of history. Amy watched his movements with close interest.

'Baptist or no Baptist,' Mrs Owen said, 'he's the perfect Welshman. Standing in the courts of the world like a prophet in arms!'

63

The Rector stretched out his arm, his fingers spread out like a blind man feeling for a wall.

'Yes,' he said. 'That's it. Evensong. The English-language service. Just this.' He breathed deeply before giving his text. ' "All these men of war, that could keep rank, came with a perfect heart to Hebron, to make David king over all Israel, and the rest also of Israel were of one heart to make David king." '

Miss Owen smiled nervously. 'That sounds very stimulating, Rector.'

The Rector gave a worried nod. 'I haven't finished it,' he said. 'That's the trouble. You see these things, you know . . . quite clearly . . . and then they elude you . . . gone . . .'

Miss Owen moved her head so that he could see the full sympathy in her eyes.

'I'm dying to join up,' he said. 'But the Bishop won't hear of it. "It's not easy to stay home, Philips," he said. "And do the hum-drum things. The lights may have gone out all over Europe, but we're not going to let them go out here." '

'I understand your dilemma,' Miss Owen said. She held the edges of the sideboard tightly with both her hands. 'I really do.'

'We must *all* pull together.'

Mrs Owen made the dramatic announcement as she handed Amy the milk-can.

'Take that one back my love and tell them to watch the smell. I can smell turnips on the milk. Remember to tell them now. "Mrs Owen has smelt turnips on the milk." That's what you say. Now that shouldn't be at this time of the year. I'm a farmer's daughter myself so I know what I'm talking about.'

Amy looked demure and obedient.

'Here.'

The Rector thrust his hand into his trouser pocket, stretching his trousers as he fumbled charmingly among his small change. He offered Amy a penny. The schoolmistress and her mother smiled their approval at his generous gesture. Amy hesitated to take it. The Rector stretched forward and dropped the penny neatly into the small pocket of Amy's pinafore.

'Thank you, Rector. I'm going to help my Auntie now.' She gave a brief curtsey. 'May I go around the back, Miss Owen?'

'Of course you may.'

Miss Owen pressed her hands together under her chin. As she walked away Amy just caught the headmistress addressing the Rector.

'Isn't she sweet?'

The note of approval made her jump with sudden joy. She ran into the school swinging her empty milk-can and calling out for her aunt. Her voice echoed in the long dim corridor that separated the school from the schoolhouse. Esther stood in the centre of the main schoolroom, rubbing her brow with a hand that held a large scrubbing brush. She had just finished an area of floor board. The stack of desks now had to be replaced.

'What is it? What is the matter?'

Her back was hurting and she tried to massage it with her other hand.

'A lady gave me a shilling. And the Rector gave me a penny.'

Amy held out the coins in the palm of her hand for her aunt to see. Esther frowned wearily.

'Lady? What lady?'

'Miss Van's track. Mrs Owen said she's going upstairs to shoot her.'

'What are you talking about? Why should this lady give you a shilling?'

'She wanted me to find out if the Rector was in the school-house.'

'That's none of our business.'

'She gave it me anyway. She was very nice. She said she was English not German. Her best friend in school was called Amy. Amy Silk.'

Esther looked at Amy, uncertain whether or not to believe her.

'Where is she then? This Miss whatever her name is.'

'They've come to live in Meifod Hall.'

Amy gave the information importantly.

'Where is she now, I'm asking?'

'In her trap. In the road.'

'Well you just take that shilling back to her. Your uncle would be furious if he knew. You must never take money from perfect strangers.'

'She said she was my friend.'

'Friend indeed. I've never heard of such a thing. Give that shilling to me.'

Reluctantly Amy handed the coin over to her aunt. Esther's footsteps echoed heavily in the empty schoolroom as she marched towards the door. She emerged from the shadowy school porch on to the tiled verandah shielding her eyes against the bright light. She peered down the drive and saw nothing in the road.

'Where is she then?'

They moved together down the drive. Amy kept behind her aunt. There was no sign of the pony trap or of Miss Vanstrack.

6

AT A QUARTER-TO-TEN ON A TUESDAY MORNING, AN ATMOSPHERE of industry, application and good order prevailed in the main schoolroom. Miss M. A. Owen sat in her polished oak chair making a final check of the beautifully kept class registers. She set them aside with a brief sigh of satisfaction. She opened a drawer low in the desk on her left side and extracted the leather-bound school log-book. There was also a diary she wished to consult. She paused in the act to stare discouragingly at heads in standards five and six which had been lifted from their written task by the force of irresistible curiosity. Her desk occupied a conspicuous forward position towards the middle of the room. It was midway between the upright piano and the great sandstone fireplace in front of which a more modern stove had been installed. Her back was at that moment getting too hot and she wriggled with genteel restraint in her chair. With a sweeping movement of her well-groomed head Miss Owen could supervise with her protruding brown eyes the work of four standards. She could also watch her younger colleague at work, although at the moment a blackboard on an easel obscured Miss Bellis from her view. But the time-table decreed that standards three and four were deeply engaged in arithmetic exercises. Throughout the whole room the monastic silence was so profound that the wall-clock could be heard ticking. Something squeaked high up in the rafters, but Miss Owen restrained herself from looking up. The children were trained to reflect her disciplined responses. The great arched windows at the gable end gave the whole schoolroom an ecclesiastical appearance which encouraged sober and subdued behaviour.

Amy sat to the right of the centre in the front row of standards five and six. It was a privileged position and she was young to occupy it. Higher up the class behind her older girls envied her. But Amy sat in her place as if it were an hereditary stall. A year ahead of her age-group she was more easily summoned to go on messages than any other pupil in the room.

Next to her sat Gwyneth Mair, a large diligent Calvinistic Methodist. A prosperous farmer's daughter. She wanted a glimpse of the ink figures Amy had inscribed in the squares on her arithmetic exercise book. Amy blocked her view with an instinctive movement of her elbow and right shoulder. She knitted her brows and stared absently at the great map that hung on the expanse of yellow wall between the piano and the ornate fireplace. The shiny surface had cracked in the hot air that ascended daily from the stove on its way to the dim spaces among the varnished rafters. In Mercator's generous projection, the expanse of Empire was coloured a deep emotional red and only the green translucent seas and oceans were bigger. The same heat had kippered the wall charts that hung on either side of the impressive map of the world: on the left, tonic sol-fa in thick black letters; on the right, a rigid drawing of an imaginary Norman manor tilted upwards so that the children could see the armed men inside the bailey as well as the faceless peasants toiling in the sterile outlines of strip-cultivation and ditches.

Amy returned her attention to the next sum in the exercise. She lowered her nose close to the paper in an all-out attempt to work through it faster than anybody else. When she had finished she

67

took up a fresh pose. She shifted her exercise book so that she could study the wall opposite Miss Owen's desk and at the same time still innocently obscure Gwyneth Mair's short-sighted inquiring view. Inside the shallow vaulted recess there was a newspaper photograph of David Lloyd George stuck to the wall with saving stamps' edging.

'Amy . . .'

Miss Owen thrust the upper part of her body low over her desk. She spoke in a subdued tone that gave warning that no one should allow the floated call to disturb their concentration.

'Will you come here a minute.'

Although she responded promptly, Amy found time to close her exercise book and slip it in the slot beyond the ink-stained penholder hollow. She stood to attention at the top corner of Miss Owen's large desk, while the schoolmistress finished writing a note in red ink.

'Just a moment, Amy.'

Miss Owen rose with ghostly grace and tip-toed in wide steps to her colleague beyond the standard four blackboard. Amy could just catch the drift of a whispered conversation. Miss Owen reappeared to pick up the log-book and her diary. She returned to display a wrist-watch in support of her case.

'He's late . . .'

Amy lowered her head to show she was trying not to listen. Miss Owen was trying to convince herself and her colleague of the critical nature of the situation.

'This is the day,' she said. 'And this is the hour laid down. The Inspector will want to see the log-book. And the visitor. And the results will have to be entered. After all it is an exam, the Scripture exam . . . and this is a church school.'

She had convinced herself and had gained as much support as she felt she needed from her colleague. She returned to her desk, folded the note and placed it in a brown envelope. She gave Amy a sign to follow her through the narrow space between the high back of the teacher's chair and the brown dado of the classroom wall. With familiar ease, they both skirted a cluster of maps and wall-charts. Miss Owen held the loose brass doorknob with both hands to reduce the rattle as she opened the door. She frowned at herself for the noise she made. They stood among the coats in the cloakroom. The great door was open but the fresh air could not displace the smell of the heavy clothing. Miss Owen shivered a little at the autumn chill.

She moved to a window-sill where her mother had left for her a fortifying glass of raw egg beaten in milk. A clean piece of blotting paper lay on the glass to protect it from the dust that could so easily rise in the cloakroom. Miss Owen removed the blotting paper and sipped at the beverage, grateful for the fresh access of strength it brought. There was a faint smell of sherry about the glass.

'Now, Amy.'

Miss Owen spoke more confidently. She wiped flecks of the yellow drink from the corners of her mouth with her little finger. Her instructions were precise and urgent. She began in a low voice but her words began to bounce off the bare floor tiles and soar into the wide space above their heads. Amy listened with loyal intensity. She held on to the end of the brown envelope in Miss Owen's hands as though she were taking an oath of loyalty before dashing off bravely with a vital message through enemy lines.

'See that he gets it in his own hands. Don't give it to anyone else. It's most important.'

If only the classroom doors had been thick glass instead of varnished pine, the children could have seen her off without overhearing a word of the secret message being entrusted to her.

'What is it, mother?'

Mrs Owen's broad figure blocked the light in the open doorway behind Amy. She spread herself on the top step so that Amy could not easily pass. She bent her head inside to check whether the contents of the glass had been consumed.

'You haven't finished your egg and milk, my pet.'

The authoritative note in her concern irritated her daughter.

'I shall do, mother, when I have time, thank you.'

'I'm thinking of your health, my jewel. That's all. You have a lot of responsibilities to carry.'

Miss M. A. Owen was staring with open disapproval at her

mother's feet. With incongruous childishness they were shod in a pair of plimsolls with the uppers holed to accommodate her bunions. Mrs Owen shuffled over to a neutral position on the verandah halfway between the two front doors. As if to explain why she had emerged during school hours and moved about in forbidden territory, Mrs Owen pointed to a strange group apparently picnicking on the school steps.

'I thought there might be trouble,' Mrs Owen said.

'Trouble? What trouble?'

The schoolmistress emerged with official confidence to stand on the school side of the verandah. At the bottom of the drive there were four children sitting on the steps being fed by a large shambling unshaven man and a boy who looked like his eldest son. The boy looked sturdy enough but the smaller children were thin and pale and the clothes they wore were not warm enough for the time of the year. The father was cutting up a loaf. When he saw Miss Owen he touched his tattered hat with the blade of his knife. The smallest child had begun to creep over the curbing stone to play with a heap of fallen leaves the wind had piled up in the gap between the steps and the border of the schoolhouse lawn. His bare buttocks were exposed and his thin legs were blue with cold. The man lifted his boot to push the child back into line. Amy saw wet cardboard sticking out of the hole in the sole of his boot. When the child started to whimper he sprinkled cheap sugar on a lump of bread and stuffed it in the child's mouth. As he bent over he wiped the child's runny nose with his sleeve. Miss Owen was moved to take action.

She held the brown envelope in the air and waved it at the intruder as she took sufficient steps down the drive to place herself in a convenient position to address them. Her mother dodged with surprising agility into the schoolhouse. She opened the door wide so that the group on the steps could see if they looked hard enough, an ornamented glazed pipe containing heavy walking sticks and a shotgun and, on the polished banister, a man's black bowler hat. As she came down the drive in support of her daughter she moved diagonally to the school side so as not to obscure the limited view of the schoolhouse interior.

'This is school property,' Miss Owen said.

She waved her hand at the steps where the family had presumed to accommodate themselves. The children turned around to gaze at her. The child in the middle was a beautiful but fragile girl. Amy looked at her with some fascination. Her golden hair was the same colour as her own.

'That I know it is, Missus. And that is why I am bringing them here. This is Lawrence, ma'am.' He laid a heavy hand on the head of his eldest son. 'This is Joseph.' He turned with apologetic deliberation to the smaller children. 'This is Benedict. This is Peter. And this is Theresa, my one and only little girl. I couldn't send them to school with empty bellies now could I, ma'am, as a Christian father. But they've finished now. You've finished, haven't you? Is there any of that cow's milk left, Larry my lad? If there is, give it to Theresa.'

'Are you vagrants?'

'We've got the end house, if you can call it a house, your ladyship. One of the three cottages all unfit for human habitation. We were moving in you see. I've got to work on the land with the potatoes and that. I'm a travelling tinker but I'm setting my trade aside for the sake of the children here reading and writing and that and for the war effort of course. I'm doing my bit you see.'

'This is irregular,' Miss Owen said. 'You'll have to see the Attendance Officer.'

'A very civil man, and he's the one that sent me here. We're a little late I admit. But we were moving in you see. And I needed their labour, as they say, God bless their little hearts.'

'What is your name?'

'John Joseph O'Brien-Wood, your ladyship. Believe it or not, it's double-barrelled. Too much you may think for a travelling tinker. But I have to use it all. I don't want to get mistaken for a gipsy.'

When she saw that her daughter was uncertain what course of action to follow, Mrs Owen moved forward to whisper energetically in her left ear in a strange species of abbreviated Welsh.

'Send for the police, pet. Look at that knife . . . We'll all be murdered in bed. Move them on, jewel, or I'll never sleep nights. Send for the police . . .'

'Do be quiet please, mother.' Miss Owen was very firm. 'And do go back into the house. Now Amy, will you take this note to the Rector directly?'

Miss Owen turned her back for a moment on the O'Brien-Wood family to mutter a further message. 'And tell him what's happening here. Do you understand?'

Determined to exhibit fearless enterprise Amy marched down to the steps and waited for Theresa to move so that she could go on her important message. Theresa looked up at her innocently. She was not inclined to budge. As Amy waited, she let her mouth sag in a manner that could only be understood as derisory. Amy looked angry. The father scratched his head and looked amused by the encounter between the two girls. Had a fight broken out, for some time at any rate, he would have watched it with pleasure before pulling the contestants apart.

'Bring the children forward.'

Miss M. A. Owen had stretched out her thin arm with all the authority she could summon. Her mother was still watching from the steps of the schoolhouse. She had moved the ornamental glazed pipe into a more conspicuous position. It was almost beside her in the doorway. The tinker waved his hat and his coat swirled. Amy stood back as he seemed to sweep his entire family forward like a drover with a well-trained herd near the end of their journey.

'They are disciplined, ma'am,' he was saying. 'But they lack a woman's guiding hand. Their mother, bless her golden soul, she went with the consumption three years ago and has left me with them all on my struggling hands.'

Once out into the road, Amy broke into an urgent run, clutching the brown envelope in her hand. She climbed over the Rectory gate instead of opening it. The straight drive was flanked by tall coniferous trees. The gravel had been raked recently and Amy interrupted her run with long jumps that allowed her to land with a satisfying crunching sound in the gravel. There was a second more ornate white gate to open before she could approach the Rectory itself. The gravel drive flowed into a well-kept forecourt. The house and its outbuildings were set back among more trees and bushes and completely concealed from the public highway. It was a late-

Georgian house, granite-built with broad eaves and low-pitched roofs. The front door, painted white, was surmounted by a canopy supported on scrolled brackets. Amy considered the letter in her hand as though she were measuring its importance in relation to the black iron claw of the front-door bell. Somewhere inside the large silent house was the man with whom she had to make direct contact. She moved backwards to look at the upstairs windows and then darted through the space between the stables and the side of the house. In the open coach house a load of potatoes had been recently tipped. In the stable next to it there was still hay in the curved iron racks but no horses to eat it. A black cat was poised on the edge of the manger and stared balefully at Amy. She shooed the cat away and took a bold step forward to examine a bulky motor-bike that occupied the centre stall. It was being repaired and mysterious parts of heavy metal covered in black grease were strewn over the bevelled stable tiles.

Across the stable yard Amy could see through the low kitchen window a plump dark woman with an angry face bending over the corner range with a steel fish-slice in her right hand. She was turning over long slices of bacon. In between turns, she held the slicer up like a sceptre and stared gloomily into the flames of the fire. Behind her back another cat was on the table, licking the bacon grease off a large plate. Amy took a deep breath. This was the Rector's sister, who kept house for him: the obstacle implied but never named by Miss M. A. Owen when she despatched Amy on her important errand.

The first back door was open. Amy knocked it firmly but respectfully. There was no reply. No one emerged from the long damp corridor that led from the deserted rear rooms that included a workshop, a washroom and a dairy, to the front kitchen where the Rector's sister was cooking bacon. The corridor smelt of tom-cat. Amy held her nose for a moment and then ran back to the window and tapped it. Miss Philips looked up startled, guilty, worried and disturbed by the intrusion. The cat on the table also looked up but made no attempt to move.

'Yes? Who's there? What is it?' She spoke first over her shoulder and then when she saw it was only a child she came to the window and waved the fish-slice in the air. 'Who are you, then? What do you want?'

Amy held up the brown letter. 'I have a message for the Rector.'

'Message? Message? What message?'

She flourished her fish-slice to indicate that Amy should enter the house via the back door. Amy tiptoed down the smelly dark corridor uncertain at the end of it which door to open.

'In here. In here.'

Amy knocked the door before opening it.

'Who are you then? You're not one of those tinkers are you? You haven't come to live in the terrace under the bridge?'

Amy flushed heavily. If her feelings were hurt, Miss Philips did not notice.

'I've come from school,' Amy said.

'I didn't ask you that. I asked you who you were.'

Miss Philips was in a bad mood. There were two more cats circulating around her thick legs and waving their tails about in the air. The smell of fried bacon was deceptively friendly like the flames of the great fire that roared inside the range. There was a sour smell in the room. There were dirty supper dishes still on the table from the previous night.

'It's always a good thing to know who people are. Then you know where you are.'

'Amy Parry.'

'We've all got names, haven't we? Where would we be without them. Now where are you from? Who's your father and who's your mother? Whose daughter are you in other words?'

'My father and mother are dead.'

Amy made the statement as though she had never realised its full pathos before. Miss Philips sighed loudly and turned over a slice of bacon.

'I live with my aunt and my uncle. In Siloam chapel house. My aunt cleans the school.'

Miss Philips cheered up quite suddenly.

'I know, I know,' she said. 'I thought I'd seen you before but I wasn't going to admit it. I'm very cautious you see, bach, I always have been. Your aunt is a good clean woman. An excellent worker.

74

You don't think she'd like to come here do you and give me a hand? This place could do with a good clean.'

She waved the fish-slice at the cat on the table. Reluctantly it jumped down to the floor. Miss Philips became smiling and friendly. Her face shone with the heat of the fire and her eyes became merry slits in the folds of fat. Amy took a little time to adjust to the change.

'Would you like to come and work for me, Amy Parry? Good food and good wages. Live in if you like. There's plenty of room in this old place I can tell you. I want a nice clean girl. And you're a nice clean girl aren't you? Do you like cats?'

Amy looked pale and frozen with embarrassment but Miss Philips did not appear to notice. Like her brother, when she was in the mood she was greatly amused by everything it occurred to her to say. It seemed the one point of resemblance between them since she was as fat and as plain as he was thin and handsome. She never made any effort to modify her heavy Cardiganshire accent whether she spoke in English or Welsh. She had developed a way of confusing the two languages that was peculiarly her own.

'Duw, duw, chapel or not. It's a nice clean girl I want. Lodes lan. Lodes lan. My mother was an Annibun, 'sa hi'n dod i hynny. I'm not narrow you see. 'Sa'i 'n gul o gwbl. Nobody can accuse me of being narrow, nage wir.'

'I'm in school,' Amy said.

She sounded a little desperate. She lifted the envelope in her hand in the hope that Miss Philips would notice it. Miss Philips waved her fish-slice.

'Poof!' she said. 'It doesn't matter about that. What good does school do you? I never liked it I can tell you.'

'I have to stay in school.' Amy murmured her explanation apologetically. 'I want to be a teacher.'

'Do you indeed?' Miss Philips transferred her attention to the frying-pan. 'You want to be one of those, do you? One of those women teachers.'

'I've brought a note for the Rector.' Amy held up the brown envelope.

'Have you indeed? And what is that to do with me? Am I my

brother's keeper?' She waved her fish-slice in the direction of the
ceiling. 'I can't do anything with him. He's a law unto himself. He
says he's ill. I don't think he's ill. Do you think he's ill?'

She peered into Amy's face and waited for some reasonable
answer.

'I cook him a lovely breakfast and he won't get up to eat it. I
don't know what to do with him. What would you do with him?'

'I have to give him this,' Amy said.

Miss Philips stared at the envelope.

'Red ink,' she said. 'What's it written in red ink for? Why do
people write letters in red ink?'

'It's from Miss Owen,' Amy said. 'She said I was to give it to the
Rector.'

'They're all after him! Well, they can have him. That's all I'll say.
If they only knew what I know they wouldn't want him. I can tell
you that much. That's more than half the trouble with people in
this world . . .'

Her mood was changing again. She began to gurgle in her throat
with uncontainable amusement.

'Everybody wants what they can't get. And if they get it they
don't want it any more. Don't you think I'd make a good preacher?
Won't you give a Sunday in Siloam?' She waved the fish-slice
exultantly. 'Better than him anyway. Spoiling a good mechanic to
make a poor parson. Rector of Melyd indeed. That's what my
uncle used to say. And he was right too. Although everyone used to
laugh at him. Prophet in his own family you see. What shall I do
with this bacon? Will you tell me that? I can't eat it all myself. And
I can't give any more to the cats. It would make them sick. Now
would you like some, Amy Parry? On a piece of dry bread. Do you
good. I gave some to the tinker's little girl yesterday and she
gobbled it up.'

'No, thank you.'

Amy was staring dutifully at the envelope. Miss Philips's
goodwill evaporated swiftly.

'Well take it up to him. And tell him to get up while he's at it.'

Amy hesitated.

'Go on. Open that door. And march up those stairs. You'll find him. He'll be either snoring or coughing, one or the other. It's time somebody got him up. He won't do a thing for me.'

On the wall of the stairs there were views of the Oxford colleges. Amy stopped to look at her boots as though she were considering taking them off. There were four bedroom doors in sight and a corridor which led to more rooms at the back of the house and an old servant's staircase. She stood on the landing with one hand on the banister rail, looking from door to door. A tired groan from behind a closed door solved her problem. Resolutely she tapped the door.

'Who's that?' His voice sounded weak and irritable. He began to cough.

'It's me, Rector. Amy Parry. I've brought you a letter.'

'Who?'

His coughing had drowned her name.

'Amy, Rector. Amy Parry.'

He groaned dramatically. But when he spoke again he sounded more cheerful.

'Amy! Esther Parry's little girl. Come on in, Amy.'

He lay in the middle of a double bed deep in a feather mattress with the clothes over his head. The bedroom was large but sparsely furnished and most of his clothes were on the floor. The internal shutters of the long window were only partially closed. The view southwards was all fields and fertile valley with the glimpse of an ivy-covered water mill that had fallen into decay. To the left of the bed an open door led to a large dressing-room which the Rector used as a workshop. He made models there, mostly of sailing ships and a pleasing odour of glue and resin emerged through the open door. The Rector peeped out of the bedclothes.

'Close the door,' he said. 'For God's sake! Those damned cats. I can smell them from here. I'd like to drown the lot of them. Now what have you got for me?'

He stretched out a long bare arm to accept the letter. He sniffed and coughed and tore open the brown envelope, dropping it on the floor. Amy looked inclined to tidy it up if she only knew where to dispose of it. She craned her neck to take a closer look at the workshop. Sails made of thin wood were being fixed to the masts of a brigantine: she also caught a glimpse of a small open drawer with

77

birds' eggs resting on cotton wool. The Rector let out a sudden yelp of protest that made her jump.

'How can I possibly do it? A Scripture exam! You can see for yourself I'm ill in bed.' He sat up a little to cough and fall back on his pillows in order to demonstrate his complete exhaustion. 'It would be the death of me to go out on an autumn day like this and all the leaves falling. The worst time of the year.'

He shut his thin mouth and a melancholy silence descended on the bedroom. He stared at the ceiling with open eyes.

'To think of me,' he said. 'An Oxford man. Ending up in a place like this.'

Amy screwed up her courage to speak.

'Excuse me, Rector. Miss Owen asked me to tell you there was a family of tinkers on the school steps.'

'Tinkers? Tinkers. What have I to do with tinkers?'

Once more he listened to the silence, his head on the pillow and his eyes searching the ceiling. He coughed and his lips began to tremble.

'It's the saddest day of the year for me today. Six years ago to this very day I lost my dear sister, Megan. And Lizzie Anne doesn't even remember the date. What does she think of all day except her stomach and her cats?' His head rolled sadly from side to side. 'Her spirit fled through the dark vale to the bright light of a better world. "I am worn out," she said. Those were her last words. And she smiled as she said them. She was not twenty years old. The most beautiful, pure thing on earth. And I lost her.'

'I'm very sorry, Rector.'

Amy murmured her respectful sympathy so quietly, he did not hear her.

'Her body lies out on a Cardiganshire hillside. But her spirit is in heaven. I shouldn't grieve I know. She is with the Resurrection and the Life and I am down here among mortality and corruption. Among the silent company of graves. I shouldn't grieve. It's just that on this day, I am filled with an overwhelming sense of loss.'

He drew the bedclothes slowly over his head. Amy watched him, her mouth open. She stood quite still, overcome with awe, until she heard him speak in a muffled voice.

'Tell them I'm ill,' he said. 'Tell her I'm not coming.'

7

IN THE TOP CORNER OF THE GARDEN WHICH SLOPED UP THE HILLSIDE behind the chapel, Amy was scraping the bottom of the big iron kettle with a piece of slate. The crust of soot and carbon fell on to the damp soil next to the rhubarb patch. She squatted down, absorbed in her task and determined to do it well. She had an old black-leading brush in the pocket of her coarse apron ready to finish off the job. Only a few cabbages still grew in the empty garden. The bare soil was drying quickly. High clouds were being driven across the blue sky by the prevailing wind. Amy was so intent on her task, at first she did not hear her aunt calling her name in the kitchen doorway.

'I'm coming now, Auntie.'

On her way down the path, she managed a few strokes of the brush on the sides of the heavy kettle. She held it up in the doorway so that Esther Parry could see it.

'Leave that now, Amy.'

Esther's face was red with effort and confusion. She was a woman fighting against time with inadequate equipment. Her sleeves were rolled up as high as they would go. Her hands and forearms were red and cold with salt water. On the scrubbed kitchen floor lay the carcass of half a pig, blocks of salt, sacks, earthenware pots, a tin bath half full of salt and water. Esther was eager to take pleasure in her work, to show proper appreciation of the privilege of disposing of such an exciting and important consignment of winter food: but she was also nervous. The butcher's knife she had in her hand needed to be resharpened on a grindstone. The pots were not the right size. The right quantities of salt and saltwater had to be determined, and the most advantageous methods of cutting the meat.

'Lay the coal fire in the parlour.' Her anxieties made her short tempered. 'You can do it now while your hands are dirty. I'll cut a piece of pork-rib for Richard Parry. Then you can wash your face and hands and take it to him. And his bread.'

Amy put the kettle down on the iron stool inside the fender. She opened the oven door to collect the heather and charred furze that had been left there since the early morning to dry. She loaded them into her sack-apron, kicked off her clogs and stepped carefully across the floor. The parlour smelt soothingly of the turpentine and the linseed oil of the homemade beeswax polish that Esther used to make the modest furniture shine. Vigorously applied it almost obliterated the lingering smell of damp. Amy laid the fire with care. Even the bottom rails of the fire basket had been black-leaded by her industrious aunt. The room was cold but spotless enough for immediate use. A lit match had only to touch the kindling and it would burst into flame around the economical mixture of fresh coal and riddled cinders.

'Wash your hands.' Back in the kitchen Esther panted out her instructions. She was on her knees before the carcass. 'Then get me the little meat-basket from the pantry.'

Amy washed her hands outside in an old enamel basin under the tap of the rainwater cistern. The cistern took the water from the roof of the chapel. It fitted in between the chapel wall and the damp rock where fern and harts-tongue still flourished late in the season and fluttered endlessly in the eddying wind.

Amy shivered as she rushed back to the kitchen to dry her hands on the roller towel behind the back door. She pushed the door to as she dried her hands. Esther cried out crossly.

'Don't close the door,' she said. 'I can't see what I'm doing.'

In the small pantry, Amy took down the basket from its hook. She removed the wooden lid that fitted over the large earthenware pot where the home-baked bread was kept and took out the smallest oval-shaped loaf and put it in the basket. She placed the basket on the slate slab under the kitchen window next to the washing-up bowl. Her aunt told her to put the liver and piece of pork wrapped in separate greaseproof papers into the basket. Esther had more instructions to impart as she wrestled on with the carcass on the kitchen floor.

'Don't stay there, Amy. You know what your grandfather's like. And don't say too much to him. If he knows you've got to hurry back he'll do his best to keep you. I need your help.'

Amy nodded obediently. She held her hands together and watched her aunt with interest engaged in her unfamiliar task.

'Don't stand there,' Esther said. 'Put your coat on.'

'It's not cold.'

'Yes it is cold. Put it on. And put the cape on. There's no need to be ashamed of that coat. It may be a bit long but it's good material.'

Amy bit her lip, still reluctant to wear the coat.

'You like Miss Bellis,' Esther said. 'You know you like her.'

'It's too big for me,' Amy said.

'Listen.' Esther sat back on her heels and pointed the knife she was using at Amy. 'Listen to what I'm telling you. Clothes don't count. I'd like you to remember I said that. Clothes don't count. I know women make an awful fuss about them. But they're not important. It's your character that really counts.'

While she was speaking she heard voices outside the front door. She held the knife up in a gesture of frozen desperation.

'He's got somebody with him.'

Amy could barely hear her whisper.

There was a scraping of feet at the front door and Lucas Parry called out his wife's name. 'Esther!' He sounded loud and social, uncharacteristically cheerful.

'Who has he got with him?' She asked Amy the question as though she expected the girl to be able to answer. 'On a day like this.'

It all seemed suddenly a clandestine operation. Esther waved her knife helplessly. Had there been time, she would have swept up the carcass, the salt, the pots, the sacks into the pantry and closed the dark varnished door on her winter hoard. She was desperate to keep her secret.

'Are you there, Esther?'

He opened the kitchen door and leaned forward, one hand on the knob, the other arm raised high against the door frame like a railway signal. His smiling face and freedom of gesture was so unfamiliar that Esther forgot her concern about concealing the meat. She stared back at him with her mouth open. For once he showed some kind of resemblance to his father. Amy quickly withdrew her arm from the sleeve of the Ulster and shook out her hair. There was a visitor standing demurely behind her uncle: a small man in a high clerical collar, his plump shining face already

81

wearing a smile as though practising in the shadows for a sustained effort in geniality.

'I have with me the Reverend Parry-Bell, Esther. He has come early as you can see, but I am sure we are very glad.'

Momentarily the Reverend Parry-Bell went out of sight as he put down his Gladstone bag on the front-door mat. Hampered by his left leg, Lucas rolled to one side so that Mr. Parry-Bell could pass him. The minister entered the kitchen with his right arm almost fully extended . . .

'Mrs Parry! How very nice to see you.'

His cordiality came with a whirlwind delivery. As he jerked his head his little eyes twinkled like fireflies behind the tight spectacles he wore.

'And here is little Judith . . .' He paid Amy the closest attention as someone who had studied her progress with benevolent attention since earliest childhood. 'My goodness, how she had grown! She is going to be a beautiful woman. You mark my words. Like the rest of her family.'

'Amy,' Lucas said, pointing helpfully at his niece.

He was in no way put out. As a man long on the brink of the ministry himself, he knew how difficult it was for the shepherd to remember the baptismal name of every single member of a very scattered flock.

'Amy, of course. I'm getting old you see. And muddled. "Ffruxed" as we used to say in Machynlleth.'

He bent his knees unnecessarily to snatch up Amy's limp right hand from her side and hold it in his as he shook it slowly and solemnly.

'Now tell me, Amy. In all seriousness. What are you going to be when you grow up?'

'She wants to be a teacher.' Lucas made the announcement, not without a certain sober pride.

'A teacher!'

Parry-Bell held open his mouth in a dramatic circle of astonishment. His reaction could not have been bigger if Lucas had said 'Empress of China'. Lucas was obliged to introduce an element of restraint.

82

'A teacher like Miss Bellis of course. I tell her she'll have to work hard.'

'I'm sure she will. You will work hard won't you, Amy?'

Amy blushed and nodded. The minister shook her hand with continuing warmth and seemed content to go on doing so until they inspired him to do something else.

'Have you got a nice piece of pork there we could give Mr Parry-Bell, Esther?'

Lucas behaved like a man who could never prevent himself from being open-handed and generous. At last the minister let go of Amy's hand. He wanted both his to demonstrate intense and active opposition to Lucas's reckless proposal.

'I won't hear of it,' he said. 'Dear me, no. I won't hear of it. This is war time, Lucas Parry. There is a war on, as they say.'

Esther looked down sadly at the carcass on the floor. It lay with its ribs uppermost on the spread of washed sacks. She lifted her knife to examine the unsatisfactory edge.

'If you put this knife on a grindstone,' she said. 'That's what it needs.' She took a hesitant step towards the spot occupied by the minister on the crowded kitchen floor. 'There isn't much room,' she said.

'Please,' Mr Parry-Bell said. 'Think no more about it. I appreciate your generous offer and let us leave it at that. What do you think of this old war, Lucas Parry? Will it ever come to an end?'

'It's so restricted . . .' Esther's voice was faint and unenthusiastic. She looked at Lucas and at the carcass alternatively as if she were pleading for guidance about what kind of a cut to make.

'I've turned against it.' Mr Parry-Bell made a frank confession: a man speaking freely among friends. 'I'll admit at the beginning I was for it. So was everybody, if we set about counting. But where are we by now? Where has it got us?'

'I agree with you,' Lucas said. He smiled to show that he was still intent on being generous. He pointed at the carcass on the floor. 'Don't misunderstand my wife. She's the most generous woman in the world. She was talking about the kitchen not the pig.'

The latent humour in Lucas's remark made Mr Parry-Bell's shoulders work up and down like pistons. His beaming face did all it could to generate a festive atmosphere. Esther felt along the high shelf above the fireplace for a box of matches. She reached out to hand the box to Amy.

'Put a match to the parlour fire,' she said.

Lucas shifted his position to allow Amy to pass. He had news for his wife and he could not contain it any longer.

'You may have a bigger kitchen soon, Esther Parry. It looks as if we'll be moving from Melyd.'

Mr Parry-Bell kept his shoulders still. He watched Esther with an anxious smile.

'I am to be sent to work as a lay-preacher on the Shotton and Queensferry Circuit.'

Esther seemed to be having difficulty in taking in the news.

'This could be a step forward,' Mr Parry-Bell said. 'As I said to Mr Parry on the hill, this could lead to something.'

Lucas breathed deeply.

'There is work there,' he said. 'The Lord's work to be done. Chiefly among the munition-workers. I'm a worker myself. I know how to speak to them. We speak the same language.'

His eyes widened with inspiration as he stared hard at Mr Parry-Bell.

'It's a great challenge,' the minister said. 'A great challenge.'

Amy stood listening in the parlour doorway. Behind her the dried wood crackled and roared. Esther was finding it difficult to be enthusiastic. 'What about your principles, Lucas?'

'Well, what about them?'

He looked so full of conclusive arguments his face was already glowing with triumph.

'The blood is on their hands.'

Mr Parry-Bell looked at her as though she had made a scriptural quotation.

' "Thou hast shed blood abundantly and hast made great wars" ... That will be my first text,' Lucas said. 'Head-on! I don't want to avoid anything.'

Esther closed her eyes. 'Well I'm sure you know what you're doing,' she said. 'Why don't you go in the parlour now, both of you. I'll bring you some tea shortly.'

'How about some pork for Mr Parry-Bell and his little family!'

The minister shook his head energetically. He made a determined effort to change the subject.

'This war,' he said. 'It can't go on much longer. Prayer will be answered. It's got to come to an end.'

Esther lifted her hand to deal with the hair which was falling over her face. 'What will they do, then?' she said.

Mr Parry-Bell raised his eyebrows. 'I don't quite follow,' he said.

'The munition-workers.'

He indicated that he had no immediate answer to her question: he could only move into the parlour and sit by the fire and think about it.

'Amy!' Esther called sharply.

Lucas shepherded the visiting minister into the parlour. He looked at Amy before he closed the door. 'Have you learnt your verses?'

'Nearly, uncle.'

He showed his approval and then turned his attention to the visiting minister. He made an odd nasal sigh as he closed the door. It suggested that they had weighty matters to discuss, as churchmen, on either side of the fire in the parlour of the chapel house, but that the discussion would be agreeable and warmed with goodwill.

Respectfully Amy closed the kitchen door.

'Put your boots on,' Esther said. 'And watch how he packs the eggs, Amy. They are tenpence each you know now, in the shop.'

As she was speaking, she packed and unpacked the basket more than once. In the end she left out the piece of pork rib so that she could give it to the minister.

'He won't like it,' she said. 'But I can give him another piece next week tell him. Walk in the middle of the road and don't let anyone see what you've got in your basket. It's none of their business. And don't loiter. Stay in the middle of the road.'

Amy set out with the basket on her arm. No sooner had she closed the back door than Esther opened it again. She carried a piece of oilcloth with which to cover and conceal the contents of the basket. As she placed the oilcloth in position she repeated her instructions. Then she followed Amy down the path, pushing and patting her back with a sort of urgent affection, until she seemed to reach the end of an invisible tether, and was plucked back to the concerns of the kitchen.

Below the chapel, Amy was already walking obediently in the middle of the road. She was a solitary figure between the steep hillside and a tall hedgerow strengthened with ash trees which hid the roofs of the village from sight. As she descended the hill she became aware of the noise of shouting in the village and she could tell there was a popular game in progress long before the clock on the village hall of Melyd came into sight. From her vantage point on the hill road, she saw boys lined up against the wall below the village hall. One of their number stood halfway between their line and the cobbled forecourt of the stables of the Red Lion Inn. It was his business to capture a companion as the line of boys broke and they rushed across the square to press their hands against the stable wall. Amy hurried down the hill excitedly as though she were longing to take part herself. She paused when she saw that all the participants were boys: such girls as were present only watched from a safe distance. On the doorstep of a terrace house, next to the Central Stores, a toothless woman wearing a man's cap watched the game with evident enjoyment. With arms folded she leaned against her own front doorpost, a devoted spectator. From time to time she felt obliged to take on the function of a referee and waddle out into the middle of the game, wave her arms and make some loud but unintelligible pronouncement. The game swirled on around her and the boys took little notice of her judgements.

A girl on the high doorstep of an old house on the edge of the village had turned away from watching the game and saw Amy approaching. She lifted her hand in an eager wave.

Briefly Amy waved back. She made a sudden change of course. She crossed a fallen wall into what had been the large garden of a ruined cottage. It was used now as a rubbish dump by the people living at the top end of the village. Tracks made by dogs and stray animals and children blackberrying among the brambles led through the dying dock leaves and nettles to a stone doorway that opened on the narrow back lane that was only passable downhill to the main road. Amy hurried down the lane, glad to pass unobserved. The boisterous wind had dried the mud surface and she was able to pick her way without dirtying her boots. From watching where she put her feet, she looked up and saw that the way ahead was barred by three of the tinker's children.

The back yards of a single-storey terrace of three cottages were separated from the lane by a straggling thorn hedge full of gaps down which the three children had slid silently as story-book Red Indians. Their cottage was the only habitable dwelling in the row. The other two were empty with broken windows. The three children had a confidence Amy had never seen in them before. They were in territory they had made their own: the back yards of three decaying cottages. Theresa occupied the centre of the lane. Benedict and little Peter stood just behind her. Theresa folded her arms and stared back boldly at the intruder. Although her pretty pale face was dirty, her hair was neatly combed and shone with a gold light around it when the low sun broke through the clouds. Amy seemed to glance at Theresa's hair with grudging admiration before she advanced towards them. She looked determined not to have her way barred by children who were not even natives of the village; fringe people without any recognised territorial rights.

'You are blocking the road.' Amy spoke sternly, but Theresa refused to move.

'Our Joe's in the house.'

Her voice was light and husky. The statement was intended to support her boldness.

'He's got a knife.'

Red spots of excitement appeared in Theresa's pale cheeks. Little Peter watched her with absorbed interest, his finger in his nostril and his weak eyes screwed up against the late afternoon light.

'It's a knife for killing people. For cutting throats. I saw him kill a sheep with it.'

Theresa poked a stiff finger into the side of her neck.

'What you got in that basket?'

They were staring at the basket with an open longing that was stronger than curiosity.

'No business of yours,' Amy said. 'Get out of my way now. I'm late already.'

Little Peter had crept close enough to the basket to smell it. He began to sniff excitedly.

'There's white bread in there,' he said. 'And pig's liver! I can smell it.'

Amy looked down thoughtfully into the basket and then at little Peter. 'I can smell you too.'

She moved with angry speed. Her arm shot out straight into Theresa's chest. The girl's body was without any strength at all. Her legs collapsed under her. They were as thin as sticks. The two boys scrambled up the bank to the gap in the hedge. Theresa lay breathless and half-stunned on the bare earth. Amy knelt down to grasp a fistful of the golden curls and pull up her head.

'Listen,' she said. 'If I had the time I'd take you to Mr Ellis the policeman.'

Theresa began to tremble like a chick held in the hand. When Amy pulled her hair her head waggled helplessly like a doll's. Benedict had retreated through the hedge. He began to shout and scream urgently for his elder brother.

'Our Joe! Our Joe! Come quick!'

Still trying to be adult and dignified Amy let go her victim's hair and picked up her basket. She marched down to the bottom of the lane and crossed the main road with her head high, no longer caring, it would appear, whether she was observed from the centre of the village or not. The stony lane on the other side was wide enough for horse-drawn vehicles. She tried to ignore the shouts and taunts behind her. Even the rhythmic chant based on her name. The first word was 'smelly' and 'Amy Parry' was made to rhyme with 'never marry'. It was difficult for her to decipher the exact nature of the insult without standing still to listen. When she paused a small stone landed on the hem of her long coat. She turned around, her face red with anger. She saw that the three children were being urged on by the older brother, Joe. He stood behind them, a squat sturdy figure carving a clothes peg. Another stone was thrown. It fell harmlessly at her feet. Amy put down her basket. The stony surface of the lane provided an unlimited supply of ammunition. With sudden energy, Amy picked up a stone, shut her eyes and threw it. When she opened her eyes she saw Theresa sinking to the ground and a patch of dark blood beginning to ooze into her golden curls. She saw Joe drop his knife and clothes peg to kneel down and lower his close-clipped head near his sister's. Amy clutched her basket in both arms and turned to run as awkwardly as if she had suddenly acquired web feet. Breathlessly, she stopped to look back. The lane stretched back as straight as a shooting gallery. She was not being pursued. The tinker's children were all attending to their sister Theresa. Amy watched with growing horror as Joe picked her up. Her thin white legs looked so frail and limp and lifeless hanging down from his strong arms.

8

FROM THE VERANDAH STEPS TO THE SCHOOL GATES THE SMARTEST and strongest children in the school were paraded in their dark Sunday clothes. Those whose long overcoats were not dark enough wore black armbands. The schoolhouse door was open. A chair had been placed in the doorway for Lance-Corporal Owen, Miss M. A. Owen's brother. His mother stood behind him, massive in a black velvet hat and a black fur over her shoulders. The soldier was smoking and every time his mother bent to whisper some solicitude he inhaled deeply and waved the sound away from his ear. Miss Owen and her colleague Miss Bellis were in charge of the party. Miss Owen felt the cold. She shivered inside her thick coat like the trimmed yew trees either side of the school drive. Miss Bellis moved up and down the line, her cheeks glowing in the east wind, admired by her pupils who responded instantly to her softly spoken instructions. A boy had been posted on the wall, by the gate pillar to keep watch on the road that led eastwards to the village centre.

When he saw the funeral procession preparing to move from the village he raised his arm in a pre-arranged signal. The Rector was watching him through a small window in the church vestry. He emerged through the vestry door, his white surplice billowing freely in the brisk wind. He was followed by the part-time verger in his cassock. Among the gravestones the bow-legged verger stumbled as he hurried forward so that he could proceed to the lychgate ahead of the Rector.

The signal from the boy on the wall also served to start off the column of schoolchildren. With Miss M. A. Owen at their head and Miss Bellis at the rear they crossed the road to take up their appointed positions on either side of the minor road that led down to the churchyard. In the schoolhouse doorway Mrs Owen paused to fuss over the rug that covered the lance-corporal's knees and then moved down the drive with dignified haste and some concern for her large hat. The hatpins were not enough to keep it secure. She had to hold it down with her prayer-book and pay special attention to the steps that led down to the main road.

When the children had taken up their positions, Amy found herself under the large oak tree that leaned out over the road from the Rectory field. She looked up at the branches apprehensively: the brown leaves that were left rustled in the wind and attracted her attention. The teachers were making a last survey of the ranks. Miss M. A. Owen was straightening the round shoulders of the boy on the opposite side of the road. The Rector had arrived too soon at the lychgate. He opened the large prayer-book to glance quickly at the order of service. He saw Amy and seemed to consider smiling at her. Instead he shut his eyes tightly and lifted his face to the grey sky.

'Are you all right, Amy?' There was a soft note in Miss Bellis's modulated voice. Amy saw her teacher's bare hand coming closer, a shape of concern, totally unlike the indifferent branches of the oak tree. Her face began to crumple up. Tear drops bumped out of the corners of her eyes. 'Now we must be brave . . .'

Her hand had settled on Amy's shoulder. The little girl twisted her neck to bring her hot cheek closer to the comfort of the cold fingers. Miss M. A. Owen was not so sympathetic.

'Now then, Amy Parry,' Miss Owen said. 'We are all grief-stricken. All of us. But we must try and control ourselves. So that we can pay proper tribute to the memory of our little friends.'

Miss Owen crossed the road. The sterner note was ineffective. Amy was crying as though she would never stop.

'I think she may be unwell. Are you unwell, Amy?'

Amy nodded willingly. Miss Bellis felt Amy's cheek with her bare hand. There were traces of chalk on her soft fingertips.

'It feels hot. She may have a temperature. Do you feel a chill, Amy?'

Again Amy nodded. Miss Owen looked very put out.

'She had no business in that case to come to school. I've warned all the children. The slightest hint of influenza they should go to bed. I'm surprised at Esther Parry. Usually she's such a responsible woman.'

'I expect she wanted to pay tribute to her little friends.' Miss Bellis was firm in Amy's defence. 'I had no idea she was so fond of Theresa Wood. That poor little thing. That golden hair. To think it all fell out.'

Overcome, Amy let her wet open mouth sink in the material of the sleeve of Miss Bellis's coat.

'We don't know how friendly these children can get with one another, do we? If they find something in common. Shall I take her into the schoolhouse?'

Miss Owen turned her head about uneasily: it was not a decision she wanted to take. The two teachers hurried back to the main road with Amy between them. They joined Mrs Owen who stood in the middle of the road dividing her attention between the motor car parked down the road and the slow approach of the enlarged funeral procession from the village. Miss Bellis gave Amy a clean handkerchief. Amy looked up towards the procession and clapped the ironed handkerchief over her mouth. The road was packed with people mourning the child victims of the epidemic. Amy's eyes widened. At first the coffins were barely visible. There were three side by side, new and neatly made. The boots of the bearers and the brass fittings were highly polished. The only sound was the strange slow shuffle of many feet, the creak of boots, an occasional suppressed cough and the crows cawing in the Rectory trees. Behind the centre coffin one white face stood out among the mourners. The tinker was washed and shaved and his thin unruly hair was greased down on his domed skull. The women around him wore veils. The tinker's face was as white as a bone. The procession as it advanced ate up the remaining comfort of distance. Amy's sobbing came closer to hysteria.

'What's possessing this girl?' Miss Owen sounded repulsed and a little frightened. Miss Vanstrack, wearing a long leather driving coat, was striding masterfully towards them from her car.

'What's up?' she said. 'Anything I can do?'

Miss M. A. Owen was too preoccupied to answer her. The proper order of the ceremony was being disrupted. The girl was turning into an irritating liability. If the Rector could see what was happening he could be holding her responsible for an unseemly diversion. Her mother was being unhelpful, trying to catch her eye to request permission to speak severely to the erring pupil who was showing such ingratitude for all the grace and favour bestowed upon her. Miss Vanstrack was threatening to interfere and undermine her authority.

'She ought to be somewhere warm, I think.' Miss Bellis tried to speak in a reasonable manner. Miss Vanstrack nodded approvingly.

'Absolutely right,' she said.

Miss Owen looked at her mother who shrugged her shoulders under her black fur.

'I don't think I can have her in the schoolhouse,' she said. 'There's a risk of infection. My boy is in a low state still. He's a wounded soldier remember.'

Amy had buried her face in Miss Bellis's warm overcoat. But she could not stop up her ears against the ominous advance of feet on the dry surface of the road. She began to push so that Miss Bellis was obliged to stagger back and then brace herself against the strong shove.

'It's all right, Amy.' She spoke softly. 'There's plenty of room.'

'Oh my goodness!' Miss Owen thrust her hand in her coat pocket and extracted a small metal pitch-fork. 'The hymns.'

Her protruding eyes stared at Miss Bellis.

'I should be in front,' she said. 'Can I leave this with you, Miss Bellis?'

She slid down the church lane, touching first one child and then the other, moving sideways and trying to be as unobtrusive as she could. She was ahead of the cortège which proceeded with great calm and dignity down the church road. The villagers seemed intent on supplying solid warmth and sympathy to the bereaved families. They crowded together and the standing children were completely hidden from view. When Amy lifted her face minimally from the shelter of Miss Bellis's coat, the procession was coming to an end. It was now much shorter than it had appeared as it advanced from the village. At the very end she saw her grandfather, Richard Parry. He stood with his hands behind his back and he was craning his neck to try and see what was going on down at the lychgate.

'You know what it is, don't you? It's not Spanish at all. It's not 'flu.' Mrs Owen was murmuring sepulchrally into Miss Bellis's ear. 'It's the smell. All the dead bodies on the battlefields. The smell carries away the weak children with no resistance. That's what it is.'

Amy began to shudder.

'I say,' Miss Vanstrack said. 'Just look at her. She's got a fever surely. Do you think I ought to drive her down to the Isolation Hospital or something?'

Miss Bellis and Mrs Owen both considered the suggestion. Each for her own reasons seemed inclined to agree.

'It could be just hysterics,' Mrs Owen said. 'She's had rather too much notice. Singing and so on. I've always found that. Especially with girls.'

'She ought to have a blanket,' Miss Vanstrack said. 'I could wrap her in a blanket and stick her on the back seat. What's her name?'

Amy let go of Miss Bellis's coat. With her head lowered, she darted up the road to where her grandfather was chewing excitedly and standing on tiptoe to get some idea of when the singing was likely to start. He wore no overcoat. Amy plucked at the long tweed jacket he wore.

'Hello, little Miss Fraction. What are you up to then?'

'Taid,' Amy said. 'I want to go home. I don't feel well.'

'Is that a fact?'

He turned his head to spit tobacco juice to the side of the road. He bent his knees to take a closer look at Amy's face. She lowered her glance to avoid returning the grin on his face as he made his eyes small to examine her face in a mock medical manner. While he was looking at her, the hymn singing began unsteadily. He screwed up his eyes tightly as though the action would keep the unlovely noise out of his ears.

'She's pitched it wrong,' he said. 'The silly bitch. Church people got no idea about singing. Just listen to that. The crows would do better. And singing in English. Just imagine.'

The singing stabilised itself with male voices in the ascendant. The words of the hymn became clearer.

> 'Oh how peacefully a child
> In the grave is sleeping
> Free of anguish free of sin
> Pale but safely gathered in . . .'

Richard Parry took Amy's hand in his. He scratched his head as he wondered what to do with her. He realised the three women by the school gate were watching him. He cleared his throat and hummed sol-fa through his nose. Amy tugged his arm.

'All right,' he said. 'Off we go. It's a rotten hymn. That parson has got no taste at all. And he calls himself an Oxford man. I've had conversation with him and I can tell you he doesn't know much either. He didn't know John Wesley and the Duke of Wellington were cousins. More or less told me I was a liar. And do you know what I said to him? I'm surprised at you, Mr Philips, I said, and you so fond of the English.'

He straightened his back slowly and in doing so he managed to catch a fleeting smile on Amy's face.

'I thought as much,' he said. 'Are you ill, Miss Fraction, or aren't you?'

He began to chew more rapidly and blow his cheeks in and out. He stretched out a rigid index finger. Amy shifted her ground quickly in anticipation of the familiar threat he was going to make to tickle her.

'Shall we try Doctor Parry's tickling machine? Tickle three times a day after meals.'

Amy suppressed a giggle and shook her head. She held on to his hand and they began to walk slowly up the road to the village. As they put more distance between themselves and the children's funeral, Richard Parry grew more outspoken.

'There's nothing wrong with you is there? Say the truth and shame the devil.'

'I *have* got a headache,' Amy said primly.

'Um.' Richard Parry went through a bout of rapid chewing, took aim and spat at a target on the road. 'I don't know what your game is, Miss Fraction. But I know what mine is. No school this morning, eh? How about a game of draughts?'

He winked and Amy accepted the change of atmosphere. From now on they were fellow conspirators. They ignored the hymn-singing in the distance and hurried on to the wide lane where Amy had put down her basket to pick up a stone to hurl blindly at the tinker's children. Richard Parry was in a gay mood. To make Amy laugh he sang two lines of an old revival hymn.

'I have cast aside my crutches
And both my feet are free'

and then began a slow shuffling dance to illustrate his words. As he danced, he stole a glance at her laughing face. She looked pretty and healthy. No one was about. Most of the village was attending the funeral. He grasped Amy's arm and made her imitate some of the antique steps he was making.

Richard Parry's cottage was on the roadside. It consisted of two rooms, one on either side of the door. The doorstep had been freshly decorated that morning, while it was wet, with a chalk design that gave it a white edge and a diagonal cross. When Richard Parry opened the door they both stepped with super-stitious care over the threshold. When Amy passed the wooden screen on the right of the doorway, she saw a bright fire burning in the grate. Richard Parry stretched his hands out to the fire and rubbed them together gleefully.

'Very important,' he said. 'When you've been to a funeral, have a nice big fire waiting for you when you get back.'

His aged terrier dog was stretched out on the washed sugar sack in front of the fire.

'Look at him,' Richard Parry said. 'He's glad to see me but he's too lazy to wag his tail.'

There was a dark oak settle on the left of the fireplace. The floor was bare earth, but beaten so hard it glittered in the comforting firelight. Richard Parry moved the round table closer to the settle. Amy opened the middle drawer of the dresser and brought out the draught board. The pieces were kept in a triangular oat-cake tin with a picture of Queen Victoria on the lid. Richard Parry put his foot on a block of oak and watched Amy intently as she set out the pieces. He fed himself a fresh quid of shag tobacco.

'Taid . . .'

He seemed to know at once that there was an important question she wanted to put to him.

'Where is hell?'

Amy fingered the pieces on the board while she waited for an answer. Her grandfather had begun to chew excitedly and she knew it was unlikely he would say anything until he had spat with dramatic accuracy, into the heart of the fire.

'That's a good question,' he said. 'A very good question.'

She lifted a white and a black counter from the board, put her hands behind her back and mixed them about before holding out her fists towards him.

'Hell is a prison,' he said.

'Where though, Taid? Where?'

'I'll tell you exactly where it is.'

He spoke so solemnly that Amy kept her fists clenched and her arms rigid. Richard Parry tapped her right knuckles with his finger and then pointed at Amy. She opened her hand and a black piece lay in the centre of her palm.

'Inside you!'

Richard laughed triumphantly as they turned the board around.

'My father heard it in a sermon when he turned to religion in 'fifty-nine. And it did the trick. He was a serving man in Plas-y-Llan living in the stable loft. Following the plough. He was very worried at the thought of ploughing a field of everlasting fire for all eternity. Very worried indeed. Then he got his new idea and he took to religion like a duck to water.'

Having answered her question he began to concentrate furiously on the game. As he studied the board he pushed his eyebrows down over his eyes with his fingers and stared through them like a pet dog, blowing his cheeks in and out. When the old terrier on the mat groaned in his sleep, he pushed his belly with the toe-cap of his boot to stop the noise.

'Do you think God watches everything we do?'

'Of course he does.'

Richard Parry took a piece with open satisfaction. Calmly, in return, Amy took three of his.

'Everything? All the time?'

He stared crossly at the draught board as he quoted absent-mindedly:

> 'God lives in every space
> As easily as air
> So when you walk alone
> Remember He is there . . .'

He made his move. Amy took more pieces. He stared at her sulkily and conceded the game.

'Set them up again,' he said. 'And don't think you are going to win every time.'

While he waited he frowned and spat moodily into the fire.

'Why should He bother?'

Amy grasped her hands together under her chin, ready to play.

'What are you talking about?'

'God,' Amy said. 'Why should he bother to watch everything? Your move, Taid.'

Richard Parry peered at her suspiciously through his eyebrows.

'You are not getting too big for your boots, are you? Just because you're good at school. Let me tell you something. School is nothing.'

Amy was staring at him with polite disbelief.

'What are they anyway? Teachers. What do they know worth knowing?'

97

'Miss Bellis is a B.A.' Amy spoke primly, her eyes on the board.

Richard Parry shifted his jaw about as he searched for a disparaging phrase.

'B.A. Ba-ba,' he said, not altogether satisfied with the invention. 'Something for sheep. That's the way I look at it.'

Amy concentrated on the game. Longing for victory but uncertain how to proceed, Richard Parry waved his hand over the board as though he were casting a spell before descending on a piece and moving it. The move was a mistake. He saw this as soon as he had made it. He was losing a second time. Angrily he bent his finger, wedged it under the corner and tipped the board so that the pieces that were left rolled over the floor. The action restored his good humour. He began to laugh happily.

'Taid!' Amy sounded cross. 'That's very childish. Very childish indeed.'

He rubbed his hands delightedly.

'Now then,' he said. 'Now then. When you've finished picking all those up, every single one of them, would you like me to give you a lesson in the strict metres?'

Amy was on her hands and knees searching for the pieces.

'I don't like verse,' she said. 'Not Welsh verse anyway. Not the strict metres. Miss Owen says they're not worth the bother of learning.'

'That one!' Richard Parry brought his fist down on the round table so hard the draught board bounced in the air. 'Don't we get cheated all ends up. No matter which way you look at it. Disestablishment. What a fraud! I keep telling Lucas, the great preacher. But he won't listen. He's green enough to get lost in a lettuce.'

He stopped himself abruptly to watch a bulky figure passing the window. 'It's Ellis the policeman,' he said. 'In his uniform too. Now then, Amy Parry. What have you been up to?'

Amy went white. She sat back on her heels and looked around desperately for somewhere to hide.

'Did you ever see such a slow mover? It would take him half a morning to put the handcuffs on you.'

Amy crawled on her hands and knees towards the siamber.

'What's the matter with you?'

98

Richard Parry bent down to see what was going on. Desperately Amy put her finger to her lips before she hid behind the door. The policeman knocked three times before lifting the latch and bowing low to step over the clean threshold.

'Is there Peace?'

He made his greeting in a sonorous bardic tone. He carried a brown-paper parcel under his arm. He had a large expressive face and it seemed to be a pastime with him to make grimaces inside the constriction of his chin-strap. He also liked to make his large brown eyes roll about.

'A little bird told me you had a visitor.' Ellis the policeman spoke in his most playful manner.

'Come on now,' Richard Parry said. 'Let me see them then. When do they have to be in by?'

'My englynion?' the policeman said. 'Alas I haven't written them yet.'

'You don't expect me to write them for you?' Richard Parry wanted to make a joke. 'That's against the rules.'

Ellis made a large circle with his slack lips. 'Oh,' he said. 'This is business, Richard Parry. Not poetry or pleasure. This has to do with a theft.'

The unpleasant word disturbed Richard Parry and the policeman went through a series of grimaces to show that he too was joking.

'Look here, Ellis. You are paid to be a policeman not a clown. What have you got in that parcel?'

'I thought you were a man who enjoyed a little relaxation.'

The policeman sighed reluctantly and dropped the parcel on the round table. Richard Parry opened it. Inside was a chenille table-cloth with tassled edges, neatly folded.

'Esther Parry's table-cloth. Where the preachers eat. The chapel house.' The policeman sighed again and stretched his jaw inside his chin-strap. 'I'm a better detective than I look,' he said. 'Solved this one in next to no time. Esther Parry hung it on the line. It vanished. That little tinker boy took it. Now then, in view of their sad bereavement, I don't want to pursue the matter any further. That's the way I feel about it. Now if Amy will help me out, she can take it home. If she likes she can pretend she found it.'

His thick boots shifted about on the beaten floor; his large eyes rolled in his head.

'Where is she then? Where is my little girl?'

9

THE BRAKES OF THE AUSTIN TOURER SQUEALED LOUDLY AS MISS Vanstrack pulled up in the road below Siloam chapel. She wore a manly navy-blue Henry Heath hat, a woollen scarf with tassles and a belted leather overcoat. The top half of the windscreen was bent down but she looked warm enough. At her side Miss Bellis, wearing a raincoat over a thin dress, was shivering with cold but smiling enthusiastically.

'That was fun,' she said. 'I enjoyed that, Berta.'

'Yes, well, you'd better find a stone and stick it under the back wheel,' Miss Vanstrack said. 'This hill looks as steep as the side of a house to me.'

Miss Bellis remained poised athletically for a moment on the running board, holding onto the open door. She saw the limestone dry wall across the road shining white in the fitful spring sunlight. She crossed the road and lifted a stone from the top of the wall, studying the moss, the white and yellow lichen spots and the primitive fossil marks with habitual interest.

'Buck up!' Miss Vanstrack said. 'I want to let go of this blasted handbrake.'

Miss Bellis wedged the stone in front of the offside rear wheel. She stood back to brush the palms of her hands against each other. Miss Vanstrack stretched out a gloved hand to squeeze the rubber ball of her motor horn. Her companion waved a hand to stop her.

'Better not, Berta . . .' She spoke apologetically. 'The uncle is a bit touchy . . . You know what I mean?'

There was already a smile on Miss Vanstrack's heavy face.

' "Dauntless the slug-horn to my lips I set . . ." '

Miss Bellis nodded hard to show approval and appreciation. 'You are doing a marvellous thing, Berta,' she said. 'And I know they'll respond. I'm sure of it. Esther Parry is a good woman. I have the highest opinion of her. And I'm sure he's a good man too in his own way. But he can be touchy and difficult.'

'He'd better watch his Ps and Qs with me . . .'

Miss Vanstrack drew off a driving gauntlet to examine first one side of her hand and then the other.

'You've been away,' Miss Bellis said. 'You've been in London doing valuable war-work and you've seen a great deal. But these people have never been anywhere. And they've seen nothing . . . do you know what I mean? Don't be hard on them.'

Miss Vanstrack opened the low door of the tourer and swung her legs jauntily out.

'You are a good sort, Bellis,' she said. 'Much better than me. Where's the child do you suppose?'

Miss Bellis raised her arm. 'Up there.'

She waved her arm to indicate that Amy could be anywhere on the hillside. 'I thought I caught a glimpse of her as we came along the top. Flying a kite. A brown paper kite. With a long tail of coloured bits.'

She made a floating gesture, giving a smile to represent a brief nostalgia for the timeless freedom of children. Miss Vanstrack approached the chapel gates. She looked up at the building with the interest of a tourist in a foreign country.

'Do you know I've never been in one of these. What make is it?'

Miss Bellis smiled. She tapped Miss Vanstrack's elbow playfully. 'Wesleyan. Welsh Wesleyan.'

The chapel doors were open.

'Can't we pop inside and have a decko?' Miss Vanstrack rolled her eyes naughtily. She opened the gate and climbed the steps and looked back challengingly when she reached the top. Miss Bellis remained in the road.

'Just a peep,' Miss Vanstrack said. 'Just a squint. Curiosity killed the cat and all that.'

Cautiously she stepped into the chapel porch. She could hear the echoing rasp of a scrubbing brush on bare floorboards. She touched her nose against the green frosted glass but she could see no one. She pressed on a door to peep inside. Over the pulpit a Welsh biblical inscription had been freshly painted. A silver scroll unfolded in the shape of an arch. The gothic capitals declared THE LORD IS RIGHTEOUS IN ALL HIS WORKS WHICH HE DOETH. Miss Vanstrack located the scrubbing sound. Esther Parry was at work with a scrubbing brush in the area where the church members knelt to receive their communion with their elbows on the rail of the deacon's pew. When Esther raised her head her face was flushed with the physical effort she was making.

'Good Lord,' Miss Vanstrack said. 'Why don't you use a mop? You'll never get to the end of it doing it that way.'

Esther wiped the sweat from her brow. She looked embarrassed and disturbed.

'I say,' Miss Vanstrack said. 'Is it all right for me to creep in like this? Am I trespassing or something?'

'I wasn't expecting you.'

Esther cleared her throat and spoke more loudly.

Miss Vanstrack nodded understandingly. She stretched out her arm magnanimously inviting Esther to stop working, get up from her knees, and walk down the aisle to join her.

'Yes, well you see, this afternoon I've arranged to take the Pulfords for a spin. To Colwyn Bay we thought if the weather holds. Mr P doesn't get out much you know. Motoring takes him out of the dumps. Good for him the doctor says. So I said to Glenys Bellis, "Let's nip over to the Parrys' and get the Amy business all over and done with."'

Esther took off her sack-apron and rolled it up tightly in her red hands.

'I promise I'll be very tactful,' Miss Vanstrack said. 'Where's Daniel? Show me the way to the lion's den.'

Esther gazed at Miss Vanstrack as though she were seeing her in a totally new light.

'Shouldn't make jokes in church, should I? Or in chapel I suppose. It's those Zeppelin raids, you know. They made me quite jumpy. The result is I can't stop making jokes and frivolous remarks. I was never like this before. It's changed my whole nature.'

As she burst out laughing again Miss Bellis arrived in the porch on tiptoe. She smiled and nodded in the friendliest fashion at Esther.

'Hello, Mrs Parry,' she said. 'We've come rather earlier as you can see. I hope it's all right.'

'He's studying,' Mrs Parry said. 'He tries to do two hours solid every Saturday morning. Every chance he can get really. He doesn't get much of a chance.'

'Lead on, MacDuff.' Miss Vanstrack waved her driving gauntlets at the chapel doorway.

'I'll just go and tell him you are here. Prepare him a little.' Esther was nervous and uncertain what action to take.

'Doesn't he know . . . ?' Miss Bellis let her voice trail tactfully into silence.

'Yes, of course. In a sense he knows. And he wants the best for her. Of course we both do. And we are deeply grateful too. Please don't think we are not.'

She turned her knee towards Miss Vanstrack as though she were contemplating making her a curtsy. Instead she lowered her head in an abbreviated bow.

'I've thought about it a great deal and I'm sure it would be the best thing for Amy. But he's very quiet about it. We are fond of her you see. She's made a great difference to our lives. We think of her as our very own. It won't be easy to part with her.'

Miss Vanstrack struck Esther lightly on the back with her loose glove. 'Good heavens, woman,' she said. 'You're too soft by half. I went away to school when I was eight, for heaven's sake. Best thing that ever happened to me. Jolly good school it is too. One of the best in England in my opinion. Talbot Manor Collegiate, *Fac et Spera* and all that.'

'I hope you don't think we are ungrateful . . .' Esther appealed humbly first to Miss Vanstrack and then to Miss Bellis.

'The place is in such a mess. He won't let me touch his books you see when he's working. I was going to make you a nice tea. I was going to make some fresh griddle-cakes. I know you like them.'

Esther inclined her head towards Miss Bellis and stared at her dumbly, appealing for help and support.

103

'Well, let's get on with it.' Miss Vanstrack sounded brisk and efficient. 'This sort of thing has got to be settled once and for all. There are arrangements to make, as poor dad used to say. And he was always right. Nearly always anyway. It's my old school, I know that. But there are arrangements to make. And old Ma Henman likes plenty of warning I can tell you that. She's a tough old bird is Ma Henman.'

'I'll go in.'

Esther backed away from them. Once out of their sight she hurried down the steps, squeezed herself between the motor car and the rock face to get to the little wooden gate and the path to the back door of the chapel house. In the kitchen she paused to inspect the fire and push the heavy kettle on to the coals. She tapped the parlour door gently before opening it. Lucas Parry sat in his shirt sleeves at a small round table he had placed near the fire. Both his hands supported his forehead as he pored over his books. He screwed up his eyes as he lifted his head like a man emerging from a cave trying to find his bearings in the unfamiliar light of day.

'What is it?'

'They are here.' Esther smiled nervously. She was making a great effort to speak calmly.

'Who are "here"?' Lucas spoke pedantically. He raised a weary hand over the pile of books that lay between himself and his wife.

'Miss Bellis. With Miss Vanstrack. I told you they might be calling this afternoon. They've arrived this morning instead. It's about Amy. Going away to school.'

Lucas pushed back his chair and stretched himself carefully. 'I've been thinking about that,' he said. 'I've given it a lot of thought. I don't think she ought to go.'

Esther trembled with sudden alarm.

'But Lucas,' she said. 'They're here. They're outside now. Miss Vanstrack's car is outside.'

'It would be a mistake. A grave mistake.'

'But Lucas, you said it would be a chance for her. You said that. We can't stand in her way now . . . can we? They're here. Listen. They're outside the front door!'

'In that case you had better let them in.'

Very deliberately, he rolled down his shirt sleeves over his forearms, concealing the tight sleeves of his woollen vest. He lifted his jacket from the back of his chair and put it on.

'Do come in, please.'

He could hear Esther making welcoming noises in the little hall.

'And please don't notice the mess. By this afternoon I would have had the whole place in proper order . . .'

'Now don't worry.' Miss Vanstrack's voice sounded too loud for such a small house. 'It's all very spick and span I can tell you that. It's a great credit to you Mrs Parry. The world of the scrubbing brush and not the mop. Down on your knees. That's what I'd call it. I only wish you'd come and work for me, I can tell you.'

The narrow hall and the steep stairwell did not seem large enough to contain her laughter. Miss Bellis stayed outside on the front door step until Miss Vanstrack's leather bulk had moved into the parlour.

'Now where is this mysterious husband of yours. Do you realise, woman, I've never clapped eyes on him? How do you do, Mr Parry.' Miss Vanstrack smiled cheerfully and offered him her hand. 'I'm sorry if I make too much noise,' she said. 'I was telling your wife. It was the Zeppelins really. My poor old father complained about it bitterly sometimes. "For God's sake Berta," he used to say, "try to make less noise." And I did you see. I tried very hard indeed. Poor old dad. He was such a wise old bird. I do miss him.'

Lucas pressed his hands together and bowed his head gravely. He seemed anxious to express his sympathy to her in her bereavement.

'May I say . . .' He paused to choose the English words carefully. 'On behalf of us all as a family how much we sympathise with you, Miss Vanstrack, on the occasion of your bereavement.'

'Thanks very much. I'll sit here then, shall I?' Miss Vanstrack spoke briskly.

She sat on a mahogany dining chair wedged between the glass-fronted bookcase and the wall. Lucas pressed her to come nearer the fire.

'No thanks. I want to keep as far away as I can from the Flames as long as I can manage it.'

Lucas seemed disorientated by her laughter.

'Working are you? Working?' She flicked her glove in the direction of his books.

'New Testament Greek,' Lucas said. 'Latin and geometry.'

'My goodness,' Miss Vanstrack said. 'It sounds stiff.'

'Oh it is. Especially to someone my age. I dare say it would be nothing to Miss Bellis. May we congratulate her on her new appointment at the County School. Very well-deserved promotion if I may be allowed to say so.'

Glenys Bellis had entered the room. She stood by the aspidistra in the window, trying to make herself as small as she could. Esther hovered in the open doorway.

'I'll make a cup of tea,' she said.

'No, don't you bother. We shan't stay long.' Miss Vanstrack beckoned her in. 'The more the merrier. And then we can make the arrangements. "Get the arrangements cut and dried," dad used to say and dad was always right. Nearly always anyway. What I suggest is this. I'll take care of everything. All fees are absolutely inclusive. There's no messing about at Talbot Manor. Every bit as good as Roedean. Especially at lacs. Thirty-five guineas a term. And then there's three guineas termly for piano lessons. I'll take care of all that. And I've got a lacs stick she can have and a tennis racket. And cricket pads. But cricket is optional. She'll go in Nelson I expect. My old house. Now all you have to do is to find the train fare and take care of the clothing outfit. Uniform and all that. How does that sound?'

She smiled at Lucas Parry and then turned to Miss Bellis for approval. 'Have I left anything out?'

Miss Bellis kept a steady eye on Lucas Parry while she spoke with the measured care of an authoritative but tactful adjudicator. 'Amy is a clever girl,' she said. 'And she's good at games. She would do very well at a public school. She has an outgoing personality. And she has very good manners. I think she ought to be given a chance.'

'Hear! Hear!' Miss Vanstrack said. 'And so say all of us.'

Lucas's mouth was closed tightly. The women were all waiting for him to speak.

'The first thing to be said . . .' He breathed very deeply and lowered his head. 'The first thing to be said is to express our deep and heartfelt thanks to Miss Vanstrack for her most generous offer. My wife and I are deeply appreciative and deeply grateful. And we are grateful, too, to Miss Bellis for being such a wonderful teacher and for taking such an interest in our little Amy. We are very appreciative. I am confident you must be aware of that.'

He spoke with stiff but practised chapel eloquence. By force of habit, he was leaning forward as if his right fist were weighing against the rail of the deacon's pew rather than the round table at which he had been working.

'But there are difficulties.'

'Oh? Are there?' Miss Vanstrack sounded mystified.

'Naturally one wants the best for the child. We have always cherished her as if she were our very own. And when my wife first intimated to me the possibility of such a generous and kindhearted offer I was overjoyed. I still am. I still am deeply grateful as I said before. But I know from bitter personal experience that the educational process is long and arduous.' Lucas made a graceful gesture with his right hand that suggested the majestic progress of education. 'It's not over in a matter of one or two years.'

'We all know that.' Miss Vanstrack was impatient. 'If it's a written guarantee you want, my lawyers can easily draw up something.'

Lucas raised his hand with the palm outwards to protect himself from mercenary procedures.

'I mean it.' Miss Vanstrack was being firm and fair. 'Get the lawyers to draw up an agreement, dad used to say. And dad was always right.'

'Education for what,' Lucas said. 'That is the point I am trying to make. What path are we taking? Which direction is she going to follow? Do you see what I'm getting at?'

He showed his discoloured teeth in an intense effort to be agreeable but Miss Vanstrack looked the other way.

'She has the potential for any course, I would have said.' Miss Bellis was again ready with a fair and rational judgement.

107

'Well for goodness' sake,' Miss Vanstrack said. 'A public-school education is always worth having. For one thing it would get rid of her Welsh accent. She'd be living and talking with well-bred English girls all day long and she's the kind of girl that would pick it up in no time. Take to it like a duck to water.'

She laughed loudly and Esther, still standing in the doorway, tried to contain the waves of sound with an anxious smile.

'That really brings me to my next difficulty,' Lucas said. 'Would there be any provision in Talbot Manor Collegiate School for Amy to receive lessons in Welsh?'

An uneasy silence fell in the parlour of the chapel house. The question seemed to take them all by surprise. Miss Vanstrack spoke at last. 'I shouldn't think so,' she said. 'I never heard of it in my day certainly.'

Miss Bellis showed she had been thinking quickly. 'But, Mr Parry,' she said. 'We only have Welsh in the church school two lessons a week. She won't be missing much, will she?'

She smiled lightheartedly, but Miss Vanstrack was over-eager to press the point home.

'After all,' she said, 'it's not much use outside Wales is it? You've got to learn good English if you want to get anywhere in this world. That's what it amounts to in the end. We have to face it.'

Lucas was tapping his chest. 'Here,' he said. 'This is where it's important. In the heart. In the soul. We don't depend on the church school for this, Miss Bellis. It wouldn't be much use if we did, to be frank with you.'

He pointed at the wall in the direction of the chapel and then he pointed at Esther to indicate the home.

'In the chapel, and in the home,' he said. 'That's what we mean when we say "Welsh". And how can you replace that?'

'Religion you mean?' Miss Vanstrack frowned like someone trying to solve a riddle.

'Of course, religion. Exactly. Religion in all its aspects.'

'Well,' Miss Vanstrack said, 'the point there is, the religious training at Talbot Manor Collegiate is in accordance with the principles of the Church of England, *but*, girls of other denominations *are* accepted. I believe they have even had Jewish girls, although I wouldn't swear to that. I think I'm quoting there, word for word, from the prospectus. I should have brought you a copy really. I think there must be one in the car. Should we nip out and get it?'

'Thank you. No.' Lucas Parry was beginning to look more like a man whose mind was made up.

Miss Vanstrack lifted a finger and settled it by her lower lip. Lucas waited politely for her to speak.

'Her real father. Her natural father or whatever you like to call it. One has to ask these questions. What about him?'

Lucas looked solemn. 'Missing believed killed. At Vimy Ridge.'

Miss Vanstrack's jaw fell. She looked uncomfortable, almost disappointed.

'Hefin Price, the singer.' Esther made the quiet identification with the kind of qualified respect she felt was due to her dead sister's husband. Miss Vanstrack nodded sagely.

'Anyway,' she said. 'He did his bit.'

Lucas allowed a moment's silence before resuming his argument.

'As I say, there is the burden of a choice to make. And it is that much *more* difficult for me because we are as close as any daughter and father. Aren't we, Esther?'

Esther nodded a little sadly.

'I teach her to recite and to sing you see. And we are very proud of her. You know about her eisteddfodic successes. We would miss her grievously if she went away. I admit that. But I have tried to put all my personal feelings to one side in coming to my decision. The choice is clear. Is Amy to be sent away to be turned into an English young lady, with an upper-class manner and an English accent? Or is she to be brought up a Welsh girl with the chapel in her heart and the language of her forefathers on her tongue? It's a moral question. Now how am I to choose? How would you choose if you were in my place?'

Lucas raised his eyebrows and an index finger in a gesture of rhetorical triumph, as if to say he had made a case that was unanswerable. Miss Vanstrack looked cross. Miss Bellis searched about in her mind for effective counter-arguments.

109

'Mr Parry,' she said. 'I don't see it. Honestly I don't. Why can't she have the best of both? The best English education that money can buy and the best possible Welsh upbringing. Look at Mr Lloyd George.'

Lucas began to frown.

'I don't mean his politics. The way he brings up his children. Roedean and the chapel in Cricieth. There are plenty of examples. It's perfectly possible.'

Miss Bellis stretched out a hand appealing to them all in turn. Miss Vanstrack preserved an ominous silence. Lucas frowned harder. Esther looked at him with the forlorn hope on her face illuminated by the pale sunlight through the parlour window.

'I have searched my heart on this.' Lucas sighed deeply. 'I am a man of principle as Esther will tell you. I've guided my whole life by principles. It's not just a balance sheet of profit and loss. I believe in education. I'm struggling for it myself. But there are more important things. I'm sure of that. Deep things you can't put into words.'

'Well . . .' Miss Vanstrack jumped to her feet and slapped her gloves across her left hand. 'That's all there is to it then. We won't waste any more time. You've made your choice.'

'Please don't think of us as ungrateful,' Lucas said.

'Yes indeed . . .' Esther held her red hands together in a pleading attitude. 'We are more grateful than we can say.'

'Come on, Bellis.'

Esther opened the door and backed away into the kitchen to allow Miss Vanstrack uninterrupted passage. Miss Bellis was biting her lip and still searching her mind for more arguments.

'It seems such a waste.' She spoke to herself. 'I could see such a brilliant future for the girl. I really could.'

Esther nodded her head sympathetically because she knew Lucas could not see her in the kitchen doorway. Miss Bellis left the chapel house without saying any more. Esther stepped outside the door. Miss Vanstrack turned around to call out to Esther.

'Look here,' she said. 'The girl can have the tennis racket if you send her down to the Hall to collect it. And the lacs stick. It's no earthly use to me.'

110

'Oh thank you,' Esther said breathlessly. 'Thank you very much.'

She would have followed them to the road with her thanks but Lucas was in the front doorway, calling her back.

'Come inside,' he said. 'And close the door. You've thanked them enough.'

She shut the front door carefully.

'I didn't want them to think we were ungrateful, Lucas,' she said.

He was fidgeting with his jacket. He began to scratch the back of his hand.

'I think I saw through her,' he said. 'That's what they are like. When they're put to the test. There's your English gentry for you.'

Esther was amazed by the tone of satisfaction in his voice.

'Restore her reputation. That was her motive you see. After the German trouble during the war. They've moved to the Hall and she will be the bountiful lady of the manor, sending a poor girl off to school at her own expense. And a girl whose father was killed in the war. And to think he claimed an army allowance for her and I was keeping her.'

For a moment he was overwhelmed by the enormity of the offence. Then he saw Esther before him and her innocent ignorance seemed only a degree less offensive.

'Don't you see it?'

Esther shook her head miserably. 'But she's Dutch, Lucas, isn't she?'

Lucas glared at her impatiently.

'What's the difference?' he said. 'Big people with money. Exponents of the Balance of Power. Please do not disturb, when it leans so very nicely in our favour. Don't you understand anything, woman?'

'Lucas . . .' Esther's voice wasn't strong enough to register as a protest.

'You should never have encouraged her. That Bellis girl. She's church. Don't you understand that? Church folk are natural serfs. They try to deceive themselves into thinking they're some kind of honorary English because they tip their hats to the Parson and the Squire and have the Book of Common Prayer stuck to their armpits . . . I thought you understood all this.'

111

Lucas looked angry and puzzled.

'Of course I do,' Esther said. 'You know I do.' She was blushing that her husband could think her so stupid. 'But I was thinking of Amy's education, that's all. I was thinking of her good.'

Lucas picked up his grammar of New Testament Greek and looked at it as if it would help to calm him down.

'Well you've seen what they're like. That large coarse female. Thinks she's a lady. In fact she's just a fool with too much money looking around for a new plaything.'

Esther's mouth opened wide with shock. 'Lucas! Do you really think that?'

'Yes I do. She doesn't really care about Amy. And she doesn't know a thing about education. Did you see the way she looked at my books? I've told you about the English. The English Big People – no, all of them. They are tough, aggressive and unpleasant. When they laugh they don't mean it. That's the way they want to be. They're not like us at all. Not in any way. I've always felt that. They're not sensitive about anything. And they're not a pattern-making people, Esther. But we are. We are.'

Lucas sat down in his chair and stared into the fire while he savoured the full flavour of the perceptions he had just managed to express. Esther watched him, overcome with respectful awe until she heard the back door open and Amy calling.

'Auntie! Auntie!'

She turned to meet her. Amy's overcoat was open. Her smooth cheeks were flushed with running down the hillside. Her eyes sparkled excitedly. She still carried the brown-paper kite Richard Parry had made for her. It was the shape of a shield almost as large as herself made with a frame of bamboo sticks and trailing a long tail of coloured paper wings.

'I saw a motor car outside the chapel. A big one. Who was it, Auntie?'

Esther smiled at Amy as fondly as she could. She stepped back into the parlour so that she could see Lucas's face and take some guidance from it. She seemed inclined to tell Amy anything except the truth.

'Amy!' Lucas's voice was firm and gentle. 'Come in here. I want to talk to you.'

112

Amy leaned her kite against a kitchen chair and walked into the parlour, confident of her aunt's affection and her uncle's approval.

'Have you done all your homework?'

Amy nodded complacently.

'And have you learnt your verses?'

'Yes, Uncle.'

'And done your practice on the harmonium?'

'That's this afternoon, Uncle.'

Lucas smiled tolerantly.

'I'm going to be honest with you, Amy. The people that came here wanted to send you away from us. A long way away. We didn't want to lose you, did we?'

He looked at Esther for support and confirmation.

'Oh no. No. We didn't.'

Esther's eyes were filled with tears. Amy looked at her aunt's face. A tension in the atmosphere which she could not understand excited her. She watched her aunt and uncle as closely as she could and listened enthralled to every word they had to say. It was at the least a story in which she herself was the central figure and heroine.

'Do you want to leave us, Amy?'

'Me?' Amy simpered self-consciously. 'Of course I don't.'

She could see that the answer had pleased them both. Lucas stood up and lifted his right arm. He could have been taking an oath or giving a blessing.

'We'll struggle on,' he said. 'We'll go forward. In the strength of Heaven. We shall smile in the face of all the storms. Our Father is at the helm.'

He sat down abruptly. Esther judged that he wanted to be alone with his thoughts. Gently she put her arm around Amy's shoulder and steered her into the kitchen, putting her finger to her lips to indicate that Lucas would be in need of peace and quiet for his meditation.

'Yes, but Auntie . . . Whose motor car was it?'

'Miss Vanstrack. From the Hall. She has some old sports things you can have. A tennis racket.'

'A tennis racket?' Amy's eyes went big with wonder and delight. 'But that's just the thing I want most in all the world. Oh Auntie!' Impulsively she put her arms around her aunt and gave her a hug.

113

10

I N HER EMPTY BEDROOM, AMY KNELT ON THE LOW WINDOW-SILL trying hard to follow the movements of her uncle in the chapel-house garden. The window was open a few inches so that she could hear the thud of his heavy boot as he moved about his task with clumsy speed. The new moon rode into sight from behind the massed clouds and it showed clearly the outline of the long hillside swelling between the enclosed garden and the night sky. She saw Lucas Parry encumbered with a can and a home-made hayfork in one hand and a battered storm-lantern in the other. He threw the hay-fork to a certain centre point in the empty garden and entered the earth closet in order to pull out old newspapers and magazines he had stacked there in an awkward collection of boxes.

'Esther!'

Amy could hear him breathing heavily as he dragged out a large box overflowing with papers.

'Esther!'

Her aunt appeared on the path, her clogs knocking against the stones that marked the edge of the cultivated ground.

'Don't you think you should take a look at them, Lucas? There'll be nobody here tomorrow. Just in case you need something.'

'I never want to come back to this place. Not as long as I live.'

He spoke quietly but with so much intensity that Amy could hear what he was saying.

'Hold the lamp.'

Now that Esther was there to witness his action, Lucas Parry began to work with more determined effort. Breathing hard he dragged the boxes to the centre of the garden where he had already assembled dead gorse, broken bits of furniture and household rubbish as the basis of a bonfire.

'It's all got to go.'

'They're very damp,' Esther said. 'These are covered in mildew.'

'There's plenty of paraffin. That's one thing we've never been short of.'

Lucas hurried up to the shed at the top of the garden where even older papers were stored. Esther followed him. She put the lamp on the ground so that she could carry loads of paper herself.

'You can light it,' she said. 'And then we'll be able to see what we're doing.'

Lucas felt about for the old paraffin can. Amy heard the rusty stopper squealing in its thread as her uncle turned it before sprinkling paraffin liberally over the damp pages. Out of the darkness Esther brought an armful of old newspapers to toss on the pile. Lucas told her to wait. Awkwardly he went down on one knee to strike a match. When the paper spurted into flame his right arm stretched out for the hay-fork stuck in the ground within his reach. The pole acted as a crutch and helped him to his feet. He stood back to study the progress of the flames with satisfaction. He inverted the hay-fork and held on to the base of the prongs with an outstretched arm like a biblical illustration of a prophet standing before a king.

'Throw it on!'

Esther obeyed. She stood back from the growing heat.

'To the flames!' Lucas spoke masterfully. 'We should have done this long ago you know, Esther. This church was never built on the rock!'

He turned to point the handle of the hay-fork disdainfully at the back of the chapel.

'Don't raise your voice, please Lucas. You never know who may be passing.'

'I don't care who hears me. The truth against the world! That's always been my motto.'

Esther moved closer so that she could wave a warning hand in his face and put a finger to her lips. She pointed at various points behind the garden wall and her gesture showed plainly that she believed that already there could be spies and persons of ill-will behind the wall, watching and listening.

'Let them!' Lucas raised his voice and yet there was less volume and it trembled a little. 'When I think of the way they have treated me. Made use of me. Made a cheap tool of me. I marvel at my patience putting up with it so long. The Wesleyan Connexion has dealt very shabbily with me, Esther Parry.'

115

'I know that, Lucas.'

If in fact there were someone listening the eavesdropper should be made fully aware of the loyal and complete support she gave her husband. In her bedroom Amy turned her back on the scene outside, resting her chin on her knees, staring at her empty bedroom.

'I have sacrificed everything to work on the Shotton and Connah's Quay Circuit. And what thanks did I get? None. None at all. Only blame. As if it was my fault the Munitions were closing down. As if I was to blame that the Mission wasn't a success. I never wanted to go there. Never. Not near the place. You heard me call it a Temple of Moloch, didn't you?'

'Yes, Lucas.'

'I allowed them to persuade me. I went against my better judgement. Against my principles really. It's always a mistake to do something against your principles.'

He could no longer control the trembling in his voice. He seemed to find some relief in pushing the material lying on the fringe of the bonfire towards the centre. He stuck out his hip and turned his face away from the smoke. He stood back and Esther watched the firelight dancing on his narrow face. He was brooding over a new thought. He opened his clamped jaw.

'I'm not suggesting I've been persecuted,' he said. 'I'd never claim that. Perhaps it would have been better if I had been. I could have spoken out more against the war. You know how I felt. But I listened to my Superintendent and I kept silent. I did it because he said it was important not to divide the churches in our care over controversial issues. And that was why I kept silent. And what reward do I get? Complete neglect. A man can't go on all his life being overlooked.'

He was becoming passionate again. Esther moved so that he should see all the sympathy and support in her face illuminated by the firelight.

'We mustn't dwell on the past, Lucas. We must look forward now to a better future. A brighter future.'

From his position higher up the sloping garden he looked down at her as though once again she had surprised him with the unshakeable strength of her faith and optimism.

116

'It's a big decision I have taken,' he said. 'A terrible decision. But there's no going back on it.'

'It's a decision you were fully entitled to take.'

Esther was roused. If there was such a thing as an unseen audience and even if it contained half the people of the village, she was now prepared to welcome their witness. She and her husband were making a public declaration of faith.

'People will say all sorts of things,' Lucas said. 'They'll call me a turncoat.'

'People are always people.' Esther's face was youthful and enthusiastic in the glow of the fire. 'It doesn't matter what they say.'

'They'll say that it's your money that bought Swyn-Y-Mynydd . . .'

'*Our* money!' Esther became indignant. 'If she had lent me money when I asked her before the war we would have been there long ago making a decent living. Butter was ten shillings a pound during the war. Don't forget all those years we've been slaving to clean schools and chapels. Don't forget all we've gone through.'

Lucas lifted his head and smiled as if he were listening to the strains of an old much-loved song. Had he now the untrammelled use of both his legs he might have launched himself into a slow heavy dance around the fire. All he could do was shift his position in order to drink in the cool night air more deeply. He squared his shoulders like a man determined never to give way to feminine sentiment and returned to the fire to poke urgently around the edges with a hay-fork.

'They are Armenian.' He stated the fact with loud satisfaction. 'There is no doctrinal difficulty. And as far as church government is concerned, I've been inclined towards Congregationalism for years. I was never happy about the Wesleyan Conference. Or what I used to term the anti-democratic tradition. Remember?'

'Indeed I do, Lucas.'

'The importance attached to worldly wealth. And the practice of settling vital issues in committees behind closed doors and then coming out to use the Conference as a rubber stamp. You heard me say it many times.'

'I did indeed.'

'The gathered Church.' Lucas sighed deeply and contentedly.

'That's where I belong. You know Esther, there are new ideals abroad in the world now. A new spirit. The war has destroyed so much. An old civilisation has been swept away. All right. It's happened. That's what I say. So let us set about building a new and better society. I want to compose a sermon about it. It's a big theme. But I've got the text. Do you know what my text will be?'

'No, Lucas. I've no idea.'

' "Sing unto the Lord a new song and his praise in the congregation of saints." Psalm one hundred and forty-nine. A part only of the first verse.'

'Of course. That's wonderful, Lucas.'

A solemn silence fell between them that was like a celebration of their identity of purpose. When the fire began to die down Lucas picked up the rusting paraffin tin and shook it before he sprinkled the last drops on the fire. The last flames flared up. With a gesture of release, Lucas shook the can for the last time before hurling it away to the top corner of the garden. They were still rapt in solemn stillness when they heard Lucas's father's voice calling urgently some way off up the road.

'What is it? What is he saying?' Esther was instantly alarmed. 'There's something wrong isn't there? What's he saying?'

They listened. Richard Parry still had the most powerful voice in the district, but it sounded old, strained, forlorn against the massive indifference of the mountainside and the solitude of the moonlit late autumn night. In the farm buildings that spread lower down the hill halfway between Siloam chapel and the village, a sheepdog began to bark and rattle his chain.

'Something the matter with the load.'

Lucas inclined his ear in the direction from which the shouting came. His face wore an angry expression as he deciphered the message.

'How can you trust him with anything . . .'

'What is it, Lucas? What's happened?'

'He's toppled the waggon, that's what he's done. The load is all over the road.' His head waved from side to side in helpless anger. 'Where's that girl? She must have finished her homework by now. Isn't she giving you a hand?'

118

'She's a little upset, Lucas.'

Even in the midst of her anxiety about the removal of her furniture Esther did not forget to be diplomatic.

Amy crept away from her window. The floorboards of her bedroom were bare and the room was empty except for a small tea chest filled with books and a tennis racket lying near it on the floor. Amy was wearing her thick overcoat. She could see rectangular patches of wallpaper that had been hidden all her life by familiar pieces of furniture. Where the wash-stand had stood against the wall there were patches of black damp calling attention to themselves like asterisks in the moonlight. Outside in the garden Lucas was still talking.

'She could do a lot more,' he was saying. 'She could have gone with him and seen to it that he didn't start showing off to that young Gwynfryn from the farm. The boy is a giggler. I should have thought of that. A giggler always sets him off. He can't resist showing off to a giggler. But I can't think of everything. It's always the same. There are so many things that can go wrong. It's like running around trying to plug all the holes in a leaking dyke, that's what it's like. Get that girl downstairs, Esther. It's all hands on deck as they say, or the ship will sink before we get off it.'

In the poor light of what was left of the fire Esther moved with cautious speed down the narrow path. The back door stood open and a forlorn-looking lamp stood burning on the range where the fire had gone out. It gave little comfort in a cold empty place about to be abandoned. Unable to break her habit of cleanliness and good order, Esther snatched up a cracked saucer left on the hob and the stale crust of a hefty home-baked loaf that stood on the slate slab by the door, tilted among its own crumbs like the model of a wreck on a beach. As she cleared them away and swept up yet again with an old floor brush that was to be left behind, she called out Amy's name, assuming the girl would appear before she had finished. Amy did not appear. Standing in the middle of the deserted kitchen Esther took her feet out of her clogs, again from force of habit, before going upstairs. She clicked her tongue and stepped back into them, prepared to accept the uncivil clatter on the tiles and the hollow banging as she tramped on the engrained strips of old linoleum left on the stair treads.

119

Hearing her loud approach Amy stepped across to her bedroom door and quickly turned the key in the lock. She pressed the palms of both hands against the bedroom wall and slid silently across to where her bed had been. Outside Esther lifted a rough hand and then with a visible sign of conciliation that was wasted tapped the door with one knuckle.

'Are you ready, my love?'

Amy said nothing. She pressed her cheek against the wallpaper. It smelt of plaster and ancient flour paste.

'Your uncle is very upset. There's been an accident. Leave your homework now if you haven't finished it. All hands on deck, he says. The waggon has turned over.'

Esther held her breath to catch the slightest indication of a reaction from inside. She heard nothing at all.

'Amy! Are you listening?' Esther grasped the door knob and tried to open the door. She rattled the door knob. 'Amy! What are you doing? Unlock this door at once!'

She was distracted by another noise. Richard Parry had arrived in the road outside the chapel. Instead of coming up the path and giving a quiet explanation of all that had happened he was shouting his angry version of the accident all over the neighbourhood. It was not his fault. A stone had been laid deliberately in the track of the inside wheel by some person or persons of ill-will in his opinion. There was a lot of indiscipline among the youth of the next village. It had happened before, last month. Esther moved about at the head of the stairs torn between dashing downstairs to quieten the old man and dealing with Amy inside her locked bedroom. She heard her husband's rasping voice and instantly returned her attention to Amy, bringing her lips close to the panel of the door and muttering urgently.

'We are moving somewhere better. Our very own little small-holding. It's what we've always wanted. Not like this. A chapel house belongs to a chapel. At everyone's beck and call. You've always been a sensible girl. Well you are a big girl now. I know it's a change Amy, but you'll like it when you get used to it . . . You'll see.'

'I'm not coming.' Amy's voice was almost smothered in sulky saliva but Esther caught the words at once.

120

'How can you talk like that? A girl in the County School, for heaven's sake. And top of her form too. I've never heard anything so silly in all my life.'

'I'm never going there. Never!'

Esther squeezed her hands together. Downstairs Richard Parry was stamping his feet in the kitchen and demanding, unreasonably, why there wasn't even a chair he could sit on and why the fire had been allowed to go out just when he most needed a hot drink.

'They are downstairs,' Esther whispered into the door. 'So keep very quiet and come outside. We'll say no more about it. We mustn't upset your uncle. He's going through a very difficult time.'

'I don't care.'

Esther breathed very deeply. 'Oh yes you'll care my girl, if I tell him how you are behaving. He's never used the rod on you before, Amy, and you've never given him cause. But I'm telling you now he will use it if you drive him to it.'

'I don't care. I'm never going there. Buried alive in the middle of nowhere. I don't care if you kill me.'

'Keep your voice down, Amy. If he hears you like this I don't know what he'll do. He's very upset as it is. He's not a cruel man, but he's upset. He'd break down this door. I can tell you that for a start.'

'I don't care. He's not my father. My father was killed in the war.' Amy's voice was slightly less loud and defiant. Downstairs in the kitchen Lucas raised his voice. It echoed in the empty house, both stern and urgent.

'What is going on upstairs? Esther! Is the girl ill or something?'

Esther held on tightly to the banister rail and stretched her neck down so that she could speak with the greatest clarity and sweetness without raising her voice.

'We'll be down directly, Lucas. We shan't be a minute.'

She returned to Amy's bedroom door and pressed her forehead against it.

'Listen to me, Amy, please. You are old enough to understand. We have to leave. We have no choice. Your uncle is changing his denomination. So we can't stay here. Do you understand that?'

She waited impatiently for an answer.

121

'I could have gone away to school,' Amy said.

'Never mind that now. That's water under the bridge. You can't stay here. Another family will be moving in next week. Do you understand?'

'I'll go to the Rectory,' Amy said. 'Miss Lizzie said I could go there any time I liked.'

'As a maid.' Esther punched home her points with muted but remorseless energy. 'As an unpaid skivvy. My goodness if that is what you want from life. Where's your pride? If that is all you want . . . now listen. I'm prepared to help you. For the sake of your uncle and for the sake of peace in the home. He's sacrificed his whole career so that you could have a good home and a good start in life. I'm not going to see all that in ruins. I've got to be responsible. And you've got to learn to be responsible too. Unlock this door now and I promise you by the end of the month, you'll have a bicycle of your own.'

Esther closed her eyes and waited for the girl's reply. Her knees bent and she lowered her head in an attitude that could have been prayer or desperation. Downstairs Richard Parry was declaring himself rested and ready to move again. He and Lucas were discussing the possibility of the existence of a second stormlamp in the small out-house at the back of the chapel. At any moment Lucas would raise his voice again and ask her to go out and find the lamp. Her knees sagged further as if the last strength was ebbing from them.

'A bicycle.'

She spoke the words into the wood. 'I promise.'

She heard Amy move and the key turn in the lock.

11

FROM THE TOP FIELD THERE WAS A TANTALISING VIEW OF THE SEA: IT was a deep blue curtain on the northern horizon, visible through a gap in the last high ground before the smooth contours dropped suddenly to the invisible coastal plain. Esther, wielding her wooden hay-rake, looked up briefly from the dry ground and the rustling hay as though a glance at the blue sea would momentarily quench her thirst and make it possible for her to work on without stopping for literal refreshment. Lower down the field the red cart creaked ominously under the weight of the load of pale hay as their neighbour, Evans Tŷ Croes, turned the horse's head to move forward a few cautious steps nearer the next heap to be lifted. Mot, the sheepdog, crept low after the cart so that he could continue to rest in its shade while Lucas, his master, on top of the load, spread out his arms like a swimmer out of practice and lacking in confidence, making an arrested breast stroke. His father Richard Parry extracted his tobacco box from the pocket of his corduroy waistcoat and allowed himself a rest, his sinewy arm embracing his pitching-fork while he prepared a quantity of tobacco to plug into his smiling mouth.

Where the field merged untidily into the bracken and gorse of the rabbit-infested summit of the hill behind Swyn-y-Mynydd, Amy was engaged in raking the coarser hay that had been cut with a scythe. Her job was to tumble the stuff down into a more convenient area where Esther and Mrs Evans Tŷ Croes could deal with it and prepare it for loading. The field was little more than seven acres, but spread out on the rising slope it seemed trouble-somely large and inclined to diminish the power of the six figures in the summer landscape and the simple tools they had to work with. Accustomed to hard physical labour all his life, Richard Parry worked in a relaxed manner and in a merry mood as though they had all the time in the world to carry the hay in. Lucas, like his wife, was much more anxious. When the cart stopped moving and it was safe for him to stand on his feet, he frowned and looked up at the sky.

'It's so warm and heavy,' he said, addressing no one in particular. 'There could be a storm.'

Esther heard his words distinctly. They seemed to hover over his head in the still air. Nervously she looked up at the sky. Far over to the west there were black clouds forming, burnished by the afternoon sun so that she found them hostile and menacing.

'Faith!' Richard Parry shouted cheerfully. He wanted everyone in the field to hear him. It was just possible that he might say something witty.

'Faith is the substance of things hoped for, the evidence of things not seen!'

'Don't mock, father!'

Lucas just had time to utter the reproof before Evans Tŷ Croes swung up a smotheringly vast forkful of hay that smelt as good as brandy. Evans was a man that took pride in the strength of his arms and the skill with which he arranged the pile before he pierced it expertly with the shining prongs and levered it high in the air and across into the unsteady arms of the loader. On the other side of the cart, Richard Parry worked at a slower pace altogether. He was capable enough, but there were privileges of age and an open-air freedom of speech that he felt the urge to exercise at regular intervals.

'You've become a proper old dry Dissenter,' Richard Parry said. 'Where are all your sweet Wesleyan juices gone, my boy? "Where are the melting promises, where are the words like wine?"'

He stopped work to sing, pleased with the open-air effect. He was plainly a little disappointed when no one else stopped work to listen. He cocked his ear to catch any reaction from his fellow worker concealed from him by the cart. Evans just carried on working, a dry smile on his saturnine sunburnt face. When he stopped to lift his cap briefly to scratch his hair, a white band of upper forehead was revealed between the pickled features and the dark flat hair.

'General Booth is back from the States,' Lucas said.

He was waiting for the other two men to scrape the ground around them for the last wisps of dried grass. Kneeling on the load, he could have been making a statement that was of direct importance to them both.

'He says they are better off without it.'

'Without what?'

Working unhurriedly, Richard Parry looked willing to be entertained.

'Intoxicating liquor. Prohibition. The people look better fed and better dressed. They live in fine houses. They are enjoying a level of prosperity such as the world has never seen before.'

'You don't say.' Evans Tŷ Croes showed genuine wonder and interest. His new neighbour was commonly known as a big reader and to listen politely was not merely amiable: it coupled a degree of respect with a display of good manners. For full measure Evans added another sincere comment. 'Isn't this old world of ours getting to be a strange place?'

He approached the horse's head and held on gratefully to the familiar metal of the bit. Foam from the horse's mouth spilt over the back of his hand.

'It's going to be a better place,' Lucas said. There was a note of restrained fervour in his voice. 'I'm pretty certain of that. A lot of the old things have gone for good you know. There's going to be a League of Nations you see. And a new kind of statesman. Men who think of the poor and the needy and the ageing. It's going to be a better world, Evans. I'm pretty sure of that.'

'Well let's hope you're right.' Evans spat on his hands before taking a fresh grip on his polished pole. 'We could do with that.'

Richard Parry was shaking his head. 'I've never seen anybody like you for swallowing stuff, Lucas,' he said. 'It all goes down like a train of raw eggs.'

'What do you mean?'

Richard showed amusement at the instant indignation shown by his son. Lucas ventured to stand up, his legs wide apart.

'Come on,' he said. ' "Tomorrow is on its way!"'

'No. Just a minute, father. You tell me exactly what you mean.'

'Come on,' Richard Parry said. 'Let's get on with it.'

He made a sudden, teasing show of anxiety to get on with the work; stirring the hay with his pitching fork like a dexterous cook using a long ladle.

'No, wait a minute. Just explain yourself.'

'Don't be so touchy, boy.'

'No. I'm not touchy. But this is how you are, you see. You drop these innuendoes . . . what do you mean about me swallowing stuff?'

Richard pulled his hat over his eyes and looked up at his son perched high above him.

'Opening a pit in the Big Pew,' he said. 'For a start.'

125

His shoulders shook with amusement at the thought of the bizarre enterprise: he was also clearly pleased with his own phrase.

'Aha! So that's it. Well, we weren't so wrong there either, were we?' Lucas's voice struck an excited note. Crows in the adjoining field suddenly took to the air and flew off croaking to the wood far away at the bottom of the valley. Everyone stopped working to listen to the argument.

'It was so childish . . .' Richard Parry seemed to be regretting the example he had chosen already.

'Ah, but was it?' Lucas dropped on his knees and leaned over the edge of the load to grin at his father. 'It discomfited the church authorities. It proved them wrong. Absolutely and completely wrong. What about that then? The authority of the Established Church not only proved wrong but also caught out lying.'

Richard Parry sighed and nodded. He turned to look up at the sky as a man who has been caught in a sudden shower waits patiently for it to blow over.

'Adolphus Wynne *was* a Dissenter,' Lucas said. 'He lived and died a Dissenter and was buried in front of the pulpit in the Congregational Church where I happen to have the honour to be a member. He never as they falsely claimed went back to the Established Church. He never as they falsely claimed was buried in the parish church. The money he left was to maintain a school for the children of Dissenters. Now that fund was appropriated illegally by the absentee incumbent of the living in 1788 . . .'

'All right, all right.' Richard Parry waved his hand and then slapped it against his forearm in a vain attempt to kill a horse-fly that was sucking his blood. 'Ancient history.'

'Nothing of the sort. By fraud the Established Church took control of the school, a control which it still maintains – disestablishment or no disestablishment! I am a reformer, father, and reform means reform. And I don't mean socialism. I mean reform according to the highest principles of liberal Christianity!'

'I don't want to interrupt . . .' Evans Tŷ Croes was studying the bland face of his turnip watch. He returned it safely to his waistcoat pocket before venturing to speak further. 'I make it

126

twenty to four,' he said. 'We must move on, friends, if we want to get this field finished today.'

'Twenty to four!' Lucas sounded appalled by the news. 'What about my letters?'

The only answer to his forlorn question was a cloud of hay hurled up by his father, quickly followed by a heavier but more accurately placed forkful from Evans Tŷ Croes. Lucas emerged spluttering from the avalanche, retrieving his cap and pulling hay out of his hair.

'Wait a minute,' he said. 'Just a minute. Those letters have got to go.' He put his right hand to his mouth and shouted urgently. 'Amy! Amy! Come here a minute.'

Amy lifted her hand rake and waved it to show that she had heard. She raced eagerly down the slope. She took off her straw hat and shook out her fair hair as she stood obediently where her uncle could see her from the top of the load.

'On the parlour table,' Lucas said. 'There are two letters and a postcard. Take three pennies and a halfpenny out of the lustre jug on the dresser and go down on your bicycle and post them in the village.'

'Can we spare her?' Richard Parry stretched out his hand in a mockingly oratorical gesture. 'Half the harvest not gathered in.'

Lucas was not prepared to treat the matter as a joke.

'We've got more help coming in the evening,' he said. 'And Amy will be as quick as she can be on her bicycle.'

Amy placed her straw hat between her face and Lucas's line of vision as if it would help to prevent him giving her further orders or in any way circumscribing her impending freedom.

'Letters . . .' Richard Parry spat to his right and wiped his lips with the back of his hand.

'They are important,' Lucas said. 'The card confirms my engagement at Horeb next Sunday. And I've written a letter to the *Gazette* in defence of lay-preachers.'

His tone invited comment, particularly from his father, but Richard Parry had his back to the cart and appeared to be absorbed in assembling the next heap of hay.

'You'd better take a look at that letter,' Lucas said to Amy. 'It's in

127

English. Just check the grammar and the spelling. Use the dictionary if necessary. If you see anything seriously wrong, you bring it out here to me and we'll correct it on the spot. It's got to be good English.'

He had time to make a brief nod before the pitchers were again at work, overwhelming him with hay. Amy bolted down the slope and then tried to restrain herself a little in case anyone looking should imagine she was making a gleeful escape. The sheepdog had chased after her, his tongue hanging out, ready to bark any minute and attract attention to her liberated behaviour. She rebuked the dog by making suppressed threatening noises in her throat and sending him back up the field before she climbed the five-barred gate. She was confronted by a group of store bullocks, all staring in a doleful trance at the aromatic hayfield from which they were excluded. Amy glanced back briefly. The five people in the field were absorbed in their labour. She landed alongside the bullocks, breaking the spell which held them still. They scampered back untidily bumping against each other in their haste to get out of her reach and Amy ran on with outstretched arms swerving like a bird that delights so much in the freedom of flight that it disdains to proceed in a straight line.

A brief lane led down from the fields to the house and the modest out-buildings. It was stony and narrow and wisps of hay were stuck to the dusty hedges on either side. Amy's boots as she ran kicked up a lot of dust. The exterior of Swyn-y-Mynydd was picturesque enough. A small wall and a gate protected the front door from the comings and goings of the animals. Rosemary grew in the narrow garden and a holly which needed trimming. Alexandra roses in bloom leaned boldly across the front door as if to prove it was never opened. Amy made straight for her bicycle inside the small barn.

The half door was open. There was a swallow's nest on the roof beam. The identical heads of five chicks in a solemn row made the nest look shrunken. Their droppings had accumulated on the rear mudguard and the leather seat of the bicycle. Angrily Amy kicked at two brown hens that were stalking about innocently pecking at the dusty floor. She pulled the bike out into the yard and leaned it against the wall between the water butt and the anvil so that she could clean the seat with a wet rag.

It was a ladies' model. The fine yellow lines painted on the chain case and the frame were wearing off and some of the stringing of the rear mudguard that prevented long skirts from tangling with the rear wheel was missing. She pressed the tyres with her thumb. She removed the pump from its sockets on the frame and fixed the flexible connection to the thread on the valve of the rear wheel. She pumped the tyre hard until the handle of the pump barely responded to the pressure from the damp palm of her hand and she could no longer hear the satisfying pant of the compressed air inflating the tube. It was warm work and she stepped back into the shade of the old cart-house. She studied the shadow of her bicycle on the yard while she replaced the connection inside the pump and seemed to make a series of rapid decisions.

Inside the house Amy stalked imperiously from one small room to the other, and appeared to be dissatisfied with everything she saw, including her own reflection in a square mirror that hung crookedly from a nail to catch the light from the little window above the low kitchen sink. There was hay and dust in her hair and clearly no time to wash it. She found a brush and comb in the area under the stairs that was shelved in order to serve as a kind of pantry. The comb was dirty and she began to clean it under the rain-water tap. Impatiently she dragged the wet comb through her matted hair so that her waves and curls temporarily disappeared and she pulled out her tongue with distaste for what she saw.

In the dimly lit parlour Lucas's letters lay conspicuously clean on a round table covered with an ink-stained protective grey sheet. As she had been instructed to do, Amy sat down and read the letter to the editor of the *Gazette*. Lucas took pride in his handwriting. It was large and bold and easy to read and the letters were rounded with orderly innocence like rows of fat-cheeked children.

Dear Sir,
I fail to see how any fair-minded reader could support your correspondent's unwarranted attack on the scriptural practice of lay-preaching . . . To call a modest recognition of their services a 'corrupting practice' and 'profiteering' is surely, sir, a grave slander? . . .

Describing lay-preachers as 'black-legs' in relation to the ordained ministry is not only an absurdity, it flies in the face of the known facts . . . No person can be a success as a lay-preacher in whatever denomination without enormous self-sacrifice and self-denial . . . The work of preaching is a labour of love . . . The lay-preacher must prepare and must provide himself with a goodly library of expensive books . . . He rarely makes a fixed charge for his services. He is content to accept whatever small recognition the church is generously disposed to give . . . By the time he has subscribed to all the church causes he is in honour bound to support there is little left for the purchase of those books so necessary for earnest and conscientious study.

I remain your humble servant, A Lay Preacher.
(Name and address supplied to the editor)

A blue-bottle buzzed in the warm window pane as Amy read her uncle's letter and a drowsy butterfly on the dusty geranium leaf opened and shut its wings.

Amy picked up a penholder and scraped the steel nib against the bottom of the glass inkwell. It seemed possible that she was contemplating drawing a line through the whole letter as the charged nib hovered over the paper. She pushed her lips judiciously in and out, pressing the hard end of the penholder with the tip of her nose. She scratched out the letter 'Y' in the printed nom-de-plume and substituted 'ME'. Having done it she looked about quickly for a piece of blotting paper. She let it rest for a moment over the wet letters before she thumped it with a tight fist.

With a deep sigh, like a form-mistress just contemplating the task of correcting a slow pupil's work, Amy jerked back the mahogany study chair which her uncle always used so that the legs scraped the linoleum on the floor. With a sudden shift of mood, she lifted the blotting paper and exclaimed theatrically at what was revealed. She rushed upstairs singing throatily for comic effect a popular Sunday School hymn with a jaunty tune. The words were about the unfortunate black and yellow children of the world living in dark ignorance without the advantages of the Sunday School.

Upstairs there were three bedrooms separated from each other by wooden partitions. In the hot afternoon the windows were closed and the confined interior smelt strongly of woollen blankets and moth-balls. In her tiny back bedroom there was little space between the bed and the window. The wash-stand was in the spare bedroom. The ewer was filled with rainwater. Amy took off her working clothes and stood naked on a worn towel to wash herself in the cold water. Critically she smelt the piece of coarse flannel she used before soaking it in the soapy water, squeezing it and rubbing her neck, under her armpits, around her breasts, between her legs and every available inch of her skin with unrestrained enthusiasm until she was covered with a thin soapy film which dried quickly in the warm bedroom. She placed the ewer on the towel and plunged in her arms so that she could rinse herself as thoroughly as possible in clean water. Her singing now was unself-conscious, naturally melodious. There was a mess to be cleared up. The dirty water to be thrown away, the ewer refilled, the linoleum to be wiped and the room restored to its drab but respectable neatness. The window was smaller than the basin so the dirty water could not just be thrown out into the nettles of the overgrown back garden. Amy put on clean knickers and carried the ewer downstairs. In the dark cramped dairy she put her feet in cold clogs. She peeped out of the door into the sunlight to make sure there was no one about before she stepped outside and hurried awkwardly to the midden to cast the dirty water over the dried dung.

In the silent house Amy hurried to get herself dressed. But she was faced with a problem. All her clothes hung on two pegs on the back of her bedroom door. The blue summer frock she wanted to wear was too tight under her arms and around her growing breasts. Angrily she took it off again and removed her vest. The frock was still too tight. And in any case the hem needed lowering. Her knees were in sight. She removed the frock a second time and the sound of tearing as she pulled it over her head helped to assuage her anger. The dress lay in a heap on the floor. Amy flung herself on her bed: she would lie there on her own, sulking and naked, in protest against a world that did not provide her with the necessary appropriate clothing to enable her to emerge and move about with the colourful freedom that was her due. With her hands under her chin and her little finger in the corner of her tightening mouth, she

131

considered the situation. Her trance was broken by a sudden commotion beyond the open window: a wood pigeon bursting out of the heavy leaves of the old sycamore tree that overshadowed one side of the garden. The narrow confines of the room made it harshly plain that it was herself that was being punished and deprived and not the delectable world outside. The only remedy was to wear her school uniform. The green serge gym-tunic would be heavy and hot. To compensate she would leave off her vest. And the white blouse would be left unbuttoned so that the cool breeze could play about her neck as she rode her bicycle down hill. She had no liberty bodice and she would wear no stockings. Her legs would look long and white below the green serge, but strong and healthy. She would wear her sandals without ankle socks as she had seen some of the senior girls do at the school sports.

In her haste to escape from Swyn-y-Mynydd, Amy had gripped the handlebars of her bicycle before she remembered to collect her uncle's letters. The letter to the editor of the *North Wales Gazette* had to be folded and placed in the envelope he had already addressed. And there was the card to confirm that he would keep his preaching engagement at Horeb. There was also a letter to the editor of a denominational magazine offering an article on the discovery of the authentic burial place of Adolphus Wynne. It was unfinished and Amy screwed up her eyes as she considered impatiently what to do with it. The three pennies and the halfpenny from the lustre jug on the dresser she dropped into the pocket inside the fold of her green gym-slip. There was room there too for the letter and the card she had to post. She was ready at last for her mission.

The farm track from Swyn-y-Mynydd was rough and narrow. Amy concentrated on riding carefully so as not to do any damage to a machine which meant so much to her. She stared at the surface of the lane, adroitly steering the front wheel between large stones, holes and cart ruts. Startled young birds fled before her, briefly trapped between the high hedgerows. A hare amazed at her approach stopped to look before fleeing forward in front of her meandering advance. The final descent to the by-road between Melyd and Trerhedyn was so steep Amy decided to dismount. Her concern was clearly for the condition of the bicycle rather than her own safety, because as soon as she reached the road and as soon as the tyres came into smooth contact with the metalled surface, she began to pedal as energetically as she could. Showing complete faith in her brakes she let go of the rubber grips on the handlebars and stretched out her arms so that the breeze could reach her armpits and cool her sweat.

12

THE VILLAGE POST OFFICE AT MELYD HAD ITS OWN FORECOURT IN which a Victorian letter box stood in important isolation. The post office was all that was left open of what had once been a general stores. A bell clanked importantly above Amy's head as she pushed the door open and echoed itself when she closed it. She stood patiently in front of the grille. She studiously avoided showing any interest in the trestle table to her right, where boxes containing humbugs, aniseed drops, liquorice balls, Mint Imperials, dolly mixtures and jelly babies seemed to be laid open and tilted towards the customer to tempt flies and children to illicit tastings. Behind them in tall glass jars stood columns of treacle toffee, butterscotch, chocolates and sugared almonds. From a brass knob surmounting a corner of the grille a bunch of triangular paper bags hung ready for use. Fragments of paper from bags already plucked away still clung to the white string.

Amy knew she was being watched. A mirror hung high on the wall, above faded local government notices. It was opposite the open door which led into the room next to the shop where the aged proprietor sat with his flat cap on his bald head toasting his toes in front of a coal fire regardless of the hot summer weather. He was putting the young customer to the test, observing her behaviour closely in the mirror. His sitting-room was full of the furnishings which had once graced the general store: dummies and cardboard displays of vanished products, all sorts of empty shelves, and glass cupboards. A dog slept on the hearth-rug. With his cap on his head and shawl over his shoulders the old man could very well have been waiting for a removal van.

When an approved testing period had elapsed, he bent stiffly to pat his dog. He shrugged off his shawl and shuffled to his official position behind the counter. His pipe was wedged firmly in the centre of his false teeth and since he was smiling, his round spectacles gleaming with a dangerous benevolence, his spittle ran freely down the smooth stem of the briar pipe. Amy was approved of. She had resisted the temptation to snatch up jelly babies or Mint Imperials and pop them in her mouth or conceal them about her person. Whether by moral rectitude or common prudence the temptation had been overcome and he was satisfied.

'How is Mrs Roberts today?'

He did not answer Amy's clearly spoken question immediately. He stared at her through the grille, his round cheeks flushing with a new wave of approval. The sight of the polite, good-looking growing girl seemed to restore his wavering faith in the future of humanity. She was not only honest and beautiful, she was polite. She showed sympathy for the elderly and her pleasing voice was resonant with tactful concern. His voice was hoarse when he answered her.

'She's not at all well,' he said. 'She had another heart attack last night. I've kept her in bed today as a matter of fact. This is her seventh, you know.'

He referred to the fact with a tinge of melancholy pride as though his wife had now overtaken a well-established record.

'Three penny stamps and a half-penny stamp, please.'

His face darkened, showing mild displeasure. He was not to be hurried. He opened the large book with greasy black binding in which the stamps were kept. He tore out the stamps with the steady care of a government official obligating a still unfranchised member of the general public.

'The Archbishop is in the Rectory.'

He gave out the information with the stamps. It was a fact he desired for his own reasons to be more generally known, even by

134

the younger members of the community. It was a news item of some interest. He was also prepared to comment on its implications.

'You can tear down a bag,' he said.

'Thank you, Mr Roberts.'

With a restrained eagerness that gave him pleasure and made him lean forward to watch her actions more closely, Amy tore down a bag, blew inside it to open it out and held it like a cup in her hand to await his further instructions.

'There have been complaints.'

Mr Roberts's pipe wagged up and down as he spoke and the saliva began to hang down in threads that caught the sunlight from the window behind him.

'Cars parked in the Rectory drive. Women's cars. That yellow one with a dicky seat. That's been seen several times. And he doesn't visit. He doesn't visit the sick.'

Amy listened to the old man's high complaining voice with unnatural stillness as if a bat were flying about her head in the confined space of the shop. Mr Roberts was leaning even further forward to make sure the girl had absorbed his announcement together with the explanatory comments. He examined Amy's features closely. She belonged to a non-conformist family, but his noted generosity was enough to win attention to parish church affairs. Even though she did not take her eyes off the thick black print of a County Council Election notice, he judged from some minute alteration in her colour that the criticism of the Rector had been registered. He relaxed a little.

'Six Mint Imperials and six jelly babies,' he said. 'And one or two others if you like. Just as samples.'

Amy carried out his instructions exactly. She gave the top of the bag a twist when she had finished and placed it in the pocket of her gym-slip.

'Thank you very much, Mr Roberts.' Her voice rang out loudly in the shop. He gave a single benign nod and the trail of saliva caught on to the stained tweed of his waistcoat.

Outside, Amy still had to push her uncle's letters into the letter box that had the initials V.R. raised in the cast of the red door.

135

When she had completed her duty, she weighed on the seat of her bicycle and rocked it to and fro, clearly reluctant to abandon her freedom. She held her head down and watched the spokes of the wheels revolve like a novice gambler looking at a roulette wheel. In theory and in fancy, the bicycle could carry her anywhere, more realistically than a magic carpet. It was her machine and she was entitled to take any road. She stood on the pedal and using the bicycle as a scooter and thereby only borrowing a fraction of its potential she arrived in no time outside the road gate at the end of the Rectory drive. She hesitated a moment before proceeding further. The straight drive between the tall trees was a cool inviting tunnel in the hot afternoon. The Rectory was hidden from sight, but she could see beyond the second ornamental white gate the bonnet and front wheels of a large imposing motor car parked in front of the house. Cautiously she opened the road gate and wheeled her bicycle through. As a visible mark of respect she did not ride down the drive, except to step on the pedal from time to time when she felt confident no one could see her. When she reached the second gate, she saw that a chauffeur sat in the motor car with his gloved hands clutching the substantial driving wheel. His grey uniform and peaked cap gave him a military appearance. Amy began to blush as if she realised her erratic approach down the drive had been under observation all the time. She strove to look as if she were there on business, lifting her head with some effort and staring intently at the wooden gates between the stables and the house. Before she could reach it clergymen had appeared in the open doorway. A plump young man stepped jauntily into the open air, holding a straw boater with a black band. He was full of approval for the fine afternoon and he turned to walk slowly backwards as though to demonstrate to someone inside that he had inspected the weather and it was safe for his superior to come forth.

'Mind the step, your Grace,' he was saying.

The Rector also emerged anxious to prepare the way for the Archbishop. Solemnly the chauffeur descended from his exalted seat, and opened the door of the interior of the saloon. Amy saw that the lower half of the door was upholstered in buttoned red

136

leather. She saw the Rector walk in a light circle like a man in a slightly dazed condition. The Archbishop stood in the doorway. He was a vigorous old man and the blue veins in his flushed stern face showed themselves as clearly around his bald white head as in an anatomical illustration of the circulation of the blood. The red silk vest under his clerical collar made the veins appear more blue. Overcome with awe, Amy pushed her bicycle back and concealed herself behind a hydrangea bush. She remained in a position that would allow her to watch the Archbishop's departure unobserved.

'Thanks for the tea, Philips.' The Archbishop placed his silk hat squarely on his head and gave his host a frosty smile. The hat in position made him look permanent and immutable as a statue. The Rector shifted about as he spoke.

'My goodness, our pleasure, my lord . . . I mean thank you for coming like this, your Grace.'

'Do stand still, there's a good fellow. You're making me quite dizzy.'

The plump young man lifted the rim of his boater to hide his sycophantic smile.

'Take my advice, Philips,' the Archbishop said. 'Get married the first chance you get. It's the only way you'll ever get any peace. And start a Scout Troop. I strongly advise that. It's one of the best ways the Church can help to instil the youth of Wales with a love of Empire and the Empire ideals.'

'Yes indeed, your Grace.'

The Rector was stuttering in his anxiety to express his appreciation of the Archbishop and his gratitude for the honour of a visit and every detail of his timely suggestions.

'We parish priests, your Grace, we appreciate you, our leader and I say this everywhere, every chance I get you know, because we know you are one of us. From this stems the burning loyalty we all feel . . .'

The Rector swung his long arms in an effort to make himself more eloquent. He pointed desperately at the Rectory and the Archbishop glanced back apprehensively at the building. The Rector's extreme gesture could have meant it was in danger of falling down.

'From a cradle such as this . . .' The Rector's face began to flush with triumph. He clearly felt he had found the right words at last. '. . . You were sent by heaven to lead us in our hour of trial!'

The Archbishop stared at him with a measure of uneasy and silent severity. He looked like a headmaster deciding reluctantly to give an unstable pupil a second chance to prove his worth.

'H'm. Stick to the hum-drum thing, Philips. Regular visiting. And societies. Mother's Union. Scout Troop. I recommend a Scout Troop. This is the day of the small matters, Philips. The day of the small matters.'

The Rector swung his body around and stretched out his arm to open the door of the limousine: but the chauffeur in his grey uniform was there already, as still and as stiff as a guardsman, confident in his ability to carry out the customary drill with elegant precision. The Archbishop's secretary murmured a neutral farewell to the Rector before he followed his master into the interior of the motor car. He sat facing the Archbishop in the opposite corner, ostentatiously silent with concern not to interrupt the old man's train of deep thought. The Rector rushed off to open the ornamental gate. Amy pushed her bicycle into an empty stable and hurried to the back door of the Rectory. She found it open. She tapped it confidently and then walked down the dark corridor calling out the Rector's sister's name.

'Miss Philips! Are you there? It's me, Amy. Would you like me to give you a hand?'

Miss Philips sat on a kitchen chair in an attitude of extreme exhaustion, one plump arm extended across the table, the other hanging loosely to the floor, her legs wide apart and her small mouth open.

'Can I help you, Miss Philips?'

'Men.' Miss Philips uttered the word in a voice of doom-laden finality. 'Men,' she said. 'World without end, Amen. Men, men, men.'

Amy stood still, her head a little to one side, waiting like someone familiar with the vagaries of the weather for Miss Philips's mood to change.

'Bishop, archbishop, what's the difference, I said. He doesn't like cats. All right I said, we'll scrub the whole place from top to bottom, et cetera et cetera. And do you know what he said? To me. His sister.' Miss Philips stared at Amy as if to see whether her imagination was capable of comprehending the enormity of the indignity she had suffered. 'He told me to shut up. That's the way he talks to me now. That's what it's come to.'

The features of Amy's face were struggling to show sympathy.

'And after the first day's cleaning, Mrs Evans let me down. "I'm sorry Miss Philips but my father's brother is ill." Well what a time to be ill, I said. With the Archbishop coming. And she left me high and dry at eleven-thirty this morning. Church people too. You'd think they'd have a little loyalty.'

'What would you like me to do?'

Amy's voice and presence began to take effect. Miss Philips sat up in her chair and began to look a little less dejected.

'You've come to help me, Amy fach? You're a good girl aren't you? A very good girl. I didn't give the chauffeur a cup of tea, you know. I tell you what I did.'

Miss Philips stood up, prepared to re-enact the event so that Amy could see it as closely as possible as it happened and then give her judgement.

'I walked over like this and tapped the window. I tapped it quite hard. He must have heard. He must have seen me. I beckoned to him like this. Come in, I said. Around the back and I'll give you something to eat and drink.'

Once again standing by the tall window she mimed the action of eating and drinking. She wore a heavy green knitted dress and her sallow skin glistened with sweat. The slanting sun brought a halo of light around her thick curly black hair. 'He must have thought I was a maid or something. Should I have gone outside, do you think, Amy? Anyway he's gone now, so it doesn't matter.' Miss Philips pulled out the nearest chair from under the table and sat on it despondently. 'He just sat at that wheel like a graven image and took no notice,' she said.

'Is there any hot water, Miss Philips?'

'Hot water?' Miss Philips took a little time to adjust to the change of subject. 'Well that's another thing. She went off without filling the boiler. She's that kind of woman you see. You have to tell her every single little thing.'

'I'll fill the big kettle, shall I?'

Miss Philips watched the strong young girl working with open admiration. Amy took the heavy kettle through to the dark scullery and filled it from a large brass tap. She used both hands to carry it back and place it on the fire.

'Shall we clear the dishes?' She smiled politely at Miss Philips as she made the suggestion. The Rector's sister rose from her chair and bustled about the kitchen as though she was winding herself up for a prolonged bout of physical activity.

'Come with me,' she said. 'Come with me.'

The drawing-room door was ajar. Inside they found the Rector sprawling in an armchair smoking a pipe and staring with melancholy fascination at the action of the gleaming brass balance-wheel of the clock on the white marble mantelshelf. Under the glass dome the wheel carried out its horizontal alternating motion in eerie silence. Amy looked at the reflection in the mirror behind it.

'Look,' Miss Philips said, pointing at the food on the table. 'They've hardly eaten a thing.'

On the white damask cloth was an array of plates with cakes, meringues, sandwiches, scones and thinly cut bread and butter both brown and white, and several sorts of home-made jam.

'They've hardly touched any of it,' she said. 'Didn't you ask them then? Didn't you press them?'

The Rector sighed deeply without taking his eyes off the ornamented wheel that seemed to be swimming majestically in some element heavier than air but less resistant than water.

'He's a great man,' he said. 'The Moses of the Welsh Church. I'm glad he's been in this room, Lizzie Anne. I'm proud of that.'

'Well he could have eaten something. After all the trouble I've gone to.'

'Do you realise that but for him, but for him . . .' The Rector repeated the phrase and raised a warning index finger while he struggled to think of the most effective phrase.

'Bishop, archbishop. What's the difference? If you ask my

opinion he's not so wonderful. He's been married three times for a start.'

The Rector's eyes opened wide to show how difficult he found it to comprehend his sister. 'What are you talking about, woman?'

'Don't call me "woman". I'm your sister. I'm your only surviving sister who sacrificed nearly all her cats. But I'm not good enough to preside over a tea-party for the Archbishop. And look at the mess you've made of it.' She pointed angrily at the loaded table, and in particular at the large silver teapot under its elaborately decorated tea-cosy. 'I dare say you didn't even offer him a second cup of tea.'

'This was an official visit,' the Rector said sharply. 'A visitation, not a tea-party.'

'In that case what did he have to say? Are we moving or something?'

The bluntness of her manner offended him. He stood up and Amy shuffled back a little to take more protection from the open door.

'When I said Moses,' the Rector said, 'I meant Moses. He has taken the fragile Ark of the Covenant across the Red Sea of hostile radical non-conformity! You have just seen the only man on earth who has plucked a hair out of the nostril of David Lloyd George.'

'I didn't see him.' Miss Philips shut her small mouth obstinately and turned to see where Amy had got to. 'You sit over there, Amy fach, and eat as much as you like. Don't let this good food go to waste. That's all I ask. And then clear up if you feel like it. I'm not too well myself. I think I'll go on the bed for an hour. I've got one of my splitting headaches.'

She turned on her heel so quickly Amy had to step back out of her way. She watched her walk down the corridor towards the white staircase with her head lowered as if to indicate that she had blocked up her ears and would not listen to any remarks that might be called out after her. Amy turned to see how the Rector had taken his sister's sudden departure. He had turned to look at himself in the mirror above the mantelpiece. He raised the hand that held a pipe to smooth down the waves on either side of his centre parting with the back of his hand. There was a calm

141

philosophical expression on his face. He looked pleased with his cultivated appearance and prepared to accept things as they were with lofty resignation.

'Poor Lizzie Anne,' he said.

Amy could not prevent herself glancing down the corridor to see whether Miss Philips could hear what her brother was saying.

'Lack of education,' he said. 'That's her whole trouble. The Archbishop is quite right. It holds her back you see. The lack of a full command of English. Now that's what he wants for every boy and girl throughout the Principality. A man of vision. How's your English getting on, Amy?'

'Very well thank you, Rector.'

'That's the spirit. It's a pity you're a non-conformist, you know!' He chuckled happily and pointed his pipe first at her and then at the table. 'Now you sit there, Amy Parry. And tuck in. Don't be shy. Eat all you can. Make hay while the sun shines. I've got to find some tobacco.'

Amy looked shy. She bit her lower lip.

'Sit over there. Where the Archbishop sat. Let's be broad-minded today above all else. That's what the country needs. What the world needs. Broad-mindedness.'

He waved his pipe and took wide steps towards a door in the far wall that led to his study. When Amy was seated and had begun to eat, he returned nursing a jar of tobacco. It was empty. He came up to the table and held the jar so that Amy could see inside it.

'Would you believe it? I've been so nervous these last few days I've smoked the lot.'

He left the room again. Amy was very hungry but she did her best to eat decorously. There was a table full of food at her disposal. She began with plain brown bread and butter and graduated to scones and from scones to cakes. The tea was no longer fit to drink so she filled her cup with milk, holding up the bulbous porcelain jug to admire it openly before putting it down again.

The Rector reappeared. This time he had his hands in his pockets. Momentarily he stood like an undergraduate posing for a photograph. He smiled approvingly at Amy.

'At the head of the table,' he said. 'Having a tea-party all by herself.'

He paced about the room in an aimless manner driven by his emotions like a fallen leaf in an eddying wind. Amy went on eating, unconcerned by his erratic movements and apparently making no effort to understand what he was saying.

'Great men always have hangers-on. I'm not blaming him. But he has his favourites. Anglicise, My Lord, I said. Our policy in one word. Why not use it? The Anglican church must Anglicise. And Farley-Thomas started laughing. In front of the Archbishop. I was quite put out. We mustn't say these things, Philips. Not in so many words. I looked at the Archbishop. And do you know, he didn't say a word!'

The Rector was standing by the long windows looking at the view of the valley through the trees which grew on the south side of the Rectory. On the hillside in the far distance hay-making was in progress. The little figures were visible in the long sloping field and the waggon moved like a toy slowly from one heap of hay to the other. The faint scent of the honeysuckle from the garden hedge wafted through the open window. The Rector turned round and stood behind Amy's chair. She saw his hand reach over to help himself to a small scone on a plate. It was large and rough and hard. His hobbies were carpentry and tinkering about with machines and motor-bikes. In spite of scrubbing there were traces of black grease still in the lines on the palm of the hand. He smelt of tobacco as he leaned over her. Amy went on eating neatly. Suddenly both his hands were slipping down her open blouse and resting on her half-grown breasts. They lay still there and Amy herself did not move. She wore no vest and her face grew red with embarrassment.

'They're coming along nicely,' the Rector said. 'Very nicely indeed.'

Amy closed her eyes while she waited for him to take his hands away. She felt the hard sides of fingers rough against her nipples. She could not wait for ever to take his hands away. The longer they hung down from her neck and lay heavy on her breasts, the more they resembled a yoke of servitude, a sign of inferiority.

'I'd better clear the dishes.'

As soon as she spoke he took his hands away. He began to pace about the room again, confused and agitated. Amy could not eat any more. She concentrated on clearing the table as efficiently as possible: it seemed the best way to retrieve her dignity and independence. She loaded up the mahogany trolley and tried to ignore the tall man pacing about the room.

'I should have joined up,' the Rector said. 'That was the mistake I made. I'd have had more respect then. On all sides. As an ex-service-man I would have had more respect. I felt it very much the day they dedicated the War Memorial. I couldn't help feeling how manly old Ffestin Edwards looked. And he used to be the sloppiest-looking man in Jesus. It's a wonderful combination: the uniform and the cloth.'

He marched smartly into his study and left the door open so that Amy could see him standing in front of his roll-topped desk. On the wall above were two small wooden shields on which were printed the coat of arms of his college at Oxford and the University. In between hung a plain oak wooden cross. He came back into the drawing room and stared hard at a large picture over the polished sideboard of a maiden in distress clinging to a cross planted on a pale green globe. He turned to look at Amy as she continued to clear away in steady silence.

'Look, Amy,' he said. 'Let us kneel together. Shall we?'

Amy put down the plates she was holding and watched the Rector take two steps forward to the hearth rug and sink upon his knees. She noticed the cake crumbs on the carpet were also on the rug, just where he was kneeling. His eyes were already shut tight, before she herself sank obediently to her knees.

'Oh Lord,' the Rector said. 'Forgive us our sins. Forgive us our trespasses.'

Amy opened one eye and caught a glimpse of the balance-wheel of the clock on the mantelpiece glittering solemnly as it swayed from side to side inside the glass dome.

'Keep this young girl pure. Keep her on the path of righteous-ness. Keep us all from the snares and traps of the Evil One. Watch our steps as we travel through the teeming jungle of modern life. Keep our thoughts pure when the busy world is hushed.'

Amy shut her eyes tight until she heard the Rector give so deep a sigh that she opened her eyes again to make sure he was all right.

'Amen,' he whispered fervently. He opened his eyes and smiled at Amy as if to show the prayer had come to an end. 'No fervent prayer has ever failed to reach the Throne of Grace,' he said. 'Remember that, Amy. Remember it as you travel forward along life's road.'

Amy nodded respectfully. She jumped to her feet ready to resume the clearing up. The Rector watched her and when she pulled the large trolley down the corridor he followed her. She had difficulty in turning the trolley into the scullery doorway.

'Let's see,' he said. 'Let's see.'

He helped with one hand only, putting his right hand on Amy's shoulder. Involuntarily she shrugged his hand away. He backed away quickly, walking through the kitchen and into the scullery so that he could draw the trolley in and prove himself effective and disinterestedly helpful. In the scullery there was a strong smell of onions. There were old tea-leaves in the yellow sink. It was a part of the house that had escaped the great clean-up before the Archbishop's visitation. The Rector bent his knees to peer under the table. His nose wrinkled up fastidiously as though ready to record the trace of a smell of tom-cat.

'Do you know what the Archbishop told me?'

He looked at the heavy table for a clean spot to lean against. He sniffed and folded his arms, leaving both his little fingers delicately extended.

'He told me to get married.'

Amy stood politely by the sink not wishing to interrupt the Rector with the clatter of dishes. The Rector nodded his head towards the ceiling.

'She didn't hear it, thank goodness. But just think of my problem. If I did get married, where would Lizzie Anne go?'

He accepted Amy's polite silence as sympathetic understanding. A strand of ivy hung down outside the window. There were cobwebs in the top of the window-pane. Amy began to work. She carried in the heavy kettle from the kitchen and poured the hot water over the dishes in the sink.

'How old are you, Amy?'

'Fourteen, Rector, the week after next.'

'You're a fine-looking girl you know. In the springtime of your life. Why can't I marry you?'

Amy's face grew red in the steam from the sink.

'Quite common you know. Among the Chinese. A man of forty and a girl of fourteen. Not that I'm forty yet thank goodness. Adam and Eve were Chinese. Did you know that, Amy? And it was standard practice here in the Middle Ages. But then of course priests didn't marry. So I wouldn't have had any problem. Interesting people the Chinese. Very ancient civilisation. Cradle-snatching. That's what they'd say. What an excuse for scandal.' The Rector's forehead creased in a heavy frown as if he were confusing himself with the inconsequential sequence of the thoughts that came tumbling out of his mouth. 'Not to mention Lizzie Anne. But I like the idea. Quite seriously.'

He put a warning finger to his lips. Amy had begun to laugh.

'Don't laugh,' he said. 'This is a secret. Just between us two. Not a word to anybody. Not a whisper. A secret pact. When you are seventeen and haven't been kissed, I'll ask you again.' He cocked an ear towards the ceiling. 'She's getting up,' he said. 'I'm getting out. Or she'll be at me again. I'll go and do some visiting.'

He took a quick step towards Amy and touched her lightly on the cheek with the tips of his fingers. He looked at her, waiting for her to return his friendly smile. When she smiled at last he thrust his hand in his pocket and took out a florin.

'Here you are then,' he said. 'Just between you and me.'

Amy accepted the coin with a wet hand and dropped it into her gym-slip pocket. The Rector flicked the tops of his fingers together as he walked rather mincingly towards the door. When he got there, he turned back frowning with an afterthought.

'There is one thing,' he said. 'Don't let anybody kiss you. Not if you can help it. Not on the lips anyway. Not till you're seventeen.' He listened for further movement from his sister upstairs. 'I'm not joking,' he said. 'I'm serious. You can see I'm serious, can't you?'

He heard his sister's footsteps on the stairs and did not wait for an answer before hurrying away.

Book Two

1

THE WHITE MOTOR-BUS LOWERED ITSELF DOWN THE STEEP HILL
in a cautious first gear. It panted and shook with restraint
like a working sheepdog creeping down a hill with its tongue
hanging out. The noise of the engine drowned the habitual riot
of the waterfall that was the conspicuous pride of the lower village.
A cyclist in vague uniform drew his heavy push bike into the
gutter and waited respectfully for the long white machine to pass.
Two women in the doorways of their terrace houses overlooking
the road stopped gossiping to admire the triumph of public
transport over a hill which formerly had such an awesome
reputation. They released their bare arms from the sack-aprons
rolled around them, to raise them in salute, in the random hope
that the bold bus-driver might notice their signals of allegiance.
They were supporters of the White Bus Company and when they
joined the privileged class of passengers, they would wait for this
very bus to be carried across the plain to the delights of the seaside
town.

Amy sat halfway down the bus, her school satchel resting on her
knees and a notebook in her hands. Her eyes opened and shut and
her lips moved as she memorised lists of Latin irregular verbs. She
ignored the noise of a group of senior boys in the back of the bus.
They were rough unruly types who had failed examinations: their
manners were bad, their hands were unwashed, their collars tight
and frayed. They bulged in their untidy clothes as their boils and
pimples bulged under their skins. Closer to Amy sat three young
women who worked in offices in the seaside town and always
travelled together. Each day they took it in strict turn that one
should sit alone and turn sideways during the journey to continue
amiable contact with the other two. There was a minister on board.
He sat alone, his neck upright in his high clerical collar and his
right hand outstretched, grasping the rail on the seat in front to
maintain his balanced posture. He stared ahead as though he were
memorising the agenda of a denominational committee. A farmer's
wife with a basket full of fresh pounds of butter at her feet sat near
the door and looked around in vain for someone to talk to. The

149

conductor was far away, leaning against a perpendicular steel rail behind the driver and letting his small body shake with the sprung motion the whole bus was making. She caught his eye and smiled in a friendly way. He nodded and stirred the coins in his leather bag. She smiled when she heard the merry jingle. He rubbed his ticket punch with his sleeve. Then he held up his fingers to show her they were green from constant contact with the copper coinage.

The daily route was familiar. Amy had no need to take her eyes off the list of verbs to tell where they were. The bus stopped outside the public house opposite the waterfall. The sounds and smells were as solid as signposts. Voices identified faces with the accuracy of bird song. The driver leaned out of his window and in a hoarse voice called out his daily joke to a woman wearing a man's cap who was scrubbing the steps of the public house. Not wishing to rush his colleague, the conductor glanced slowly at his pocket watch before lifting his arm to tug twice at the leather line that made the bell ring above the driver's head.

When the bus was in sight of a crossroads outside the village the driver pushed his fist into the rubber ball of the horn. Amy looked up and saw two girls from the house next to the smithy run out of their front door. Amy closed her eyes and muttered her way quickly through the Latin verbs. She put away the notebook in the satchel before the bus had stopped. The older girl came to sit beside her. Even before she had settled in her half of the seat, she took on an air of authority. Eager to remain inside the orbit of her sister's power, the smaller girl sat down in front of them, ready to listen as she played with the pliable straps of her satchel. She seemed to know her sister was about to make an interesting announcement.

'Johnny Angorfa has broken his arm.'

As she waited for Amy to take a proper degree of interest, she looked as proud as a carrier-pigeon.

'How did he do it?'

The bus rattled between an orchard and a walled garden. From her seat Amy saw geese grazing under the pear trees. The bus-driver changed gear to take on a sharp incline. At the top they gained a pleasing view of Llanelw across the alluvial plain. In the morning haze, the domes and spires and pavilions seemed to lie like an exotic mirage along the edge of the sea.

'Playing football. When his father told him strictly not to.'

The small girl studied Amy's face for her reaction to the moral content of the news. Her sister's tone of voice inferred that the misfortune was the predestined result of disobedience.

'They have taken him to Liverpool. So as not to lose his arm. They have better surgeons there. They are all Welsh of course.'

Amy was obliged to nod. Respectful allegiance was due not only to particular knowledge, but also to providential wisdom. The smaller girl became suddenly restless and anxious.

'Nesta Wyn . . .' She addressed her sister with becoming diffidence. 'You haven't said he could still lose it.'

Nesta Wyn frowned to show that she did not like having her pauses curtailed. She spoke sharply. 'Keep it or lose it, it will cost them a fortune. It could be cut off above the elbow. That's what my father said.'

Amy's fingers moved instinctively to protect her elbows. From the back seat of the bus a roar of raucous laughter from the rough boys drew a glance of disapproval from the travelling minister: his neck swivelled inside the high round collar. The conductor frowned absent-mindedly and reached up for a board on the luggage rack on which papers covered with sheets of numbers were kept flat by elastic bands. He was so short he had to stand on tiptoe to reach it.

The bus now travelled at twenty miles an hour. From their high seats the passengers could see over the low hedges. Nesta Wyn shaped her lips in preparation for further revelations. Her sister, still eager to please, tapped the window to draw her attention to tents and a marquee being put up in the largest field in view.

'Nesta Wyn.' Pride in her sister's omniscience glowed in her pale face. 'You know what it is!'

'That's the Air Circus,' Nesta Wyn said. 'That's what that is.'

She turned around to ascertain whether her announcement had registered with those within earshot. The three office girls were so patently puzzled, she repeated her announcement in an obliging tone.

151

'Air Circus,' she said. 'It's the Air Circus. They charge five shillings for a ride. My father says it's cheaper to go on a donkey . . .'

'Oh look!' Her sister clapped her hand over her mouth to suppress her unseemly interruption. Outside, a flying machine was about to land in the big field. All the passengers, even the minister, scrambled to the left-hand side of the bus to gain a better view of the unexpected marvel. The wheels on stiff supports threatened to touch the grass. They would see the machine meet the ground with the grace and power of a mythological bird. The bus-driver, his mouth hanging open, leaned over his large steering wheel to see all he could. There was a bend in the road ahead and his right foot came down hard on the brake. All the passengers were thrown forward. One of the office girls squealed as she disappeared under a seat. She was speedily rescued by her two friends and restored unharmed to a position at a window that gave her a good view. The stationary bus completely blocked the narrow road.

'I'd love to go up.' Amy spoke quietly but Nesta Wyn heard. She stared down disapprovingly at the golden curls that hung under Amy's velour school hat.

'You'd have to cut your hair,' she said. 'I can tell you that much.'

Her sister was shouting again. She was the first to notice that the wings of the aeroplane were wobbling like the stiff arms of a man on a ledge trying to keep his balance. The boys from the back of the bus were punching each other with excitement.

'He's going to crash, I tell you . . .'

They began to push their way to the front of the bus, still trying to keep the aeroplane in view.

'Any minute . . . It will be a smash . . .'

The conductor stood in his way, doing his duty. 'Take your seats. This is not an official stop. The bus may move at any moment.'

From the bus the view of the aeroplane was now excitingly complete. The wheels had touched the grass but the machine swept nearer and nearer towards them. Suddenly it stopped. The tail lifted, the nose tilted downwards and the long propeller splintered into the ground.

An uncontrollable surge by the senior boys thrust the small conductor aside. He looked in vain for help from his colleague. In a trance of curiosity the driver had already clambered out of his cabin. Out on the open road, the boys careered around like bullocks, bumping into each other in their eagerness to find the first point of access to the field and the immobilised aeroplane. A wide ditch clogged with rushes totally frustrated their efforts.

'He may need help, you see.' The minister easily persuaded the conductor to stand aside so that he too could descend to the road and be ready to serve in a private or official capacity. The rest of the passengers hurried to follow his example. Only Nesta Wyn, copied by her younger sister, hesitated.

'We could have to pay to get on again . . .'

'Come on.' Amy pushed her impatiently.

The bus was empty, except for the conductor who stood loyally on the step while still able to observe the aeroplane not twenty yards away across the ditch and the low hedge. The pilot was climbing out of the cockpit. He could be heard shouting as he gesticulated.

'He's swearing,' Nesta Wyn said. 'He's swearing something awful.'

A senior boy with pock-marked cheeks and pale blue eyes stood in front of Amy, his school cap clutched in his right hand.

'I'm going to jump,' he said. 'Down there. I'm going to jump across the ditch. Will you come and watch me?'

Amy studied his excited face as if she were seeing him in a new and more interesting light.

'Amy . . .' Nesta Wyn had taken hold of her arm. Her voice was low with warning. Amy nodded at the excited boy.

'Go on then,' she said. 'If you think you can. I'll come and watch you.'

Nesta Wyn whispered rapidly in her ear. 'That's Raymond Henbont.'

'I know,' Amy said calmly.

'You can't go and watch him. He's a bad boy. He does bad things. He does.'

Her small sister scuttled back to her side from a brief reconnaissance to make a quick report. She had been as observant as ever.

153

'There's a car coming,' she said. 'I've seen it. It will be here soon. It won't be able to pass.'

Nesta Wyn barely acknowledged the fresh data. She was too intent on directing a gaze of concentrated reproach towards Amy's moving figure. Swaying in the middle of the road his legs already bent in rehearsal for his jump, Raymond was urging Amy to come closer. He behaved as though he knew the hedge well and had selected the best crossing-point while the rest of the boys were still vainly chasing about. The motor car was almost upon her before Amy took in its arrival on the scene.

It was a bull-nosed Morris with the hood up. Behind the wheel sat a striking woman made up with the confidence of a film star, wearing a wide-brimmed hat. Amy could not prevent herself staring at her. She was even more fascinating than the aeroplane. A red cloak was held together at her throat by a silver clasp made in the image of a serpent swallowing its own tail. Beside her sat a girl Amy's age. She was wearing an unfamiliar school uniform. She was smiling broadly and seemed so glad to see her, Amy smiled back. The girl had a large mouth and her eyes were the colour of bluebells.

'What's all this, then?'

The lady driver's voice was rich and friendly and infinitely confident.

'It's an aeroplane,' Amy said. 'We saw it crash. In the field. We all saw it from the bus.'

To Amy's surprise the lady showed much more interest in her school uniform.

'You are Llanelw, aren't you?'

Amy nodded.

'Well now then, my dear. This is my niece, Enid. Enid Prydderch. A new girl. What's your name, my dear? Jump in, in fact. We're on the way to your place, if that bus is ever going to move. And we are going to be late. Shall I blow my horn?'

She asked the girls their advice and Enid nodded merrily. Amy stood on the running board, and Enid offered to shake hands with her. The aunt pressed the accelerator up and down so that the engine of the car roared sportily and the chassis shook although they were standing still.

154

'I've got to keep this stupid engine running,' she said, shouting. 'What name was it?'

'Amy,' Enid said. She moved up so that Amy could have plenty of room to sit beside her. 'My Auntie is an Inspector of Schools,' she said. 'It's only fair to warn you. Just in case you say anything that could be taken down and held in evidence against you.' Enid laughed delightedly. Amy joined in although she had not seen any joke. The aunt was becoming impatient with the bus.

'He's blocking the public highway,' she said. 'If I stop this engine it will never start again.'

Further down the road Raymond Henbont was shouting crossly for Amy by name. He was about to jump and he could delay his effort no longer. Enid and Amy turned to watch his antics through the celluloid window in the back. They giggled together and with a tolerant smile Miss Prydderch turned her head to see what they were laughing at.

'There you are,' she said. 'That's the male for you, all over. They always want attention. Both of you take a pinch of advice from a sour old maid. Always keep them waiting.'

Enid laughed and looked at Amy as if to say she was free to laugh as well if she wanted to.

'It's what they want themselves in the end. Believe me. Celtic man, anyway. Never run after them. That's fatal. I wouldn't care to speak for the Saxons. They are altogether a different kettle of fish . . . Hold tight, girls.'

Amy grasped the frame of the hood. She nodded to Enid to indicate how much she was enjoying herself. One last look back told them that Raymond Henbont had made his jump and stood in low water with mud over his ankles. Men were running across the field from the tents to the aeroplane, followed by a clumsy tractor with steam rising high from its radiator. The bus-conductor was recalling the passengers to take their seats. The driver waved gallantly to Miss Prydderch to show that he was returning to take charge of his vehicle as fast as he could.

'I'll show you around the school.' Amy spoke quietly to Enid. 'We might be in the same form.'

'Oh, yes,' Enid said. 'I really do hope so.'

2

THE WINTER SUN, LOW ON THE SOUTHERN HORIZON, FLOODED THE school field with a deceptively bright light. The heads of hockey players were blurred by their own breath, except for Enid Prydderch keeping goal, who stamped her feet to keep warm, and, wearing heavy pads, moved about in front of her goal like an elephant on a short tether. She grinned cheerfully as she watched the bursts of organised movement of the two sides. Her side was winning. But she looked the kind of girl who would grin cheerfully in any case.

The girls on the side line kept each other warmer by standing close together. Behind them, under the high wall and in the shadow of the bare beech trees, hoar frost lay out of the reach of the sun's rays. The school colours were everywhere in evidence: long knitted scarves in gold and azure blue wound twice and even three times around their necks. There were boys watching too, on the opposite touchline. They had strayed across from the football pitch where a second-eleven match was dragging itself to an undistinguished conclusion. They no longer knew or cared about the football score, but in the hockey match the school was in the lead and they came to cheer and encourage. They were also attracted across by the referee, Miss Lewis, the Latin mistress, whose sporty gym-slip was so short it gave glimpses of cold bare thighs and suspenders above her brown stockings as she raced about the field, energetically dispensing advice to the school side, as well as an impartial interpretation of the laws of the game. The boys studied her splendid legs with mesmerised interest until the game came to a halt near them and they made way sheepishly for a panting girl in order to allow her to roll-in the ball by hand with both feet and hockey stick outside the line. Miss Lewis seemed intent above all to keep up the pace of the game.

'That's the stuff,' she said. 'That's it. Keep the thing moving.'

Enid Prydderch came out of her goal to catch a flying ball in her right hand. She released it to fall perpendicularly to the ground, manoeuvred it around the striking circle until she was in a position to make a long direct pass to Amy in her centre position. Amy stopped the ball with her foot, turned swiftly and began to advance towards her opponent's twenty-five, eluding first one defender and then another. Her ball control gained a quick shout of approval from Miss Lewis. The girls on the side line began to jump up and down in their excitement. The action also helped to improve the circulation of blood in their chilly feet. Amy was now running on their behalf and the least they could do was scream out their encouragement.

'Amy! Amy! Amy! On your own now, Amy!'

The boys caught her name and took up the cry. 'Go on, Amy! Shoot now! Shoot!'

Amy steadied herself. She appeared to be preparing a strike for goal. She tempted the last defender, a large girl playing full back, to lumber wildly at her. Deftly she tapped the ball, side-stepped and sped on, on a diagonal course, her golden curls flying so romantically in the wind they roused her school fellows to a new level of frenzied support. Protected by massive leg-pads, the opposing goalkeeper was more formidable opposition. She was not to be tempted out. Amy conjured the leather ball with her stick. The opposing players were racing towards her. Agonising shouts and cries of conflicting advice rent the still air. Miss Lewis stood holding her whistle, a grim smile on her narrow masculine face. Amy used her speed to race the ball across the striking circle. She eluded an opponent whose passionate intervention momentarily unsighted the goalkeeper. Abruptly Amy changed course, took aim and struck the ball as hard as she could through the narrow gap between the goalkeeper's stick and the right-hand goalpost. The ball hit the net.

'Goal! Goal!'

The spectators were beside themselves with delight. Girls hugged each other. The school was now two goals in the lead. Enid went forward as far as she could to let Amy see how delighted she was. Amy's team-mates were crowding around her. Under the watchful eye of the Latin mistress, Amy struggled to restrict her own overwhelming joy to a modest smile. She gave Enid a little wave to thank her for the original pass before the teams lined up for the bully to restart the game.

Their opponents mounted a last desperate attack. Twice Enid saved powerful shots with her pads. Amy threw all her energies into helping the defence. She robbed an opposing winger of the ball and launched herself on a break-away run that roused her supporters to fresh ecstasies of excitement. She moved so lightly and with such elegance she might have had wings on the ankles of her borrowed hockey boots.

'And another, Amy. And another.'

Her name was on a hundred lips. For a brief moment the sound seemed to make her hesitate, as if her vision had been clouded suddenly with the responsibility that everyone was eagerly thrusting upon her. Her shot at goal was accurate enough, but this time it was stopped by the broad goalkeeper. Amy struck herself angrily on the hip, but no one else reproved her. Soon the final whistle blew and the game was at an end. The spectators made it clear that Amy was the heroine of the match. The teams made their way to the cloakrooms on the girls' side of the redbrick County Intermediate School. The sun sank nearer the horizon and the shadows of the players seemed as long as the shadows of the trees. Some stopped to talk, but Miss Lewis made them all move along quickly. Enid, encumbered by her leg-pads, caught up with Amy.

'I'm so glad, Amy. I'm so glad.' Her face was lit up with happiness and for a moment Amy stared at it as if she were looking at herself in a burnished mirror. She squeezed Enid's arm.

'It was you,' she said. 'Our team has been great ever since you were picked.'

There was little space in the cloakroom for the two teams and the supporters who were still milling around them.

'Now look here,' Miss Lewis said. 'Let's give our worthy opponents room to breathe for heaven's sake.'

Enid and Amy sat next to each other on a narrow ledge under the rows of iron coat-pegs. They took off their boots and rolled down their stockings. Amy's were spattered with mud. Miss Lewis held on to a cast-iron coat-peg and leaned over them.

'Look here, Prydderch,' she said. 'You ought to have a word with that aunt of yours. She's an H.M.I. after all. Tell her this school needs changing rooms, will you? And that's for a start. Athletics

158

and sport don't seem to count for anything in this country. *Mens sana in corpore sano* and all that. You tell her from me.'

Amy listened intently. Enid was nodding her head and laughing merrily.

'Yes, Miss Lewis. I will tell her.'

'Facilities, tell her. That's the latest word. *Facilis Descensus Averni* and all that. Especially with a hockey stick. You tell her from me. Is this your stick, Parry, or the school's?'

Miss Lewis's manner was pleasant enough. Amy blushed and looked at the red tiled floor.

'The school's, Miss Lewis. And the boots as well.'

'Right,' Miss Lewis said. 'I'd better take them then so that I can lock up the tackle room. Facilities for ever, Prydderch. Don't forget!'

'I shan't, Miss Lewis.' Enid raised her finger gaily and almost winked at the Latin mistress. As soon as she had moved away, she said, 'She's nice, Miss Lewis. I like her. She's so jolly always.'

Amy carefully drew a clean black stocking up her leg. 'I prefer Miss Bellis. When she was here I mean.'

Enid looked puzzled. 'But you said Miss Lewis was much better at games.'

'I'm not denying it. I just said she was nicer. That's all I said.'

Enid did not pursue the topic. 'Will you come home with me for tea?' she said. 'You could have a bath at our place if you liked. I'll be having one anyway. I asked my mother. She said it would be all right.'

Amy looked at her friend's wide sympathetic eyes. 'Beti Buns asked me,' she said. 'She asked me yesterday. I said yes. I can't really put her off now, can I?'

Enid was disappointed. Her smile vanished from her face. She bit her lower lip and blinked to clear any moisture that could be accumulating against her will in her eyes.

'What about next week, then,' she said. 'I'd better book you in good time, hadn't I?'

'I'm sorry,' Amy said. 'I'm very sorry. I'd much rather come with you, Enid. You know that.'

'Of course you can't let her down. I wish I wasn't so horribly selfish.'

159

Girls waiting in the porch began to call for the players by name.

'I suppose she's waiting for you now, isn't she? Beti Hughes I mean.'

'She could be. Don't you like her, Enid?'

'It's not her. I don't mind her. It's that awful father of hers. Councillor Buns.'

Amy smiled at the nickname. 'Why? What's the matter? What's he done?'

The girls in the doorway were edging their way in.

'I'll tell you about it another time,' Enid said.

As she stood up she looked unexpectedly mature and sad. Nesta Wyn followed by her sister came into the cloakroom.

'I've got your bag Amy,' she said. 'Are you coming on the four o'clock?'

She spoke loudly as though she wanted as many people as possible to know that she and her sister travelled to school every day on the bus with Amy Parry. Amy took her school satchel from Nesta Wyn and shook her head.

'I'm going on the half-past seven,' she said.

Nesta Wyn waited for more information but it was not forthcoming.

'You played very well,' Nesta Wyn said.

She made her toll of compliment before hurrying on to an item of news she was anxious to impart.

'Have you heard about Miss Bellis?'

Before she could gain Amy's undivided attention, a girl of short stature, wearing a belted navy-blue overcoat of outstanding quality, pushed past Nesta Wyn and her sister to take hold of Amy's arm and shake it proudly with both hands.

'You were a marvel.'

She raised her eyebrows and looked around at everyone so that they were obliged to agree.

'Wasn't she, kids? Wasn't she a marvel?' Her enthusiasm made her breathless. 'And I'll tell you something.'

Still clinging to Amy's arm, she lowered her body and spoke rapidly in a low voice to indicate her remarks were being made in confidence.

160

'She ought to be Captain. She ought. There's no doubt about it. No doubt at all.'

Amy blushed and looked anxiously at Enid. 'You shouldn't say that, Beti,' she said. 'Not on any account. I don't want you to.'

'Well, I've a right to my opinion.' She looked at Nesta Wyn for support. 'Everybody's got a right to her opinion.'

Nesta Wyn was obliged to agree.

'Nesta,' Amy said, eager to change the subject. 'What were you going to say about Miss Bellis?'

Nesta Wyn drew herself up, stiff with information.

'Only that she had to get married.'

The features of her face tightened with righteous disapproval. Other girls who could hear were making noises of disbelief.

'Keep your voice down,' Amy said.

'To a postman. Just think of that. She's had a baby and they're living in a cottage on the road from Denbigh to Mold. Just think of that.'

Amy had gone pale. She sat down on the narrow ledge. Her back was bent with a load that was more than weariness after a hard game. Beti did not notice. She was itching to make a joke.

'Playing postman's knock,' she said.

No one responded. Beti quickly covered her mouth with her hand, revealing an eczema rash on the inside of her wrist. Enid touched Amy gently on the shoulder.

'I say, Amy. Are you all right?'

Amy swallowed the saliva that had accumulated in her mouth before she spoke.

'She was always so nice. She was my teacher in Melyd. Before she came here. She was always so nice to us.'

The girls were silent together thinking of Miss Bellis. Beti made another attempt to be cheerful.

'Guess what's on in the Cinema Royal. Harold Lloyd in *Safety Last*.'

Gloomily the players put on their overcoats. They moved together in a tight group through the side entrance to the drive on the girl's side of the school. Amy stretched herself to demonstrate stiffness. Beti tried to keep as close to her as she could. Nesta Wyn

161

had more to say but nobody seemed disposed to stand still and listen to her. She hurried ahead so that when they reached the school entrance she had turned in the open gateway to face them.

'The baby arrived five and a half months after they were married.' She stared at her listeners as though she were defying them to challenge her relentless accuracy.

'She should have tried *Safety First.*'

'Oh Beti . . .'

Amy tried to show complete disapproval of Beti Buns's tasteless joking. Enid had moved away in the direction of her home. She came back to speak to Amy again.

'Are you sure you won't come to our place?'

She spoke as quietly as she could but Beti's eyes showed clearly that she had overheard. Amy behaved indecisively. With the whole group watching her she plainly wanted to make some kind of decision that would satisfy them all. Beti suffered from asthma. A wheezing noise was already being generated in her chest as though she were working herself up. Amy appealed to Enid.

'Next week. Can I come next week?'

Enid was ready to understand. Her large blue gaze rested briefly on Amy's face before she smiled cheerfully, bade them all good-bye and went her own way. Nesta Wyn and her sister moved to the bus stop across the road. Beti was breathing heavily as Amy walked beside her towards the centre of the town.

'She's a stuck-up thing.'

Amy affected not to hear, only quickening her step a little. Beti was still talking in a dark menacing tone.

'I don't want to be the first to say it, but all I can say is I hope you won't have to choose between us. That's all I can say.'

Amy kept her mouth firmly closed. They walked on until Beti's mood was changed. She linked her arm with Amy's and sniggered asthmatically.

'Eccles cakes,' she said. 'Hot from the oven. And Harold Lloyd if we hurry. First-house.'

3

ESTHER PUSHED THE SEWING MACHINE UNTIL IT WAS AT RIGHT angles to the bedroom window to gain the best light she could. She was wearing cheap spectacles that were clearly not made for her in the first place and staring hard at the needle as her rough hands pushed the material of the dress closer to it. Outside the window the weather was cold enough for snow. Black and white clouds towered on the eastern horizon burnished by fitful light. A sudden shaft of sunlight illuminated the brown bracken on the hill south-east of the farm house. Rabbits could be seen clearly scampering about the openings of their burrows. Then, as if drawn by the desolate cry of the curlew in the still air, a shadow fell over the uplands. Only a single gull high in the sky flew on calmly towards the sea, a solitary white object in the full light of the sun.

Amy was standing behind Esther's chair, shivering in her petticoat and rubbing her stockinged feet together to keep warm.

'It's not right,' she said. 'It will never really fit me.'

'Of course it will.' Esther was optimistic. 'And this is lovely material,' she said. 'You've got to say that much for the aristocracy. They know what's what when it comes to material.'

'But it's wrong, Auntie. Over the shoulders. It doesn't hang properly. It's crooked.'

'That's your Lady Diana for you. Curvature of the spine I shouldn't wonder. And to think that Connie Clayton dances attendance on her night and day in the County of Hampshire. Where's her pride? Where's her dignity?'

Esther flourished a large pair of scissors and shook her head sadly. 'They are no good really.'

Amy stared petulantly at a heap of old clothes on the bed: overcoats, dresses, skirts and blouses, all in varying conditions of wear.

'Nothing will make them fit me,' Amy said. 'Not really. Those dresses are tight under the arms. These are too long and too narrow. And these knitted things. You need to be ninety to wear them. I don't think they all belonged to this Lady Diana either.

163

They're all shapes and sizes. I think Connie Clayton must have been to a jumble sale.'

Esther pushed her head closer to the needle and pulled her mouth into strange shapes as she concentrated on the unfamiliar work. She stopped to breathe with deep relief as she came to the end of a hem. She bit off the end of the cotton with her front teeth. She lifted the dress by the shoulders and shook it out to examine the hem critically.

'Beggars can't be choosers,' she said. 'Goodness knows I never liked Connie Clayton. But she takes some interest in you, Amy, and I'm grateful for that. Here. Try it on.'

Amy thrust her head with nervous reluctance into the dress. Esther stood up to help her.

'It's an awful colour,' Amy said.

'Oh, I don't know . . .' Esther plucked at the back of the frock cheerfully. 'Primrose would you call it? It suits you, Amy. I wouldn't say it if it didn't.'

'She must have round shoulders or something . . .'

Amy bent her arm so that she could grasp loose material on the back of the frock.

'It will be cold in the hall,' Esther said. 'You can be sure of that. So you can leave the coat on. You must admit the coat does look nice now we've re-shaped the collar. It looks as good as new.'

Amy was not easily consoled.

'You should see the new frock Enid Prydderch's had for Christmas,' she said. 'Pleats in the skirt. Extra low hips. And a lovely blue artist's bow here. It looks lovely on me. Marocain they call it. The material.'

Esther was on her knees, snipping off bits of cotton from the hem.

'Don't worry,' she said. 'There'll be no one in that village hall to compare with you. I can tell you that much now.'

'Enid said I could borrow it. But I didn't like to. I could tell by the look on her mother's face she was annoyed with her for offering.'

'You did quite right. Never get into anyone's debt. My mother used to say that and I used to think she was awful. Strict and mean.

And of course she was in a way. But she was always upright, I'll say that for her. And you can't say that about everybody nowadays. Not by a long chalk.'

'I wish I had,' Amy said. 'I wish I had borrowed it. Better than wearing cast-offs. I know that much.'

Esther did not choose to pursue the argument. She began to pick up the bits under the sewing table.

'Have you seen Doctor Peter Prydderch yet?'

She sat back on her heels looking up at Amy and smiling with frank curiosity.

'I don't think he comes out of his room,' Amy said.

Esther shook her head in sad amazement.

'To think of it,' she said. 'Dr Peter Prydderch, Liverpool. A famous name you know. When I was a girl. One of the eight-inch nails as they used to say. A man ahead of his time. That was his trouble. My mother wouldn't have his name mentioned in the house. That heretic she used to call him. She couldn't stand the mention of his name. But William thought he was wonderful. And that was another thing for them to quarrel about. Calvins you see. They are very narrow as your uncle says. When you're narrow its much easier to fall out among yourselves. I ought to know, I used to be one of them. Before your uncle rescued me.'

Amy pulled the dress over her head. She looked around for her old clothes and put them on.

'The Prydderchs aren't narrow,' she said. 'I wouldn't say so anyway.'

Esther found the comment deeply interesting.

'Tell me about them,' she said. 'What kind of a house is it? I never hear or see anything or anybody in this place from one day to the next.'

'It's big,' Amy said.

'I think I should know that.' Esther spoke drily. 'How many people live there? Can you tell me that?'

Amy was reluctant to pursue the topic.

'Enid's father and mother.'

'What's he like? Dr Peter's brother.'

'He's a surveyor for the Llanelw Town Council.'

165

'Amy fach, I know that,' Esther said. 'What's he like? Is he like his brother? That's what I'd like to know.'

'I suppose so.'

Esther sighed patiently. 'And who else?'

'Miss Sali Prydderch. The H.M.I. She's nice. She wears gorgeous clothes. Like a film star. She had two brothers away in college. Emrys in Cambridge. And Ifor in Paris. They are older than Enid. They're all clever.'

'Is Enid clever?'

'Oh yes.'

'Cleverer than you?'

'That's a silly question, Auntie. Do you want me to feed the calves?'

'Oh dear . . .' Esther looked for somewhere to dispose of the bits of material in her hands. '. . . here's me sitting down if you please with all the work waiting . . .'

Her arms and legs became animated with stiff but habitual concern. Amy followed her downstairs. Through the open door, she saw her uncle Lucas. His shirt sleeves were rolled up to reveal woollen combinations that ended at his wrists. With a pipe gripped between his teeth he was cutting out articles from weekly papers to paste in his scrap book. Totally absorbed in his task, he took no notice of Esther's agitation.

'Would you mind, Lucas, feeding the pigs shortly?' Esther said.

Lucas lifted his head like a man surprised. He turned to look at the grate where the fire was burning very low.

'The fire needs coal,' he said.

He spoke as if someone other than himself had neglected a duty.

'And there is wood to be chopped, Lucas,' Esther said. 'If you could give it your attention for a moment.'

Amy pushed ahead of her aunt, clearly eager to get on with the job in hand. In the dark scullery they found old working coats. They tied lengths of binder twine around their waists and pushed their feet into their clogs. Still in his shirt sleeves and nursing his pipe Lucas followed them and stood on the kitchen step to watch their hurried preparations.

'Why all this haste? The week-night Seiat isn't until seven o'clock. You are like goats in a storm, the pair of you.'

166

'Amy is going to the Christmas thing,' Esther said. 'The Christmas Treat.'

'What Christmas Treat?' Lucas's voice was as impartial as he could make it, but the word 'Treat' seemed to give him difficulty.

'The school's,' Esther said. 'It's for the school children. Miss Owen has asked Amy to go along and help. She's also going to get the Wynne Prize.'

'Why wasn't I informed, may I ask?' Lucas spoke very calmly without in any way apportioning blame.

'You were, Lucas. Just over a week ago. But you were reading something. You just didn't take it in.'

Lucas pointed the stem of his pipe towards Amy who was about to dash out to the wash-house to collect the buckets for feeding the calves.

'You be back in time for Seiat then. Take care of that.'

'But how can I be?' The protest burst loudly out of Amy's tight lips.

'Well, see to it.' Lucas was edgy but reasonable still. 'You've got a bike,' he said.

'But how can I tell when the thing is going to end? Or how long it will take? And I'm sure they won't give the prizes until the very end. How on earth can I ever get to Ebenezer by seven o'clock? From Melyd to Trerhedyn. I would need wings not a bike.'

Esther said nothing. She held her head on one side and stared at her husband in silent appeal.

'And who is giving this Christmas Treat may I be allowed to ask?'

This time his voice made no attempt to disguise his contempt for the phrase. The English word 'Christmas' was alien enough, with pagan and commercial overtones, but 'Treat' was worse, a disposition of worthless trinkets to gullible natives.

'A church function for the so-called church school no doubt. Presided over by our eloquent friend, the Rector. And is the Archbishop in attendance as well? That guiding star of the English tide . . .'

Amy shook her head vigorously.

'No,' she said. 'It's Miss Vanstrack, Uncle. Or Mrs Pulford, rather. Captain and Mrs Pulford to be exact.'

167

'That creature!' Lucas's harsh voice rang out between the stone walls. ' "Captain" Pulford. That drunken lout!'

'Now Lucas, please.' Esther waved her hand pleading to quieten her husband. 'Forgive me for saying as much, but I don't think you've ever met the man, have you?'

'Parading as a war hero.' Lucas brought the note of indignation down. 'All he does is drink in the Llanelw Conservative Club and drive his wife's cars into ditches. And he only married the woman for her money.'

'Lucas.' Esther spoke mildly. 'This isn't like you, if you don't mind me saying so. You are condemning the man without ever having met him. That's not your way, Lucas.'

'I'm dealing in established facts,' Lucas said. 'The bricks and mortar of history. I knew that man's father. I faced him in what you might describe as Class Conflict. Now see how closely the family runs to type.' Lucas was eager to gain their undivided attention for an impromptu lecture. 'Or more correctly, how the class runs to type. Here you have a perfect example of the would-be capitalistic class trying to buy its way into the ranks of the landed gentry. What ignorant people like to call county folk. What it means in practice of course is buying and marrying their way into positions of privilege, influence and power. It's all quite clear, Esther Parry, if only you learn a little about economics and political science. You ought to come to the W.E.A. on Wednesday evenings. It would open your eyes.'

'Well Lucas my dear, the calves and the pigs can't eat economics and politics, can they?'

Esther wanted to press on with the work and at the same time end their conversation on a cheerful note. But Lucas ignored her attempt at laughter.

'I know my authority doesn't count for much,' he said, in a sarcastic voice. 'But I don't think she should go.'

The very pronouncement that Esther had striven to avoid had now been made. As Amy stamped angrily across the yard, Esther turned on her heel as helplessly as a goalkeeper watching a ball fly past out of his reach into the back of the net. With her hands half lifted in a gesture of restraint, she heard the girl banging empty buckets together as she collected them from the slate slab in the outside wash-house. The banging and stamping as Amy entered the small barn to measure out calves' powder from a worm-eaten wooden chest made her flinch as if blows had been aimed at her face.

'Lucas . . .' Esther lowered her voice and moved away from the door so that Amy would not hear her. 'She's a good girl, Lucas. She's passed all those subjects in her Junior, with three distinctions. She's the only girl from the village school who has ever done that well. So we must be proud of her, Lucas, mustn't we? We must always look on the best side of things. You say so yourself. I've heard you preach it and I'm sure you're right. Well in that case, Lucas, let the girl enjoy her little triumph. Perfectly harmless it will be and it will help her to work that much harder for her Matric.'

'Matric.' Lucas muttered the word as though it described a chronic complaint from which he had suffered all his life.

'We want her to do well. You've always said that, Lucas. From the beginning.'

'Beginning' was the wrong word. It made Lucas frown heavily. It was so dark in the scullery Esther was obliged to light the small paraffin lamp that hung from a nail in the wall. Lucas stood close behind her. His hands wandered down to the pockets of his fustian trousers and back up to his waistcoat.

'Are we seeing the father coming out in her?' He muttered his misgivings just loud enough for her to hear. 'I saw him once. Before they were married. Singing in a concert. Wearing a white suit and a gold watch chain. He had a waxed moustache. Unreliable. You could see it written all over him.'

Esther waited for the right moment to speak. She had arguments that could dispel all his misgivings, she seemed to be saying, and they were all drawn from the wisdom she had learnt from his superior intelligence.

'It's upbringing that counts. You've always said that, Lucas. If she's got a mind of her own and a will of her own as we must admit, aren't they just like yours? She's very like you, Lucas. You are her real father. Let her go and see for herself. You've brought

169

her up to see the world as it really is and I'm sure you were right to do so. So why not have faith in her. Like a real father. Show that you trust her. Show that you can rely on her to see it all in the way that you see it. Why not, Lucas?'

'She should accept a reasonable analysis of the situation.' Lucas was still stern. But Esther reacted as though he was giving way. 'Apply logic. Cold logic. Reason tempered by Christian principles. The way is clear and she should see it. Shun that which is evil. Cleave to that which is good.'

'I am quite sure you are right, Lucas. So why not let her see for herself? An object lesson. It could be a good experience for her.'

Lucas looked at his pocket watch.

'Going to chapel would be a better experience,' he said. 'If we don't accept that, where on earth are we?'

'Of course, I agree with you. And so does Amy. We'll both be there as regular as clockwork as we have always been. But just this once, Lucas . . . Let her collect her special prize.'

Lucas replaced his watch in his waistcoat pocket.

'I wouldn't want anybody to think of me as a tyrant,' he said.

'Of course you are nothing of the sort.'

'All I ask of the girl is to use reason as a cautious guide along the narrow path of righteousness.'

Esther pressed her hands together to suppress an overwhelming urge to get on with her work. She nodded obediently to her husband who stood above her on the kitchen step. Behind him the lamp on the oilcloth-covered kitchen table created shadows out of the fading daylight.

'The old ways were very strict,' he said.

'Too strict.'

He was surprised by the note of bitterness in Esther's voice.

'As far as I was concerned anyway,' she said. 'My mother was too strict. I still respect her memory, but I still remember she ruled us with the rod of fear. Let her go, Lucas. Just this once.'

He nodded briefly and Esther smiled to show her delight.

'And don't forget the pigs, if I might remind you, Lucas, while there is still some light.'

Esther restrained herself from rushing to give Amy the good

news. She passed through the small barn into the stack-yard and collected an armful of loose straw to spread under the calves. She returned to the pen at the end of the outbuildings where Amy was now feeding four strong calves with a warm mixture of powder and skimmed milk. The calves nuzzled greedily into the battered buckets. With some dexterity Amy used her hands and feet to prevent them tipping the buckets over before they had finished drinking. She also tried to keep herself clear from the wet manure which was some way up under the calves' feet. Helpfully Esther spread straw to absorb the excess of liquid.

'You can leave me,' she said. 'You can go and wash, Amy. He's quite willing you should go.'

Amy held on grimly to the buckets. The strongest calf had finished and had begun to suck blindly at her knuckles.

'There are the others to do,' Amy said. 'And the milking. I'll stay and help you.'

Esther tried to read her face in the failing light. It was possible she could have been crying.

'Indeed you won't,' Esther said. 'The sooner you start off the better. Especially since you've been invited to help. Now hurry. And see that your bike is all right. The lamp I mean.'

Amy's voice was low with discontent. 'He doesn't want me to go,' she said. 'He never wants me to go anywhere.'

'Oh yes he does.' Esther was kind but firm. She smacked the nose of the greedy calf that was sucking her sleeve and gently pushed Amy away from her position of control over the buckets. The last calf to finish had to have his share protected from the butting heads of the other three.

'He means well,' Esther said. 'Always remember that. He's suffered a lot. Disappointments as you know. In a way he's sacrificed his life for us. We've always got to remember that. Now, off you go.'

4

AMY HUMMED CHEERFULLY TO HERSELF AS SHE BOWLED ALONG the final stretch of the upland road from Trerhedyn to Melyd. When she reached the shadowy bulk of the Wesleyan chapel with the chapel house attached, she knew she could freewheel all the way down to the village. Her cheeks burnt in the cold air of the clear winter night. From time to time she squeezed the brakes to restrain the headlong descent of the bicycle. She saw the impressive silhouette of the Memorial Hall in the moonlight. There were stars in the violet sky in spite of the full moon. Inside the hall the lamps were already lit. They were not bright but they seemed to draw attention to the romantic outline: ornamental buttresses cast tent-like shadows and the towers at either corner of the façade had black crenellations in clear outline against the night sky. Halfway down the hill Amy decided to dismount. She had ridden hard to arrive in good time: now, in order to establish an appearance of calm and tranquillity she would walk decorously down the hill.

The children, in numbers, were already making their way up the steps. They were all lumpy figures in scarves and overcoats. Some of the smallest were escorted by the more massive padded forms of their mothers who greeted each other on the steps and seemed to take a quiet pride in an extended civic building which had added distinction and interest to the centre of their village. At the foot of the steps, Amy turned down the flame in her bicycle lamp so that it went out. Leaving it in safety was something of a problem in front of the hall on such a night as this. While she was undecided what to do, she studied the new War Memorial. It stood between the corner tower of the hall and the retaining wall of the small garden of remembrance. The base of the plinth was just above the level of Amy's head. Still holding her bicycle, she moved as close as she could to see if it was possible to read the names of the dead in the light of the moon. A bulky woman with arms outstretched like wings behind two little girls managed to bring her white face into Amy's line of vision. The very swing of her head on her shoulders suggested that she missed nothing.

172

'I can't pass without asking,' she said. Her honeyed voice and expression of intense concern immediately stiffened Amy's back. 'How is your taid, the poor old thing? How is the poor old creature?'

'He is as well as can be expected, thank you.'

'Oh how pleased I am to hear it.' She made a funnel of her lower lip and her phrases poured out with the slurred gleam of golden syrup. 'And it's the best place for the poor old man. That's generally conceded. Where he can have what you might call medical care. Your poor aunt has more than enough to do as it is, more than enough as the wide world knows . . .'

'We hope to have him home as soon as he is better.'

The sharp defensive note brought the woman's moving eyeballs to a stop as they studied Amy, a grown girl able to look after herself, in a new light.

'Of course you do, bless your honest heart. Of course . . . And no one calls it the workhouse any more, do they? It's far more of a hospital as is generally conceded and there's no shame at all attached to it.'

Amy was silenced. At last the woman was willing to respond to the plucking of her thick sleeves by each little girl in turn. Amy held her head down in an engrossed examination of the pedals and crank-shaft of her bicycle. She managed to spirit herself through the shadows around the hall in the direction of a side entrance. The site on which the Memorial Hall stood had been levelled out of the rock so that the village street was higher than the back of the building. Her access to a narrow gate was impeded by two motor cars parked close to each other. It was just possible for her to push the bike between the two cars. She considered for a moment leaving the bicycle tilted against the bonnet of one car or the luggage rack of the other. But the gate was open and it would be safer inside the railings. Concrete steps descended abruptly to the stage door. The way was difficult to make out in the deep shadow cast by the buttressed building. The stage door itself was shut, and the faint light in the billiard annexe attached to the rear of the hall did not reach the steps. Amy pushed her bicycle forward and held on the seat bracket with both hands when she could no longer reach the handlebars. When she had squeezed through the gate herself she attempted to regain control of the front of the bike but before she could do so the front wheel passed over the edge and the weight of the whole machine began to tip first one way and then the other. Amy held on to the seat. Her knitted cap slipped back on her glossy hair and threatened to fall off. From the billiard room she could hear the ominous ululation of older boys who were probably using the table without the caretaker's knowledge. While Amy was still muttering angrily between her teeth, the stage door opened. Light fell on the fair hair of the bold youth who looked out into the night and called out impatiently to the occupants of the billiard room. He got no reply. Lazily his head moved and he took in Amy and her predicament. He kept his hands in his pockets and leaned against the half-open door.

'And where are you off to?'

His voice was impressive. It was soft but arrogant. Unemotional English with a public-school accent. In spite of her concern for herself Amy listened as though she were hearing an attractive musical instrument for the first time.

'I'm coming to help.' Amy struggled not to sound inferior and apologetic.

'You won't be much help hanging on up there, will you?'

'Miss Owen asked me.'

'Did she, by jove? Good for her.'

When his head turned towards the billiard room as though he were contemplating calling out the occupants to come and see the fun, Amy's back arched like a cat that senses the approach of stray dogs.

'This is the village hall,' Amy said. 'I've got a perfect right to be here.'

She tried to move forward. The bicycle wobbled dangerously from side to side. She was about to let go. The young man sprang forward with sudden agility and grasped the loose handlebars with both hands.

'Memorial hall,' he said. 'Get your facts right. Where do you want it?'

'Village hall.' Amy spoke stubbornly. 'That's what it was before the war.'

174

'I don't care what the world was like before the Flood. Where do you want it?'

Amy let go of the seat. She pointed hesitantly to the shade of the closest buttress.

'Somewhere there,' she said. 'Should be all right.'

'Sure you wouldn't like it on the stage?'

He tested the bike, pushing it back and fore and leaning over the handlebars.

'You could do some tricks. Get the party going.'

'No, thank you.'

Amy spoke so primly, he laughed at her. She could see that his nose was crooked and the end of one of his front teeth had been chipped off. He was gay and self-possessed. Openly pleased with himself. In case he would force her to smile at him, Amy stood in the doorway with her back to him. She examined her hands closely in the poor light to see if they were clean. As she moved inside he called out.

'I say!' He was bent over her bike in the shadow of the buttress. 'This doesn't look too good, does it? Just look at this.' He sounded alarmed as though he had suddenly discovered some serious fault in the condition of her bicycle. 'Just look.'

Amy stepped gingerly towards him, her head thrust forward as she peered into the darkness. As she raised her arm, he suddenly grasped her wrist and plucked her towards him. He caught her as she fell and planted a sudden kiss near her lips. She could feel his body shaking with suppressed laughter.

'A little something for my trouble,' he said. 'How about another?'

Amy said nothing. It was clear that she was furious, but he was not afraid of her. He was strong and confident and treating her like a mountain pony he knew how to master. He tightened his grip on her wrist and drew her closer to him. He made a mock romantic noise.

'One more little kiss . . .'

Amy breathed deeply. She moved her free hand and planted her finger nails as hard as she could into the back of his hand. The strike took him unawares.

'Cripes,' he said, nursing his hand. 'Hell's bells . . .'

He gasped with pain and anger. But there was also a new note of respect in his voice. Amy smiled to herself and slipped inside the stage door. She hurried down the short corridor to the Ladies' Room. She had the room to herself and although it was chilly and damp, she took off her overcoat and her dress to wash in the cold water under the single tap. She dried her face with the clean towel and stared at her own reflection in the tarnished mirror above the washbasin. She could not see very much in the pale light of the flickering lamp, but she was able to comb the thick waves of her golden hair by instinct, her fingers pushing the curls and ringlets into the positions they were familiar with. The hair was allowed low over her forehead and the ends curled over her ears towards her glowing cheeks. When she had slipped back into the dress her aunt had worked on, the knitted belt seemed to present an insoluble problem: whether to wear it tight, or high or low, or whether not to wear it all. While she was still trying out styles, there was a brief knock on the door. Miss Philips, the Rector's sister, entered the washroom clutching a black fur tightly around her throat. She whispered cautiously.

'Is there anyone else in here?'

She was looking at the water closet cubicle.

'No.' Amy shook her head and smiled. Miss Philips looked greatly relieved as she closed the door behind her.

'Isn't it cold? It's very cold, bach, isn't it?'

She was dressed in black. Her small face appeared squeezed between her black fur and her black hat. She approached the cubicle and contemplated the W.C. There was no seat and the white porcelain shone in the gloomy interior like frozen snow. She sighed and muttered to herself. Amy buttoned up her coat and placed her knitted cap carefully over her hair. She prepared to leave. Miss Philips turned to her suddenly and touched her arm.

'Tell me something, Amy fach. Does my breath smell of pickled onions?'

Politely Amy bent her knees to bring her nose on the same level as Miss Philips's open mouth. Her nostrils twitched involuntarily as they were assailed by a specimen of hot breath.

176

'Just a little.' She spoke tactfully. Miss Philips shook her head and turned to stare again at the W.C.

'I should never have touched them. The trouble is I can't leave them alone. I'm not going in there. You'd think that at least they would provide a seat wouldn't you?'

Outside the Ladies' Room, Miss Philips held Amy's arm to make her stand and listen. Her whispering echoed in the high ceiling.

'I wish I'd never come. I can tell you that much. He made me come and now I'm here he's ashamed of me. That's my brother for you. You won't be ashamed to sit with me, will you?'

'Of course not, Miss Philips. But I promised to help.'

'You want to watch them.' Miss Philips's warning was both general and mysterious. 'I tell you one thing, Amy fach. Don't let them make you a pawn in their game.' She paused to listen to the echo of the impressive phrase she had just uttered. 'You watch, as soon as he sees me back in there, he'll start frowning at me. That's how he is. That's how he always is.'

She pushed Amy's arm and they moved side by side down the narrow corridor, Amy slightly in front, as though she offered Miss Philips some form of cover against unexpected attack. Once more Miss Philips squeezed her arm and they halted.

'This Captain Pulford is an odd sort of chap, isn't he? Do you like him, Amy fach?'

'I've only just seen him from a distance,' Amy said.

'Do you know what he said to me? You wouldn't believe it. "And who's little girl are you, may I ask?" Those were his words. And he'd been drinking too. I'd sooner have pickled onions than whisky.'

Miss Philips was taken with a fit of giggling. Her hand shook Amy's arm up and down and only stopped when she became serious again.

'That was no way to talk to the Rector's sister. So you know what I did, bach?'

Miss Philips paused to give Amy a chance to guess.

'I just didn't answer. I think that settled him, you know. I really think it did.'

Miss Philips frowned as she struggled to consider objectively the effect of her not supplying Captain Pulford with an answer to his question.

'Except that he's English of course. Skin like a wall of leather.' Miss Philips gazed sadly up at Amy's face. 'Tell me one thing Amy, before we go in. Will you always be my friend?'

Amy hesitated a fraction in case the question was not being put with total seriousness. Miss Philips's expression did not alter. The pupils of her small eyes were fixed in an unblinking stare.

'Yes I will, Miss Philips. Of course I will.'

When she opened the door they stood together just inside the hall without closing the door behind them. Amy stared wide-eyed at the unfamiliar sight. As many as a hundred schoolchildren were seated in two long rows on forms and benches almost the full length of the hall. The boys were even stiffer and more still than the girls. Under short hair plastered down with grease or water, their white faces were subdued with wonder and curiosity. Opposite them, narrow trestles were laid end to end to make one long table, covered with white cloths, where there was room for them all to sit. The light from the hanging lamps under their clouded white glass shades shone with equal lustre on the jellies laid out at intervals in different colours, shapes and sizes and on the children's eyes. Between the trestle tables and the stage stood a large Christmas tree. A painter's steps in the corner behind it showed how it had been decorated from top to bottom with silver tinsel, glass bells and coloured balls and dummy parcels. The real presents were heaped on the floor around the stout tub filled with earth which sustained the impressive tree.

'Oh, isn't it wonderful?'

Amy's enthusiasm was unrestrained. Miss Philips had asked her to be her friend and she was eager to share this first surge of delight with her.

'I don't think I've ever seen such a big tree before. And so many presents. Aren't they neat? The parcels.'

Miss Philips was inclined to be critical.

'It's all right I suppose. But work it out for yourself. One hundred presents at an average of sixpence each. Fifty shillings. Two pounds ten. And a few more shillings for putting up the tree. Not a very expensive way of making a big impression.'

178

Amy's face went pale with disappointment. Silently she shifted her feet so that she would not be standing quite so close to such a sceptical companion. Miss Philips had not noticed but the slight movement was enough to attract the attention of a plump military-looking man who was talking to the Rector. He took hold of the Rector's arm and steered him round so that he could see Amy and his sister standing together by the side entrance. His beady bright eyes and clipped moustache were animated as he moved the reluctant Rector towards them in a slow march.

'Jiw, jiw.' Miss Philips made a frightened noise and stepped back into the corridor. 'It's that Captain Pulford,' she whispered desperately and tried to lure Amy into a quick retreat into the Ladies' Room.

'You never know what he's going to say next.'

'Just look at this! Just look at this!' The Captain's penetrating tenor voice was consistently jovial as though he had just won a large prize in a lottery. 'What about it then? Here she is. Saint Gwenny – what's it – what's-her-name in the flesh. Rector? Can't you see it?'

The Rector screwed up his eyes and blinked as though he were unable to get Amy's image into focus.

'This is Amy,' he muttered nervously. 'Amy Parry. She's a non-conformist. Aren't you Amy? Not church you see. So you couldn't have her in a pageant in praise of the Church in Wales, could you, Captain Pulford?'

'No.'

The Captain continued to study Amy's person with the objectivity of a keen producer. Amy blushed with embarrassment but he did not seem to notice.

'I take your point. But we could stretch it a bit, couldn't we? Your point I mean.'

He addressed Amy directly. 'What firm are you? Calvin is it?

> Calvins cruel without grace
> Keep a chapel in this place
> Rent their pews to well-off people
> And leave the parson in his steeple.'

179

He recited the jingle in a quick monotone and ended by slapping the Rector heartily on the back.

'You didn't know I knew that one, did you? It's a bit of a hobby of mine to tell you the truth. I call it social geometry. Now did you know that if the hall is taken to be the hub of a wheel all the chapels, Wesleyan, Congo, Calvin, Baptist, are related to it in relation to their numerical strength, and that this figure in turn is related to their respective distance from the centre as points on a compass? Now the disestablished established church, the old mother as you call it, doesn't fit in at all. It's down there in the south somewhere. Guarding the entrance to the underworld.'

The Rector was barely listening. He was engaged in an attempt at silent communication with his sister who lurked in the shadows of the corridor. By twitches of his thin mouth and his eyebrows which had developed a tendency to peak at the ends, he urged her to step forward with quiet dignity and take up some useful but inconspicuous position among the assembled people. Captain Pulford tugged happily at his arm.

'There's one about the Baptists too, you know. And I particularly like the one about the Wesleyans.

> John Wesley jumped up on a hedge
> And made the workers take the pledge
> Shouted till his throat was sore
> "Holiness is for the poor."'

Between the Captain and the Rector, Amy had a view of Miss M. A. Owen. The schoolmistress had taken up a key position behind a green baize table under the stage. Restless as she was, she never wandered far from it. If she sensed that she was under critical observation, she consulted the lists on the table written in her own copperplate handwriting, or rearranged the books and prizes on the desk or touched the small handbell which would be used to make general announcements. Sometimes she moved to her right to be nearer the small group of gentry around the wheelchair occupied by Mr Pulford senior. He had suffered a stroke and his mouth was fixed in a crooked salivating smile. His patient wife

180

sat with her back to the schoolchildren. She nursed a large white handkerchief in her lap. From time to time she wiped her husband's mouth. Invariably Mr Pulford pulled at her arm impatiently because it blocked his view of some detail of the occasion that he wanted to observe.

Miss Owen also kept in touch with the room used as a kitchen on the other side of the stage. The door to this room was open, but partially concealed by the great Christmas tree. Women appeared from time to time to give Miss Owen signals concerning the progress of their preparations. Captain Pulford's wife, the former Miss Vanstrack, walked across to the table to speak to Miss Owen. She was smoking a cigarette. But as far as Amy could see the schoolmistress did not seem to mind. Amy stared at them with awe. Mrs Captain Pulford was smoking in public. Her elbow rested on one protruding hip. A long cigarette-holder seemed to float above her fingers. She looked like a substantial copy of an advertisement from an illustrated magazine. Miss Owen gave her polite attention and continued to do so even when her mother appeared in the doorway behind the Christmas tree making urgent signals. She raised her left hand and waved a finger with some delicacy along a suggested route from the doorway behind the tree to the end of the long table. When she had repeated the gesture, Mrs Owen passed on the message. Two burly women emerged carrying between them a steaming tea-urn. They made their way to the far end of the table. They were followed by a smaller pair with a slightly smaller urn, who made the shorter journey to the end nearest the Christmas tree. A rustle of excitement swept through the two long rows of children. Captain Pulford began to chuckle.

'Now for it, chaps,' he said. 'Stand by for the stampede.'

He shifted about to obtain a better angle to view the total reactions of the schoolchildren. As a recognised authority on discipline and an ex-regular, he showed conspicuous tolerance of the schoolmistress's performance. As soon as the Captain's back was turned, Miss Philips slipped back into the hall. She paused briefly to glare at her brother before pushing Amy forward so that they could both take up positions at the far end of the table. Women were emerging from the kitchen. They took up posts at

181

intervals between the windows and the long table. Having inclined her ear to Mrs Pulford to accept a final suggestion, Miss Owen rang the handbell. The children shot to their feet. Miss Owen lifted a warning finger. It was enough to hold them. Captain Pulford raised his eyebrows to show approving surprise. Miss Owen rang the bell the second time and grabbed the clapper with her left hand. The children crossed the open space. Captain Pulford caught the Rector's eye, put a hand to his ear and leaned down as if he were listening to the approach of buffalo along a level plain. The bell tolled a third time. The children stood still above the places they had found for themselves. Miss Owen's thin high voice brought about complete silence.

'I now call upon the Rector, the Reverend J. J. Philips, M.A., to say grace.'

The Rector shut his eyes tightly, squared his shoulders, raised his chin, and rushed through the grace with devout but unintelligible speed. There was an extra silence while the children wondered whether or not he had finished, since his eyes were still closed. The more enterprising took advantage of the uncertain interval to begin eating, planting their teeth enthusiastically into the thick tinned-salmon sandwiches that had to be disposed of first before the ladies were prepared to lean over and sink their serving spoons into the trembling jellies. Miss Philips took a close interest in the performance of two little twin girls seated in front of her. They were both very polite and answering her constant questions left them behind in the consumer's race. The plates in front of them were emptied by eager hands that shot out like snakes' tongues for sandwiches and cakes. Miss Philips became concerned. She gave Amy two empty plates.

'They're starving,' she said. 'You're starving, aren't you, girls?'

The twins nodded politely. Identical pairs of eyes with highlights from the lamplight under the pupils were fixed longingly on Amy. She squeezed between Miss Philips and the window and hurried down the empty space in the middle of the hall. She glanced at the group around Mr Pulford's wheel-chair and saw that they had been joined by the arrogant youth who had tried to kiss her. He had one hand in his trouser pocket. Captain Pulford tapped his arm reprovingly. He pulled out his hand and Amy saw that he had wrapped a clean handkerchief around it.

Inside the kitchen Mrs Owen and two helpers were still cutting bread and butter.

'Miss Philips would like some more sandwiches, please.'

Amy smiled pleasantly and held out the empty plates. Mrs Owen's breasts and long double chin swung about loosely as she sawed away at a large loaf she held below her bosom.

'She would, would she?' Mrs Owen's lips stretched with the urgency of her effort. 'I don't suppose she'd like to come and cut them herself. That's how it always is in this world: some in the engine room, some on the bridge. And how are you, Amy Parry?'

Mrs Owen stared hard at Amy and the empty plates in her hand.

'I'm very well, thank you.'

The self-possession in the answer gave Mrs Owen no pleasure.

'You did very well in your Junior, didn't you? Distinctions all round I hear. And the Wynne Prize. I am sure you are very grateful to your teachers, Amy Parry. All the care and attention they've given you. All the help and encouragement. Especially the good grounding you had. You don't get anywhere without a good grounding.'

'I am very grateful.'

Mrs Owen showed qualified approval. She nodded to allow Amy to put down the plates on the table. When she spoke again her voice had a sweeter tone.

'And are you going to sing for us tonight, Amy?'

Although she was anxious to please the schoolmistress's mother Amy shook her head.

'I don't think so, Mrs Owen. I never sing in public now.'

'Don't you?' Mrs Owen's thick fingers were arranging the bread and butter on the plates. 'Why not may I ask? You used to sing very prettily when you were a little girl.'

It was gently phrased and still an awkward question. Amy's face flushed as she searched about in her mind for the most diplomatic answer.

'I get so nervous,' she said. 'I get frightened in front of an audience.'

183

Mrs Owen showed complete disbelief. 'You don't look to me like a girl who gets easily frightened,' she said. 'You're not too proud, I hope? You're not too proud to sing for your old school?'

'Oh good heavens no,' Amy said.

Even as she spoke she tried to replace the words and the manner in which they were spoken in favour of something she could be sure Mrs Owen would approve of. She went on much more demurely.

'What I mean is, I don't sing anywhere. I couldn't. It's nerves I suppose. My legs go all to jelly. I can't stop my left leg shaking. It's awful.'

Mrs Owen looked grudgingly satisfied with the last piece of evidence.

'You have to command your nerves,' she said. 'In this world you have to. There's a piece of advice for you, my dear, and I'd say it was worth taking.'

'Thank you very much, Mrs Owen.'

Amy picked up the plates loaded with thick slabs of bread and butter.

'The tinned salmon is finished,' Mrs Owen said. 'You can tell her that if she asks you. We could have done with some more. You can say that too. Our supplies didn't come from a bottomless pit. Not by any means.'

Between the door and the Christmas tree, Amy's passage was blocked by Mrs Pulford, the former Miss Vanstrack, who was bending down, the long cigarette-holder sticking out from the corner of her mouth, examining the parcels heaped on the floor. Her husband stood beside her, cheerful as ever.

'There should be one for Jack,' she was saying. 'In fact I'm sure there is one. I put yellow string on the family ones. Can't you help me find it?'

'Don't bother,' the Captain said. 'Young rascal doesn't deserve one anyway. He's done absolutely damn all to help. God knows what he's been up to . . . Oh hello . . . Here's Saint Gwenny-what-you-may-call again. Carrying plates of bread and butter. Having a good time, my dear?'

Mrs Pulford straightened herself with some effort to study the object of her husband's interest.

'It's Amy, isn't it? Amy what's-her-name. Done very well, haven't you? Jolly good show.'

The words were patronisingly kind but there was no warmth in their utterance. As if she had no more time to waste Mrs Pulford called her husband's attention to the parcel she was trying to find as she bent down to resume her search. Amy shifted sideways, lifting the plates of bread and butter in the air so that they passed over Mrs Pulford's prominent posterior. But her way was still not clear. She was confronted boldly by the fair-haired boy, with his right hand in his pocket. He did not speak but he was smiling as if to invite her to examine his whole personality in the brightly lit corner of the room near the Christmas tree. Among the largesse and the gifts, number me, he seemed to be saying.

'Jack . . .' Mrs Pulford had turned her head enough to recognise his feet. 'Help me find your present for goodness' sake.'

Jack continued to smile at Amy. Less boldly perhaps. Just asking for some small smile in return. Amy kept her eyes down until she heard the Captain's voice bark out angrily.

'Don't you hear, young brother o'mine? And take your hand out of your pocket for goodness' sake. And get out of the path of this charming young lady.'

Mrs Pulford was straightening her back again as Amy moved away with a plate in each hand. She could hear Mrs Pulford's voice saying something that sounded derogatory. She hastened her step as if putting more distance between herself and a possible detractor would diminish any aspersion.

Miss Philips appeared to have forgotten her. She was leaning benevolently over the twins watching them eat with their faces close to their plates.

'I'm afraid you are too late,' she said as Amy put down the fresh supply of bread and butter in the centre of the table.

'We started on cake, you see, Amy fach, and we got in first. I took the liberty.'

Both the twins turned their heads to look at Amy with equal bulges in their cheeks.

'Hilda and Laura.' Miss Philips tapped each of their heads in turn. 'There are their names for you. This is Hilda and this is

Laura. And I've learnt to tell them apart. As long as they don't move anyway.' Miss Philips chuckled to herself. 'They sing duets,' she said. 'And there's always confusion whey they say their verses. They get quite fed up with it. Don't you girls?'

The twins nodded quickly before filling up with more cake. The concentrated eating and drinking along the whole length of the table had sent up the heat of the hall by several degrees. Miss Philips's face was glistening with sweat between her black fur and her black hat.

'It's all very well,' she said. She began to lose interest in the twins and wanted to confide in Amy. 'Parties and things. They're all very well in their way. But they never live up to expectation, do they? Do you think they live up to expectations, Amy fach?'

Amy looked at the children. A boy who was still hungry was reaching sideways for the fresh bread and butter.

'They seem to be enjoying it,' Amy said.

'Yes. They do, don't they? You're quite right.' Miss Philips sounded deeply surprised. 'But *I'm* not a child any more you see. And you won't be for much longer either. I mean what does it all amount to? A big feed, prizes, a few games, cheap presents, speeches. Thank you very much Captain and Mrs Pulford. The vote of thanks and all that sort of tommy-rot. I'll be off before that. I've got a good excuse. I didn't turn all the cats out.'

Miss Philips nudged Amy in the ribs so that she was obliged to laugh. As she did so she glanced across the length of the hall to where a group of people stood apart around old Mr Pulford's wheel-chair. She noticed at once that Jack Pulford was watching her. She moved her head with a pretty show of independence as if she were willing for him to see from a distance just what she looked like when she was agreeable and happy.

'You do me the world of good, Amy bach,' Miss Philips was saying. 'You must come down to the Rectory, some time, and have tea with me.' She waited for Amy to reply to her suggestion. 'Would you like that?'

Her voice had dropped, weighed down with instant doubt and she rubbed her snub nose in the black fur around her neck. She glanced up at the handsome young girl who stood at her side.

186

Amy's face glowed with the confidence of a flower opening in the sun.

'Oh yes, Miss Philips. Thank you very much.'

Aware that Jack Pulford was still watching her across the room Amy was particularly kind to the Rector's sister and courteous to everyone around her.

5

TOGETHER ENID PRYDDERCH AND AMY STOOD ON THE SUMMIT OF the highest sand dune. The sand was still wet after an intense early morning shower and, where they planted their feet on the tough marram grass, the sand crumbled in lumps like shattered masonry, but did not fall away. Behind them the tide was out. Shallow pools and lakes of sea water left behind in the great expanse of sand reflected the light from the cold blue sky and the shadows of the high cloud scudding along in the morning breeze. The vast shore was completely deserted but below them people crowded everywhere, all over the dunes, and stared at the hospital buildings where the patients and the nurses were leaning out of the windows. The Prince was due to open the new wing. It was a three-storey building in red brick built in the most modern style. There were long balconies attached to the first and second floors, where the patients' beds could be placed, for them to enjoy the view of the distant mountains, the expanse of flat sand, the sea, and nearest of all to them, the dunes. Four arches gave each balcony a cloistered effect. When the weather was bad they could be blocked by large windows in wooden frames. In the side road below the balconies, two charabancs were parked. One for the Silver Band and one for a male-voice choir from a mining village ten miles away. The choir stood on stout benches behind the Silver Band on the left of the hospital steps. On the other side local dignitaries and officials looked dangerously crowded on a wooden platform which had been specially built for the occasion. A detachment of Territorials formed a guard of honour. A flagpole was planted in the centre of the circular lawn in front of the hospital. At the top a large Union Jack flapped in the brisk March wind. The wet flag rope struck the pole from time to time like the crack of a whip.

'Oh dear,' Enid said. 'Poor Tada.'

Amy studied her face enquiringly. Their arms were linked to give them a better balance in their precarious position. Enid's cheerful face was unusually gloomy. The cold wind had turned the tip of her nose red but the rich curves of her bold mouth were unusually pale.

'They'll be out for his blood again.'

'What's the matter?' Amy spoke anxiously.

'That platform is too small. Not big enough for all the bigwigs. You can just hear them . . .You wait till the next full meeting of the Council. They'll be out for his blood. Especially Councillor Snapes. And Hughes Cakes I'm sorry to say.'

Amy bit her lower lip and shook her head to show she knew Beti Buns's father could be difficult.

'Poor old Dad. He's got nothing to say to all this ceremonial rot. He wouldn't give tuppence if the whole of the Royal Family emigrated to Siberia tomorrow morning.'

Hearing herself make such a daring remark raised Enid's spirits substantially. She stamped her left foot and part of their sandy pinnacle began to topple. They clutched tightly at each other and began to laugh: Amy more restrained than Enid, more conscious that they were conspicuous, that many heads were turning, including, immediately below them, a stern-looking man in a bowler hat who was wearing a row of medals pinned to his overcoat. It was evident that he was on the point of rebuking them openly. His walking stick looked dangerous and his black moustache was stretched in readiness to deliver some crushing caustic remark. More sand gave way under Enid. She held on to Amy and dragged her down with her. As she toppled she was taken with an irrepressible fit of giggles.

'Oops!' Enid laughed happily. 'The foundations are moving! The earth is giving way!'

She had sunk to her knees. Amy pulled her to her feet. Wet sand stuck to her stockings. They were nearer the stern-looking man now. He turned to address them in a fierce whisper.

'Look here,' he said. 'His Royal Highness will be here any moment. If you can't conduct yourselves properly, I shall ask you to leave.'

Enid's mouth opened wide with surprise. 'Good Lord,' she said. Amy pressed her arm in an attempt to restrain her.

'I always thought this was a "free country". I must have been mistaken.'

She winked daringly at Amy and climbed back as nearly as she could to the height they had formerly occupied. She held down her hand so that Amy could take it and she could pull her up.

'It's a bit lower,' she said. 'But we can still see.'

Amy was breathing hard in her agitation, but Enid seemed unnaturally cool and self-possessed.

'Didn't you see all those medals? Weren't you afraid?'

Enid pulled a face. She was ready to laugh again. They heard a thin cheer in the distance. A grey-coloured limousine followed by three black cars was being driven sedately from the centre of the town. Police and soldiers lined the route. Children on bicycles raced recklessly along the promenade, trying to keep parallel with the Prince's car. They avoided pedestrians, but rode at full speed into the stultifying sand, hurling themselves in mock sacrifice into the softness of the sandhills that brought the promenade to an end. Their antics were tolerated and allowed to continue as a form of surrogate excitement to supplement cheering that seemed meagre in such a vast open-air setting. During the night the unruly wind had blown sand off the dunes to form new drifts across the highway. For some yards the front car had to follow a zig-zag route to avoid them.

'Poor old Tada.' Enid, overcome with curiosity at last, was watching the procession closely. 'He'll get the blame for that too. You mark my words.'

Below them the man with medals had raised his hat and was eager to lead the cheering. 'Hurrah! Hurrah!'

Women turned their heads like members of a choir suddenly

189

presented with a new conductor who had rearranged the piece they had learnt. Most of them had brought along silk handkerchiefs which they wanted to wave at the Prince. Their dilemma was solved by the Silver Band which began playing 'God Bless the Prince of Wales' to everyone's relief. The choir sang lustily and many of the spectators on the dunes joined in. Enid and Amy had a clear view of a slight figure in an overcoat that buttoned tightly at the waist. As he raised his bowler hat they saw clearly the neat waves of his fair hair. Amy clutched her friend excitedly.

'Look,' she said. 'His hair is exactly the same colour as Jack's. Isn't he wonderful?'

Enid had become sad again. She shook her head and looked mournfully at her friend's elated face.

'Gosh,' she said. 'Talk about the magic of Royalty. Poor old Dad. I shouldn't be surprised if they send him to prison. For lack of zeal. For having disloyal thoughts.'

Amy wasn't listening. She was totally absorbed in trying to follow every detail of the ceremonial outside the hospital. From the other cars the Lord Lieutenant and the High Sheriff of the County emerged. The Mayor of Llanelw had taken off his hat and was clutching excitedly at his special commemorative programme which was proving to be something of an encumbrance. He handed it to the Town Clerk. But then he realised his brief speech was printed in it and he turned in some agitation to reclaim it. The Prince coughed politely while he waited for the Mayor to descend the two wooden steps to greet him on the ground.

'But he does look wonderful, Enid, doesn't he? Every inch a Prince Charming. You've got to admit that.'

'That's what everybody says. So it must be true.'

Abruptly Enid turned her back on the public event. She ran down the deserted side of the sandhills and when she reached the shore she kept on running until Amy saw her as a small solitary figure halfway to the edge of the sea. She hesitated, her feet apart and firmly balanced on her vantage point, as though there was more drama for her to witness. The eager crowd was scattered all over the south side of the dunes. There were more vehicles moving on the road. The band was still playing and the nurses and patients were waving little flags from the hospital windows. Enid was too far away to be called back. At last, smacking her lips impatiently, she gave way to the obligation to follow her friend. She ran across the wet sand, jumping the water wherever she could, anxious for speed, but also anxious to preserve her best shoes from the ill-effects of salt water. When she was close enough, she called out.

'Enid! Stop, will you? Enid! For heaven's sake. Where are you going?'

Enid stood still when she heard her voice. She was staring westwards towards the mountains which came down in terraces from the clouds to join a long snake-like promontory that ended in a great bastion of rock far out in the sea. The keen sea wind was making their eyes water. As she wiped her own eyes, Amy saw that her friend had been crying. There were long tear stains on cheeks that were usually so plump and cheerful.

'Enid . . . What's the matter? What is it?'

Enid continued to stare at the mountains. For her they possessed a mystical power. They could understand what she felt: all the emotion she was incapable of putting into words.

'Enid, why don't you tell me what's the matter?' Amy sounded businesslike but not unsympathetic.

'Oh my country. My poor little country.'

Enid began to cry again. Amy moved closer to her so that her friend could put her hand on her shoulder and lean on her.

'I had a vision up there. A sort of vision.' Enid nodded towards the sandhills which now concealed the whole of the east front of the seaside town from their gaze. 'What's to become of it?'

'Wales you mean?' Amy was trying to understand.

'The whole thing of it. That awful flag. The mark of our subjugation. And all those silly self-important people loving it. Don't you understand?'

'He's the Prince of Wales, after all,' Amy said. 'It was all in his honour really.'

'Prince of *Wales*?' Enid sounded so angry, Amy moved away from her.

'Don't you know *any* history? The Prince of Wales had his head cut off on Tower Hill in London. And they stuck an ivy crown on

191

his head instead of the crown of Arthur which they had stolen from him.'

'Oh Enid . . . That was all so long ago.'

'Was it? Was it?' Enid wiped first one eye and then the other with the back of her hand. 'Well I can remember being away in school. In England. And the teacher was on about 1282. And she said, "In 1282, the history of Wales came to an end." And I burst into tears. Much to the amusement of the rest of the class. But I was right. I was absolutely right. There I was, a little Welsh girl, and this damned woman was more or less telling me I had no right to exist. Don't you see?'

There was an urgent, pleading note in Enid's voice that almost compelled Amy to nod.

'Well there you are then.'

She breathed deeply and thrust her hands deep in her coat pockets. Turning westwards, she marched towards the pier which had suffered damage in the recent storms. Amy ran to catch up with her. They walked side by side, both turning their shoulders against the prevailing wind. All work on the damaged pier had stopped in honour of the royal visit. Two cranes stood idle, their hooks like inverted question marks in the sun. The girls turned their backs to the wind and began to walk towards the open-air theatre on the end of the promenade.

'This place is a shambles if you like.' Enid spoke authoritatively. 'You wouldn't believe it. They skimped on the foundations, and the outer wall on the sea side is giving them endless trouble. And all the woodwork inside is rotting. You never saw such a mess. It's symbolic really.'

'Symbolic of what?'

Amy seemed to find her friend's omniscience oppressive and wanted to challenge it. Enid gave a wave that included the drinking fountain, the new public lavatories, the amusements centre and the pavilion.

'All this,' she said. 'Cheap and nasty. If ever a people were falling over themselves to sell their birthright for a mess of pottage . . .'

'But you said you liked Llanelw.'

'Did I?'

192

'You said you liked living here. I've heard you say it lots of times.'

Enid frowned as she considered her own lack of consistency. 'Living at home, yes. Not being away at school. Yes. Being here? Yes, I suppose so. There are worse places. But that wasn't what I was talking about. I was talking about values.'

Amy was not prepared to shift to such a lofty level of argument.

'What about the Tudors?' she said. 'After Glyndŵr I mean. You know, the Tudors. They were Welsh, weren't they? And he's descended from them.'

She stretched out her arm in the general direction of the hospital.

'He's German,' Enid said firmly. 'If he's anything. But he's English now, of course. But that's not what I'm talking about.'

'Well, what *are* you talking about?'

Enid made gestures to express speechless exasperation.

'I'm asking you. I want to know.'

They sat on the promenade wall and looked at the sea.

'You're not against all change are you? It's a new world, isn't it, after all? You can't put the clock back.'

Enid was staring at Amy's mouth as though her friend possessed a strange soft machine made to repeat words that made her wince. It was so quiet around them they could hear someone pull a chain in the new public lavatories and beyond the dunes the faint noise of the Silver Band playing outside the new hospital.

'We've got to get on, haven't we? We can't stay stuck in the same mud for the rest of our lives, can we? Just look at me. I feel sometimes like that girl who turned into a stick. What was her name? Here's one spot and you can stay there for ever! A few leaves in the summer and shivering all winter. Life must be more than that. Don't you think.'

Amy was bringing her head closer to Enid in order to stare in a comical schoolmistressly way into her eyes. She made Enid laugh and they giggled happily together.

'Oh gosh.' Enid tried to be serious again. 'I wish Val was here.'

Amy raised her eyebrows and Enid began to blush.

'No, I mean it. He's got such a lucid mind. He puts things so

193

clearly. He has the French way of looking at things. You ought to hear him, Amy.'

'My dear, I can't wait . . .'

'No. I mean it. He's brilliant. There's no other word for it. Even Emrys admits it. And he doesn't like him really. I think he's jealous.'

Enid brooded over the sad word. They stared together across the expanse of empty sand to the distant margin of a bottle-green sea and the tiny shape of an ocean-going liner on the horizon.

'Jealous of what?'

Enid prepared to make the effort to explain. 'Emrys is very ambitious. When he sees anybody brilliant like Val he immediately thinks of him as a rival. I shouldn't say this about my own brother – Ifor is different.'

'I'm afraid of him,' Amy said. 'He's got such a deep voice. Perhaps it's because I haven't got a brother?'

Enid laughed. In her enthusiasm she took hold of Amy's hand to show that she was as good as included in the family and could say what she liked about her brother.

'He's so stern,' Amy said with delicate frankness. 'Ifor. He stares at you as if you've just done something wrong. Remember when he borrowed my bike? "I'm afraid I took your bike," he said. He said it as if it was my fault. "That's all right," I said. As if I were apologising.'

'Ifor . . .' Enid was overwhelmed with affection for her brother. 'He can't help his voice, poor thing. He's so shy really. It's just a little boy trapped inside all that Adam's apple . . . I'm not making fun of him. I think the world of Ifor. And Emrys isn't so bad really. It's being the eldest you see. In a family of failures.'

' "Failures . . ." ' Amy repeated the word to show how ridiculously inappropriate it was. 'The Prydderchs!'

'We are.' Enid insisted on the definition. 'I can't begin to tell you. Tada a failed composer. Well . . . an unacknowledged one anyway and that amounts to the same thing. Definitely a failed surveyor. You ask Councillor Cakes. And then there's Uncle Peter. And Sali. All talent and no success.'

'I think you have a wonderful family.'

194

Amy sounded so sincere and envious Enid gave her hand a squeeze.

'So Emrys feels obliged to make up for it. He's too shy for politics. So it has to be a scholarship. Degrees. Prizes. He works like a beaver.'

'Don't talk about work,' Amy said. 'Don't remind me.'

'Well, now Val, you see. He's just naturally brilliant. And Ifor keeps on saying how brilliant he is. And that gets on Emrys's nerves. So there you are. That's how we are.'

Enid talked about her family as though it were an inexhaustible source of amusement, but Amy listened as if she were learning new secrets about living. The promenade behind them was almost deserted. The population was elsewhere. A terrier dog with brass studs on his collar ran first one way and then the other, appreciating the open space. He stopped by the drinking fountain and then turned sideways to cock up his hind leg. As the girls talked their heads were close together. It was cold sitting on the wall and they both began to shiver at the same time.

'Let's go home, shall we?' Enid said.

Amy made her teeth chatter noisily to show how cold she was.

'Unless you want to go back and stare at your Prince Charming?'

Amy made a token show of self-defence. 'He is good-looking,' she said.

'Wait till you've seen Val. Would you like to see a drawing of him?'

Amy lifted a finger and pointed it close to Enid's nose. Enid blushed again and shook her head.

'No,' she said. 'Seriously. It's rather good. An artist in Paris did it. He threw it away but I kept it. Would you like to see it?'

'My dear,' Amy said. 'I can't wait.'

6

As soon as they saw Amy standing by the gate the ponies raised their heads high in the air. There was dried mud on their winter coats. The field was grazed bare. In the untidy hedge the pith of gorse branches gleamed white where the horses had scraped off the bark with their long teeth. The boldest advanced towards the gate and then paused to scar the turf with his right hoof. He could see that Amy's outstretched hand had nothing in it. Around the gate the churned mud was drying in the wind. It was a bright day. Primroses were showing near Amy's feet. The mountain pony came closer to sniff the outstretched hand – Amy's fingers touched the sensitive nostrils and the young animal shot back in a startled flurry.

Amy stepped into the lane. On the wide verges grass grew undisturbed by hungry animals. Trees leaned over the banks of a bright stream that flowed parallel with the lane. On the branches nearest the water the buds were ready to break into leaf. Amy bent down to harvest the first growth of spring grass with her bare hands. She offered it through the bars of the gate. A hungry mare made the approach. Amy spoke in a childish coaxing voice.

'You've got a little foal inside you, haven't you, my pretty, so how can they expect you to live on nothing? The wicked things . . . hey!'

The mare had snapped hungrily at the limp grass. Amy withdrew her hand quickly and let what was left of the grass fall into the mud. She pulled more grass for the other two ponies who had pushed forward to the gate. She was less concerned now with their hunger or about the bald condition of the section of the field into which they were paddocked. She frowned anxiously in the direction of the square dovecote that stood in conspicuous isolation in the centre of the full field. It was a handsome stone tower constructed in two tall storeys. In the south face, she could see a small rectangular window and much higher up, directly above it, a diamond-shaped hole which once gave the birds access to the columbarium. Above this a date in softer stone had been worn away. The roof was crowned elegantly with a cupola that itself was square with a gable roof echoing the shape of the tower. Beyond

196

the fence that kept the ponies in, black bullocks grazed. Two of them were rubbing their flanks against the exposed angles of the dovecote.

Amy continued to stare at the building expectantly. The ponies became used to her. They nuzzled against her elbows. She climbed over the gate and they retreated in alarm. When she crossed the paddock, they followed her at a safe distance. She made a direct course for the window in the south wall. Standing precariously on a heap of stones, she was able to put her hands on the cold sill and push her head inside. Startled ewes scrambled to their feet and, having flared their nostrils, broke the first trance of their panic and bolted between the stone posts of the doorless entrance. Amy called out softly. Then she uttered a name.

'Jack!'

She waited for an answer. Inside the tower, a stone stairway against the north and west walls led up to the second floor. Someone could have been hiding there. In spite of the heavy silence, Amy forced herself to smile. She called his name again, very softly, conjuring up his appearance in some way that would amuse them both without startling her unduly. At last the cold damp of the deserted tower persuaded her that there was no one hiding inside. The place became antipathetic. She shuddered when she saw a bat hanging from a corner of the vaulted roof. She could stay there no longer. She jumped back and the startled ponies scattered in three separate directions kicking up lumps of turf. They ran on until they had rejoined each other at the furthest point of the paddock. Apprehensively they eyed an angry young woman march across their worn grazing area to the gate.

Amy retrieved her bicycle from the trees at the stream's edge. She rode down the lane as far as a crooked notice which read, MEIFOD HALL. PRIVATE ROAD. TRESPASSERS WILL BE PROSECUTED. Ahead of her beech trees grew in an ordered fashion on either side of the road. The sun was shining through the bare branches and made the way seem both forbiddingly enclosed and beautiful. A slow incline made the riding harder. Amy's mouth was resolute with effort and her shoulders pressed low over the handlebars. Her goal was beyond the west gates of the Hall. She

197

rode past the out-buildings of the Home Farm. The austere limestone wall came to an end and was abruptly succeeded by a high ornamental hedge that concealed the lawns and gardens in front of the Dower House.

Now that she had arrived, she was overcome by indecision. Her bicycle was an encumbrance and yet she hesitated to let go of it. She tugged moodily at the handlebars so that the front wheel pointed first one way and then another. When she let it go it fell against the bank like a discarded friend. She thrust her hands deep into her coat pockets and stood still in the middle of the road. She was there, defiantly herself, if someone should choose to emerge from the house or from the garden and discover her. But no one came. Almost by stealth she moved closer to the iron gateway to take in a complete view of the house. It was a neat rectangular stone building with a steep slate roof. A gravel path led directly to the ivy-covered portico. With spring hardly arrived, the lawns had already been cut. The borders and flowerbeds and isolated trees were all obsessively well cared for. A stone sundial situated on the centre lawn looked as if it had been washed and scrubbed. Amy rested a hand on the wrought-iron gate. While she was plainly gathering her courage to open it and walk straight up to the house, the front door opened. Like a swimmer before disappearing under the surface of the water, Amy gulped a quantity of air and flung herself out of sight behind the gatepost. With more drama than perhaps was necessary she rolled her stiff form into the wider screening of the privet hedge on the left.

With her face close to the leaves, she saw Jack Pulford in his shirt sleeves manœuvring his grandfather's wheel-chair down the steps. The old man, his face twisted in a permanent crooked grin and his face a dark red, gripped the arms of his chair apprehensively. From inside the house came the voice of the Rector. He spoke loudly so that old Mr Pulford could hear what he was saying.

'You are quite right, my dear sir. Quite right. It doesn't seem at all just, does it, whichever way you look at it.'

Once on the path, Jack steered the wheel-chair around in a wide half circle so that his grandfather could see the Rector emerging from the house. He wore a dark overcoat with a velvet collar and carried a small black case that Amy had seen before. It contained the elements and equipment of a portable communion. He was followed by Mrs Pulford. Her long pallid face wore a pained expression. The pockets of her overall bulged with handkerchiefs and she held a large white one at the ready in both her hands. Over her arm she carried a folded travelling rug.

'I've never preached on it. Never. I can tell you that much. Work an hour or work a day and you get the same pay. Where's the sense of it? As you rightly say: it's not strict justice and its bad economics.'

Mr Pulford had raised his arm to address the Rector, but Amy could not hear what he was saying. She only saw Jack's broad back in his sleeveless pullover and the Rector leaning forward with his eyebrows raised and his right ear inclined towards the man in the wheel-chair. He nodded in vigorous agreement.

'Oh it is a difficult book. It's a difficult book all right. I sometimes think it was a mistake to let every Tom, Dick and Harry read it.'

The Rector pumped his shoulders up and down to show that his remark was intended as a rather daring joke. Mrs Pulford came forward to wipe her husband's mouth after his effort of speech. She arranged the travelling rug over his knees. He made the task more difficult by pushing at her arms as she tried to wrap him up warmly. Amy became aware of the steady noise of a garden fork turning over the earth in a corner of the garden to her left. It was a sheltered arbour concealed from the road and from most of the lawn by a trimmed yew hedge. Jack began to push the wheel-chair along a garden path which led to the arbour. Inside there was a wooden shelter where Mr Pulford could be placed to watch the gardener at work. The Rector and Mrs Pulford followed the wheel-chair, speaking in low tones.

'If he wants sausages, Mrs Pulford, I really don't see why he can't have them. If that is what he fancies . . .'

Amy strained her ears to listen. She crept along the hedge to find a better position, but the back of the shelter blocked off most of the sound and she was more cut off than before. At the corner of the property she noticed a decaying wooden stile. A blocked path ran alongside the garden of the Dower House. Amy's fists closed and shook with determined urgency although there was no one to see her on the quiet road. The stile was rotten and had to be negotiated with care. In summer the path would be closed with brambles and nettles. But now she could progress a few yards to reach a gap where the tight hedge came to an end. Through a hole in the blackthorn she could see an old gardener bent low over the soil, weeding with one hand while he supported himself on the handle of the fork with the other. A strip of green tweed had been sewn along the lower edge of the back piece of his waistcoat to give more protection to his lumbar region. Mr Pulford was already watching him intently, issuing suggestions and orders by waving his arm like a voluble spectator at a football match. The gardener had a rhythm of his own. He straightened his back and turned to take his shining spade, lift it deliberately and cleave a tangled mass of root in two. Mr Pulford waved his hand in disapproval but the gardener paid no attention.

'I'll be off now then.'

Amy heard Jack's voice. He was doing his best to be polite and agreeable.

'Oh yes.'

The woman's voice was plaintive and unemphatic: apparently no sort of a restraint and yet he waited.

'Off where, may I ask?'

'To see the fellows. That sort of thing.'

The gardener moved and Amy caught sight of the Rector. His mouth was open, his square jaw stretched forward in a nervous yawn. It shut abruptly. Jack could have been staring at him.

'To play rugby?'

The Rector nodded helpfully. 'Games, Mrs Pulford. Sport. Nothing like it for strong young men like Jack here.'

'I'll be off then?'

Jack sounded as though he were waiting for some formal dismissal.

'Keep away from that common Welsh girl. That's little enough to ask.'

Her voice was low and casual. She moved to talk to the gardener about the positioning of the plants. He straightened his back to give her respectful attention. Amy pressed her hands against her burning cheeks. She looked around as though her position behind the hedge had become a trap from which she could not escape. Jack was watching the Rector who cut himself off from such a bold stare. Jack marched away, the thick soles of his boots crunching the gravel. Mrs Pulford returned to the side of the Rector. With a dexterous flick of the handkerchief in her right hand she wiped the saliva running out of the corner of her husband's mouth.

'Thank you, Rector.' Her voice was low but clear. 'A word in time can save a river of tears.'

The Rector stretched his jaw again, squeezed his eyes and raised his eyebrows. She waited for him to speak.

'Suitability.' He found the right word at last. 'That was my point. There's absolutely nothing against the girl herself. Excellent character. My sister is very fond of her.'

He watched the gardener walking away at a steady pace. He carried an empty wooden bucket. Mrs Pulford moved around the wheel-chair to face the Rector.

'Illegitimate?' The finality of her tone suggested there was nothing else to expect.

'Good heavens, no.' His denial was so emphatic he started blushing.

'It's been looked into,' he said. 'Her father was a noted singer. Hefin Price. Her mother was Esther Parry's twin. There is a birth certificate. He's down on it as a quarryman. The mother died and the father was killed on Vimy Ridge. There's no question of illegitimacy. None whatsoever.'

'Well. I suppose that's something to be thankful for.'

The Rector turned his head about like a blind man testing the breeze with his cheeks. He was having difficulty concealing his embarrassment. The gardener was returning, his bucket filled with water.

'I must get back,' he said. 'With your permission I'll take the back way to the Hall. Captain Pulford is waiting. He says he's got something for me to shoot. Shoot I said is one thing. It's another thing my dear fellow to hit the target.'

201

While he was still laughing at his own remarks, Amy crept out of her hiding place. As she picked up her bicycle she wiped the tears from her eyes. She looked down into the ditch. There were small stones all over the sandy bed. She knelt down to scoop up a handful. She moved the bike with one hand until she stood behind the arbour. Determinedly she tossed the handful in the air so that they rained down on the other side. The gardener was the first to react. Without waiting to hear any more Amy mounted her bike and rode away as fast as she could.

7

ESTHER PARRY AND AMY WAITED ON THE UNEVEN PAVEMENT WHILE Miss Connie Clayton tugged at the door of her terraced house. With her left hand she turned a large iron key.

'Poor uncle,' she said cheerfully. 'To think I've got to lock him in. But he will wander off and leave the door open. Just any of these people around here could pop in and pinch anything they fancied.'

Esther set her lips disapprovingly, but she said nothing. Her long coat looked drab alongside Miss Connie Clayton's smart knitted two-piece suit in pale green, with cuffs and pockets and lapels in a darker shade. The curved brim of Miss Clayton's summer hat hung so low over her head that she was obliged to tilt up her chin in order to see. It was evident that she considered the pose becoming. She touched Amy on the arm.

'Why don't you take your mackintosh off, dear? That's such a pretty dress. You look so nice in it. Powder blue, Lady Diana's favourite colour.'

Amy bit her lower lip. She looked embarrassed. 'I'm all right, thank you,' she said.

The street narrowed and there was no room for them to walk side by side. They passed the forecourt of a large chapel and almost immediately came to the rear of another.

'You never saw so many chapels.' Miss Clayton spoke to herself, but she wanted Esther to hear. She seemed to imply that chapels were some sort of offence that took away from the beauty of her native town. Esther's lips moved silently as though she were rehearsing a brief speech of thanks. Then she spoke aloud.

'I must say, Connie, that Amy and I, and Lucas of course, are very grateful for the trouble you have taken . . .' She paused to clear her throat. They walked along the side of the new post office. Miss Clayton made a dramatic gesture and produced a letter and four postcards.

'Excuse me,' she said. 'I just must post this to Lady Diana. She'll be waiting to hear from me. Why don't you wait for me by the Memorial? I shan't be a trice.'

They watched her enter the doors of the post office.

'Lady Diana,' Amy muttered rebelliously. 'I can't stand it, Auntie. I really can't.'

Esther's eyes narrowed as she looked across the square to the grey walls of the castle. Three buses were lined up side by side between the fountain and the statue of a famous son of the town. 'More buses every time I come here,' she said. 'And every colour under the sun. Purple. Blue. Red. White.'

'She'll be going on about the aristocracy and the British Empire every step of the way to the churchyard.'

'Be patient,' Esther said sharply. 'That's all I ask.' It wasn't a subject Esther wanted to hear about. 'Everything changes,' she said, looking around the square. 'Everything changes so fast. You can't keep up with it.'

Amy was determined to make her aunt listen, even though she was closing her eyes wearily.

'You should hear what the Prydderchs say about the aristocracy,' Amy said. 'And the British Empire come to that. Dr Peter has published a new pamphlet. Calling for an international conference to outlaw war. He says the British Empire is the greatest single obstacle to world peace.'

'Does he?' Esther made an effort to show polite interest. Amy kicked her heels against the edge of the pavement, exasperated by Esther's neutral manner.

'So you can see how awful it is, Auntie. For me to have to listen to her.'

Esther was smiling with fond pride at the girl she had brought up with so much care and effort.

'It's nothing to laugh about, Auntie. Don't you understand? These are world issues. Issues of life and death. This old Connie Clayton doesn't know what she's talking about.'

Esther still smiled, her eyes focused somewhere in the middle distance, her mind in some cloud of nostalgia. A bus exhaust snorted angrily as the large vehicle with its complement of passengers all seated snugly on board nosed forward out of line.

'That's going to Llandudno,' Esther said absently. 'Via Llanfair-fechan and Penmaenmawr.'

Amy made a more extreme bid for her aunt's attention.

'I think I'm a socialist,' she said.

To her disappointment, Esther did not hear the dramatic announcement. She was absorbed in a memory from the past.

'You ran up the mountain,' Esther said. 'When she first came to see us. With your kite.' She gazed at Amy fondly. 'Do you remember? She came to tea to the chapel house and you were nowhere to be found. She had to leave without seeing you.'

Esther turned her head to catch Miss Clayton re-emerge from the post office. She saw where they were standing and raised her hand to show her correspondence safely stamped. Esther gave Amy a warning glance.

'It's like that new fly paper,' she said, sighing.

'What is?' Amy frowned impatiently.

'The world.' Miss Clayton had turned her back on them to study closely a printed schedule of posting times. 'It makes us stick together. Whether we like it or not. I never liked Connie. Yet today I've got more reason to be grateful to her than anyone else. We have to learn to be grateful, Amy. It's a hard lesson sometimes. Be civil to her now whatever you do. Don't aggravate. For my sake.'

Amy's restlessness still threatened. Esther was obliged to go a step further. 'And for the sake of your mother's memory.'

Connie Clayton hurried to join them.

'I sent a card to Dame Alice as well. She's just back from the

South of France. She says she likes to hear from me. Isn't that nice of her?'

Esther nodded politely. She was already looking around as they sauntered along the north side of the square. She touched the back of a tree with a gloved finger.

'Everything changes and nothing changes,' she said. 'It's a nice old town.'

Connie Clayton was willing to respond. She gazed at the new marble War Memorial with profound approval.

'It's beautiful,' she said. 'It's really beautiful.' Contemplating the monument made her more graciously disposed towards the old town that had erected it. 'I must say I like the place much more than I used to,' she said. 'A home town is a home town after all.' She paused outside the imposing premises of a bank to turn and wait for Amy. 'Come along, my dear.' She offered Amy her arm. 'It's quite a step you know. I did think of ordering a carriage and taking uncle with us. But it was such a fuss and bother. And these townspeople would only say we were putting on airs.'

Amy allowed her hand to rest lightly on Connie's arm in a token of submission. Before they moved away a motor-bike made itself conspicuous on the square. Amy recognised the rider. Quickly she withdrew her hand from Miss Clayton's arm. The young man wore dust goggles but his head was bare and his short fair hair blew about as he rode with a certain impudence around the fountain.

'Well I never,' Miss Clayton said indignantly. 'Just what is the world coming to? Did you see that, Esther?'

The motorcyclist drove up to the post office, turned to pass through the narrow space between the pavement and the back of the War Memorial and rode as close as he could to where Amy stood with the two older women. He raised his hand in a brief salute before roaring up the High Street and out of their sight.

'My goodness. Did you see that, Esther? Do you know that young man, Amy?'

Both women were watching her face with deep curiosity.

'I'm not sure,' Amy faltered. 'It's difficult to tell when they've got those things on.'

She was obviously evasive. Esther was frowning. Amy was clearly relieved when Connie Clayton spoke again.

'Well whoever he is, I shouldn't encourage him. He's a very bold young man. Anyone can see that. And a girl should never encourage bold young men. I'm right about that, am I not, Esther?'

As they walked up the street, Connie held out the crook of her arm for Amy to take. She continued her observations on the subject. 'It's something that has spread since the war I think. There seem to be so much more of them. That's what I think. Chauffeurs are very often bold, you know. I've noticed that in recent years. You must have read about Lady Nathan's chauffeur?' Esther shook her head. 'Haven't you really?' Connie's incredulousness was quickly superseded by her urge to demonstrate her own intimate knowledge of the case. 'It was such a scandal. I don't think the family will ever get over it. Not as long as they live. He ran away with the second daughter. Such a sweet-looking girl. She had her picture in *The Tatler* just a fortnight before. Just eighteen she was. You must have heard about it?'

During their progress up the street, Connie Clayton did all the talking. Sometimes she broke off to greet people from the town she knew. Outside an ironmonger's shop, she paused to introduce Amy and Esther to the proprietor who stood in the doorway wearing a long green overall and a bowler hat and holding his large hands behind his back.

'We are going to the churchyard.' Connie Clayton smiled sadly as she gave the information. 'To show her poor Gracie's grave.'

The ironmonger nodded with solemn approval. His large face was giving Connie Clayton such total attention he could have been memorising what she was saying.

'We have had a new kerb built. A new kerb surround. And new gravel. It's much tidier, I think. Don't you Mr Griffith?'

The ironmonger cleared his throat and nodded again, a little anxiously. The intensity of his attention had slackened. Miss Connie Clayton moved her head and saw that two women customers were waiting to pass.

'Oh dear . . .' Her apology was immediate but genteel. 'We really mustn't hold up your business, Mr Griffith. So nice to see you. Good afternoon.'

206

The tall ironmonger raised his hat and stepped into the street so that the customers could enter the narrow doorway of his shop.

'Such a good man . . . and always so well mannered,' Connie confided in Esther as they continued their walk up the hill. 'A churchwarden you know. At St Peblig's. Don't you remember him, Esther?'

'I remember the shop.'

Esther looked as though she were enjoying the walk. They were passing trim little gardens in front of the houses on the hill.

'But he didn't know me from Adam and Eve.'

Amy grew impatient with their slow progress. She quickened her step and within a minute or so she was so far ahead she had to turn around and watch her aunt and Connie Clayton coming up the hill towards her. She was high enough to see above the roofs of the houses, the towers of the castle and beyond a glimpse of the sandy bar and the sea.

'Are you in a hurry?' Esther asked the question when Amy touched her arm in a concealed hint for greater speed.

'It's not that,' Amy said. 'But I promised Beti Buns I'd meet her at half-past three. And the charabanc starts back at half-past five.'

'Beti Buns?' Connie wanted the name explained.

'She's my friend in school,' Amy said. 'One of my friends anyway. We call her Beti Buns because her father owns the Foryd Confectionary in Morlais Street. Just off the Promenade.'

'Confectionary?' Connie Clayton raised her eyebrows to show professional interest. 'That's very interesting. Doris Winters did that, you know.'

She looked at Esther as though she should know the identity of Doris Winters. Esther looked back at her blankly.

'She was cook-housekeeper with Sir Jeremy Murray, the distinguished surgeon. They were our neighbours in Pont Street. Sir Jeremy dropped dead in the street. Just outside his club. We were all so worried about Doris. But she'd been ever so sensible. She'd put by a bit. Enough to open a confectioner's in Broadstairs. So she was able to put her skill to good use.'

Amy had walked ahead again. She stopped to look at the Roman ruins as she waited for them to catch up. When they came within earshot, Connie Clayton was still engrossed with her thoughts on the subject of confectionery.

'I suppose I could do it.'

Esther struggled to show an intelligent interest.

'Even the business side. I'm used to keeping accounts. Lady Diana depends on me almost entirely over the house-keeping. And I deal with the tradesmen. But buying of course, not selling. That's the big difference. You know what I mean? That would be more difficult. In a shop you have to be nice to everybody, no matter who they are, so long as they pay. That wouldn't be easy.'

'Shopkeepers can't be proud,' Esther said sagely. 'I'm sure that is true. That's the same all the world over.'

'Can't we hurry please?' Amy pleaded as politely as she could. Voluntarily she took Connie Clayton's arm. 'It's just that Beti gets so peevish if I keep her waiting.'

Connie Clayton hastened her steps obligingly. She was visibly pleased that Amy had taken her arm.

'But won't you be coming home for a cup of tea?' she said. 'It's all prepared. Everything is ready. Such a nice tea-set Lady Diana's aunt gave me. There are only a few pieces missing.'

When they arrived at the lychgate they were all three walking at a brisk pace. Once inside the churchyard, Connie Clayton automatically slowed down. She sought to take hold of Amy's hand. But the girl anticipated the action and moved out of her reach. Connie fumbled about in her handbag for a handkerchief. The churchyard was well kept. The grass had been cut and carried away for burning in a corner of the extensive burial ground hidden by evergreen trees. The gravel paths had been raked. Connie's voice sank to a whisper as they walked respectfully between the imposing monuments and gravestones.

'It's such a peaceful place,' she said. 'And so dignified, I think.'

Amy lifted a hand to point at the more ostentatious funeral monuments, weeping angels in marble, cherubs holding open books, and then let it fall again. It was not an occasion for criticism. They arrived at a corner site between paths. Here the graves were overshadowed by an ancient yew tree. Connie stood still to admire the slate kerb that had been set to mark the confines of Amy's mother's grave. She waited for Esther to make a suitable comment. Amy herself hung back on the path while her aunt came close enough to the grave to touch the slate headstone.

'It's very nice,' she said.

Connie accepted the tribute graciously.

' "I hope it's simple and tasteful," I said to John Williams. "Oh I can assure you it is, Miss Clayton," he said. He's a very reliable man. A reliable craftsman. Uncle always spoke very highly of him. And his charges are reasonable. There's that to be said about him too . . .'

Esther forced out words of appreciation. 'As I've said, Amy and I, and Lucas of course, are deeply grateful to you for going to this expense, Connie. We . . .' Esther frowned. The words seemed to be congested in her throat.

'I always wanted to do it. Always.' Connie sounded elated. 'Grace was my best friend in all the world.'

A choking noise escaped from Esther's lips. She sank to her knees. Her shoulders shook with a sudden storm of sobbing and her forehead rested on the new kerb of the grave. She moaned her sister's name. 'Oh Grace. My poor Grace . . .'

Connie Clayton too began to cry. She lifted her white handkerchief and applied it gently to her eyes. Amy, who had stood watching them in an attitude of sullen stillness, turned her back on the scene to stare at the swelling contours of the range of mountains that rose abruptly on the southern horizon.

8

A CLOUD PASSED IN FRONT OF THE SUN AND AMY CLUTCHED HER mackintosh more tightly around her body. Jack Pulford lifted the rear of his motor-bike and tugged it back to make it stand on its steel parking rest. It was almost hidden by the low branches of overgrown rhododendron bushes.

'How did you find this place?' Amy was curious. He turned to give her an admiring glance. Then he winked knowingly. Amy lifted her head, a young woman illuminated with confidence in her own beauty.

'I had time to waste,' Jack said. 'I scouted around. I saw this was for sale so I thought I'd buy it. You must tell me what you think of it.'

With an airy possessiveness he put his arm around Amy's waist. His smile appeared to be made broader by the chipped front tooth. The leather motorcycling coat he wore hung open and he twirled the dust goggles gaily as he came to join her. To elude his reach she quickened her step. They approached the empty house at a little distance from each other. Grass grew to its full height on the neglected lawns, almost hiding the pieces of weathered sculpture that had been part of an ornamental fountain. Inside all the windows, the shutters were closed. Some of the panes of glass had been broken.

'I wonder why it's empty,' Amy said.

She was showing much greater interest in the house than the young man. He waited impatiently, clearly longing to touch her.

'Spooks,' he said cheerfully.

'Oh Jack!' Amy shivered theatrically.

'Let's peep round the back, shall we?'

The out-houses were in a much worse state than the house itself. The roof of the coach-house was caving in. A single-storey scullery attached to the back of the house had been broken open. The walls were discoloured with damp and the branches of an elderberry bush had thrust themselves through the broken window. Amy stepped inside to look at the rotting shelving. She wrinkled her nose with disgust. Jack stood in the doorway barring her exit. He took his hands out of the pockets of his leather coat and held them out, ready to grasp her.

'Now I've got you cornered,' he said.

Amy showed her displeasure. 'Don't talk like that,' she said.

'Like what?' Jack put on a baffled expression.

'You know what I mean.' Amy spoke severely. He stood to one side to let her out.

210

'I think it's an awful place.' She delivered her verdict standing under the tall trees at the side of the house. 'It's an awful place to bring a girl. You should be ashamed of yourself, Jack Pulford.'

She was smiling a little to take the sting out of her reproof, but he began to look sulky.

'You told me,' he said. 'Find somewhere where the rest of the Sunday School trip won't see us. And so I found this. I thought I was being quite clever, to tell you the truth.'

The sun burst suddenly through the clouds. The deserted garden brightened with the warmth of the early summer. Amy moved away from the trees and the sudden sunlight added a golden halo to the outline of her hair. She gave him a more direct smile and he was encouraged to take off his heavy coat. Underneath he was wearing a cricket blazer with brass buttons. He led the way to a corner of the garden that was sheltered by a brick wall.

'Just look at this,' he said, beckoning persuasively to Amy. 'The remnants of a shrine, I should think!'

A marble bust with blind eyes stood on a plinth in the shadow of the wall. In front of it a stone font lay toppled over on its side almost hidden by the long grass. Jack trod down the grass and spread his coat so that they could lie on it. He lay down himself first, closing his eyes as he turned his face to the sun. Then he patted the place next to him and invited Amy to sit. With a prim mouth, Amy considered the invitation.

'It's warm here,' he said. 'You'd better take your coat off or you'll be lying in a pool of sweat.'

'Don't be so crude. You can be so crude sometimes. And so vulgar.'

'Comes of training to be a vet. Blood and guts. Goes with the job.'

Amy sat down carefully. She had removed her mackintosh. Jack admired her summer dress. Playfully he pulled at the loose ends of the decorative belt. Amy moved a little further away. She drew up her knees and looked around at the marble bust behind them.

'I wonder what they were like,' she said. 'The people who used to live here, I mean.'

211

Apparently charged with such speculation, Amy stretched out to bask in the warm sun, her head pillowed on her hands. While her eyes were closed, Jack Pulford crept closer to her and lowered his head close enough to kiss her on the lips. She kept her head still for a moment and then opened her eyes to find his eyes open as well. She moved her head to speak, her face turned away from him.

'What do you say?'

She whispered the question. Jack hesitated. Quickly he brought his hand down around her waist.

'You are so beautiful, I can tell you that much. I can't sleep at night thinking about you. I can't keep my mind on my work either. Look at me today for God's sake. Coming all this way on a borrowed motor-bike, just to see you.'

' "Just to" . . . ?'

In spite of the emphasis, Amy seemed to be pleased with what she was hearing. She turned to look at the face that was looking down at hers. She lifted a hand timidly to stroke his hair.

'You're a nice boy, Jack. A very nice boy.'

He accepted the commendation as a permit to advance. He kissed her again. Amy's hand clutched at the back of his well-shaped head. His hand shifted from her waist to feel her breasts. As their embrace grew more passionate Amy disengaged her lips with difficulty to speak. His wet tongue prevented her. She shifted her head. Her voice was husky with fear and excitement.

'Oh Jack,' she said. 'Jack darling. We must be careful.'

He pushed her hair aside to mumble soothingly in her ear. Before she could understand what he was saying, she felt the tip of his tongue licking the lobe of her ear. She leaned forward as though to listen more intently to the sound inside a sea shell. He moved with her. The emotion she felt was making her tremble.

'What is it, Jack?' she said. 'What is it?'

He stopped whispering. His tongue caressed her ear with a worrying intensity.

'Jack,' she said. 'What are you doing? What are you trying to do?'

'Do you like it?' he whispered excitedly in her ear. 'Do you like what I'm doing?'

Amy giggled nervously. 'Calves do it,' she said. 'Calves suck each other's ears.'

Jack did not seem to hear her. His hand groped over the features of her face and his fingers felt for the lobe of her other ear. She tried to make out what he was whispering so urgently.

'Why not,' he was saying, 'Why not? You love me, don't you? Say you love me, Amy.'

'It's your place to say it . . .'

Amy struggled to remain lucid in spite of her increasingly sensitive state, but the words had difficulty in coming out.

'Wonderful,' he said. 'It's wonderful. In the open air. In the sun.'

'What is?' Amy asked the question in an uncharacteristically stupid tone. Impatient with the slowness of her response, he took hold of her hand and pulled it towards his crotch. Partly with her fingers and partly with his own he undid his trouser buttons.

Amy gazed with horrified fascination at the purple head of flesh and the shadowed pubic hair. She listened to his words as though they had acquired a cutting edge that sliced into her consciousness.

'Why can't we then? Why not? If we love each other. Satisfy each other. It's sure to be wonderful. Nothing like it. Nothing.'

Amy shook her head. She pulled her hand away from his grip and turned her back on him, her face close to the trampled grass. Green insects climbed the damaged stems. In the silence the sound of a grasshopper invisible and yet very near was loud and mechanical like the spring of a clock being wound up. There were sounds also behind her back. Jack was stretching some elastic substance but she did not turn around to look. Silence and stillness seemed her best refuge. From him and from herself. She did not move when she felt his heavy hand on her shoulder.

'Come on,' he said. 'Come on, Amy. Be a sport. There's my lovely girl. Just leave it to me. You've got nothing to worry about.'

Her passivity encouraged him. His hands slid down from her shoulders. He murmured soothingly as he slid his hands under her dress and began to stroke her thighs. When she moved her legs away, he used all his strength to turn her on her back. Before she could prevent it, he was lying on her and her dress was around her waist. She saw his face just above her own, laughing cheerfully as

213

though he were winning a friendly wrestling bout. Her lips stretched angrily.

'Get off,' she said. 'Get off me.'

'Now come on, Amy . . . what's the harm . . .'

Gradually their struggle became more intense. Absorbed in his own desire, he was slow to realise the depth of her resentment. At first he paid no attention to her fierce muttering.

'What's up?' He held her down by force but his voice was still friendly. 'Have you got the monthly thing or something? Have you?'

Her face had become dark with anger and embarrassment.

'Don't talk to me like that . . . that's what you think of me . . .'

'Well, we're all human.' He was complacent as she struggled to release herself from his grip. 'All of us.' He was so pleased with the all-embracing nature of the statement that he seemed ready to adopt it as a motto if not a philosophy of life. 'No point in beating about the bush.'

'We are not animals . . .'

He laughed in her face. Her anger exploded. She managed to get her hands into his hair. She tugged as hard as she could. His body lifted enough for her to draw up her knee into his crotch with enough force to make him double up with pain. She scrambled away out of his reach.

'You bitch. You little Welsh bitch . . .'

He rolled on his stomach, his bare buttocks exposed and his trousers still below his knees. Amy stretched out an arm accusingly and brought it back to help rearrange her clothes and her hair, and stretched it out again.

'If you had any respect for me,' she said, 'you wouldn't talk like that.'

'Respect . . .' He barely managed to gasp out the word with ironic wonder.

' "Common little Welsh girl." That's what you think I am, isn't it? You and your awful old grandmother. Think you can do what you like with me. That's why you plotted to bring me here. So that you could do what you liked with me.'

'What are you talking about?' He had recovered sufficiently to

214

start tidying himself. But his puckered face showed that he was still more concerned with his own condition than with what she was saying.

'Keeping it all a secret,' Amy said. 'A dirty secret. That's what you thought of me, Jack Pulford.'

Amy was working herself up to a fury. He made a gesture intended to calm her down. It only seemed to make her angrier.

'You never wanted to love me. You don't know what love means. I've learnt that much anyway. This afternoon.'

She reached down to pick up her mackintosh. Jack was still kneeling on a corner of it. She tugged at it frantically until he moved. He sat down on another spot. He held out his hands appealingly.

'You wanted to come,' he said. 'What did you expect?'

There were tears in her eyes. 'If you don't know, there's no use me trying to tell you.'

'I'm a straightforward chap,' he said. 'Or I try to be. I don't know what the future holds, do I? I had one brother killed in the war.'

'My father was killed in the war,' Amy said promptly. 'What's that got to do with it?'

'I'm pretty certain to go abroad. When I'm qualified. The colonies I expect. So that's bound to affect my outlook, isn't it?'

'Is it?' Amy was challenging and unsympathetic.

'Well of course it is.'

'And I'm just a bit of stuff to pass the time with. Handy for the hols . . .'

'Amy, you said you loved me . . .'

'Did I?' she shouted down at him, her face wet with tears. 'Do you know where I was going to take you this afternoon? Have you any idea?'

'Of course I haven't.'

'You've got no idea, because you've got no respect. And respect is the only foundation of true love. That's why you've got no idea.'

'Where?' Jack felt in his pockets for a hair comb.

Amy's voice fell.

'To see my mother's grave.'

215

She fell into an awed silence, her head lowered as she stood in front of him in the deserted garden. There was the noise of a swift-flowing stream somewhere out of sight and in the far distance children playing on a hillside. Jack had struggled to his feet. He was putting on his leather coat.

'Gosh,' he said. 'I had no idea.'

Amy started walking through the long grass to the path, dragging her mackintosh behind her. Jack hurried after her. He began to speak, anxious to be friendly.

'I tell you what, Amy . . .'

'Don't you ever come near me again, Jack Pulford,' she muttered without turning round. 'Do you hear me? Don't you ever come near me. Not as long as you live.'

9

IN THE NARROW DRAWING ROOM OVER THE SHOP, BETI HUGHES WANTED to show Amy their new gramophone working. Smiling, she wound the silver chrome handle. In the middle of Saturday morning she was still wearing her dressing-gown.

'It's a Consol model,' Beti said. 'That's what it's called.' The name was important. 'They say it's the best kind of gramophone you can get.'

Amy studied the model respectfully and then moved her head to take in the whole room. It had been redecorated recently and she could be called upon to appreciate it. The floor was covered with a new Axminster carpet and the stained surrounds were highly polished. The curtains were heavy velvet. Wooden pelmets covered in the same material had been cut to fit the awkward shape of the two bay windows, one wide, one narrow, overlooking the street. All the furnishings were a conscious display of comfortable circumstances, intended to alleviate the stubborn reality that the drawing room was situated over the shop.

216

'Not bad, is it?' Beti had noticed that Amy was studying the redecorations.

'It's lovely.' Amy made a large appreciative gesture to satisfy her friend.

'Just right for a party. Roll up the carpet. That's what I said. You should have seen her face.' She was referring to her mother. 'Dad won't mind though. Not when I've finished working on him. I reckon we'll have something to celebrate when the exams are over. Like they do in colleges.' Beti gave a wheezy laugh. She pulled out a battered packet of Players White Label cigarettes from her dressing-gown pocket. 'You can ask Jack Pulford then,' she said. 'And tell him to bring that Reggie.'

Amy looked cross. 'Beti! You shouldn't smoke! You really shouldn't.'

The packet was empty. Beti squeezed it in her small fist and stuffed it back into her dressing-gown pocket. She pulled up her sleeve to scratch the eczema on her forearm.

'What's wrong,' she said shrewdly. 'Did I say the wrong thing?'

'If it comes to that you should be in bed.' Amy was beginning to blush under the close scrutiny.

'Had a tiff?' Beti murmured the tentative enquiry. She was watching Amy with the closest attention. In unconscious response Amy had stretched herself to her full height. She held her head high and Beti stared at her with open admiration. 'League of Wandering Hands,' she said. 'Like his friend Reggie.'

Amy was not prepared to respond. Her voice was firm and a little patronising. 'You ought to be in bed, Beti. You shouldn't be up at all really.'

Beti gave her a wink. 'All right,' she said. 'If you'll come up and tell me all about it.'

Amy followed her up the short flight of steps to the next floor. Beti went into her sister's bedroom first and then led the way into her own, carrying a pair of silver-backed hair brushes. She sat up in bed and flourished the brushes in the air like hand puppets.

'Here you are,' she said. 'The best that money can buy. Too good for our Phyl's rats' tails. Sit on the bed and I'll give your lovely hair a brush and you can tell Auntie Beti all about it.'

Amy moved across to the narrow window and looked down into the street. There was a fresh sea breeze blowing across the promenade. The shadow of the open window fell on the white wall of the building opposite. The noise of the Saturday morning traffic came up from the street. Beti was suppressing a cough. Carefully Amy closed the window. Sitting in bed, Beti was hungry for confidences. The small features of her face seemed fixed tight in a state of warm excitement.

'It's all over.' Amy spoke at last. Beti nodded encouragingly. Her eyes darted about as she waited impatiently for Amy to say more.

'I bet you feel really cut up.' Beti whispered the comment with soft speed so that it could evaporate quickly into the anonymity of the air if it wasn't the stimulus Amy really needed. Without saying anything Amy turned to look out of the window. 'He was a catch after all, wasn't he?'

'What do you mean?' Amy swung around angrily. In the morning light her golden tresses rose and fell with a sinuous life of their own.

Innocently Beti pressed the bristles of the hair brushes into each other as though she had not noticed Amy's reaction. 'After all, you are the best-looking girl for miles around, you lucky thing,' she said in her swift whisper. 'You don't need me to tell you . . .'

'What do you mean "a catch"?'

'Did I say that?' Beti looked surprised.

'Yes. You did. Are you suggesting that I set out to get him? Is that what you're suggesting?'

'Good Lord, no.'

'Well? What are you trying to say?'

'I was just trying to help . . . He was good-looking and rich and English public school, all that sort of thing . . .'

'Rich.' Amy spoke the word contemptuously.

'Isn't he?'

'Do you think I care about that sort of thing?'

'I thought they lived in a hall. A mansion. County folk sort of thing. Didn't his brother marry the rich woman who wanted to send you away to school when you were little?'

Beti hugged her knees to show that she was ready to make do with any details Amy might care to provide. When Amy remained

218

ominously silent, she bowed her head in an awkward sign of submission.

'I don't want to talk about him. Ever.'

Amy's words were quiet but awesomely final. Beti pressed the cold back of a hair brush to her lips.

'Let me brush your hair then.'

Amy sat down on the edge of the bed. Beti removed the pins and the neat black ribbon and Amy shook it out impatiently.

'I'm going to have it cut,' she said.

'Oh no. You shouldn't. You shouldn't really.'

'It's such a nuisance.'

'I love your hair, Amy. I really do.' Beti made soothing remarks as she brushed it down. 'My goodness,' she said. 'It's so fair and so thick. You've no idea how I envy you. You've no idea. I can just see them lining up when the word gets round. I can just see them bowing and scraping and smiling and grinning.'

'It's ridiculous.' Amy pulled her head away until the hair stretched out straight from her white neck. 'It's humiliating.'

'What is, love?' Beti's voice was a mere whisper, a technique of speaking that put the least strain on her asthmatic chest.

'Women depending on men. And talking about them all the time. That's what I mean.'

'Oh golly.' Beti wanted to make a joke but she could see it wasn't the right moment to make it.

'As if they were the lords of creation.'

Amy drew away from the brushes as though her long hair was an encumbrance she was resolved to be rid of.

'I'm going to cut it. The first chance I get. I can tell you. That's what I'm going to do.'

Beti's face was radiant with a secret smile. If she kept silent and brushed her friend's hair with proper rhythmic skill, the flood gates might still open and her spirit would be refreshed and given a new strength from the swirling reservoir of confidences that Amy was keeping locked up in herself. The only sound in the room was the steady swish of the brush as it worked smoothly through the hair. When Amy spoke her words dropped into the silence like the phrases of a litany in an empty church.

219

'If there is one thing I want to do in this world,' she said, 'it is to stand on my own feet.'

Beti breathed a pious agreement through her nose, without opening her mouth.

'You look around you,' Amy said. 'At married people. Or any people anywhere. The man is always the master.'

Beti smiled again without Amy seeing her. But she made no comment.

'Look at my uncle. He never dreams of cleaning his own boots. Or putting coal on his own fire. Look at the Rector of Melyd. The Oxford man. He drops his dirty handkerchiefs on the scullery floor and his poor sister goes on her knees to pick them up.'

Beti began to giggle openly. It was no longer inappropriate to do so.

'No. I'm serious, honestly. Look at our school. Which teachers work harder. The men or the women? The women of course. And they get half the pay.'

'Amy,' Beti said. 'I had no idea you were a suffragette.'

'It's time things were changed. I know that much . . .'

'Listen!' Beti was sitting up rigidly in bed. 'Listen!'

Hurriedly she replaced the pins and the ribbon in Amy's hair. The sound of a drum and distant bugles blowing made it impossible for her to stay in bed a moment longer. She dropped the brushes and rushed across to the narrow window, opening it in spite of Amy's protests. She threw off her dressing-gown and rushed about her bedroom trying to get dressed.

'It's the Terriers,' she said as Amy closed the window. 'The Territorials from Birkenhead. They've got a weekend camp by the Pleasure Lake.'

Amy stood on the narrow landing while Beti rushed to and fro between her sister's bedroom and her own.

'I'll borrow Phyl's new frock.' She was breathless already but utterly determined.

'Won't she mind?'

'I'll say she'll mind. She'll kill me and that's a fact. But she won't be back till tea-time. I'm pretty sure of that.'

Amy gazed sympathetically at Beti's thin little figure as she stretched her sister's frock between her arms over her head.

'It's an awful thing to say but I'm saying it to you Amy. I can't stand my one and only sister.'

Amy looked worried and embarrassed. 'You can't go out Beti. You're not well. They'll never let you go out.'

Beti looked up from adjusting the hem of the frock to wink at Amy. She wheezed dramatically and then laughed at her own voice. 'You know me,' she said. 'I can make it come and go like boiling up a brass kettle. I didn't want to have to help with the first rush in the shop this morning. Aren't I awful?' Her small face squeezed up. She was giggling too much and she was obliged to sit on the edge of her bed while she struggled for breath. 'There's one thing you can say for me, kid,' she said. 'I'm sure to die laughing.'

Amy was disturbed and worried. She tried to sound sympathetic but stern. 'Beti,' she said. 'You can't go out.'

Beti pulled her best overcoat out of the wardrobe. She struggled into it as she led the way downstairs. Amy handed her a scarf anxiously as she sank against the wall to recover her breath.

'Beti,' Amy said. 'Really, we shouldn't go out. I don't want to anyway.'

'Well I do.'

Firmly she gripped Amy's arm. She spoke in jaunty gasps giving most of the things she said the cadence of popular songs, so that Amy could not tell which words were her own and which came from the Pierrots on the promenade.

'You are the only bait I've got, kid. So let me hang on to you, beautiful. That's all I ask. We'll sit in a shelter and watch the soldier boys go by.'

'Rubbish,' Amy said. 'Utter rubbish.'

But she allowed Beti to lead her down the ill-lit staircase. The passage to the front door proper was permanently blocked with heaps of cardboard boxes and cake cartons. The room to the right, intended as a sitting room, was Mr Hughes's office. It contained two roll-top desks, one open and one shut, and a table covered with papers that almost filled the space that was left. In abrupt contrast, through the full-length glass of the door on their left, they saw the interior of the confectioner's shop glittering at its own reflection in wall mirrors, as resplendent as a wedding cake in a rococo reception hall. They saw the reflection of Beti's father, Councillor Hughes, in his stiffly ironed white overall with his hair brushed laterally across his bald head, responding with restrained but practised courtesy to the whims of a large capricious matron with a fur around her throat and a diamond ring on her pointing finger. There were two young women also busy serving, conspicuously neat in their white caps. Beti's mother was in a more shadowed corner, selling their celebrated fresh bread. Beti lifted her nostrils and sniffed with exaggerated delight.

'Can you smell them, sweetie? Fresh eccles cakes. My pride and joy. Shall I get some?' She hesitated before opening the shop door. 'When Mrs Thing-a-me-diamond-ring has skid-addled.'

There was a draught in the passage which came from the open back door. Across the cobbled yard, one of the bakers in his dull white vest was washing his brawny arms in a bucket of warm water. The flesh of his arms was bright red, but his face and cropped hair were still white with flour. The bakery had been scrubbed and washed and the dirty water had been brushed out to leak away between the cobbles. Beti nudged Amy.

'Come on,' she said. 'The coast is clear.'

Amy sighed and followed her friend into the shop. It seemed that with instinctive skill Beti had hit on a lull in the morning's trade. She made straight for her father. He gave her his immediate anxious attention, watching her closely for the symptoms of her disability, but Beti continued to control her breathing and her speaking so that there was no wheeze at all.

'Morning, Councillor Hughes.'

Her manner was gay and confident. He was plainly relieved to see that she was so much better.

'Can I have two delicious eccles cakes, please? Two of your famous delicious eccles cakes.'

Her mother, serving a customer, held out a large loaf wrapped in tissue paper. While her other hand was still extended to receive the customer's coins, she took crab-like steps behind the counter to get closer to her husband and her younger daughter.

'Amy thinks a short stroll to the shelters would do me good. We could sit in the sun. All nice and warm out of the wind.'

222

Amy went pale and looked up quickly at the pattern of mouldings on the white ceiling. Mr Hughes pulled his nose between his finger and thumb and frowned hard. His wife had come close enough to start claiming his attention. She uttered his name but he waved her to silence. With practised precision he opened two paper bags and dropped an eccles cake into each. Still holding the open bags in the palm of one hand, he bustled out into the street. Beti tugged quickly at Amy's sleeve and slipped out to join him. Her mother wanted to speak to her but she succeeded in avoiding her gaze. Outside Councillor Hughes was testing the keenness of the breeze.

'I shouldn't be long,' he said.

He addressed Beti first and then repeated the appeal to Amy. When he stared up the street at the promenade it was not without a proprietory air. To his obvious displeasure small boys on hired bicycles could be seen weaving about among adults taking the air.

'Just look at that,' he said, stretching out the hand that held the paper bags. 'It's a public nuisance. It ought to be stopped.'

He was emphatic and decisive on this public issue. There was no trace of the diffused anxiety he had shown when faced with the domestic problem of his younger daughter's welfare. His mouth opened ready to cry out when he saw two boys on tricycles aim themselves deliberately at a line of four nursemaids in uniform all decorously pushing smart perambulators in front of them. The boys were ringing their bells furiously as they pedalled. They yelled out savage warnings. Just in time, before they could even utter a protest, the nursemaids scattered. The boys rode on in their impudent triumph, waving their arms in obvious imitation of cinema Red Indians breaking up a waggon train. Mr Hughes's lips protruded out of his face, frozen with outrage. He handed Beti the paper bags so that he could wave both his fists.

'They should *not* be on the promenade. That's the whole point.' He was addressing Amy who showed that, if it would help in any way, she was ready to agree. 'Councillor Snapes was in the shop first thing this morning. Where's the sense in it?' he said. 'Six hundred tricycles hired out in two days last week. It's like the Plague in Egypt. And the point is you see, it will give Llanelw a bad name.'

The bugles had begun to blow again. This time they sounded much nearer. Beti shifted so that she could nudge Amy without her father seeing: but Amy could not disengage herself from the obligation of listening intelligently to Councillor Hughes.

'I put it to the Council last winter and it was passed unanimously: limit the number of tricycles for hire and confine them to a properly enclosed sunken garden area. It's in the minutes. And what happens? Thanks to Prydderch, our brilliant musical surveyor, it's not ready. As Councillor Snapes was saying in the shop this morning anyone would think our Council staff was a rest home for absent-minded musicians.'

Amy was blushing as if she had some personal responsibility for the surveyor's negligence. She was relieved to respond to Beti's excitement at the sound of the Territorial Band.

'Now Dad,' she said. 'Amy would like to see the soldiers marching along the promenade. Wouldn't you, Amy?'

Her father was gazing at Beti's pale face. His ear was tuned to the slightest suggestion of a wheeze in her breath, but his eyes, shifting anxiously, betrayed that he had no means of warding off the unpredictable bouts of asthma when they came.

'Don't be long,' he said.

His head began to rock slightly as though it were being reoccupied with familiar worries that flowed in like the customers filing through the open doors of the shop.

Beti was elated by their release from her confined quarters above the shop. She sniffed in one direction and then the other as though freedom was a smell in the air. She pointed grinning to a photographer setting up his tripod on the corner of the street. Passers by, carrying carrier bags and coats on their arms stopped to watch the intriguing process. Across the road a long primrose yellow charabanc was parked parallel with the promenade. The passengers had paid for their places and they were waiting with patient pride to be photographed. Some of the hardier men wore open-necked shirts and among the sprinkling of children a small boy in a black and orange beret held on to the brass hood-bracket and leaned over the half-open door pretending to be sick. Beti was very taken with his antics. The boy's father in a flat cap tugged him back into position with a sharp reproof and then nodded politely to the photographer to indicate that all was well for him to continue with his work. As the photographer once again settled his head and shoulders under his black camera cloth the military bugles blew in sudden proximity. With one accord, all the passengers turned their heads to watch the parade. While the cloth remained over his head the photographer threw up his arms in a gesture of frustration and despair. The crowd had grown dense in no time at all. Beti became suddenly active. Her chest heaved as she grabbed Amy's hand. She dragged her forward and in spite of her expression of reluctance and distaste, Amy gave in. A butcher's van barred their way across the street. The driver had slowed down to watch the soldiers. He seemed indifferent to the fact that he was blocking the traffic. With an elbow on the steering wheel and a hand under the top half of his striped apron he was content to stare and ignore the motor horns that were being blown behind him. Beti rapped the palm of her hand smartly behind the side of the van and the unexpected thunder made him creep forward a little. But by the time she had persuaded Amy to cross the road and achieve a place on the promenade, the column of Territorials was already diminishing in size as it marched resolutely westwards. When the bugles blew again they already sounded distant and a little forlorn.

'Let's go after them,' Beti said. 'Let's.'

'Don't be silly.' Amy was firm and dignified. 'Even if you were fit and well Beti, I wouldn't dream of it. And you know it.'

Beti held up the paper bags and offered one to Amy. They walked reflectively to a shelter with a glass screen that gave protection against the breezes from the sea.

'Remember the Boys' Brigade from Birmingham? Last summer. Those two officers or whatever they were supposed to be. Jerry and Lawrence. He was mad keen on you.'

Amy was striving to look indifferent. 'Who was?'

'They both were if it came to that. I was second best for Jerry. Soppy pair. Believe anything. You know what he asked me? Lawrence. Is she really an orphan?' Beti's mouth full of cake, stretched in a sly grin. Amy's face was growing red.

'Well I am an orphan,' she said. 'It's true if it came to that.'

'And does she really live in that Thing-a-me Hall.' Beti was in danger of choking from her amusement. She turned her back and invited Amy to slap it.

'I never said any such thing.' Amy's denial was over-emphatic. She restrained herself as she slapped Beti's back, but her voice was hot with anger. 'And don't you ever say I did. All I said was I went there sometimes. Which is true. Not that I'll ever go there again. So don't repeat it.'

Beti coughed and flakes of eccles cake fanned out in the air. She shook her head and gasped as she tried to speak. She wanted Amy to take a lighter view of the whole matter.

'It doesn't matter what you tell them anyway, does it?'

'The truth does matter.' Amy had become stiff and prim.

'Yes, but not to a lot like that. Total strangers. Foreigners really. All part of a game. I'd never repeat it anyway.' She looked up respectfully into Amy's face. 'You know I wouldn't, Amy.'

Amy nodded briefly and turned her head to look down at a sunken garden behind the shelter. It had been laid out to surround a bandstand with an oriental roof supported by ornamental cast-iron pillars. The base of the bandstand was hidden by drifts of fine sand. Between the angular stones of the rockery immediately below the sand was choking the aubretia and alyssum planted by the Parks Department. Beti was frowning hard as she seemed to cast about for a topic that would please Amy and make her behave more warmly towards her.

'Did I tell you what Willie Fudge told me last week?'

Amy barely appeared inclined to listen.

'I've been meaning to tell you. He said you had a bad effect on Lloyd Music.'

'What's that supposed to mean?' Amy showed interest in spite of herself.

'That's why he always puts you as near as he can to him in the Choir Practice. Hadn't you noticed?'

'Of course not.'

'That's what Willie Fudge says. He always notices everything. The little sneak. He wanted me to tell you, you had a bad effect on him as well.'

'Rubbish.' Amy finished her cake and screwed up the paper bag in her hand.

'It must be nice.' Beti touched Amy wistfully on the arm. 'What does it feel like, Amy?' Her voice was quiet and insinuating. 'It must be great to have it. Have the power. You know what I mean.'

Amy jumped to her feet. She marched determinedly towards a wire litter basket fixed to a silver painted lamp post and tossed the paper ball. From where she stood, far away from the shops and buildings and the busy streets, the promenade was so wide and spacious it looked incapable of ever being crowded. The long distance from the estuary to the sand dunes was marked out by a line of equidistant tall ornate lamp posts. In such an area, designed as a great forum for the sustained pursuit of public happiness, the pavilion, with its large glittering central dome guarded fancifully with four lesser domes at each corner, was a dedicated temple. A broad band of lettering repeated on three sides the message FORTHCOMING ATTRACTIONS. Beti came up to her friend.

'Am I getting on your nerves?' She asked the question humbly. Amy looked at her fingers to see if they were still sticky.

'I don't like talking about sex all the time,' Amy said. 'It's not nice.'

Beti was prepared to accept the rebuke.

'Anyway. There are much more important things in life. Much more important. Sex isn't everything.'

'No. But it's a heck of a lot, isn't it?' Beti glanced stealthily at her friend to see if she were in the mood to accept the last remark as a joke.

'There are all sorts of problems we have to face.'

'Oh gosh.' Beti pulled a face and dragged the sole of her shoe over the thin film of sand on the surface of the promenade.

'No. I'm serious, Beti. I spend a lot of time worrying about them. I can't begin to tell you.'

'Like what?' Beti was sceptical but sympathetic.

'Religion, for instance. And politics. And social problems. The international situation. We have to think about these things.'

'Do we?'

'Are you going to join the League of Nations Union?' Amy put the question in the most challenging fashion. Beti looked dismayed and a little baffled.

'What the heck's that?'

'You don't mean to tell me you don't know?'

'I suppose I do.' Beti looked beyond her friend and was quick to seize on a diversion. 'Who's that lot over there? I think they're waving at us. At you anyway.'

On the edge of the promenade an open tourer had come to an abrupt halt. With its front wheels looming over the kerb, it looked like some awkward amphibian trying unsuccessfully to transfer itself from one element to another.

'That's Miss Prydderch's new car,' Amy said. She declined firmly to notice the expression of distasteful apprehension on Beti's face. 'Miss Prydderch, H.M.I. It is, Beti. I'm sure of it.'

At the wheel a young man with a large mouth and horn-rimmed spectacles had half-risen to his feet, still undecided whether or not to drive forward on to forbidden territory. Some of his passengers appeared to be urging him on and the others urging him back. In spite of herself, Beti began to show interest.

'Gosh,' she said. 'He looks just like Harold Lloyd.'

'It's Ifor!' Amy sounded pleased. 'And that's Enid waving. Let's go and meet them. Come on.'

The car was in some difficulty. A pony trap had returned with its small load of visitors from one of the circular trips around the town and the pleasure lake. Ifor had driven into an area reserved for the pony traps and an indignant driver was already waving his whip at him accusingly. Ifor made appealing gestures with one hand. He took his foot off the clutch and the long car lurched clumsily on to the promenade. Enid fell back into her seat.

Of the three young men in the back of the open car, the one furthest away wore a hat and tried to look as anonymous as possible in the corner. The man in the middle was gesticulating vigorously in protest against his younger brother's driving. His seat was at a disadvantage so that he had to exert himself to appear purposeful and assert his authority. He worked hard to show that he had a plan in mind that he wished them to follow. On the near side Amy and Beti saw a dark-haired handsome young man with a flashing smile. He made no effort to compete with his friend's bid for authority and attention. He had given himself up completely to enjoying a lark. Amy thought she recognised him.

'That must be Val,' she said. 'I'm sure of it. And that's John Cilydd More. He's a poet. Come on, Beti. We ought to go and meet them.'

When she reached Amy's side, Beti was already showing a connoisseur's interest in Val. 'Just look at him,' she murmured urgently. 'My Latin lover. Amy! He is the spitting image of Rudolph V or is it Ramon Navarro?'

The problem of resemblance intrigued her so much, Beti pressed a knuckle against her teeth and lifted her knee.

The car with its load of charming young people drove around in a dignified circle before jerking to a sudden stop, just in front of them.

Book Three

1

ENID STRETCHED HERSELF INTO A POSITION OF DELIBERATE discomfort on the iron railing of the balcony outside her bedroom. Her books were scattered over the dusty tiles. She shoved first one and then another into the shade so that their open pages should not curl in the rays of the afternoon sun. She leaned back recklessly to take a detached look at the wall of the house. The window frames needed painting. The shutter hooks were covered with rust. The whole place was large enough to meet the needs of all the occupants: but since they all went their separate ways, no one carried the responsibility of maintaining the appearance of the property. The garden was mostly a wilderness. The rotting garden gates were permanently open. Grass grew in stubborn patches through the gravel of the carriage drive. The yew hedge designed to mark off and conceal the kitchen garden sprouted and straggled below her. She looked down at the nebulae of gnats and midges that rose and fell above them with perpetual energy. She shook her head, yawned and looked up at the more inspiring sight of the row of tall elms that marked the limit of the garden and gave Ivydene its faint air of consequence.

'I miss them,' she said. 'Don't you?'

She spoke to Amy who was inside her bedroom, grasping the brass knob at the foot of her bed, and leaning over in order to stare with hallucinatory stillness at a large zoology text-book open on the bed. Waiting for some reply, Enid listened to the afternoon silence of the house. She shifted her position. She bent down to select a book, turned her wrist to look at its spine as though it was something she had never seen before, entered the bedroom to pick up a chair cushion and arranged it so that she could sit on the floor with her back against the window frame. Her effort to concentrate was broken by the buzzing of a blue fly inside the window pane. She scrambled to her feet to open the window sufficiently to allow the fly to escape. She moved to the balcony to try and mark its flight. She was drawn to look up again at the irresistible blue sky. She sighed.

'I miss them.' She seemed to have forgotten that she had uttered the words before. 'Don't you?'

She leaned against the window, deliberately sad, staring into her own bedroom as though it belonged to someone else. Only Amy hanging on to the brass bedstead was a figure of life and a reassuring presence.

'Don't you, Amy?'

At last Amy gave the question brief consideration. 'Yes and no.'

'The place is so awful without them. A mausoleum of Welsh antiquities Emrys calls it. He's right too. If you weren't here, I don't know what I'd do. Run up and down the corridors waving my arms, giving off silent screams. Like that woman in that silly picture in the Cinema Royal.' Enid raised her arms listlessly and let them fall again. She struck a pose, the back of her head touching the window frame. 'He's in Paris now,' she said. 'Walking across the Luxembourg Gardens to the Sorbonne. I bet he would laugh if he could see us here.'

'I don't see anything to laugh at.' Amy glared at her book. 'I'll never memorise this rubbish. Never. Never.'

Enid stirred her books with the tip of her gym-shoe. 'What's this got to do with living? I want to listen to them all day arguing. Now that's what I call education. I know Emrys sounds nasty but he doesn't mean to be. And Val doesn't mind. Steel sharpens steel, that's what he says. That's what education ought to be like.' She sank to the floor, overcome with nostalgia. 'It seems ages until they come back.'

'Revise,' Amy muttered savagely but Enid took no notice. 'Revise and stop mooning about.'

'Conflicts of ideas!' Enid held up her hands so that the edges of her fingers became red and translucent against the sunlight. 'You know I lay in bed and thought of them until my head was swimming. I didn't know who was right or who was wrong. But it didn't matter. I just said to myself, you belong to a new generation with new ideas, Prydderch! I sat up in bed and cheered!'

She cheered now, waving her fist in the air. Amy's head shot up, listening apprehensively. Someone, somewhere in the house was bound to hear. But there was no response. Enid went on talking excitedly.

'I want to be a traditionalist and a modernist. I want to be a

Catholic and a Communist. I want to be a pacifist and I want to fight for Wales. Can you imagine anything more ridiculous?'

Amy shook her head and gazed fondly at the familiar generous mouth trembling with irrepressible excitement. Enid's broad face was so tender and so vulnerable. Her blue eyes were open as though she had forgotten how to blink.

'So you know what I've decided?' Enid came up to the bed and sank down until her chin touched the edge. 'I want to keep a journal. Will you do the same?'

Amy picked up the heavy text-book and dropped it on the bed. 'It won't go in,' she said. 'It's so easy and yet it just won't go in.'

'Leave it,' Enid said. 'Let's talk for a bit. What do you think of my idea?'

Amy frowned.

'Ideas, thoughts, impressions. Like that old man by the midden,' said Enid.

'What midden?'

'There you are, you see.' Enid's determined cheerfulness washed away her friend's impatience. 'He caught a cockerel in those big hands of his. And he sang an old song. And he thought Val was a Baptist preacher. And you've forgotten it all already.'

'Who said I'd forgotten?'

'That's what it could be you see. Moments of time like crystallised fruits.'

Amy pulled a face. 'Too much sugar,' she said. 'Ych a fi.'

Enid refused to be put off. 'Not just impressions. Thoughts. Real thoughts. I'll put mine down and you put yours. I think it's a wonderful idea. So that we can share and exchange everything. Like two sisters. I always wanted a sister. I don't mind if you know every single thought that goes through my head.'

'You are funny.'

'And I don't mind how much you criticise me. You can say whatever you like. Because we have our lives inside us and we can give them to each other. Like gifts. And that means all the time we can have two lives instead of just one. Call me childish if you like. I'll jump on the bed to prove it.' She jumped and the bed springs clanged under the impact.

'Enid!' Amy sounded shocked. Enid jumped off the bed and landed with a thump on the bedroom floor. She came up to her friend and hugged her. She leaned her head back to look into Amy's face.

'I can never say what I mean. Not what I really mean. Can you?'

Amy looked at her gloomily. Suddenly Enid began to tickle her.

'Stop it . . . stop it . . .' Amy failed to preserve her straight face. They fell apart so that they could watch each other giggle. With one accord they began to mirror each other's actions. Each retreated slowly imitating the other as the distance between them increased until both their backs were touching opposite walls. Enid relaxed completely and sank to the floor like an abandoned doll, her legs thrust out untidily in front of her. Amy did her best to do the same. They were temporarily out of sight of each other.

'Oops-oops . . .'

It was one of the noises she knew made Amy laugh. She stretched herself out and called on Amy to look at her under the bed.

'Sheep,' she said. 'All over the place.' She blew hard so that balls of fluff and dust rose and fell on the shadowed linoleum. 'Dancing sheep. Which goes to prove that I don't like housework any more than my mother.'

Amy pulled herself closer to the bed so that she could talk more quietly. She put her hand under her chin and Enid immediately did the same. But Amy had already lost her zest for the mirror game.

'I don't think she likes me.'

'Who?'

'Your mother.'

Enid peered at her incredulously. 'What on earth makes you say that?'

Amy hesitated and seemed to wonder whether she had been wise to speak.

'Tell me why. Go on. Tell me.'

'She watches me all the time.'

'What a strange idea.'

'As if I had no right to be here. Which I haven't of course.'

Enid began to look angry. 'Don't say that,' she said. 'You are my best friend and everything I have is yours, you know that. So don't talk like that, please.'

'Well, I'm giving you my thoughts,' Amy said.

'Yes, but . . .' Enid checked herself. 'I can't think what gave you that idea.'

'It's as if I would pinch something valuable if she dared take her eyes off me,' Amy muttered very quietly but what she said was designed to put Enid's theory about frankness to the test. She was startled when Enid gave a sudden noisy laugh.

'What is it?'

'Oh I'm sorry. I do make the most awful noise.'

She sat up and Amy did likewise. They settled on either side of the bed and half turned to talk to each other.

'You are so wrong,' Enid said. 'But I'm so glad you told me. Poor old Ma. It's her illness.'

'What is?'

'Some odd variety of diabetes. It makes her eyes pop out, poor old dear, in a fixed sort of way. And she has to move her head when she wants to move her eyes. If you know what I mean. That's what you've noticed. The rest is your imagination. Or your conscience.' Gaily Enid slapped her hand down on the bed. 'I remember in a train once. Coming from Chester. A man sitting opposite us got quite upset. He said my Mama was "accusing him". He moved his seat. I was so embarrassed I could have died. She just sat there as if nothing had happened.'

She had more to say, but she stopped talking to listen to the creak of heavy footsteps on the main staircase.

'Uncle Peter,' she said. 'Listen to his boots squeak. Those are his walking boots. He has boots for every occasion. He's probably going to post a letter to the paper. He prefers taking his long walks at night. So that he can look at the stars.'

Enid listened attentively to the distant squeak of leather. The old preacher cleared his throat and his dramatic sigh echoed in the sparsely furnished hall.

'It sounds much louder at night. He's writing a book. On World Peace. He says it's more important than preaching. He says the Age of Verbal Exhortation is over. We're a weird lot aren't we?'

'You ought to see *my* uncle.'

Amy was blushing deeply. She lowered her head and Enid touched her gently on the shoulder to encourage her to speak. Amy struggled visibly to make a difficult confession.

'I know you've never been, but there's nowhere you could sleep there anyway,' she said. 'I want to ask them and yet I don't. Do you understand what I mean?'

Enid nodded understandingly.

'Uncle Lucas takes up more room than the rest of us put together. Poor old Taid. He's stuck in the corner all day long. Like a mouse in a box trap he says.'

Enid waited for her to say more. Amy's head lunged forwards as if a torrent of complaint had lodged in her throat. She swallowed with some difficulty before whispering four words.

'They are so poor.' She was sweating. She rubbed her hands against her skirt. 'They do everything they can for me. It's wicked of me to complain.' She made a great effort to go on speaking. 'It's the shame. It goes right down into me. Right down. You understand?'

Enid stroked her tense forearm with the tips of her fingers.

'I never want to talk about it. Never. I couldn't keep a journal or anything like that. I'm too inarticulate, if that's the right word. I never know what to say. I can't write. There are always more things I don't want to say. I get so worried about it sometimes.'

'You shouldn't worry,' Enid said in her kindly way. 'It's nothing to worry about. Anyway you can read mine. All of it. Uncensored.' She was taken with a sudden idea. She put her finger to her lips and whispered urgently. 'Come on. I'd like to show you something.'

She widened her eyes dramatically, took Amy by the hand and drew her into the dim corridor. They hurried along the worn centre carpet and up a short flight of steps to the next floor. To heighten the excitement Enid flattened herself against the brown dado and made a comic face. She brought her lips close to Amy's ear.

'Sali. Auntie Sali. I think she's out, but I'm not sure.'

They moved swiftly and softly past the door and made for a

narrow flight of stairs leading to the attic. Enid tugged at Amy's arm and opened a thin door. A powerful beam of sunlight struck down through the skylight into the stuffy room overcrowded with stacks of newspapers, magazines and books between unwanted bits of furniture.

'Now,' Enid said, forgetting to whisper. 'Where is it?' She shut the door behind her and stood on a broken chair to push the skylight open. 'He wants all these for his book. Spends hours up here. Very bad for his health I'm sure.'

There was a second door in a partition. The inside section of the attic had no light in it except the light that fell from the open door. An ancient bookcase had been set down in a corner in two pieces. Next to it stood a wardrobe in dark mahogany.

'Secrets,' Enid said. 'Family secrets. Look in here.' She opened the wardrobe door. When her eyes grew accustomed to the dim light, Amy could see material of red, green and white colour folded on the floor of the wardrobe. 'Here it is,' Enid began to pull.

'What is it?' Amy said. 'Curtains or something?'

'Look.'

The flag was so big there was no room in the small attic to spread it out. Amy could make out the head and tongue of the Red Dragon.

'Uncle Peter's flag. He thinks the world of it. His church in Liverpool gave it to him when he went to Patagonia. He took it with him there. And he brought it back. Isn't it marvellous?'

Carefully they folded it up and put it back in the wardrobe. Enid crouched down to drag out a dusty Gladstone bag from behind one of the book cases. She looked up trustfully at Amy.

'I wouldn't show this to anybody else. Not to anybody.'

It was hot inside the attic and both their faces were flushed.

'These are from Leipzig.'

The Gladstone bag was filled with bundles of old letters tied together with string. Enid picked up a packet so that Amy could take it to the light and read the address. *Miss S. M. Prydderch, B.A., 41 Netherhall Gardens, Hampstead.*

The stamp was German. The postmark, clearly legible, dated November 16, 1905, was Leipzig.

'I want you to see them,' Enid said. 'So that you can understand her better. This was the man who wanted to marry her. His father was a count. Werner von Sternberg. He was killed in the war.' She sat down sadly on the attic floor. 'Just imagine it. It's what's the matter with her really.' She placed the packet back in the Gladstone bag.

'The clothes you mean?' Amy ventured to comment. Her voice was full of respect.

'Worse than that.' Enid looked candidly into her friend's eyes. 'I know you won't breathe a word of this.' She breathed deeply before she let out another family secret.

'She drinks.'

'No . . .' Amy was deeply shocked and made no attempt to conceal it.

'You can understand it. She wants to forget. But she can't. Isn't it terrible? When it happens she comes up here for the bag and then she goes down and locks herself in her room. She doesn't eat anything all day. It's terrible when it happens. Mama is the only one who can do anything with her.'

'I would never have believed it.' Amy was still bewildered by the revelation.

'You wouldn't, would you? She looks such a tower of strength in public. Always so strong and so made up. Marching about the schools like a visiting queen from Asia. And this is her inner weakness. Life can be so tragic.'

They crouched together in the dim attic lost in contemplation. With particular care so as not to break their devout silence Enid fingered the shrivelled leather of the handle of the Gladstone bag before replacing it carefully in its hiding place.

'Just a few bundles of letters,' she said. 'That's all it was in the end. Doesn't it make you want to write a poem about it?'

Amy was standing up, ready to leave the attic. Enid looked up at her eagerly. Amy shook her head.

'There's no poetry in me,' she said.

'Well a book of some kind. Do you find it stuffy in here?'

'It is a bit.'

'Well . . . there you are. You can see what a weird lot the Prydderchs are. And I'm one of them.'

Enid led the way out. They dusted each other down outside the door.

'I'll always want you to know everything about me, Amy Parry.' Full of high spirits, Enid marched past her aunt's door without remembering to lower her voice. 'Life has just got to be exciting, the way I look at it. And there is nothing more exciting than struggling to be more than what you are. I don't mean "more", do I?' She stopped in the corridor to ask herself and Amy the question.

'I don't know what you mean,' Amy said.

'I don't either,' Enid laughed and then changed her mind. 'Yes I do. I mean a sort of divine ambition. That's what I mean. To make things. To create things. Like poor Tada with his music. Only the whole of life. Everything. Do you know what I mean?' She swirled her arms about excitedly. 'Do you think I'm swelled-headed?'

They were back in Enid's bedroom. The trail of books led from the side of the bed to the balcony. A breeze had sprung up and there were pages blowing about. Enid went outside and knelt down to collect the books. With her arms full of books and papers she looked up at Amy, her head on one side.

'Wouldn't it be marvellous if we could be young for ever?'

Amy considered the question solemnly. 'Time never stands still,' she said.

'Amy!' Enid shouted as if she had made a sudden discovery. 'That's just like a line. You are a poet, after all.'

'It's only one of those old proverbs.' Amy didn't sound pleased.

'You look mysterious anyhow. So that's poetic. It's very poetic when people don't know what's running through your head.'

2

OUTSIDE THE FRONT DOOR OF SWYN-Y-MYNYDD, RICHARD PARRY sat rigidly upright in a plain oak chair. Esther had arranged a grey shawl over his shoulders and a crudely knitted nightcap on the bald crown of his head. His eyes were closed and his old face was tilted towards the mid-morning sun. His unlaced boots were planted wide apart on the paved path, between a lanky bush of Rose of Sharon, trembling in the mild breeze, and a border of thyme growing among white stones. He sat as still as a graven image. In his lap he nursed a substantial Bible with his arms rather than his hands. It was wedged between his thick tweed sleeves. His fingers curved out of grey mittens. They were swollen and they shone in the sun: incapable of opening a book or selecting a page.

Amy appeared in the open doorway. She was moving backwards with her neck stretched as she tried to study the ground behind her. She held on grimly to the floppy end of a rolled carpet. Her hair was hidden in an old scarf and her smooth cheeks were smudged with dust. Richard Parry in his oak chair was an impassable object.

'Auntie!' she called out desperately. Esther, in the parlour, bent down to peer out through the small window. What she saw made her laugh.

'Oh dear,' she said. 'I had forgotten about old Richard. Drop it, cariad. We'll have to move him.'

Stepping over the folds of carpet, Esther emerged from the house to stand in front of her father-in-law. With her wrists on her hips she smiled at him and shouted so that he could hear her.

'Richard Parry! Are you ready for a ride? We are going to move you. Can you hear me?'

His eyes opened and he stretched his stiff mouth so that a strange gurgle emerged from it. Esther watched him admiringly.

'He's singing,' she said. 'Can you imagine it? It's one of the old songs going through his head.'

She picked up a stout plank that lay in the shadow of the low garden wall, treading carelessly on the untended plants in the

242

narrow strip of garden. When she passed it under the seat of the chair Amy was already in position to grasp the other end. Together they raised the chair and turned it sideways so that they could convey the old man more conveniently through the narrow garden gate. Esther went through first, taking most of the strain with the confidence of a woman accustomed to manual labour. As her right foot sank down to the level of the land, Richard Parry began to tilt over to his left. Amy supported his shoulder but the Bible slid off his lap and he was powerless to hold it back. Newspaper cuttings slipped from between the bent pages. Richard Parry made angry sounds. He wanted them to drop him down so that they could save the cuttings. Esther made the soothing noises she would use to calm a startled horse while they gave their undivided attention to settling him down in the lane facing the small farm yard.

'There you are, Richard Parry,' Esther said. 'Like a king looking at his kingdom. Don't worry about the bits of newspaper. Or the Holy Bible. Amy is picking them all up for you. As good as the day they came out, so don't you fret now.'

The cuttings were fragile. Some were brown and frayed at the edges.

'What's this one, Taid?' Amy was examining a cutting as she brought him his Bible. Her voice was loud and cheerful. ' "Mayor plays billiards in open field . . . strikers out of hand. Fierce fighting in Swansea Valley." I didn't know you had been in the South, Taid.'

Richard Parry made a constricted movement with his crippled hands. His voice hissed out of his stretched lips. Amy understood that he wanted her to turn the cutting over. There in smaller print the adjudications of old Eisteddfodau were printed in close columns to be studied by devotees and passed over by the more casual reader. Richard Parry was pointing to them with a cluster of fingers. Esther stood by enjoying the familiar sight of the bond of affection between the old man and the young girl. Amy was holding the cutting close to his nose for him to read the small print. Jovially he thrust towards her hand and then pushed his lips in the direction of an underlined nom-de-plume.

'Mab y Mynydd.'

Amy read it aloud and he nodded approvingly.

'Very good,' she said. 'Son of the Mountain. Follower of Ceiriog. Double allusion. Is that it?'

He made noises to show that he wanted her to read the adjudications. Amy glanced at her aunt who smiled to show they could spare the time.

Mab y Mynydd has a most competent command of the strict metres . . . obviously an experienced versifier . . . it is regrettable that his craftsmanship should be sullied by occasional lapses of taste . . . it is quite evident that his imagination is too often excited by a desire to display his undoubted technical skill in what only too often materialises in crude and debased imagery . . . it is with regret therefore that my conscience does not allow me to award more than half the prize to Mab y Mynydd.

Richard Parry's shoulders were shaking so much with painful amusement that his shawl began to slip off. Esther adjusted it with care. Amy folded the cuttings carefully and replaced them between the Old Testament and the Apocrypha. She wedged the Bible firmly between his arms with the spine outwards. He accepted all their ministrations with passive enjoyment. He would never ask for more than there was to be given, but what there was to receive, he absorbed with the stillness of a flower in a pot.

'There you are now, Richard Parry,' Esther said. 'We'll get on with our work. But we won't be far away. You keep an eye on us.'

Together the women carried the carpet to the top of the hillock that overlooked the lane. They spread one end over the gorse bushes and beat it with a birch broom.

'Not too hard . . .'

Esther shook her head ruefully as she considered the worn patches in the relentless morning light. They pulled the carpet round.

'If we had to go, I don't think we could ever take this with us,' Esther said.

A breath of cool air rushed through the gorse. Amy frowned and rubbed her bare legs. Esther was staring westwards at a distant glimpse of the high mountains.

'They could give him a Call.'

Amy began to beat a fresh area of the carpet more gently than before.

'What do you think?' Her aunt was challenging her to give an opinion.

'I don't know I'm sure.' Amy spoke with polite indifference as though the matter was no real concern of hers.

'They could and they couldn't. You can never tell with quarrymen. They said they wanted a married man but they also said they wanted a B.A. from college. Well your uncle hasn't got a B.A. but he has got a wife.' Esther tried to relieve her own anxiety with a little joke. Amy smiled grimly and refrained from any comment. 'The money will be very small. And goodness knows what the minister's house will be like. Damp I suppose.' Esther took her turn at beating the carpet. She stopped to look at Amy. 'I don't want him to be disappointed.'

The open air seemed to encourage her to speak with complete frankness. 'I wish you would try and understand your uncle, Amy. That's what I wish.' Amy knelt down to tug the end of the carpet and put a stone on the corner. 'You could talk to him about book things. You are such a clever girl.'

'If only I were.'

Esther treated Amy's misgivings as false modesty.

'Of course you are. And he's so proud of you. But you never seem to have anything to say to him.'

'Now then,' Amy said. 'You said put the chimney on fire.'

She led the way back to the house, taking the shortest route and jumping down into the lane. Esther followed more carefully. She called out, 'Do you think I'd better do it, Amy?'

'Speed!'

From the outside wash-house Amy collected a long branch of dried gorse. She waved it briefly in front of Richard Parry's face. He shut his eyes to pretend he did not enjoy the experience.

'Fire in the chimney, Richard Parry,' she said gaily. 'So watch yourself.'

Inside the parlour, sacks and sheets of newspaper had been spread over the bookcase, the harmonium and the round table. The willow-pattern plates had been taken down from the dresser

245

ready for washing. The brasses and the lamp had been carried through to the kitchen.

'Now take your time . . .' Esther stood in the parlour doorway.

'Speed,' Amy said. 'We've got to get it all done before uncle gets back. I'm only quoting you.'

Amy rolled back her sleeve and then pushed the branch up the chimney as far as it would go. Soot began to fall as soon as she pulled it back. While her aunt kept murmuring her warnings Amy stuffed sheets of old newspaper up the chimney and placed a battered enamel basin in the square fireplace.

'Be careful, cariad. It can be quite dangerous. When I was a little girl there was a house in Flood Street that burnt down when they were firing the chimney . . . oh merciful God . . .'

She backed away as the flames began to roar fiercely in the chimney. She rushed out of the house and backed away to study the solid chimney stack. Smoke was billowing out. She looked relieved.

'No jackdaw nest. That's something anyway.'

She spoke to Richard Parry without noticing that he sat with his back to the house. His arms were twitching and he wanted to be moved but Esther was too agitated to notice. She hurried back into the parlour. Amy was using some of Lucas Parry's heaviest books as weights on the mantelshelf to hold down a curtain of dirty sailcloth which was intended to prevent a fall of soot spreading into the room.

'You are doing very well, Amy. Mind the blazing soot doesn't catch the cloth when it drops. There's been smoke striking down into this room for months. So there'll be a lot of soot . . . oh heavens alive . . .'

A renewed roar in the chimney made her dash outside again. This time she could see spears of flame emerging distinctly from the stack before dispersing into the calm air like a sorcerer's illusion.

'Oh my soul . . . it is on fire . . .'

Richard Parry could see her state of panic. He hissed at her crossly between his stiff lips but she behaved as though he wasn't there. This made him struggle to stamp his feet. Overhead out of ominous clouds of smoke random collections of black commas

246

floated slowly downwards. Some landed on Richard Parry's head. Esther was calm until she saw fragments of blazing soot fall over the yard. She ran about wildly collecting buckets wherever she could find them. To her frightened eyes the whole sky was filled with potential fire raisers only waiting to descend on a heap of dried hay to start an uncontrollable conflagration. She shouted Amy's name as she worked the water pump and muttered desperately to herself. The squeaks and squeals of the rusty pump handle were sounds of panic in themselves. Richard Parry watched her. He swayed dangerously in his chair as he made vain efforts to retrieve his fallen Bible. The water spilled over the sides of the buckets and ran in prodigal rivulets down towards the gate. Esther looked for a second in that direction and saw a man in neat Sunday clothes coming up the lane towards her. He was something so detached from her state of crisis that she did not immediately recognise her husband until she saw his limp. His broad brimmed hat was square on his narrow head. He carried his familiar worn attaché case in one hand and his walking stick in the other. His overcoat was open and his sallow features were glistening with the effort of the long walk up the lane.

'Lucas!' She shouted out his name.

'Well? What is it? What's going on?'

She seemed to have difficulty in reconciling her desire to welcome him as a saviour with her urge to postpone his arrival until the affairs of the household were restored to normal.

'I'm so glad to see you of course, but how did you get here?'

'Will you kindly tell me the nature of the trouble?'

'It's the chimney on fire.'

The smoke was dispersing. There were no more fragments of blazing soot falling from the air. Esther calmed down quickly. She tried to treat the matter lightly.

'We wanted to do it all before you got back. She's so good, Lucas. Our little Amy. Such a big strong girl. I don't know how I'd ever manage without her. She's such a willing helper.'

His mouth shut tight. He squinted up critically at the chimney.

'You must be tired,' she said. 'You must be worn out. I'll make you a cup of tea right away.'

247

They left the row of buckets and moved up the yard.

'Should he be outside?'

Lucas stopped to stare at his father. Esther stooped down to pick up the Bible. Once more the cuttings had to be collected and replaced.

'You're right Lucas. We must bring him inside. This weather is so changeable.'

Richard Parry's lips were moving. He looked beseechingly at his son.

'What is it father?'

His manner was erect and formal. Esther bent close to the old man. With her ear close to his lips she was able to decipher the whisper in his throat.

'He wants to hear Psalm 130 again.'

Esther looked at her husband almost apologetically. Lucas nodded understandingly. With his attaché case still in his hand he recited the Psalm so that his father could hear it clearly.

'*Out of the deep have I called unto thee, O Lord; Lord, hear my voice. O let thine ears consider well the voice of my complaint . . .*'

'Auntie,' Amy appeared in the front doorway. Her face was spotted with soot. 'It worked! I told you it would!'

Esther put her finger to her lips and nodded approvingly. Lucas continued to recite the Psalm.

'*My soul fleeth unto the Lord; before the morning watch I say, before the morning watch.*'

Richard Parry listened contentedly. As though he were in chapel his head moved slowly up and down.

'*. . . And he shall redeem Israel from all his sins.*'

'There,' Esther said. 'Wasn't that nice?'

Amy hurried back into the parlour. She made a scuffling noise as she began to collect the newspapers spread on the floor.

'What's that girl doing?' Lucas looked suspiciously towards the house.

'Clearing up, of course. You've no idea how fast she can work. We weren't expecting you till this afternoon so you have rather caught us out.'

'What does he want now?' He was looking at his father again.

There was the apprehension of a lifetime in his frown. Once more Esther placed her ear near Richard Parry's lips.

'He wants you to read some more Psalms. He's tired though, Richard Parry. We must give him something to eat and a rest . . . I tell you what we'll do. I'll ask Amy to read to you. Amy! Amy!'

Lucas had moved up the path to peer into the parlour through the window. 'Heaven protect us,' he said. 'What a terrible mess. What are those commentaries doing on the mantelpiece?'

Amy appeared in the doorway in answer to Esther's call.

'Don't look,' she said. 'You're not supposed to see it anyway. The whole place will be as neat as a pin in a couple of hours.'

'There's a certain respect due to books . . .' Lucas was speaking to himself, but was working himself up to a more general complaint. Esther spoke across him without any hesitation.

'Amy,' she said. 'You've been such a help. I know it's a lot to ask but could you just wash your hands and read Taid one or two Psalms? Enough to settle him down. You know what he likes. And then I can give your uncle something to eat.'

She urged Lucas to enter the house through the dim side dairy. When they were in the kitchen, Lucas sat down with a deep sigh of relief without taking off his overcoat. Esther put the kettle on the fire and busied herself in the tiny pantry under the stairs cutting bread and butter.

'It will be a problem to know what to do with him.' He spoke very quietly but Esther heard him. With the bread knife raised in her hand she stood before him expectantly.

'Lucas! You don't mean it? They've given you a Call!'

He brought the tips of his fingers judiciously together. 'Not in so many words,' he said. 'But they showed me the Manse.'

Esther strove to maintain a level of optimistic enthusiasm. 'Well that must mean something,' she said.

'As far as I can assess the situation, it's between me and a young graduate coming out of Bangor . . .'

'And they said they wanted a married man! What's the Manse like, Lucas?'

She busied herself cutting slices of cold meat while she listened. He shifted his low chair to be able to reach the table without getting up. When he began to eat, she sat at the other end of the table to care for the details of his needs and to listen to his news. When he lifted a hand she immediately reached down a bottle of pickled onions and placed them within his easy reach.

'It's not a flourishing cause,' Lucas said. 'And my message was a little stiff. A little unbending. It couldn't have pleased them all. Psalm 118. Verse 25. *Help me now O Lord: O Lord, send us now prosperity.*'

'With all this unemployment you mean?' Esther was straining to understand every shade of meaning.

'It may have been a little over their heads of course. Why do we only turn to God in times of adversity? Was mass unemployment the herald of a new and great revival? . . . That came under the introduction. It wasn't a main heading. But it seemed to be all that one of the deacons had heard.'

'You think he'll vote against you?'

'I worked on the rock face myself, I told him. Not slate admittedly. But enough to let me into their world, I told him. A working man to serve working men. That seemed to solve his problem.'

'Oh Lucas . . .' Esther was overcome with admiration.

'It's small of course. The Manse. The kitchen is very dark. It stands in the shadow of a mountain of slate rubble. But they were agreeable in principle to my attending classes at the Theological College three mornings a week. Provided I paid my own fares.'

'Lucas. That would be wonderful.'

'I could acquire a diploma you see as well as a licence. And not impossibly acquire a degree. That would make up for a lot wouldn't it?'

A tear forced itself into the corner of Esther's eye. 'To think of you both going to colleges at the same time. You and Amy. Talk of a dream fulfilled at last.'

Lucas raised a warning hand. 'We mustn't rush ahead,' he said. 'We mustn't anticipate. The Call has not come. It may never come. But I must admit the church officers gave me the impression that they favoured me.' He ticked off the points in his own favour.

'A letter of recommendation from Principal Jenkins. That made a deep impression. A worker among workers. A man from the rock face. A married man . . .'

He hesitated and frowned. 'That was one weakness. A deacon's wife who seemed to be rather full of herself said it was such a pity they had not had the opportunity of meeting you.'

'Oh Lucas.'

'The sisterhood and so on. She seemed to be the voice of the sisterhood.'

'But if they are poor themselves,' Esther said, 'they must understand. Apart from looking after the holding and so on. How could we ever have afforded the fares for two? They can't be that unreasonable.'

He considered her argument and prepared to continue ticking off points. They heard Amy shouting wildly from outside.

'What's the matter with that girl?' He resented the interruption to his train of thought.

'Oh Auntie . . . Auntie . . . Quickly . . .'

Esther rushed out through the dairy and Lucas followed her. He hung back in the low doorway, suddenly unwilling to emerge without some foreknowledge of what to expect. Amy, her face white with shock, was holding Richard Parry by the shoulders. He was still upright in the chair but his head hung down on his chest. The Bible was on the ground and one of the cuttings was blowing down the farmyard in the direction of the midden.

'Oh Auntie . . . Auntie . . .' Amy was shivering and moaning. 'I think he's dead. Auntie . . . what shall we do?'

Esther lifted the old man's head with both her hands. His eyes and his jaw were wide open. Amy moaned with quiet terror when she saw his face.

'You leave it to me.' Esther was strong and calm. 'You go over there, cariad. I'll see to the poor creature. You go and weep for him over there.'

Amy moved up the lane, dragging her legs, her body racked with sobbing. She reached out blindly for the trunk of a young ash tree.

'We must close his eyes.' Esther spoke tenderly. 'And his mouth. Lucas!'

She called out to her husband who was slumped helplessly against the open dairy door.

'Lucas. Bring me a bandage from the chest of drawers. You know where it is.' She lowered her voice. 'We must close his mouth,' she said. 'Or he'll be crying for ever.' She placed her thumbs under his jaw and her fingers on his skull and squeezed them firmly together.

3

'DRAT THIS THING.'

When Sali Prydderch raised her right hand to spin the handle of the mechanical screen-wiper, a bracelet of exotic silver coins rattled down her wrist. The handle was small and stiff to turn. The car swerved with her effort and in the back, Enid, her arm raised against the soft side of a heap of luggage, groaned aloud. From the other side of the luggage Amy peered out as far as she could to show her sympathy. Her arm was also raised. There was a black armband sewn neatly on the sleeve of the blazer. She saw that Enid's eyes were closed.

'We'll soon be there girls!'

Sali Prydderch raised her voice to encourage a spirited response. She stared at the road ahead through the wet windscreen. She was incongruously well dressed and her finery, the wide brimmed hat, the silk stockings, made her handling of the stubborn controls appear adventurous and even heroic. In the back the girls had little headroom because the wooden supports of the hood had been sawn down to make the large touring car look more sporting and rakish. The wet celluloid side-screens were blistered and opaque and smelt unpleasantly. They fitted badly, but the draught did little to prevent the interior from becoming stuffy.

'I was silly to buy this monster. I really was.'

Miss Prydderch was making another effort to spin the handle of the windscreen wiper. She failed to avoid a pothole and the car jolted up and down. The girls could hear little of what she was saying. When her hat turned slightly it seemed to direct her remarks to the vacant passenger seat.

'My old car was better made in every way than this ridiculous thing. American mass production is simply directed to make a cheap shoddy product that can be cast aside and replaced with something more up to date which is even cheaper and nastier. Now I know all this. I'm supposed to be an educated woman. And what do I do? Get rid of a perfectly spiffing little car for something newer. And why? Just to be up-to-date. It's not quite as bad as that. That mealy-mouthed salesman went on about one of your Uncle Peter's sermons he heard in Liverpool in 1909. What an extraordinary age we are living in.'

She held the steering wheel in a remote manner that suggested it had suddenly become distasteful to her. Her glance lingered longingly on the empty seat alongside her as though she had half a mind to transfer to it.

Amy had leaned forward, her arm stiffened to touch Miss Prydderch when the car gave another lurch. Her arm struck Miss Prydderch in the shoulder blade. Amy apologised but the driver had already reacted.

'Please don't do that! Can't you see I'm driving?'

Amy stretched forward as far as she could, still trying to steady the heap of luggage in the middle of the back seat.

'I'm sorry,' she said. 'Could you stop the car, please. I think Enid wants to be sick.'

'Sick?'

At some risk, Miss Prydderch squinted over her shoulder. It was enough for her to take in her niece's extreme plight. The brakes squealed dramatically and the car came to a reluctant halt. Amy struggled with the side-screen and the door. Swaying with misery Enid stretched out one foot to feel for the running board and then the other for the wet grass of the verge. Although the motor car was stationary the brown bonnet continued to vibrate urgently. Enid glanced at it briefly. Holding on desperately to the end of the wide open door, she vomited into the grass. She did not see Amy's arms stretched out behind her.

'I don't want to stop the engine if I can possibly help it,' Miss Prydderch said. 'Because of that brute of a starting handle . . .'

Enid lurched blindly into the middle of the winding road. Amy sprang out of the car to support her. A Trojan van came clanking around the corner. Its square sides advertised with bold sobriety a brand of tea. Miss Prydderch gazed with dismay at the open doors of her tourer and edged fussily to the side of the road to let the van pass. She smiled tentatively at the driver. He was a grim-faced man in a bowler hat and winged collar who plainly resented having to drive a van. A tourer with open doors blocking the public highway met with his total disapproval. With a hostile glance he took in Miss Prydderch's exotic appearance before accelerating noisily forward, compelling Enid and Amy to move into the wet grass. While she was retching, Amy held Enid's forehead in her cool hand. The sun burst through the low clouds: the wild hedge in front of them was suddenly alive with glittering raindrops.

'How is it now? How are you feeling?'

Enid tried to smile. 'Burning behind my nose,' she said. 'And in my throat.'

She fumbled about in her pockets for a handkerchief. With only a second's hesitation to admire its immaculately ironed appearance, Amy pushed her own handkerchief between Enid's trembling fingers. She watched her wipe her lips with it.

'What must you think of me . . .'

'Rubbish,' Amy said cheerfully.

'I feel so ashamed. I'm spoiling things.'

'Of course you're not.'

'Your first visit to the National. It's that awful hood. And she drives in such fits and jerks.'

'Try not to talk.' Amy stroked her back gently. Enid was overcome by a further spasm of retching. Amy held her hand with firm strength.

'I'm getting better . . . Let's walk a few steps, shall we? She can follow us.' She wanted to talk in spite of the effort it cost her and Amy's discouragement. 'It's so stupid . . . I've never been sick in a car before . . . It's the awful way she drives that thing . . . I wonder if she's been drinking. I didn't smell anything. Did you?'

'Hush.'

She looked back. Ever alert, Miss Prydderch interpreted this as a signal for her to move. The car jerked forward and the open rear doors swung on their hinges.

'I want to lie down. Do you think I could lie down in the middle of the road?'

The large bonnet was just behind them. Miss Prydderch was peering anxiously over the steering wheel.

'This thing is too big for me,' she was saying. 'That's half the trouble. All I need really is a little two-seater. A nice little Bianchi. How is she?'

Enid's face was flat and white against the dark green hedge.

'If I could move most of the stuff to the front seat,' Amy said, 'Enid could lie down in the back. We could take the side-screens off couldn't we? To get air on her face. And put coats over her. And I could ride on the running board.'

Miss Prydderch studied Amy with fresh interest.

'Really,' she said, 'what a practical girl you are. You're not a dreamer at all when it comes to it.'

Amy was already rearranging the luggage. There was room on the floor in front of the seat for the large valise and picnic basket. As she transferred other things to the front Miss Prydderch encouraged her with firm noises of approval. Enid leaned in through the door to grasp a haversack before Amy could move it.

'I'll have this under my head,' she said.

She attempted to give Amy a private stare and then closed her eyes. At the first opportunity when Amy was putting coats over her to keep her warm she whispered briefly in Amy's ear.

'It's vital . . . the haversack . . .'

But she saw that her aunt was watching and she said no more. Amy could only manage to move one of the side-screens. Miss Prydderch said it was hopeless to try and unscrew the hood without the help of a mechanic. It was yet another fault in the car. In a weak voice Enid urged her to continue the journey. Amy put on her Sunday overcoat.

'Hold tight!' Miss Prydderch lowered her head to try and smile at her. 'It can't be far, my dear. Just hold tight and I'll make a

255

special effort to drive smoothly. Off we go! Now lie quite still, Enid. I'm sure the ride will do you good.'

She talked as she drove, partly to keep her concentration on the task and partly, as she clearly believed, to keep the girls' spirits up, Enid's in particular.

'Can you see the finger-post?' she was calling out to Amy, but Amy couldn't hear. 'There used to be a finger-post at the top of the hill. With some queer spellings on it. I'm not sure whether it says how many miles to Pendraw. Are you all right in the back there?'

Enid strained to transform a groan into an affirmative.

'We might catch a glimpse of the Eisteddfod field. It's near the sea I was told. I hope to goodness those would-be-bards aren't wandering about the streets in their silly costumes. I know it's meant to be the Festival of the Common Folk and all that. But there are limits. And there are standards. That's what I've always maintained. And your father too, give him his due. He wasn't always a recluse you know. I can remember him when he was an ardent reformer. While I still am, you see. And I always will be as long as the wind goes in and out of my lungs.'

She squeezed the horn mounted outside the body. A mongrel dog rushed out of the open door of a row of cottages at the bottom of the hill and scattered the poultry in the road. When the tourer rattled past he chased the rear wheels, barking furiously. A boy ran out of the same cottage with a large slice of bread in his mouth. He stood, scratching his head, to stare at Amy who held her face to the wind so that it combed her golden hair in the right direction.

'I think I can hear the brass bands.' Miss Prydderch raised her head high to listen. The brim of her hat dangerously obscured her view. 'Can I or can't I?'

Nobody answered her. They had reached the outskirts of the town. She struggled with the gear lever. The car crawled around a sharp corner. Amy began to blush when she realised that people on the narrow pavements were stopping to stare at her. She heard Miss Prydderch calling her gaily from inside the car.

'Don't be embarrassed! Look your best and keep your head in the air! That's always been my motto. Ride in triumph through Persepolis! Through Pendraw anyway.'

The streets now were decorated. Miss Prydderch leaned forward to squint through the windscreen at the names of the streets. She disapproved of the bunting.

'Just look,' she said. 'Union Jacks everywhere. Haven't these stupid people any pride at all? Don't they know this is our National Festival, for what it's worth? Haven't they ever seen a Red Dragon?'

'Look out!' Amy shouted a warning. A grocer had left a pile of barrels in the gutter outside his shop. The car stopped just in time. Over the top of the hood, Amy could read the name of the stores printed boldly on the damp awning. Thin wet Union Jacks hung down from the edge of the frame. Miss Prydderch was already rebuking the astonished shopkeeper.

'Respect your own flag, man! Think about honour instead of pennies, just for this once!'

Passers-by turned back to see what the fuss was about. The shopkeeper retreated into the interior of his premises. Amy bent her knees to try and hide her head inside the car. Miss Prydderch smiled at her.

'It's all right,' she said. 'I feel better now I've got that off my chest. Nothing behind us is there?'

A ragged little boy had climbed on the running board to gaze with open-mouthed curiosity at Enid's still form lying in the back of the car.

'Is she dead?' He spoke to Amy with the natural frankness of one running-board rider addressing another.

'Get down. Get down.' Amy pushed at him crossly. 'Get down or I'll get a policeman.'

The boy jumped off just as the car jerked into reverse. Amy clung to the hood struts and closed her eyes until she sensed that the car had left the busier streets.

'Oh look! Just look.' Miss Prydderch was enthusiastic. They had passed the railway terminus and they were crossing the wide embankment road over the cob which led to the sea front. The old market town nestled under the hill, but two roads swept out on either side of the marshy flats to an elongated sandbank which separated two colonies of hotels and boarding houses. The

257

Eisteddfod field was visible less than half a mile away in the shadow of the sand dunes. The great wooden pavilion was surrounded by a wide circle of smaller huts and tents. The music of a brass band was carried inland on the prevailing south-west wind. Miss Prydderch wanted the girls to see and appreciate everything.

'Just look. The sunlight on the harbour! We're nearly there now, Enid. Look at those two little boys fishing in a boat. And the swans. I used to adore the harbour when I was a little girl. We came here on our holidays every summer. On fine days we would hire a boat and sail all the way to the little islands. Porpoises would play around the boat. Come right up to us. And we would sing to them. You can't see the islands yet. If we get the chance I'll take you. I promise. But you mustn't be sea-sick, darling. We'll only go if the sea is as still as the cat's milk.'

With a deep sigh of relief Miss Prydderch brought the car to a halt at the foot of a steep flight of steps leading to the ample front door of Alwyn House Temperance Hotel. The name was freshly painted in black letters on a white board wired to the balcony railings above the front door. On their left the road tilted slightly towards the asphalt promenade that descended in two stages to the shingle of the long crescent beach.

'Nothing has changed! I can't wait to take you on the old horse tram. Oh what fun we used to have.'

Carefree as she sounded, she examined her complexion in detail in the mirror of her handbag before venturing to emerge from the driver's seat. On the pavement, there were more adjustments she desired to make to her appearance.

'How is she?' She made the enquiry while deftly straightening her silk stockings and shaking a crease out of her skirt. Amy was staring at two important-looking men who stood in conversation high on the hotel steps. Red ribbons in their lapels announced that they were adjudicators in the literary section. The elder of the two on the higher step held out a sheet of galley proofs and shook them to demonstrate his intense disapproval. He also continued to keep his mackintosh open so as not to impede the display of his official ribbon. His companion had much more confidence in himself. He was barely listening to the torrent of complaint and when his eye fell on the figure of Miss Sali Prydderch he began to descend the steps. He waved to his colleague, an apologetic gesture that also indicated he had more urgent business to attend to. He raised his pale grey hat to reveal dark hair with white streaks as smooth and glossy about his small head as the feathers of a magpie. His Phoenecian face was older. Elastic features spread in a charming smile of welcome above his large nose. It was calculated to make any woman feel unique and important. He glanced down to make certain his feet would descend on the right step. The spats he wore matched his hat.

'Miss Sali Prydderch?'

Amy dodged quickly into the back of the car, suddenly anxious not to be observed and anxious too about neglecting her sick friend. The voices outside were already engaged in animated and cordial conversation when Enid clutched her arm.

'How are you feeling?' Amy's voice was soft and affectionate.

'Listen, Amy. The haversack. It must be delivered. Val is waiting for it. The Higher Grade School. As soon as you can get there.'

Outside Miss Prydderch was demonstrating concern for a misfortune which had befallen the adjudicator. He himself drew a hand over his hair and dismissed the matter as a minor inconvenience.

'But Professor Gwilym. There must be something we can do to help.'

Enid tugged hard at Amy's sleeve to bring her head closer to hers. 'He's got to get it. I promised. Into his own hands.'

Amy began to smile.

'I'm serious, Amy. It's time things were organised properly. There are so many idiots about.'

Amy stroked her forehead fondly. 'How are you feeling?'

'Awful.' Enid closed her eyes. 'Don't leave it out of your sight. It's important. And don't let anyone open it. Never mind about the rest of the luggage. This is the only bit that really matters.'

Miss Prydderch watched them both emerge from the car. 'My poor darling,' she said. 'You wouldn't think to look at her that she kept goal for the hockey first eleven.'

She drew the Professor's attention to the girls, the tips of her fingers hovering about her lower lip as she considered a notion.

259

'They are both likely to be coming up, next term, Professor. My Amy and my Enid. That's how I think of them. My heavenly twins. Now the thing is, girls, poor Professor Gwilym is without a room.'

Enid swayed on her feet. Amy was strong enough to give her complete support.

'It really doesn't matter,' the Professor was saying.

'Oh but it does, I think it's quite shocking. These little seaside places go mad when the National Eisteddfod descends on them. They double-book everything. They want to make a fortune in a week. It really is a scandal. Now girls. We could help the Professor. You could move into a double room and Professor Gwilym could have the room left vacant. What do you think of that? Would you be willing? If I can arrange it?'

Enid nodded wearily. She tried to manage a smile for the Professor as Amy, with the haversack over her shoulder, helped her up the steps.

4

THE HIGHER GRADE SCHOOL OCCUPIED A CONSPICUOUS POSITION ON the hill above the town. On her way up, Amy paused to shift the haversack strap on her shoulder and to consider the possibility of using an iron wicket-gate for pedestrians in the stone wall on her right. In the open doorway of a terrace house, a toothless woman gave a cry and a cough to gain Amy's attention. She was knitting a stocking. One needle was tucked firmly under her arm and the ball of wool was attached to the waist of her apron. Behind her, seated facing each other, two pale young girls were also knitting. As soon as Amy looked at her, the woman began to work at an increased speed. The two girls did the same. Their needles clicked in unison. The woman glanced up from her work and nodded at the wicket-gate. When Amy showed no sign of moving, she stopped knitting to wave her on and mutter impatiently. The pale girls stopped to peer out into the daylight. The woman's loose lips worked mechanically and her eyes darted about as if to demonstrate that she had territorial rights to study any movement on the hill. She was recommending the route. Out of politeness Amy was obliged to take it. As she passed through the gate she heard the needles behind her resume their clicking. The path was pleasant. It zig-zagged up the steep slope through luxuriant bushes of fuchsia, hydrangea and myrtle and passed through a gap in the low wall that marked the limit of the narrow lawn in front of the school.

The school buildings were curiously quiet. The stunted gothic gables against the northern sky looked like elaborate ramparts without a garrison. The whole place had been left clean for the summer holidays. As she moved up the lawn, Amy could see the clear sky reflected in all the windows. The front doors were locked. She stepped back to examine the building. Windows staring silently southwards made her turn and consider the view. A tiny rowing boat was circulating the kidney-shaped green island in the middle of the harbour. A train was gathering steam to leave the station terminus. Along the embankment road which was the western bank of the harbour, a horse-drawn bus with an open top filled with holiday-makers was making for the beach. As though in unconscious imitation, a charabanc was crawling westwards taking the longer road to the seafront. Between the two routes lay the Eisteddfod field. The great wooden pavilion and tents, the painted huts were gay with banners, bunting and the flags of all nations. The afternoon session was coming to an end and the flow of people was turning like a reluctant ebbtide towards the exit turnstiles. From the roofs of the quiet town to the sea front almost a mile away the complex scene was laid out for her inspection like a formicarium on a laboratory bench. Her concentration was broken by the sound of precise foot-steps on the asphalt behind her. She turned to see a thin man in a dark business suit and stiff white collar studying her anxiously. She smiled cheerfully enough when she recognised John Cilydd More. He was without his hat and the palms of both his hands were pressed hard against his waistcoat as if to give extra support to his rib cage. He seemed more interested in the haversack than in her.

'It's in there, is it?'

'Enid is ill,' Amy said. 'That is, she isn't well. She was car sick. So I've brought it.'

'Car sick?' He muttered sympathy and came nearer to her. He raised his chin to look down the zig-zag path. 'You came up through the pig-gate, as they call it in Anglesey.'

She had to look closely at his expressionless face to decide whether or not he was making a joke.

'I was watching the main gate.'

He wanted to be friendly. He was a sensitive man inhibited by a strange amalgam of diffidence and pride that kept his backbone and his pale face in an exacting sequence of unbending postures. Unlike his body, his eyes were free. They stared at the world with boyish wonder. His lips appeared thin because of the tension he imposed on them. When he became more at ease they softened to the point of being feminine. He drew Amy's attention to the blue roofs of the town snuggling together under the hill.

'Look at them.' There was deep disgust in his voice. He pointed at two large Union Jacks fluttering from two flag poles: one on the Town Hall and one on the roof of the Market. His resentment was deep and personal. 'To think that I may have to go to prison because of one of those.' He glanced keenly at Amy through his gold-rimmed spectacles. 'I'm a bit old for this sort of tom-foolery,' he said. 'I'm not one of your drunken undergraduate types. I never had the privilege of university. I'm a solicitor in the Council Offices. This bit of nonsense could cost me my job.' He looked at the flags and then at Amy. 'How much do you know about all this?' His manner was both shy and brusque.

'Only what Enid has told me. I said I'd do what I could to help.'

'It's absolutely secret. You realise that?'

'Oh yes.' Amy behaved respectfully towards him. He appeared so much older than he had been on holiday with his friends.

'Well you'd better come along and see Val. We are round the back. In the cookery room.'

The words 'cookery room' amused him, articulated with mock academic precision. His lips pressed together and his shoulders shook up and down. As they walked around the school he became solemn again.

'It's an illegal act,' he said. 'There's no question about that. There have been occasions when it was described as treason.'

A surge of agitation made him hurry his steps. Amy had to break into a trot to keep up with him. They walked down a cloister past the science laboratories.

'The sign of an adult,' John Cilydd said. 'A man who realises the consequences of his actions and takes full responsibility for them. What do you think of that for a definition?'

'Very good.'

He appeared to find Amy in too much of a hurry to agree. 'Are you going to college?'

'If I've passed well enough.'

'To study what?'

'Geography. Or Zoology.'

He ignored the width of choice and considered the degree of indecision. 'Which?'

Amy's face flushed. 'It depends,' she said. 'I haven't made my mind up yet.'

Outside the door of the cookery room he looked at her as though he were making an inventory of all her endowments.

'You are a very fortunate young lady.' He spoke in a reflective neutral tone. What he said could have been interpreted as a compliment or a reproach.

The cookery room contained rows of tables and at the far end a new cooking range of exceptional width shadowed by a massive polished copper canopy. Val had taken a pinafore from the cupboard where they were hung up on pegs for the cookery pupils. It hung about his neck like a halter. He was amusing himself by showing the man in charge of making a large stew that he too knew how to cook.

'A few herbs, Sam. That's what it needs. A bouquet garni.'

Sam was a short man with curly black hair, bushy eyebrows and a substantial nose which had been broken. When the light fell on it it looked as obstinate as a rock. He raised a wooden ladle and pointed it in mock anger at Val.

'You'll want frogs in next, don't tell me,' he said. 'You'll eat what I cook, Valentine Gwyn. You and the rest of them. Or I'll resign and then where will you be?'

263

John Cilydd did not move away from the doorway. Amy was obliged to stand by his side. He was waiting until Val took proper notice and came down the length of the room to meet them. Val pulled the pinafore over his head and wiped his hands on it on his way to meet them so that he could shake hands with Amy.

'We're making supper for the troops,' he said gaily. 'An army marches on its stomach.'

John Cilydd looked meaningfully at the figure of the volunteer cook. 'Do you think we should go to another room?'

Val put his arm affectionately around Cilydd's rigid shoulder. 'He's a lawyer *and* a poet,' he said. 'You've got to make allowances for that.'

'I may appear nervous –' Cilydd was on his dignity '– but we agreed it should be a secret operation.'

Val accepted the reproof. 'I hear you,' he said. 'And you are absolutely right, as usual.' He addressed Amy. 'Always listen to this man,' he said. 'Not because he's a good lawyer. Not even because he's a good poet. But just because he is good.'

A tribute that could have been fulsome was made with such ease and charm that Cilydd could not prevent himself blushing. To cover up his emotion he turned to Amy and held out his hand for the haversack.

'Let's see it,' he said. 'Before he starts making one of his speeches.'

He took the flag out and spread it like a table cloth over one of the tables. Val examined the head of the Red Dragon and tested the quality of the mass of material.

'Just what we need,' he said. 'And you brought it to us.' The way he spoke gave her pleasure, but she was anxious not to claim any credit that did not belong to her.

'Enid brought it,' she said. 'I mean she would have brought it but she was sick in the car.'

Val had already turned to call out to Sam the cook. 'Look at this, Sam! Isn't it a beauty?' He held up a corner of the flag. Sam waved his wooden spoon and gave a shout that was muffled by the copper canopy.

'To think it's been to Patagonia and back. That must mean something.'

264

Val's eyes shone with enthusiasm as he spoke to Cilydd half expecting a poet's response. Cilydd was removing his jacket. He wore expanding sleeve bands on his thin arms. He pointed briskly to the other end of the flag. Together they folded it and solemnly began to wind it around Cilydd's chest. The cook turned around to see what they were doing. He shouted out his laughter.

'There you are . . .' Cilydd spoke testily. 'I told you this should be done in secret. In private at least.'

Val himself had begun to laugh. 'Don't get annoyed,' he said. 'Sam's hobby is rock-climbing. He is part of the plan.'

Cilydd still looked cross. 'It's not my fault I've got no head for heights,' he said.

'You are risking your job,' Val said. 'That's the biggest risk of all.'

The serious tone restored Cilydd's spirits. He concentrated on methods of concealing the large flag about his person in order to smuggle it into the Council Offices.

'You will have to leave your waistcoat off,' Val said. 'And wear a mackintosh.'

A twanging noise reverberated suddenly through the main building. Amy looked apprehensive until she realised a series of violent chords were being struck on an old piano. They could hear shouts and echoing groans of protest.

'It's quite all right. Some of our chaps were asleep in that classroom. Miners some of them. Travelled up overnight. We've been waiting for them to wake up to tell you the truth. To give them their "quarry supper". Would you like to join us?'

His manner was warm and friendly. He was concerned to make Amy feel at ease. While he folded up the flag and put it back in the haversack John Cilydd listened critically to the noise.

'It's Dyfan,' he said. 'Dyfan Davies. He's a bit of a show-off isn't he? A big noise. Always wants to be noticed.'

Val raised his eyebrows thoughtfully as he considered the content of Cilydd's rapid analysis.

'Loves making speeches. Loves being a mob orator. But can you rely on him? I don't think so. And I'll tell you why. He's seething with personal ambition.'

Cilydd paused to listen to the frenzy of piano-playing, as though the noise confirmed his worst fears. Val took his suspicions seriously.

'It's one of the hazards of our movement,' he said. 'How can we pick and choose? How can we impose discipline? Are we a sort of secret army or are we a political movement? These are big questions and we have to settle them in a hurry. That's why I want action. Action forces people to choose. This is a country that has learnt evasive habits from four centuries of servitude. We don't want our movement to become a forcing house for another generation of little Lloyd Georges.'

The piano playing stopped but the noise of the men shouting as they ran back and fore in their bare feet from the cloakroom became louder. The words were hardly intelligible but the raucous noises were unmistakably coarse. Val looked at John Cilydd a little uneasily.

'Do you think you could go and warn them, John, that we have ladies present?'

Cilydd obeyed the question as though it were an order. Amy watched his rapid narrow steps as he hurried up the cloister.

'They don't mean any harm.' Val spoke reassuringly. 'It's the hard life they lead, most of them. Miners, the pit, the rugby club. A very masculine world. I expect they are a bit unfamiliar to you?'

At the end of the cloister Cilydd was suddenly faced with a rush of men. For a second it seemed that he was in danger of being trodden underfoot or of being picked up like a rugby ball and thrown about. For his own protection a burly forward picked him up and set him to one side. Smaller men burst through and galloped yelling down the cloister. Some were still in their pyjama trousers. When they saw that there was a girl in the cookery room they stopped in their tracks like steers caught at the end of a pen.

'Jesus,' one of them said. 'I haven't woken up after all. I'm still dreaming.'

The brief embarrassment was broken. The men in pyjama trousers pushed their way to the back. When they saw that Amy held a hand in front of her mouth to hide her smile, they were inclined to resume their antics. Cilydd, who was walking forward with his hands in his pockets, was thrust aside a second time. An eager young man with thick black hair still standing on end and a smudge of moustache under his nose pushed his way forward to the front. His mouth was curved in a triumphant grin.

'I got you out of bed you lazy devils,' he was saying. 'What's holding you up? Are your legs too weak to make the journey?' As soon as he saw Amy he rubbed his eyes and started to comb his hair with his fingers.

'This is Davies the Dull.'

The burly forward held Davies back by the shoulder.

'A direct descendant of Dyfan the Dull. The last blue king of Senghenydd. I think you ought to be warned. He's only out on a licence.'

His unfamiliar lilting accent was intriguing. Amy listened intently at the ribald remarks the men were exchanging. Their easy laughter created a festive atmosphere. They filtered into the cookery room and began to tease the cook. Nevertheless they obeyed all his instructions.

'Are you going to stay and have a meal with us?' Val made the invitation but it was quickly seconded by those in earshot. Amy was clearly tempted. There was nothing required of her but to smile a little from time to time and be as still and as agreeable as a May Queen borne aloft in a procession. Her cheeks flushed in the open warmth and cheerful comfort of their admiration.

'I must get back.' She spoke responsibly to Val as if she had already learnt the kind of tone that was most acceptable to him. 'Enid wasn't well. I must see how she is.'

This brought a grave and thoughtful expression to his handsome face. He escorted her from the cookery room around the main building so that she could return the way she had come. On the school lawn he spoke about Enid.

'I can't think of her as grown up,' he said. 'I can still see her as a funny little girl on Shrewsbury station. In a school uniform that was too big for her. Coming home for the holidays. Absolutely overjoyed to see her brother. It was bubbling over. He was quite embarrassed.'

'She is very sensitive.'

Val looked at her gravely. 'You're quite right.'

267

Inspired by his approval Amy said more. 'I feel I have to protect her sometimes.'

His admiration was visible for her to see. 'You are so right. She is very vulnerable. It's wonderful that she should have you for a friend. It was something she very much needed. To have a good friend.'

They had arrived at the low wall at the end of the lawn. There was no real reason for her to delay her departure. Val appeared as though he had more to say and yet when she waited he said nothing. He looked at the view and found nothing in it to which he could draw her attention. He glanced at the black armband on her sleeve.

'I don't wish to pry,' he said, 'but I see you have suffered a bereavement.'

Amy moved her arm and looked down at the band as if she had forgotten it was there. She was ready to talk about it.

'My grandfather,' she said. 'He wasn't my grandfather really. But I called him Taid.'

'Were you fond of him?' Val asked the question so gently that her eyes suddenly filled with tears.

'When I was small, he was the only friend I had in the world.'

She turned away to hide her emotion. In the silence they could hear someone playing the tinny piano in the school. She felt his brief touch on her shoulder.

'You've got new friends now,' he said. 'Good friends.'

He waited for her to turn and face him.

'I'll tell you something,' he said. 'It's still some sort of a secret. Well it's not official anyway. I've got a job in Aber. In the library.'

Amy sniffed and prepared to look pleased and excited.

'So you won't be going back to Paris?'

He shook his head.

'Enid will be so thrilled!'

He continued to look into her eyes. 'So when you come to college I hope we'll be able to see each other again.'

'Can I tell her?'

'Who?' He seemed puzzled.

'Enid, of course.' A note of reproof emerged spontaneously but he did not show any displeasure. Instead they both laughed as if they had known each other for years.

'Tell her to keep it to herself. It's not official. The council could turn against me. People on committees don't like zealots . . .'

'Val.'

They both turned quickly. John Cilydd stood near the corner of the school. His hands were in his jacket pockets and one foot was balanced on the stone border of the flower bed. His pale tight face glimmered in the shadow of the building. He made no apology for interrupting their conversation. It was clear that he thought Amy should have been on her way to Alwyn House some time ago.

'The small committee.' His precise voice made the announcement with diffident determination. 'We should have begun five minutes ago. Are you coming?'

Amy wished them both a hasty goodnight and ran down the path through the myrtle bushes.

5

THE DOOR MARKED 'LOUNGE' IN ALWYN HOUSE WAS AJAR. THROUGH it Amy caught a glimpse of Professor Gwilym sitting low in a comfortable armchair. He was smoking a pipe, but from time to time his left hand dipped down to pick up a glass that was secreted within easy reach behind the brass fender. He was pleased with the attention he was getting. Across the room in a bay window facing the sea, a commercial traveller was hunched over his order book. The front door was wide open. The weary voices of mothers calling their children in from the beach and to bed mingled with the cries of gulls circling a fishing boat coasting on its way out to sea.

Amy turned to examine her own reflection in the oval mirror of the clothes stand. The warm damp air had darkened her hair and made it curl softly around her face. Her eyes shone and her cheeks were gently flushed. Having made sure that no one was looking she rehearsed a modest smile that brought out the dimple in her right cheek. By trial and error she tried to pin down the image that had given her such a warm and friendly reception among all the grown men in the school cookery room. While she studied herself she heard a familiar voice addressing the Professor. It was Enid's brother Emrys, speaking with uncharacteristic reverence and respect. Although she could not see him the tone of his voice suggested that he might have been on one knee.

'I must take this opportunity,' he was saying. 'You know I'm pretty friendly with Val Gwyn and what you might call the activists. As a matter of fact I happen to know he's dying to meet you – but that's by the way. What I wanted to ask was this – we all look up to you as a patriot and a man of letters. What do you think of this business of a Welsh Sinn Fein?'

The room became quiet. Amy saw the commercial traveller hold a square piece of pink blotting paper in the air as though the noise it would make soaking up the wet ink would prevent him hearing the Professor's answer. She held her breath in order not to reveal her presence. The only sound in the room was the sucking of a pipe as the question was given the most solemn consideration. The Professor spoke at last.

'Education,' he said. 'I pin all my hopes on education. Now by definition, education is a gradual process. Evolution shall we say. Not revolution.' He paused to gauge the response. 'Now this is unromantic. No Marat. No Danton. No Trotsky. Very well. But let me remind you of one interesting fact that so easily gets overlooked you know. It has never been tried before.' His nasal voice gave the words special emphasis. 'Am I right, Miss Prydderch?' He did not wait for her answer. 'Never in the history of the world. So I say to the people of Wales and indeed the world, let us give it a chance.'

Emrys cleared his throat and the Professor instantly turned the stem of his pipe in his direction.

'What does it mean? Welsh Sinn Fein. If it means anything. A newspaper phrase is not obliged to mean anything.'

Amy heard a throaty laugh from Emrys meant to inject encouragement and support into the atmosphere of the lounge.

'We are a small pacific non-conformist nation. I don't claim this as any special virtue. All I am saying is we are not designed for violent revolution and I am glad of it. And let me add now that I am speaking as a convinced socialist who profoundly wishes to bring the day of revolution nearer. So where does that leave me, Miss Prydderch?'

Miss Prydderch's silence implied that she would not presume to say.

'This calls for a little confession of faith on my part and I will gladly make it because I know I am among friends and it will not be used against me. I believe that the nature of progress always manifests itself in repeated revolt against all forms of authority. I believe this is healthy and natural in the biological sense. But this growth of repeated revolt must be channelled and controlled and even cultivated. Now the secret of the art of government as I see it rests precisely in the ability of those in power to educate the public. Do I make myself clear? Education is the secret of power.'

He paused to give them both time to catch up in the labyrinth of his reasoning and to take in the new vista at the end of the tunnel. He played with his pipe and gave a sardonic smile.

'Let us consider a concrete example from this annual festival of ours that brings us so happily together this week. It's full to the top of ridiculous nonsense. Bards in their robes tottering about the streets carrying umbrellas and their wives' shopping. Illiterate clowns like you-know-who talking about Druidic Rites and Bardic Cultures when our scholars have demonstrated conclusively that the whole jamboree as we know it is mostly an eighteenth-century hoax. And the odd smell of Victorian snobbery that surrounds it! Think of the Queen of What's-it coming here the day after tomorrow. To be made an honorary bard! And the popinjays and politicians we've had to suffer in the past. And all the other faults. No Red Dragon on public buildings and so on. How do we improve it? By taking out the chief bards to the bottom of an Irish garden and having them shot?'

'Well . . .'

Emrys was ready to toss a little joke at his feet if it would not impede the progress of the Professor's fancy. He refrained at once when he saw the professor was coming to a forceful point.

271

'We have no real choice. We are not Irish and we are not Russian. We have to be what we are to the best of our ability!'

A noise outside took Amy's attention. Ifor was bounding up the steps two at a time. She retreated hastily to the foot of the stairs and put her finger to her lips to warn him not to betray her presence.

'Where have you been?' His deep voice broke out before he saw her sign. He wiped his boots noisily on the front door mat while Amy backed further up the stairs. She beckoned him to follow her up and to do it quietly. At the top of the stairs he made an unpractised attempt to whisper. 'I was sent to look for you. They've had supper. Auntie Sali was worried. Have you been up to the school?'

Miss Prydderch was calling from the lounge.

'Ifor! Ifor! Is that you?'

'Say I'm with Enid.' Amy pushed her fist into Ifor's shoulder. 'Do you understand?'

She waited for him to show obedient understanding before she hurried down the dark corridor to the end bedroom that had been assigned to Enid and herself.

She found Enid sitting on the edge of the feather bed. She was fully dressed and she had been reading but the book was laid aside before the door opened.

'You're better.' Amy sounded astonished. 'I thought you'd be in bed.'

'Did you see him? Did you give it to him?'

'Of course I did.'

'Isn't he marvellous, Amy? Did you talk to him? What did he say to you?'

'He likes you.'

Enid clung to the bed-rail while Amy took her time to select her words.

'This is a secret. For you and me. He's almost certainly got a job in Aber. In the library.'

Enid shook the bed-rail and squealed with girlish delight. 'Oh Amy! How absolutely marvellous.'

'He was very pleased with the flag. You should have seen them. Practising wrapping it around John Cilydd's middle.'

Enid raised both legs in the air and fell back in the feather bed to laugh. While she was doing this, Amy picked up the dressing-gown she had thrown over a chair to examine it quickly and let it drop.

'You got better quickly,' she said.

'I felt awful.' Enid shuddered as she recollected how she had suffered. 'Then I felt hungry, oddly enough. So I decided to get up. I was going to follow you up to the Higher Grade. I had it all worked out and then I was trapped by Auntie and that ghastly prof.'

'Why do you call him ghastly?'

'He's a lecher.' A stern expression on Enid's face marked her determination to face unpleasant facts. 'And he thinks he knows everything. He was criticising Val and the movement in an indirect patronising sort of way. And he's afraid.'

'Afraid?' Amy showed that she found it a strange word to use.

'Yes. That's what I mean. He's afraid of growing old. He's afraid of being overlooked. He's afraid of spoiling what he considers his great reputation. Afraid of anything that will disturb his comfy position. And you should have seen my brother Emrys buttering him up. Ugh. It was disgusting. Lick. Lick. Lick. It literally made me sick again. So I pretended I was ill after the brown soup and came upstairs again to wait for you.'

She held out her hand for Amy to hold.

'Oh Amy. It's so wonderful to have you here in this room. I was thinking how awful life would be if a person wanted to be loving and trusting and the world just wouldn't let her. Do you know what I mean?'

Amy held her hand. 'Yes I do,' she said. 'I do.'

'Thank God I've got you. We understand each other. And that's marvellous. But how can I talk to my own aunt and my own brother? People I've always loved and trusted. I saw them down there in such awful glaring light. They were tumbling about like moths around a flame. No I don't mean that. I mean I could see it all so clearly. They were like half-wits falling over themselves to please a pompous professor because of his importance and influence and the position he holds. And searching for every little fault they could find with someone like Val. A man who stands for

273

something. A man of integrity. How can you be loving and trusting with such . . . How can you?'

'You can't.' Amy's voice was sad and soft. Enid was creating a passionate sound that enveloped them, close together in the chilly characterless bedroom.

'They think we are young and silly. That's what they think. I was sitting here by myself before you came and I could see them downstairs as if the walls weren't there. See them and hear them. And it was worse than that. I could almost see inside their heads. I wanted to run downstairs and punch them hard and shout "you're wrong, you're wrong". And of course I knew that would only have made them worse. So I just sat up here feeling utterly alone and lost and helpless and unable to do anything about it. Do you know what I mean?'

'Yes,' Amy said. 'I do.'

'It's no way to live. The way they are living. I'm sure of it. It's all got to be changed. If Emrys can't get on to do whatever it is he wants to do without licking the boots of men like Prof. Gwilym . . . And in any case. What does he want to do? Become another bigger and better version of Prof. Gwilym? A principal or something? Now what kind of vision of life is that. What kind of a life purpose? What kind of a country are we going to live in? I'll have to tell him, Amy. I'll have to tell him. It disgusts me.'

Enid put out her tongue and wriggled her fingers in the air as she paced about the room. The window was covered with a worn lace curtain. She lifted it to look down into the back yard of Alwyn House. A butcher's boy was pushing his bicycle through the entry door into the sandy lane. The sun had set and dusk was beginning to hide the hill behind the town. Enid turned to the wardrobe and opened and shut the rickety door.

'I don't know how I'll ever sleep tonight,' she said. 'Shall we go down and tackle them Amy? The two of us together.'

Amy was hesitant and doubtful.

'He's sitting there puffing his silly pipe as though he knew the answer to everything. Let's go down and tackle him. Unmask him so that Sali and Emrys will see him just as he really is: a poor, corrupt, helpless, frightened worm.'

'That's going a bit far, isn't it?'

'I don't think so.' Enid held up her head defiantly. 'It's only when you're young you see the world as it really is. They spend all their time trying to hide the truth from themselves. All their waking time spinning webs of illusion, deceit and lies. Come on.' Before she opened the door, she turned to face Amy excitedly. 'Do you know what I'm going to ask him? Just like this.' She cleared her throat and put an enquiring and humble look on her face in imitation of her elder brother. 'Professor Gwilym. Could I ask you something? Do you believe in Original Sin?'

'Why? Why do you want to ask him that?'

'Because he's a religious lecher.' Amy was shocked, but Enid once more wore her expression that declared her determination to face facts honestly and call things by their proper names.

'How do you know?'

'You can smell it. You go near him and it's there like stale pig food. Oh I hate him. I really do. Come on.'

Amy held back. 'I'm hungry,' she said. 'I haven't had any supper.'

Enid was instantly concerned and apologetic. 'Oh Amy,' she said. 'I'm so sorry. I've been churning away at my horrible selfish thoughts. We'll go straight to the so-called dining room. There are sandwiches under one of those railway-station glass domes. And milk in a huge jug. And bananas if there are any left.'

They hurried together down the corridor. At the top of the stairs they hesitated and looked at each other when they heard voices. Amy hung back but Enid pushed her forward. In the hallway Miss Prydderch, Professor Gwilym, Emrys and Ifor were preparing to go out. Miss Prydderch saw them first.

'Well here they are,' she said. 'The heavenly twins.'

Professor Gwilym looked up and smiled appreciatively.

'We thought of going out for a short spin. To a delightful old farmhouse on the headland. There's a Noson Lawen there. Professor Gwilym will get us in. Would you like to come?'

The girls glanced at each other and Enid shook her head and clutched her stomach.

'Don't feel like a ride again today, thank you.'

'Oh the hood's down by the way,' Miss Prydderch said. 'Emrys managed it.'

Emrys made a masterful gesture with his right hand.

'You go to bed and let Amy come then,' he said. 'I'm sure she'd enjoy it.'

He smiled at Amy to show that in spite of his post-graduate status he was prepared to treat her as an equal on this occasion.

'I wouldn't like to leave Enid,' Amy said.

He shrugged his shoulders. He found her attitude not unpraiseworthy but juvenile. He turned away to look out of doors ready to leave the children behind. Miss Prydderch began to make a show of concern about Enid's health. The professor said he had met a doctor friend earlier in the day and knew where he was staying. It would be a small matter to find him, and bring him to the hotel. If that would set Miss Prydderch's mind at rest.

'I'm perfectly all right.' Enid spoke so loudly they all stopped talking. She flushed and looked confused. 'I'm sorry,' she said. 'I didn't mean to shout. I'll be fine in the morning. We're going to get a glass of milk.' From the passage she called back in an unnaturally friendly voice. 'Oh. Have a nice time!'

Ifor hurried after them into the dining room. Enid switched on the electric light. He was pale and excited. He closed the door behind him.

'I've got it,' he said. Out of the pocket of his jacket he extracted a large key. 'The key of the market place. I don't want to go out with this lot. But it will be a good cover. Do you know what I mean?'

He looked at the girls, waiting for their expressions of approval. Enid removed the glass dome and Amy helped herself to the dry sandwiches.

'For the Action,' he said. 'Tomorrow. We'll strike! A concerted effort!' He closed his fist, shook it and put the key back in his pocket. He laughed half-heartedly. 'If I get arrested, you'll know why. I'd better go with them. As cover.'

'If it's for Val,' Enid said, 'you ought to take it up now. To the Higher Grade. Not gallivant around the countryside.'

'Strategy.' Ifor adjusted his spectacles and stared at her disapprovingly. 'You don't understand.'

His aunt and Emrys were calling his name in the front of the hotel.

'Give it to us.' Enid held out her hand. 'We'll take it. Won't we, Amy?'

Amy nodded as she chewed hungrily.

'You've no idea of the way it was obtained. Or what needs to be done. I can tell you that much.'

Ifor was in a huff. The girls laughed as soon as he had left them.

'He's sweet,' Enid said. 'He wants us to think he's a hero and he's nervous as a spoonful of jelly. Oh gosh, sometimes I wish I was a man. Don't you?'

'I'm so hungry,' Amy said. 'I'll have to fill myself up with these or I'll be without.'

'Bring some upstairs,' Enid said. 'And some bananas and milk.'

When it was time for bed, Amy went first to the chilly bathroom to change. She borrowed Enid's dressing-gown and held it tight around her body as she hurried back to the bedroom. It could not conceal all the long nightgown that stretched chastely from her chin down to her ankles. She scrambled quickly into the feather bed glad to conceal her appearance under the neutral bedclothes. She saw Enid carrying a new pair of primrose-yellow pyjamas over her arm. She lay still and rigid in the bed until Enid returned from the bathroom. Enid switched off the light. She could see her in the moonlight moving about the room. She went to the window and stared in the direction of the hill.

'You can't see it,' she said. 'You can't see anything from here.'

She threw her dressing-gown over the chair. In the feather bed they lay in two separate grooves. Enid reached across the bulge in the mattress and felt for Amy's hand. They lay for a while in silence, wide awake.

'Are you thinking about him?' She whispered softly. Amy's answer was only a sigh.

'I adore him so much it hurts. Aren't I silly?'

Amy gave her hand an encouraging squeeze. They began to move in the bed until the feather bed allowed them to hold each other in comfort and whisper to each other on the pillow.

'If he likes both of us,' Enid was saying, 'we'll let him choose. Of course he'll choose you because you are beautiful.'

277

'No he won't,' Amy said. 'He'll choose you. You're much nicer than me.'

'I dare say it will break my heart,' Enid said. 'But I won't mind so long as you tell me about it.'

'It's so silly.' Amy turned her mouth into the pillow.

'Why do you say that?' Enid lifted her head suddenly disturbed.

'He's certainly got somebody already. He must be at least twenty-four. Or even twenty-five.'

Enid nuzzled back into her pillow. 'I've never heard of anybody. I'm sure I would have heard.'

'In Paris,' Amy said firmly. 'Or in South Wales. Or anywhere, if it comes to that.'

6

THE MASSIVE WOODEN PAVILION DOMINATED THE EISTEDDFOD field. The hot sun conjured waves of steam out of the damp roof. Amy and Enid had spread a mackintosh on a sandy mound. They sat close together watching the movement of people up and down the wide ramps to the main entrances of the pavilion. They both wore similar white blouses with loose blue neckties and short sleeves. Their backs almost touching, their heads were able to scan a wide radius. Absorbed as they were in minute examination of their surroundings, there was a statuesque quality in their stillness. Each form complimented the other. When one moved, a corresponding response was evoked in the other. A continuing balance seemed an unconscious expression of mutual support.

Because the weather was close, sections of the sides of the pavilion had been removed to allow a passage of air through the cavernous interior. By stretching their necks both girls could glimpse the wide stage, illuminated by electric light, above the heads of the audience and framed by the brown varnish dimness of the interior. A small choir was huddled in isolation downstage. Far behind them was a steep rake of empty seats reserved for bards and musicians and robed personages during the ceremonial soon due to take place. Their conductor, clutching his hands together as though to stop them waving about prematurely, was waiting for a cue from the presiding master of ceremonies. This unusually small man had a great deal to cope with. He wore a perfectly cut frock coat and a large rosette in his button hole. With one hand plunged deep in his pocket and the other holding a programme of the day in the air, he walked with a confident swooping action in a diagonal line to the very edge of the stage. The audience was fluid and in a state of mounting excitement. Everyone knew the crowning ceremony was not long off, but few knew the exact time. People surged about in the auditorium. The opening and closing of numerous doors was the key to their control. A few stewards now were behaving with a certain frivolous indifference to their duties. Small though he was the Master of Ceremonies called them smartly to order. Towards the mass of the audience his manner was more wooing: an unique blend of sharp authority and the desire to please. His words were generally regarded as memorable. Many who listened with tilted heads, cocked ears and open mouths hoped to collect pieces of ready wit to take home with them and share with their neighbours as proof of their privileged attendance at the national event.

'I don't see them anywhere. Do you?'

Enid raised a hand to shade her eyes and in a moment, Amy did the same.

'He's such a scatter-brain, Ifor. I told him exactly where we would be.'

The Master of Ceremonies had cracked his last joke and the audience was quiet. The choir began to sing. Across the open field and through the spread of friendly chatter among the people in happy circulation, all buoyant with the unquenchable hope of encountering old friends, the music sounded out of tune. An ageing minister, already wearing a white robe over his black suit, halted in front of the girls. In one hand he carried an unfurled umbrella and in the other an attaché case and a laurel coronet. He was short-sighted and seemed liable to tread on them. Enid plucked at his robe and he looked down through small spectacles that made him look surprised to see her. His wife approached him from behind, took his elbow and shook it like a mother displeased with a cherished child. As she did so the glazed cherries shook on the rim of her hat.

'Tell me.' He spoke to Enid in a tenor voice still bright with youthful hope. 'Am I not supposed to know you?'

His wife shook his elbow again.

'Come away Daniel,' she said. 'Your eyesight is worse than you think. These are young ladies, not bards.'

She propelled him back at some speed while he protested hotly against such arbitrary treatment. Enid jumped to her feet, unable to sit still any longer.

'Come on,' she said. 'It's their fault. Why should we miss all the fun?'

She helped Amy to her feet and picked up the mackintosh. Standing on the mount they were conspicuous figures. From a distance away, Miss Sali Prydderch waved and called out their names.

'It's your aunt,' Amy said. She could not contain a note of disapproval in her voice. 'And the Professor. He's with her.'

Miss Sali Prydderch was resplendent in a picture hat and a flowered silk dress. Under the shadow of the hat a smile provided her powdered face with blurred illumination. The Professor stood slightly behind her. This allowed her to believe he was in faithful attendance and left him free to keep his eye on possible encounters with people of consequence. He wore a bow tie that gave him a discreetly artistic air. Enid turned so that she could mutter her feelings into Amy's ear.

'That man,' she said. 'I just can't bear him. I just don't want to talk to him.'

Amy gripped her arm. Together they presented themselves obediently before Enid's aunt.

'I don't know what it is,' Miss Prydderch said. 'But I still find it exciting. Year after year the same speculation runs riot. Will there be a crowning? Who has won the chair?'

280

'This is our version of Ascot.'

The Professor had produced his pipe and pouch. He was smiling at the girls while his eyes continued to keep an inventory of the more substantial-looking promenaders. Under his arm he carried an envelope inside his programme. Miss Prydderch tapped it playfully.

'There lies the secret of the day,' she said. 'The winner of the crown. The national winner.'

'No indeed.' The Professor shook his head indulgently. 'That's only my adjudication. There are three adjudicators. I am only one of three.' He moved one shoulder forward so that they should harken to his lowered voice. 'I can tell you this without betraying any state secret. We three are agreed.'

Miss Prydderch peered closely at each girl in turn to make sure they appreciated the confidences with which they were being entrusted.

'We are agreed. So that there will be a crowning.'

'That's always a relief,' Miss Prydderch said. 'It's always such an anti-climax when there's nobody worthy. I don't mind myself. Critical standards have to be maintained. But the public is so disappointed.'

'I'll let out one more thing. This chap – and I have absolutely no idea who he is. No idea at all. His name and address are buried in a sealed envelope until his nom-de-plume is called out by the Archdruid. This chap is potentially a poet of the first importance.'

'Well there you are, girls. Isn't that exciting? A new poet is about to appear. A new star in our literary firmament.'

Enid's face was reddening with a determination to speak.

'We need something more than poets. We need fighters. Soldiers.'

Miss Pyrdderch was smiling at her fondly. She did not appear to have understood but she could see that her niece was roused.

'She's so like me,' she said. 'Like I used to be when I was her age. Impulsive. Enthusiastic.'

Her sympathy made Enid more angry.

'All this mumbo-jumbo. All this ridiculous dressing up. It ought to be done away with.'

The Professor pointed his tobacco pouch in Enid's direction.

'Would it surprise you to learn, my dear young lady, that I completely agree with you? Indeed you can read an article of mine in the summer issue of *Y Felin*. It's all there, I assure you. It's all there.'

Enid's back stiffened. She clenched her fists. 'There's been too much writing and talking,' she said. 'The time for action has come.'

He smiled with his pipe clenched between his teeth before he looked at his pocket watch. 'Fire and sword, eh? Well, my time for action has come I can tell you that. I must report backstage.'

He made a gesture to draw Miss Prydderch aside to arrange their next rendezvous with academic precision. Enid pushed at Amy as she tried to make her walk away.

'Keep calm,' Amy said. 'There's nothing to be gained by making a scene.'

'But you heard them . . . last night . . .' Enid persuaded her to move further away. 'You heard them sniggering. And those glasses tinkling in his hands! You heard them. He wanted to make her drunk so that he could seduce her.'

'We don't know, do we?' Amy was determined to keep calm and rational. 'It's a Temperance Hotel. So they could just have been having a last drink before going to bed.'

'In her bedroom?'

'Well you heard them saying it was the best room in the place.'

'The man is a snake.' Enid screwed the sole of her shoe into the sandy soil. 'He has seduced that poor woman. Not just physically. But spiritually as well. My God, it hurts me to look at her.'

'Be quiet, Enid.' Amy spoke through a tight mouth. 'Try to be quiet. She's coming.'

Miss Prydderch was engaged in extracting a ticket from her handbag as she came up to them.

'Now what are you girls going to do?' she said. 'I've got rather a good seat here. So I think I'll go in and listen to the adjudication and watch the crowning. Do you think you'll be all right?' She peered benevolently from one to the other. 'I don't know where the boys are.' She looked around vaguely on the off chance that they would suddenly appear. 'You never know who is going to turn up on the Eisteddfod field, do you? It's exciting up to a point. But full of hazards too when you get to my age. I think I'd better get in. It's all going to start any minute you know. Why don't you find somewhere to stand where you can see most of the ceremonial?'

She lifted her arm and moved it about to suggest different directions they could follow. When they left her Enid began to breathe freely again.

'I feel so sorry for her,' she said. 'But what can you do? I want to help her more than anything in the world and there is just nothing I can do. Do you think I should talk to her?'

'If you did, she wouldn't like it,' Amy said.

'Nobody ever wants to know the truth. How can people ever understand each other properly if they'll never face the truth about each other? And it's all there in front of them. Like a landscape. And they walk through it without seeing it.'

Amy listened with grudging attention. She looked around from time to time as if something would appear to help her change the subject.

'I see things so clearly sometimes, Amy,' she said. 'It frightens me. It really does. I say to myself, if you can see all so clearly now, when you're so young, how will you feel when you are old? How will you bear it?'

'We get used to things,' Amy said sagely. 'We get used to anything in time.'

Enid shook her head. 'I won't,' she said. 'I won't ever. It's not in my nature. I suppose the world will just blaze away in my mind until I'm burnt out.'

'That's not a nice idea.' Amy made such a prim mouth that Enid burst out laughing, and shook her arm with affectionate playfulness.

'You are so solid,' she said. 'You may look like a fairy princess sometimes but inside you . . . you are nothing more than a stone-built out-house.'

Amy's face darkened. 'What do you mean by that?' she said. 'You say such silly things, Enid Prydderch . . . If there's anything wrong with me say so. I don't mind being criticised.'

Enid stared past Amy's left shoulder. 'Oh my goodness,' she said. 'Whatever next. Just look. It's coming straight for us.'

283

A large charabanc-load of bards was being driven slowly on to the field from the vehicle park. A bearded man in druidical robes stood up in front and moved his arms as if he were rehearsing some kind of Roman triumph. The charabanc was closely followed by a group of children and youths who had quickly taken the chance of getting in for nothing. As soon as it stopped it became a focal point of attention. Amy and Enid found themselves jostled apart by people anxious to get a closer view of the arrival of the main contingent of bards. Both stretched out their arms like swimmers being separated by a sudden swell. The crowd pushed them further apart. Swung around Amy found herself between a press photographer and a Scotsman in bonnet and kilt who was trying to get his photograph taken arm in arm with a small bard in white robes. The bard wanted to join his colleagues and take up his appointed position in the procession but the Scotsman was unwilling to let him go.

Amy moved as fast as she could around the edge of the crowd in an attempt to re-establish contact with Enid. She had lost sight of her completely. She turned to look towards the pavilion. There were large areas of the field quite deserted. A tall man in a black cloth cap was walking towards her, holding an open newspaper in front of him and trying to read it without standing still. Both his little fingers were extended fastidiously as he opened fresh pages. He carried a mackintosh over his shoulder. He was a familiar figure. He lowered the paper and looked over his spectacles. He recognised Amy at once.

'Well, well,' he said. 'Hello. Amy Parry. "The night is dark and I am far from home. Lead thou me on."'

'Hello, Rector.' Amy spoke carefully. Her eyes moved about anxiously as she tried to catch a glimpse of Enid. Her hand stretched out behind her feeling for support. The Rector was in a holiday mood.

'I am lost amid the encircling gloom,' he said. 'I opened my eyes and who should I see but Amy Parry. If you go round the world far enough you get back to your own front door. Are you by yourself?'

With a smile of great benevolence, he folded up the newspaper carefully and put it under his arm.

'I'm with Enid Prydderch,' Amy said. She struggled not to sound juvenile. 'And her aunt, Miss Sali Prydderch, H.M.I. We came in Miss Prydderch's car.'

The Rector screwed up his eyes and sniffed delicately. 'Prydderch? Prydderch? I don't know them, do I? No. I'm sure I don't.' He opened his eyes and peered about a little furtively before settling his gaze on Amy's face. The procession had begun to move off in ragged fashion.

'Look,' the Rector said, greatly amused. 'Just look.'

He took Amy's arm and drew her back so that they stood together viewing the efforts of stewards to move the crowd aside and allow the robed officers to lift the great banners aloft with a flourish and move steadily towards the main entrance of the pavilion. The Scotsman was anxious to join in the procession. He was pointing vehemently to a badge in his bonnet and insisting that it gave him the right to participate to the full in the ceremonial. The steward who held him back shook his head patiently. The Rector drew Amy's attention to the mottos on the leading banners.

'The Truth against the World . . . In the Face of the Sun, the Eye of Light . . . I've always liked those you know. Since I was a boy. Here they are for you. The Court of the Bards of the Isle of Britain in session. A funny-looking lot, aren't they? We may be dead or asleep, you see, but we are still on the march.'

The Rector was moved to easy enthusiasm. He gripped Amy's arm tightly. Somewhere inside the pavilion trumpets were blowing. Like a nervous horse he pricked up his ears and sniggered happily through his narrow nostrils. The crowd was shifting to get a better view of the procession moving up the ramp to the main entrance of the great pavilion. Amy tried to move with it, but the Rector's fingers fastened on to her arm. She could not shake herself free without being abruptly rude. He was demanding her attention.

'I used to think you know when I was a boy, how wonderful it would be to be the crowned bard or the chaired bard. Like a coronation, you know. All the public acclaim. Ten thousand throats opening in salutation! Ambitions of a bygone age! Do you think I would do it, Amy? Do you think I could still do it? It's in us all you see, to dream and imagine things. It's in me more than most, I should say. It's just a matter of putting it into words. And what are words after all . . .'

He shook her arm firmly to make sure that she was still noticing him and appreciating the spring of humour that was bubbling on his lips. He let go of her arm to wipe the saliva from the corners of his mouth. He perceived at last that Amy was embarrassed and self-conscious.

'Well now then,' he said. 'What about you? You've been neglecting us haven't you? Lizzie Anne was saying only the day before yesterday, "It's such a long time since we saw Amy." She misses you, you know. You lost your grandfather, I heard. Not that he was really related to you. But we were very sorry to hear it.'

Amy's lips moved. She seemed uncertain whether or not to thank him for his sympathy. He was steadily acquiring the confidence that went with his old status of authority. His familiar jerky tenor voice nudging her back into her childhood. Her head moved around constantly as she sought avenues of escape. The formal ceremonies in the pavilion had begun, but they were too far away to hear anything. The Rector for his part seemed to have lost his intense but brief interest in the proceedings. He was intent now on studying Amy. He rocked up and down on his heels immediately in front of her. His movements looked like a constricted courtship dance.

'You are going to college I hear. Is that so? You've done very well I must say. I'll have to call you Miss Parry soon. It won't be little Amy any more will it? That's it, you see. Time like an ever-rolling stream. Lizzie Anne will be bitterly disappointed not to have seen you. She wouldn't come today. But she's coming tomorrow. You've no idea how I got here?'

He challenged her to guess. Amy licked her lips and shook her head.

'With Captain Pulford. In his Buick. His wife is a bit of a trial you know. But he and I are very good friends. An interesting man, Pulford. Collects things you see. I always think that is a sign of culture. He's gone after some love-spoons this afternoon. She's a philistine through and through. Developed a passion for dogs. Set herself up as a breeder. I don't know how much she knows about it really. But of course she's got the money. Jack that young brother of his. He's going out to the Punjab. Failed his exams or something of that sort. But I was able to give them a helping hand. My cousin Elwyn in the I.C.S. has found him a place in the veterinary service. He'll be able to complete his exams out there if he specialises in water buffalo. Or something of that sort.'

He watched Amy through narrowed eyes. She was pale but apparently indifferent to the news. He waited as long as he dared to induce some reaction from her. She said 'oh' with such calm that he at once became animated and cheerful. Applause had broken out in the pavilion. The Archdruid had raised his sceptre. He was calling upon the winning bard to rise to his feet and reveal his true identity. Overcome by their curiosity hundreds of people had risen to their feet and instantly defeated the purpose of the ritual. The Archdruid was not unprepared. A flash of apparently impromptu homely wit caused a gust of laughter and made the people sit down again.

'This is the moment.' The Rector's interest had quickly rekindled. The tip of his tongue slipped out as he stood on tiptoe and stretched out a hand to rest on Amy's shoulder. 'But we can't see and we can't hear. We can only wait.' He gripped Amy's shoulder and shook it. 'But I don't mind waiting,' he said. 'I would like you to know that, Amy.'

Amy moved out of his grasp. She put her hand to her mouth and then raised it to wave energetically at someone far behind him.

'I'm sorry, Rector,' Amy said. 'But I've just caught sight of her. My friend. She's looking for me. I don't want to lose her again.'

He moved back to demonstrate that he was not keeping her. 'Of course not.'

Amy prepared to take her leave with something of her old practised politeness.

'Look here!' The Rector was struck with a pleasing idea. 'Tomorrow. I've booked a little table at the Gwalia. On the second floor. So that Lizzie Anne can have a good view of the Queen of Rumania passing through the High Street in her open coach. From the railway station to the Eisteddfod field. Why don't you join us?'

Amy bit her lip, slow to think of an excuse.

287

'We'll see you there then. Lizzie Anne will be delighted. At the Gwalia. Three-fifteen precisely.'

He moved away with confident briskness. Amy looked in the direction where she had claimed to have seen Enid. There was nothing she could do except hurry off in that direction. She soon ran out of speed, dragging her feet as she wandered aimlessly about the field. The crowning ceremony was in full swing. Trumpets blared. She caught a brief glimpse through the open side of the pavilion of a large sword in its sheath being raised over the head of the shrinking figure of the winning poet seated on the antique throne. The sword was drawn halfway out of the sheath and the Archdruid called out for the first time the traditional question: was there Peace? The crowd roared the answer 'Heddwch!'

Amy looked around her nervously. People standing near her were also shouting. Her own lips moved in polite imitation without making a sound. The Archdruid made his second call. The response was even louder. Someone ran up to Amy, grasped her by the arm and swung her round. It was Enid's brother, Ifor, beside himself with excitement.

'What do you think?' he said. 'Isn't it marvellous? Isn't it terrific?'

Amy looked puzzled. 'What is?'

'Haven't you been listening? Haven't you heard? The winner! It's John Cilydd. Our very own John Cilydd.'

'No . . .' Almost as though to humour him, Amy's face became a bright mask of astonishment and slowly dawning delight. 'Isn't that wonderful?' she said. 'Where's Enid?'

'Can you imagine him now?' Ifor laughed and then shivered all over. 'Standing up there among all those ancient Britons. He must be hating every minute of it. Isn't it marvellous?'

Ifor could not stand still. Both his legs twitched with movement but not always in the same direction. Amy watched his Adam's apple fluctuate in his long neck.

'He's a real poet. I always said he was. So it's a good thing you see. It's a good thing for the Cause. You wait. You wait until tomorrow. You keep your eyes open. When the Queen of Rumania comes.'

His left hand lifted in his jacket pocket to give her a brief glimpse of the key he had shown them the previous evening.

'You haven't lost it then.' Amy smiled at him lightheartedly, but he had a joke of his own to make and preferred to listen to it.

'He's the Keeper of the Sword,' he said.

He pointed vaguely in the direction of the pavilion stage. The first notes of a stately hymn came from the pavilion. Ifor was instantly brought to attention. He wanted urgently to join in the singing. He just managed to gasp out the end of his joke.

'And I'm the Keeper of the Key. You'll see tomorrow.'

7

STANDING ON THE EDGE OF THE HEADLAND AMY LOOKED DOWN ON sea birds contending with the mild air, rising and falling between the cliff edges and the water breaking on the rocks below. She was inclined to creep forward beyond the tufts of grass to examine old nests on the rock ledges. She dropped to her knees and then stretched herself out as far as she dared. Kittiwakes balanced on long claws were feeding plump nestlings bulging out of elaborate muddy nests. The study fascinated her until her eyes shifted and her gaze was caught by the perpendicular drop to the jagged rocks and shifting sea far below. She closed her eyes and pushed her body back, hugging the earth until she felt safe to sit up. She scrambled to her feet and looked down crossly at the soil and grass smudges on the magyar-style blouse and blue skirt. She brushed herself lightly, but there were stains that would not come off. She followed a sheep track to the top of the headland, clearly tired of being alone and eager to re-establish contact with her companion. She stood still to cup her hands around her mouth and call out Enid's name in two elongated syllables.

She studied the ridge, about to shout a second time, when Enid appeared moving down slowly through the rough grass. She was reading. The breeze blew her skirt in a billowing curve above her shadow on the hillside. One hand held her hair out of her eyes. In the other a soft-covered book was folded in half. It became apparent that she was declaiming lines quite loudly but Amy was too far away to make sense from the sound.

Amy was satisfied with the limited degree of contact. The girls moved in parallel lines along the side of the headland until the sandy cove came into view. Far below, Miss Prydderch's car stood isolated and empty on the foreshore. A shallow tide crept in over the sands, lifting the seaweed on the low rocks. Amy shouted at Enid and stretched out an arm to draw her attention to the scene below: but Enid was absorbed in her book and the sound of her own voice. She heard nothing.

Somewhat grudgingly, Amy took in the impressive panoramic view as though it was the only thing left to look at. Eastwards an isolated rock caused a break in the smooth sweep of the shore facing the open sea. It was as conspicuous and as solitary as a watchtower. Beyond it the beach resumed its slow curve until it reached the blunt edge of the promenade and the colony of boarding houses and hotels on the western seafront of the Eisteddfod town. These were dwarfed in perspective by the mountain ranges that dominated the whole length of the eastern horizon. Distant fitful sunlight picked out green patches that managed to penetrate high into the sharp skyline to soften the rugged forbidding heights.

While she watched, a miniature disturbance occurred around the base of the isolated rock. Two boys on bicycles rode out on to the shore. They leaped off with acrobatic ease when the bikes began to sink in the sand and left the machines where they fell. With intoxicating freedom they ran around, threw stones, dragged bleached branches of wood about and then turned to consider the sheer face of the rock. Amy stood still, fascinated by their antics. They began to climb and a strong beam of sunlight illuminated their effort, while the shadows of great clouds moved over the restless sea. Behind, Enid was stepping carefully through a patch of heather, and reading aloud in a critical tone from her book.

'The darkness burns
My brittle bones
The princess sang
Beneath the moon
That shone as white as children's lies.

"A daring metaphor that lifts the reader to his feet." That's what Billy Bow-tie says. But I don't agree. In what sense can darkness burn? And the moon and children's lies? Where's the connection except overstretched rhetoric?'

'There's nobody in the car,' Amy said. 'Nobody on the beach either.'

'I'm not denying that John Cilydd is a real poet. I'm sure he is. But he and Billy Bow-tie are in the grip of the same disease.'

'Disease?' Amy paid her attention.

'Cultural disease,' Enid said. 'The fag-end of gothic romance and pre-Raphaelite puerility. It's got nothing to do with the world we are living in. That's what I want to tell him.'

'Who?'

'John Cilydd of course. Not Billy Bow-tie. He's too far gone. He's so sunk in self-admiration he's buried alive in a casket of mirrors. Now just listen to this . . .

From the hill behind the heather
A bird among the amber trees
Disturbs the old age of the leaves

. . . Now that could be more authentic. More like his own voice. Do you know what I mean?'

'You are clever,' Amy said. 'And I'm so stupid.'

Enid waved the thin volume of winning compositions around her head. 'He's too clever by half,' she said. 'That's his trouble. Makes him an old man before his time. What he needs is a thump on the head. And it looks as if I'm the one to give it to him.' Playfully she tapped Amy on the head with her book.

'Oh stop it.' Amy looked peevishly at the stains on her blouse and skirt.

'What's the matter?' Enid was immediately concerned for her.

'My best clothes,' she said. 'I'm going out to tea with Miss Philips and the Rector. Today.'

'Amy!' Enid pulled a face to represent dramatic horror. 'You'll miss the open-air meeting . . . I tell you what! I'll come and get you. You know, just blunder in. Hello, hello, hello.'

Enid mimed the kind of intrusion she had in mind as they moved along the path. The bracken grew taller as they came closer to the woods on the inland slope. They lost sight of the sandy cove.

'I'm such a spineless creature,' Amy said. 'Such a serf. It's poverty that does it.'

At once Enid wanted to contest such harsh self-condemnation. She ran ahead of Amy and made signs to show how wrong she thought she was.

'The thing is, ' Amy said. 'I know very well he's nothing but a fool really. I know from experience.'

Enid waited for her to say more. They moved into the trees. She stretched her neck to admire sunlight filtering through the thick foliage.

'It was such a shock to see him.'

Amy spoke with difficulty. To cultivate patience as a listener, Enid leaned her back against the trunk of a tree and pressed against it as if it was part of her intention to push it over.

'It quite frightened me. I don't know how to put it. But I was free one minute with you. In a new world. And then suddenly I was back again. In the old life. Back in the old prison and he was standing there grinning at me.'

'Like a warder grinning through iron bars,' Enid said, her arms stiff with the effort of empathy.

'I wanted to tell him. I've got new friends. And they are all wonderful people. They are going to change the world and I'm going to be one of them.'

'Hurrah!' Enid gave an energetic cheer. It startled a wood pigeon which in turn startled her. She linked her arm with Amy's and they walked together under the trees. There were still withered leaves from the previous summer under their feet.

'He asks me to tea and I haven't even got the courage to say no. I even put on my best clothes. That's the kind of serf I am.'

'You are just too nice,' Enid said. 'You didn't want to hurt his feelings. After all, when you were a little girl they were nice to you, weren't they?'

'In a way,' Amy said. 'I suppose they were. But that doesn't alter my condition.'

They wandered apart. The number of trees between them increased. Enid was inclined to want to play a game of hide-and-seek but Amy did not respond. Enid opened her book again. She read aloud and listened to her own voice reverberating between the tree trunks.

> 'Twilight is a God that burns
> Pools of gold at cottage doors ...

A poet should sing. I'm all in favour of that. That is the Celtic tradition. But the thing is, with us, he must sing a new song. That's my point. Amy! Can you hear me?'

Amy walked towards her. 'If I'm going,' she said, 'I must go. I can't be late.' She looked at the stain on her blouse. 'If I had any courage at all I just wouldn't go. That would be as good as saying, for me, you don't exist any more.'

'There you are,' Enid said. 'I keep telling you. It's your tender heart. You don't want to hurt them.'

Together they hurried back to the bridle path. It wound through the wood to meet the lane that led down to the sandy cove where the car had been left. From the lane the enticing view was framed by the branches of trees growing across to mingle with each other in a leafy arch. Enid stood still to admire the delightful prospect. Part of the headland was reflected in the pool-like stillness of the sea that had crept so far forward that the water was only a few feet from the front wheels of Miss Prydderch's tourer. When they noticed this they both raced down the lane and up to the side of the empty car. They jumped on the running board and began to wave and shout. They looked about in every direction. Professor Gwilym's straw hat was on the passenger seat. Enid picked it up and waved it energetically as she shouted. Amy's keen eyes surveyed the headland. She saw the figure of Miss Prydderch rise up out of the tall ferns. She was joined by a bare-headed Professor Gwilym who was intent on combing his hair as he looked about him. Amy said nothing but Enid quickly saw what she was looking at.

'Oh my God.' Suddenly faint, she sank down and sat on the running board. She bent down as though she were in hiding, and held her head in her hands.

'How horrible,' she said. 'To think she's sunk so low, Amy. We must have walked right past them. When they were lying down there together in the ferns. And me shouting poetry all over the place. He gave me the book for goodness' sake.' She held out the thin volume of winning compositions. With a shudder she threw it into the back of the car.

'To let that man touch her. Apart from the fact that he's married. He is such a disgusting, vile, filthy, dishonest human being.' She clenched her fists fiercely. 'I could kill him. I really could.'

Amy watched the two figures hurry out of sight. Her voice was fatalistic. 'That's what men are like,' she said. 'They are like dogs really. Just animals.'

Enid shook her head disbelievingly. 'That's not what I want it to be like. I know about sex, Amy. In my soul I mean. It is meant to be pure and uplifting. Especially for Christians. And that's what we are after all. It's meant to be like communion. Not dirty and furtive.'

'That's idealism,' Amy said. 'I don't suppose life is like that really.'

'Well it should be.' Enid was vehement. She began to shiver and Amy touched her shoulder to comfort her. Gratefully Enid lifted her hand to cover Amy's.

'Friendship is beautiful,' she said. 'So sexual love will have to be even more beautiful. That's what I think. Don't you?'

Amy sighed and watched the sly waves reaching out towards the tyres of the car. 'They'll have to change a lot. Men I mean. That's all,' she said. 'As far as I can see.'

8

THE STAIRWAY OF THE GWALIA HOTEL SMELT OF WAX POLISH AND camphor. Amy found the tea room on the first floor. The glass doors were open and a refined woman sat on a tall stool in front of the cash desk fingering a long row of beads. The separate tables were set far apart so that the room, although it was full, did not look crowded. The Rector had a window table. He sat with his elbows on the table staring down into the street and pressing his fingers together until they were white. He sniffed from time to time and his eyebrows twitched nervously. When he saw Amy he half rose from his seat, grabbing a small napkin before it fell, and then sat down again to giggle with his own kind of guilty relief. Amy stood by the table and read the markings on the heavy crockery.

'I'm sorry I'm late, Rector,' she said. 'Miss Prydderch's motor car got stuck in the sand. We had to get a cart-horse from the farm to pull it out.'

'You don't say.' The Rector snorted rhythmically to demonstrate restrained but intense amusement. Amy smiled, prepared for the first time to see the incident in a humorous light.

'Lizzie Anne couldn't come.' He mumbled the excuse rapidly, once more rising to his feet. 'No one to feed the cats and that sort of nonsense.'

He blushed and moved away from the table, offering Amy a choice of all the seats. 'Sit where you like,' he said. 'I don't mind.'

He sat down again on the chair he had just vacated and pointed up the street to indicate its excellence as a point of view. 'We can see her coming,' he said. 'If she is coming. There have been some strange rumours flying about. Have you heard any?'

Amy shook her head. She was still standing.

'Students going to hold up the train at the junction and kidnap her. Hold her to ransom. That sort of thing. No idea what for, mind you. But the woman that owns this place was full of it. Why don't you sit down?'

With quiet precision Amy took her place opposite the Rector. It gave her a view of the market hall at the end of the street. A few people had taken up positions on the steps to view the procession as it came along. A row of policemen was drawn up behind them. Amy looked through the window, aware that the Rector was staring hard at her. She was embarrassed and uncomfortable. He raised his hand and pointed at the earth stain on her magyar-style blouse.

'I'm sorry,' he said. 'I was looking at the smudge. I'm such a perfectionist. It's a fault of mine really. I want you to be perfect. At a festival time when Fate or providence, call it what you will, has made our paths cross, so to speak.'

Amy cleared her throat. His fixed smile did not put her at her ease. 'How is Miss Philips?'

It was an attempt to keep their conversation on a formal level.

'Strong as a horse,' the Rector said. 'She'll live to bury the both of us. But I'm very glad she didn't come. I'm not saying she has any more faults than I have but she does have her own way of looking at the world and I have to confess it does get on my nerves. Since she's not here, I hope we can talk quite freely.'

A uniformed waitress arrived at their table to take their order. Her large weary eyes looked at the Rector's narrow clerical collar and then at Amy's youthful beauty with dumb curiosity. The Rector threw back both his arms.

'Well now then,' he said expansively. 'What shall we have? Welsh rarebit? Scrambled egg on toast? Are you hungry, Amy, after your adventures with motor cars and cart-horses?'

He shook with silent amusement and glanced at the waitress, inviting her to join in. She smiled bleakly.

'Afternoon tea?' He drawled the first vowel. His confidence was growing. 'Toast, home-made cakes. That sort of thing.'

He waved generously and the waitress, ready to be dismissed, dragged her varicose legs away. The Rector glanced quickly at his gold watch and leaned forward to talk across the table.

'We've got plenty of time,' he said. 'At least I hope we have. I told Captain Pulford I would meet him by the station at six o'clock.'

Amy looked down at her hands folded in her lap.

'His nerves are shattered, you know.'

The Rector's long torso was low over the tea cups as he murmured his confidences in a low voice.

296

'He loves playing the piano. But all those dogs that wife of his keeps start howling when they hear it. He has quite a hard time of it. His brother was killed in the war, you know.'

'My father was killed in the war.' Amy could not resist making the statement. The Rector opened his eyes wide as if simply making a statement of her own volition showed the girl up in a new and distinctive light.

'Of course he was,' the Rector said. 'Of course he was. I wasn't sure that you knew it.' He sighed heavily. 'I wish I had been too,' he said. 'It would have solved all my problems. All those fine fellows. Lying out there. My generation. We'll never get over it, you know. Never. I don't know how to put it quite.'

He tapped his chest with token violence.

'It's damaged me in here. All of them gone, I say to myself. And you are left behind. To what end? For what purpose? In the last ditch you see, I have only one thing to hang on to. The Resurrection. That brings me a little comfort. When the last dawn breaks, and the trumpet shall sound, they will walk out into the light of an eternal day!'

He brought his eloquence to a sudden end as the waitress arrived with the tea. He asked Amy to pour. She did so with steady care.

'I think you inspire me,' he said. He smiled and wriggled to show that he was speaking lightheartedly. 'I'm sure you do. You strike the rock and the waters come gushing out. That's it. That's exactly what you do.'

He sipped noisily at his hot tea. Made uncomfortable by the vulgarity of the sound, Amy glanced quickly over her shoulder and then fixed a glassy stare on the street.

'She's not coming, is she? The Queen?' The Rector put the cup down in the saucer with a sudden clatter. 'I wouldn't want to miss her. She is royal you see. Related to our Royal Family. Real Royal. Not one of those Balkan bandits or anything of that sort.'

He frowned with disapproval at himself.

'I mustn't waste time,' he said. 'Have you had a cake? They're home-made.'

'I've got some toast, thank you, Rector.'

He felt about in the inside pocket of his jacket. Amy caught a glimpse of stains on his black silk clerical front. He brought out a wallet and opened it. Inside was a plain postcard on which he had written a list of points, in a crabbed but embellished hand. He placed it on the table beside his bread and butter plate and studied it closely, sucking the tips of his fingers and preparing to take guidance from the points he had written out.

'How is your education progressing, Amy? That's very important.'

'It's all right, I think, thank you, Rector. We don't get our results for another ten days.'

'A university education is something of first importance. You know that, don't you?'

She showed that she did.

'Socially I mean. It's the only safe ladder to move up from one class into another. I'm quite sure of that. It makes the world of difference. What degree do you want to take?'

'I'm not sure,' Amy said. 'Zoology or Geography. That's what I thought.'

The Rector frowned, not altogether pleased.

'That's B.Sc.,' he said. 'B.A., you know, would be better for a woman. More becoming. It sounds more cultivated somehow.'

His jaw lowered as he considered the delicate balance involved. He breathed deeply and consulted his postcard.

'How long?' he said. 'How many years will it take?'

'Three or four. I'm not sure.'

'And how old are you now? Eighteen is it?'

Before she had confirmed the number he shut his eyes tight with sudden embarrassment. While they were still shut he continued to speak.

'I'm not sure whether I ought to speak to your uncle about this, before speaking to you. Or the other way round. I'm anxious to help you see. Very anxious indeed. Very eager.'

His eyes opened suddenly. He blinked to clear away the water that had accumulated in them.

'Financially,' he said. 'In that way. Given certain understandings and certain safeguards. Let me put it like that.'

298

He was staring at her so eagerly that she turned to look down into the street. The Rector leaned as far as he could over the table and spoke low and fast.

'I have certain feelings that need to be expressed. You may know what they are. They have waited long enough for expression so they can wait a little longer or a good deal longer as the case may be. I'm not an ambitious man as is only too well known I fear, but I have every hope of one day being made the Rural Dean. In Cardiganshire there are two good farms that belong to me and a number of smallholdings in the hills. I don't claim to be rich but I am independent. And I can help, that's the main thing. If we can come to an understanding.'

He halted once again and drifted back to consult his postcard. Down in the street some excitement was brewing. In spite of the police, people were moving off the pavements. Little boys were beginning to shout and point excitedly at the roof of the market place.

'What I had in mind, Amy, was something like this. Nothing hard and fast of course. Nothing rigid. Something for you to think about. Call it a grant of fifty pounds or sixty pounds a year. We won't quibble about the figure. On the understanding that some form of a marriage contract is drawn up. Privately of course. Between John Jason Philips and Amy Price commonly known as Parry.'

'Eh?' The proposal took Amy so much by surprise that her jaw dropped and she completely forgot her customary careful manners. The Rector took fright. He snatched up his postcard and put it away in his breast pocket.

'You wouldn't have to keep the bargain. What I mean to say is you wouldn't be tied down if by some unhappy turn of fate or fortune or whatever it is you met shall we say a man you felt drawn to or bound to by the hand of fate or anything like that. There could be some arrangement about returning the money. In easy stages at some future date. So as you see the way I have worked it out gives you the maximum of security and freedom. I would have been a lawyer you know if I hadn't heard the Call of the church.'

The disturbance in the street had grown to greater proportions.

The way was completely blocked by a crowd looking up at the roof of the market place. Unable to keep still any longer, Amy stood up and twisted her neck around close to the glass to get a glimpse of what was happening. On the small platform on the roof of the market hall three men were standing. One clung like a shipwrecked sailor to the flagpole, his head covered with the lowered Union Jack. His confusion brought cheers and ironic laughter from the crowd in the street. Holding to the seat of his chair with both hands, the Rector continued to justify himself.

'I don't see that it is a scheme that anyone could have the slightest objection to on ethical or moral grounds. I've given it a good deal of thought. I've spent a great deal of time working it out . . . to cover all eventualities, Amy. Why don't you sit down? I'm talking to you.'

Amy barely heard him. On top of the market hall the flag had come away and it hung over the small railings like discarded washing. The young men were having difficulty in hoisting another flag up the mast. Amy lifted both arms as if she wanted to help them. Her finger nails tapped excitedly against the glass as she recognised the Red Dragon.

'I brought that,' she said. 'I brought it.'

The Rector looked puzzled and disapproving. He rose to his feet to look through the window. He was appalled to see the street filled with people.

'They'll block her way,' he said. 'The Queen of Rumania. She'll never get through that. She's one of the Royal Family. They've got no respect. No respect at all.'

Amy pointed through the glass at the roof of the market hall. 'Look up there,' she said. 'That's Uncle Peter's flag. It's going up now. Just look.'

The Rector pressed the side of his face against the window. He was confused and disturbed. 'Jiw, jiw,' he said. 'Jiw, jiw.'

Down below, outside a grocer's stores a group of the men who she had seen camping in the school had gathered around a barrel. They set it up on end and lifted up a young man with curly black hair and a small moustache to stand on it. His short legs kicked in the air as though he resented their rough treatment. He held on nervously to the iron lamp-post and stamped his feet to make sure his platform was secure. Some of his companions plucked at his trousers and encouraged him to start speaking.

'It's Dyfan,' Amy said. 'Dyfan Davies. That's the open-air meeting. It's all working out. I can see it. It's going to be a success.'

The Rector stepped back, completely disconcerted and displeased. 'What is all this?' he said. 'What is it? What are they doing? That is the flag of our Empire.'

Amy made an unsuccessful attempt to open the large window. The orator, secure now on his platform, had begun to make gestures. His friends created a solid nucleus of support around him. The support began to spread among the crowd. He grew bolder and more eloquent. They encouraged him to continue as someone given a make-shift licence to speak on their behalf.

'They are my friends.' Amy smiled eagerly at the Rector. She seemed unaware that he was looking at her as an unfamiliar and dangerous being. The tea table spread between them. The home-made cakes on their fancy doiley paper remained uneaten.

'I must go to them. Thank you very much for my tea.'

The Rector spread his hand towards the table. 'We haven't discussed my offer,' he said. 'You haven't said anything about it.'

She was already moving away. 'Thank you very much,' she said. It was in a last effort at politeness before she turned her back on him and raced down the stairs into the shop. The proprietress with pince-nez halfway down her nose was staring through the shop window. She appeared to be talking to herself.

'There you are,' she was saying. 'I told you. I knew it would happen. I knew it. I knew it would happen. I just knew it.'

Amy pushed her way into the crowded street. She could hear Dyfan's powerful voice, stronger than the rustling noises that the crowd generated from time to time.

'It's in you, my friends! Just as it is in me.' He struck himself on the breast with his clenched fist. 'Stiff-necked officials refused to fly our national flag!'

The word 'shame' rumbled among his close supporters and then spread swiftly through the crowd.

'Jacks-in-office choose to insult our nation in the week of our

301

National Festival!' He paused again for support which came in waves of increasing strength.

'There they are!'

From the top of the market hall and the flag pole on the town council offices, two Red Dragons now fluttered in the breeze. A great cheer went up. The orator wiped his lips with the back of his hand and raised his arms wide.

'Sing! Sing so that those brave young men up there can hear you. Sing!'

The people in the street had acquired coherence. With ease like a crowd at a rugby-football match but with the growing emotional power of an open-air religious meeting, they sang. Amy joined in with all the power in her voice. While she sang she lifted her fingers to feel the tears running down her cheeks. She recognised Val Gwyn and the cook she had met in the Higher Grade School. Far above her their small figures stood erect alongside the flagpole. When the cheering started she raised her arms and started waving at them wildly and calling out their names as if she expected them to see her. Dyfan Davies had not finished.

'Now! We have to teach the officials a lesson. Officials everywhere. From Westminster to West Wales. We come to the hour of retribution.' He relished the word. 'I am going to ask my gallant friends up there to throw down the offending flag instead of the offending official as would have happened in ancient times. And when it falls . . . when it falls . . .' The crowd was silent as he raised his arm towards his friends. 'Tear it limb from limb.'

The men on the flag stand were too far up to hear Dyfan's voice and his arm signals were lost to them against the dark background of the shops. The crowd asserted its own power. A deep voice shouted, 'Throw it!'

And the chant was taken up.

'Throw it! Throw it!'

Amy joined in the cry with delighted abandon. Aloft they understood the message. The police on the steps of the market hall looked helpless and embarrassed. The Union Jack was wrapped up in the tightest possible bundle. Val and his nearer companion rehearsed the swing in an effort to make sure it would fall clear of the steep roof and the parapet. The crowd entered into the spirit of their effort and called out a rhythm for their swing.

'One . . . two . . . three . . .'

Amy tried to push her way forward nearer the market hall. Others did the same. A large woman with dark eyes, next to her in the crowd, was already muttering aloud.

'I'd like just a small piece to take home. I'd frame it and put it on the wall. Just a small piece, that's all.'

They both raised finger and thumb to show the size of the piece they wanted and laughed together as if they had known each other for years.

9

THERE WAS LITTLE TO PROTECT THE HOUSE AND BUILDINGS OF Swyn-y-Mynydd from the force of the morning storm. Water ran down the lane from the upper fields gouging new channels among the stones before spreading more evenly over the clogged farm yard. At the gable-end of the dwelling house, three ash trees had grown tall out of the ruin of a hedgerow. Their roots were a solid mass in the stony remnant of the hedge. Their grey trunks were washed smooth by the rain and their branches raked the wind with demented persistence while the blind gable of the house took the full impact of the storm. At the bottom of the desolate garden, the branches of a thorn tree bent and shook over the roof of the stone-built closet in a more effective demonstration of how to protect human habitations. With a wild persistence the gnarled shape fought the weather, breaking the force of the wind over the slate roof of the earth closet and preserving intact its own covering of modest leaves.

Pale and still, Amy hugged her knees as she crouched inside the window space of her small bedroom and watched the struggle of the thorn tree through the wet window pane. She was ready to go out, washed and dressed in her best clothes, waiting with tense impatience for a break in the weather. There seemed no hope of the clouds ever lifting. Under the floor boards she heard her aunt's clogs clapping sporadically on the stone flags of the diary floor. Among other things, Esther was preparing to go outside. In her haste she did not close the dairy door properly. It began to slam with irritating regularity. Amy shivered inside her gaberdine coat. Through the wet window pane she saw her aunt moving carefully down the cinder path to the earth closet at the bottom of the garden. She had an old coat over her head and an extra sack around her torso high above her customary apron. She carried a wad of newspaper under her armpit and a small spade in her rough right hand. She paused to glance at the overgrown potato patch as if she had half a mind to do a stint of weeding and digging in spite of the weather. Frustrated she knocked the heads of nettles with her spade. This disturbed the rhubarb leaves which released cascades of water like tipped buckets. Esther hurried to the closet and forced open the door which was sagging on its hinges.

Downstairs the dairy door was still banging. Amy seemed oblivious of the harsh monotonous sound. Her eyes were fixed on the clouds outside and her mind seemed already gone on a journey. A cold draught was spreading from the slamming door to every corner of the cramped house. Lucas Parry began to call out from his bed. He wanted his wife.

'Esther! Esther!'

With a frown Amy examined her hands, first one and then the other. They were still a little raw from the morning's work.

'Esther! If you are going out, you may as well take this pot with you.'

With silent precision, Amy stretched out for a piece of stick and began to push back the skin from the cuticles of her fingernails. While she was imprisoned by the weather she would bide her time by grooming her person. The exercise in itself would help to isolate and distinguish her from her immediate surroundings. Lucas was getting out of bed. A series of belches and groans denoted his progress and his whereabouts. He was making his way downstairs in his bare feet, carrying his chamber pot. The draught carried the smell under Amy's bedroom door. He made his way through the kitchen, down the steps to the diary and left the chamber pot in the rain outside the dairy door. He slammed the door two or three times before he succeeded in closing it against the blustering wind. Back in the kitchen, he moved into the small pantry under the stairs. Here on the highest and darkest shelf he kept a glass sweet-jar filled with a patent stomach powder bought in bulk.

Amy threw aside the piece of stick and stood up with her head bent under the low ceiling of her bedroom. She had resolved on a course of action and was prepared to carry it out immediately. She emerged from her bedroom and hurried down to the kitchen to confront her uncle. She found him preparing his dose with measured care. He wore an overcoat over his long nightshirt and a black scarf wound tightly around his neck. The skin of his face was the colour of an old blanket. With his mouth open he took in her neat appearance, and then resumed his task, holding the can to his nose before using the water and stirring up the powder with conscientious vigour, the spoon ringing against the sides of the glass.

'Can I have money to go on the bus, please?'

A spasm of pain crossed his face to show he was in urgent need of his medicine and her request interfered with its proper preparation.

'I want to get my results,' Amy said. 'I got up at six and I worked hard all morning. Auntie will tell you. I can't go on my bike. Not all the way. The weather isn't fit.'

Lucas belched unhappily.

' "Who can number the clouds by wisdom? or who can pour out the bottles of heaven!" It kept turning in my mind as I lay in bed. "Desire not the night, when peoples are cut off in their place . . ." "Call now: is there any that will answer thee? And to which of the holy ones wilt thou turn" . . . Treasures of the Mind, Amy. You should store up your mind with the Book. Ready for the sleepless nights. And the disappointments that are bound to come. Through no fault of your own. I'm not suggesting that. Just the dark days when the thing you fear arrives like a storm at the door.'

'Can I take a shilling? From the dresser. I'll bring back the change.'

Lucas drank his potion and pulled a wry face. He shook his head sadly. 'There's nothing there,' he said. 'Nothing at all.'

'There must be something.' Amy's face began to flush.

'A few pennies. Sixpence. Somewhere.'

Lucas looked at his bare feet. The big toe of his bad leg barely reached the floor. The leg itself was as white as a peeled stick.

'If we have misfortunes,' he said, 'we must learn to bear them. "Question the generation that has passed and meditate on its experience." That's sound wisdom, Amy. Always remember whenever you want to ask me anything, I am here to answer. That's what I'm for.'

He looked content with his own humility. Weighing one hand on the table he moved towards her wishing to return upstairs to his bed.

'I ought not to be down here in my bare feet,' he said.

Amy moved aside in the small space to allow him to pass but when he was on the stairs, she called after him.

'What do you expect me to do?' she said. 'My results are coming out today.'

He turned to look down at her with studied compassion. 'If the news is good it will travel fast,' he said. 'If it's bad it will travel even faster.'

Amy stood at the bottom of the stairs and pressed her fists together. 'Where's my father's gold watch,' she said. 'And his gold chain?' She stared up the stairs defiantly. 'If I go to college I want to sell them. I'll need the money, won't I? Even if I get a scholarship.'

Lucas was stern and silent.

'There'll be clothes and fares and things. All sorts of expenses.'

'It wasn't gold,' he said. 'Although it glittered enough. "Have I put all my trust in gold" . . . Rolled gold they said it was. The appearance without the reality. Only worth a few shillings. The chain was better. That was nine carat. It helped to pay for the funeral.'

Amy's face had gone white. 'It was mine,' she said. 'And you sold it. Without telling me.'

'Mine,' he said. 'That's a strange word to use.'

306

'You could have told me.'

'I'm telling you now. It helped to pay the cost of a decent funeral. How could I see my father go down to a pauper's grave? You would have been told, Miss Parry. But you were away enjoying yourself. At the great Eisteddfod. Perhaps you would like to think about that?'

He pulled himself up the stairs. There were draughts about still that were no good for his health. Nevertheless it was an occasion to be taken for saying things that needed to be said. The girl stood still at the bottom of the stairs her face turned upwards in mute enquiry.

'I have never grudged you anything,' he said. 'I would like you to remember that. Next time you start dreaming about gold watches.' Awkwardly he moved down the stairs to be nearer to her. 'I dare say you blame me for being harsh. I banged your head on the wall once, didn't I? When you were fifteen and you wanted to go out to the pictures on a Saturday night. I haven't forgotten, you know.'

'Neither have I,' Amy said.

He lifted his arm to point at her. 'Don't see me with resentment,' he said. 'Don't you fix me in a pillar of salty resentment. That's all I ask. Remember this. We are all like wild animals that need to be trained. Our passions and our instincts all have to be curbed. I've curbed yours at the risk of gaining your permanent hostility. And I've curbed myself let me tell you. All my life. Especially for your sake. And what thanks have I ever had? Not one kiss. Not one kind word.'

With intense embarrassment Amy saw that he was reaching out his hand for her to take. His fingernails needed cutting. For a moment she stared at the dirt that had accumulated under their curved talon-like shapes. Without a word, she withdrew first into the kitchen and then into the dairy. She stood very still listening for any movement he might make. The relentless wind blustered about outside, but the house was totally silent. He would be standing like a statue on the narrow stairs, a black scarf wound tight about his throat and an imprint of unbearable sadness on his long face. She was confined to the dark damp dairy as though it were a prison cell. There was no way of returning to the limited comfort and

307

privacy of her bedroom. Her whole body shook as she pressed her arms tightly together in front of her head. Under a low slate shelf she found her clogs. A sack hung behind the dairy door. She held it over her head and went out to look for her aunt. The weather made her rush into the small barn for shelter. A gust of rain folded back the brown feathers of hungry hens as they ventured out of the shelter of the cramped and filthy cart-house in search of food. Amy saw their claws grip desperately into the sodden yard before they were sent spinning by the wind in the direction of the midden. The small barn was dirty, cold and comfortless. The half door looking out on the garden path was open. She saw her aunt behind the earth closet shovelling earth into the pit under the seat. Despairingly she called out, but the wind snatched her words away. When she called again her voice almost reached screaming pitch. It sounded like a frightened little girl demanding attention. Esther looked up from her sanitary activity, catching the signal before the wind dispersed it. She wiped the spade in the wet grass and hurried down the cinder path to the small barn. As she did so a hen in the hay barn started to cluck and crow. Esther's worn face lit up with pleasure.

'A nest!' she said. 'I thought there was one. Come on. Let's find it.'

She stepped carefully down the muddy corridor between the out-buildings and the crude posts that held up the corrugated iron roof of the hay barn. The roof had no guttering and the rain water poured down in an uneven screen between the standing muddy pools and the comparatively dry interior. With a cheerful laugh Esther jumped into dry hay. Amy followed her. They climbed the stack in search of the hen's nest. Esther squinted up at the bright points of daylight that denoted the beginnings of rust holes in the corrugated roof. With rueful patience she began to mutter the words of a song to herself as she poked about for the nest. It was about building a one-day house with turf and heather.

'Auntie,' Amy said. 'He's sold my gold watch.'

Esther's arm was plunged into the loose hay up to her armpit. She felt about until her fingers touched the warm smooth surface of eggs in their nest.

'They'll be fresh,' she said. 'The hay hasn't been in a month yet. They should be all right.'

'I can't go on my bike,' Amy said. 'All the way. In this weather.'

They sat together and listened to the tattoo of rain on the tin roof.

'He shouldn't have sold it without asking me. Even if it wasn't real gold.'

Esther reached out to take her hand. 'Listen, Amy. You know he's had a bitter disappointment. They didn't give him a Call and he was much the better man, I'm sure of that. They led him to believe the Call would come. It has been a cruel disappointment.'

Amy's hand lay limp in her rough clasp.

'His hopes were dashed. We had to sell the watch and chain to help pay for Taid's funeral. Things are bad, Amy. I'm afraid his health is giving way.'

Amy was morosely critical. 'He can't be all that ill. He does so little. You do everything for him. He won't even empty his own pot.'

'Amy. No.' Esther gripped her hand tightly. Her words were something she should take back. 'Be fair to him. I love this little place you see. I don't know whether you understand. He doesn't. And you don't either. Do you?' She let go of Amy's hand. Amy did not speak. She had seen the tears in her aunt's sunken eyes. Restlessly Esther scrambled around in the hay and felt about in the forlorn hope of finding another nest. It was easier to feel than stare with eyes that were filling with tears.

'I thought I could work so hard I could make it pay. I really did. People can be so harsh and unkind to men who want to better themselves. They think they are trying to get above their station. He's too good for them you see. They want preachers who rave and shout. They don't want thinkers like Lucas. So I thought a little farm like this would give us independence. It hasn't, Amy. We'll have to give it up. I can see it now. I'll have to spend the rest of my days in a terrace house, in some dark little street. And count myself lucky.'

She had given up the pretence of searching. Slowly her body had bent until her forehead was almost touching her knees. Amy looked at her, wanting to bring her comfort. Instead she began to shiver.

'It's terrible to be poor,' she said. 'No one has any idea. It's a terrible thing.'

10

THE TOUGH LAUREL LEAVES HAD BEEN SCOURED CLEAN BY THE rain: but it had not reached the grime and traffic dust that sheathed the branches and clung to the underside of the wrought-iron railings. Amy had leaned her bicycle against the railings but both her hands still gripped the handlebars. In a trance, she stared through the leaves at the empty lawn in front of the school. The white marks of last term's tennis court were almost washed out. She was late: a solitary figure waiting for someone to appear and bring her support and reassurance.

However long she waited on the pavement, the empty school beyond the laurel hedge remained a significant part of no one's existence except her own. Her back was turned on occasional traffic and passers-by. She kept her head still as a bus rattled past. Across the wide road there were urgent shouts from young men training on the town football ground. An errand boy on a bicycle that needed oiling whistled the first bars of *Tea for Two* over and over again as he creaked down the road and out of earshot. At last an accumulation of total unconcern in everything around her, from the corner shop to the children's corner of the botanical gardens, drove her to draw her bicycle upright and wheel it towards the school gates.

The weeks of summer holidays had allowed grass to grow again on the worn patch on the base line of the tennis court. More marigolds grew in the border. Although the school seemed deserted and she was no longer a pupil, she refrained from breaking a school rule by riding her bicycle down the drive. The door of the girls' entrance was open. The lanky figure of Nesta Wyn appeared suddenly on the step. The spokes of Amy's bicycle moved clockwise and stopped. Nesta Wyn's sister was close behind her but could not emerge because the way was blocked. Nesta Wyn thrust her head forward and her long arm shot out in Amy's direction.

'Only two out of three you've got, Amy Parry! They're shocking results. The worst ever. I can hardly tell you.'

Her arm bent and the tips of her fingers slapped against her lips. She was not dressed in school uniform but she wore her familiar leather purse dangling at her hip at the end of a diagonal shoulder strap. Amy stared at the purse as if she were overwhelmed with curiosity concerning its contents. Nesta Wyn was walking forward. Her sister scuttled out to keep close to her. She was in school uniform and wore a purse and shoulder strap that was a duplicate of her sister's. Her little eyes, bright with excitement, were watching Amy eagerly.

'You can go in and look if you like.' Nesta Wyn was big with information. 'But I know them all. Johnny Angorfa's failed of course. That's no surprise. And Beti Buns, to all intents and purposes. And there's only one County Schol out of the lot. They are the worst results since the war. That's what everyone's saying.'

Her sister was nodding vigorously.

'Nobody knows what went wrong. There ought to be an enquiry. That's what I think. The Head's furious they say. He's tamping.'

Amy cleared her throat. 'Who got the County Schol?'

'Who do you think? Enid Prydderch of course. Enid P. "I wish I had an aunt who was an H.M.I." That's what I said, wasn't it?'

Her sister confirmed the report.

'I'm like you.' Nesta Wyn ventured a brief comradely smile. 'I've only got two out of three. I know it's not bad. But it's not good enough either. Is it? No Schol. No Bursary. I haven't decided yet what I'm going to do.'

Amy began to push her bicycle forward. Nesta Wyn and her sister moved out of her way.

'You go and look if you like. It's on the notice board outside the Head's study. We'll wait for you here if you like.'

The sisters watched Amy disappear inside the building,

311

preserving expressions of sympathy on their faces until she was out of sight.

'She's very upset.' The youngest sister was eager to report on her observations.

'Of course she is. Who wouldn't be? It *is* very upsetting. I expect I'll go to the Normal. I wouldn't mind being a teacher really.'

'You'd make a wonderful teacher.'

Nesta Wyn was in broad agreement with the assessment.

'Keeping control is the hardest thing,' Nesta Wyn said. 'And then making them listen.'

'I expect they will tell you how to do it in the college?'

Nesta Wyn moved back towards the entrance ready to meet Amy as she came out.

'Funny how people change,' she said meditatively. 'Big Welsh she is now. Not so long ago on the bus she wouldn't speak it for love nor money.'

'What will she do?' The younger sister whispered the question. She had no doubt that Nesta Wyn knew the answer. The only uncertainty was whether she would have time to give it before Amy got back.

'Well, she can't afford to go to college. I know that much.'

'Is she very poor then?'

'She gets clothes sent her from somewhere. I know that much. Rich people's cast-offs. But they haven't got two pennies to rub together. Her uncle can't preach for toffee. He's taken to reading long sermons and nobody wants to hear them. Goodness knows how they manage. Her auntie used to clean the schools in Melyd, I know that much. And nobody does that unless they are desperate, do they?'

The two sisters peered at each other with the complacent solemnity of a pair of birds of ill-omen. Amy was coming back. With their heads on one side they listened intently to the sound of her footsteps on the corridor tiles, like children standing to calculate in an old-fashioned mental arithmetic class. When she arrived at the door Amy shut her eyes briefly against the bright diffused light and breathed deeply. The sisters watched her and waited for her to speak.

312

'I'm glad about Enid,' she said. 'She really deserved it. I wonder if they've let her know?'

'Isn't she home then?' Nesta Wyn looked a little put out at being uninformed.

'She's in Italy. For a fortnight with her aunt. And then they're going to South Wales.'

'She's a lucky thing.'

'She's clever.' Amy was categorical.

'So are you.'

They began to walk together down the school drive. Amy shook her head. 'No I'm not,' she said. 'And this proves it.'

She pressed over the handlebars of her bike to study the front wheel in motion. Nesta Wyn was deprived of the sight of her face. She strove to say things that would gain Amy's whole attention.

'Miss Bellis that was has had another baby.'

Amy showed little interest or surprise.

The topic lapsed from lack of response. They lingered together on the school side of the open gate. Amy stared at a young mountain-ash which had been planted the previous winter and was still protected by chicken wire.

'Johnny Angorfa says he's going to run away to sea.'

Amy spun the pedal of her bike with her right foot.

'The world is full of terrible things,' Nesta Wyn made her pronouncement without fear of contradiction. 'Did you hear about Coral Mittyns?'

Amy shook her head.

'You remember Coral Mittyns? She was a prefect when we were in Form One. She went straight to a job in the Head Office of the Midland Bank in London. The manager of the Midland was a deacon in her father's chapel and he got her in. Last week she threw herself under a train in Watford Junction. Haven't you heard?' Nesta Wyn paused to allow herself a deep sigh. 'They're trying to keep it out of the papers. You can't blame them really. People can be so awful. They say there's a man in the case. And I'll tell you something else . . .'

She stopped abruptly because Amy had begun to bounce the tyre of her front wheel against the asphalt.

'What are you doing that for?'

'I'm not the type,' Amy said.

'Eh?'

She was smiling and looked so cheerful Nesta Wyn was mildly shocked.

'I'm going to get a job,' Amy said. 'This minute.'

'A job? Where?'

'I've seen an advert,' Amy said. 'I've cut it out. Just in case. Elias Thomas and Medwyn, Mostyn Road.'

Nesta Wyn wrinkled her nose disapprovingly. 'You know what they are,' she said.

'Of course I do,' Amy said. 'Solicitors.'

'Not very nice. Not for a chapel girl any road.'

'What do you mean?'

'They specialise in unsavoury cases. And affiliation orders. I went there once on a message. I saw little children sitting on the stairs. Waiting for it to open. Coming to collect their mother's money. It's a place I should think twice about if I were you.'

Amy was giving her such a careful hearing it seemed a suitable opportunity to extend advice.

'If I were you I'd do the same as I'm doing. Apply for the Normal. We could be together then. We could even share a room.'

Amy was shaking her head. 'I want to start earning,' she said. 'That's what I want. There's nothing in the world more important than being independent. That's what I think.'

Nesta Wyn pushed out her lips to make them thick with doubt. 'Oh I don't know,' she said. 'Nobody is ever really independent. Security is the thing. Teaching is good you see. Good insurance and a good pension.'

Nesta Wyn considered her sister, who seemed gripped in an instant vision of herself in infirm old age that forced her eyes and her mouth wide open. It annoyed her that Amy should be laughing in the face of her wisdom.

'That's what we are going to do. Both of us. And if you'd got any sense, you would do the same. You'd better listen before it's too late.'

'Everyone presses a finger on his own pain,' Amy said.

She mounted her bicycle and rode towards the town without looking back.

11

A MY NARROWED HER EYES AS SHE PEERED THROUGH THE PLATE glass and tried to make out, beyond her own reflection, the interior of the shop. Empty cake stands showed her much of the day's baking and cooking had been sold. She could see Councillor Hughes at the main counter. He was concentrating on converting a flat white cardboard into a box to contain half a dozen cream cakes. She saw Mrs Hughes like a late arrival in church enter through the house door and glide into the shadow of the bread counter where a customer was waiting. Another assistant was glued to her allotted place behind the opposite counter. Her mouth was set tight in her fat pugnacious face. Amy waited outside to show she would not interrupt the business without being invited in. The shop assistant had seen her but seemed wholly disinclined to communicate. Mr Hughes made no sign that he had seen her. Mrs Hughes was absorbed in paying her customer an abundance of attentive civilities. The house door opened again and Beti appeared wearing a crisply starched white overall. She saw Amy immediately. She made a silent despairing gesture and then waved her in.

Amy entered with a smile on her face but a restraining nod from the councillor stopped her in her tracks. She stood aside hastily when she realised that she was obstructing the entrance of a new surge of customers. The shop filled up. Beti took her place alongside the other assistant. Amy placed her feet neatly together and looked down at the elaborate black and white patterns in the floor tiles as she waited. Mr Hughes was the first to speak to her. He spoke over his arm as he reached out for custard tarts, a large bag in his other hand.

'You did very well then?' He managed a smile but he seemed to have a sour taste in his mouth.

'Oh no. No. I didn't.' Amy made her denial sound as pleasant and obliging as she could. 'You may as well say I failed really. That's what it amounts to.'

His nod was approving and sympathetic. When he spoke to her again a few minutes later from behind his counter his manner was altogether more amiable.

'There's some tea in the back still. Isn't there, Mother?' He looked across to his wife for obedient confirmation. 'You may find a cake there too. Why don't you go through?'

Mrs Hughes was gloomy and disapproving, in spite of Amy's smile and winning manner. 'The tea will be cold,' she said. She sniffed and wiped the sharp end of her nose with a tiny handkerchief. 'We had high hopes,' she said. 'Too high as it turns out. I don't know if there's any milk.'

Amy turned to look at Beti and caught her pulling out her tongue at her mother.

'That Prydderch girl did well, I hear.'

Mrs Hughes swept crumbs off the glass counter with the sleeves of her overall.

'Oh yes. She did.' Amy was neutral but fair.

'Just as well.' Mrs Hughes's small face darkened with grim satisfaction. 'In view of the fact her father is not unlikely to be sacked.'

A customer was bearing down on the bread counter. She demanded a loaf with a hard crust and Mrs Hughes was obliged to turn and test a few with the claw-like squeeze of her pale hand.

'Go through,' she said to Amy over her shoulder. 'Go through before the tea goes cold.'

In the crowded little office the corner of the desk had been cleared to make a place for a battered tin tea-tray. Hungrily Amy pressed a burnt rock cake into her mouth. The tea was cold but she drank it gratefully. She was picking up crumbs from the tray by pressing her finger on them and transferring them to her mouth when Beti rushed in, excited and breathless.

'Kid,' she said. 'Did you ever see such rotten results? Where have you been? I've been expecting you all day.'

She dragged in a box from the passage and sat on it in the open doorway.

'I went for a job,' Amy said.

'But aren't you going to college?' Beti leaned forward and searched the pockets of her overall for a packet of cigarettes. 'Have you got a fag?'

Amy shook her head.

'No college? Why not? You've passed. You've got a right to go.'

'No money.' Amy was struggling to sound cheerful. 'That's that. We can't afford it. So I went for a job.'

'Gosh, you're a fast mover. Where?'

'Elias Thomas and Medwin.' Amy began to blush. 'He gave me an interview.'

'Who? Elias? You know what they say about him.'

'I can guess. He kept me there for nearly half an hour in that tiny office. Combing his hair in front of me and sucking his false teeth and asking me questions and trying to touch me every chance he could get and all the time the job was taken. I could have killed him. There's no need to laugh.'

Beti was amused. She became serious again. 'I've nothing to laugh at. You can see what's happened to me.' She held out her arms so that Amy could study her new overall. 'Trapped,' she said. 'That's what I am. By my mother and my sister. Stuck on a cakestand. That's me. They must have plotted for months. I can just hear them at it.' She spoke in a mincing tone that was meant to serve as a crude imitation of her mother and her sister Phyllis. ' "If she fails again, daddy, as she certainly will judging by how little work she does, you can put her in the shop" . . . "A good idea, Ronald. Cut down the wages bill." And they still haven't told me what I'm going to get. And Lady Phyl is off to Bournemouth. Would you believe it. As an improver in a posh estate agent's office. For a year and a half. And I thought I was his favourite daughter. What a life, kid. Can you imagine it?'

She noticed how pale Amy had become.

'What's the matter?' she said. 'Aren't you feeling well?'

'It's that job,' Amy said. 'I was so sure I would get it. I could go back up there and tell them I'd got a job. I thought it would solve

317

everything. Have you got this week's *Advertiser?* I could start looking again.'

Halfway up the stairs to the family quarters, Beti stopped. Amy looked up.

'What's the matter?' she said.

'I've got it!' Beti began to wheeze with excited triumph. She sat down on the stairs and pulled Amy down to sit on the step below her.

'Listen. You can come here. You can have Phyl's room because she'll be away in Bournemouth. And work in the shop with me. If they pay you they'll have to pay me and we'll both be much better off. Just think of it.' Beti lifted her arms in triumph. 'We'll take over the place.'

Amy resisted being swept up in her excitement.

'They don't need me, do they? There are enough of you already.'

'Don't you believe it. They want to get rid of old Alice May. She won't smile at the customers and she won't wash her hands. And even if they don't there's work in the back. Oh Amy. I can just see it.' Beti began to hug herself. 'We'll have a marvellous time. Out every night and no exams to worry about. Tea-dance in the pavilion every closing day. We'll go roller skating. I've got a special ticket for the pleasure lake because Dad's on the Entertainments Committee. Have you been on the Waterways of Mars?'

Amy started laughing. 'You are funny, Beti,' she said.

'I am, aren't I? Stick with me kid, and it will be enjoyment unlimited.'

They went upstairs to the living room over the shop. There were newspapers spread over the comfortable settee. Beti began to hum the Charleston and execute a few steps. Amy picked up the local paper. 'I ought to look,' she said. 'Just in case.'

Beti danced up to her side and snatched the paper from her hands. 'What's on at the pics?' she said. 'That's more to the point.' She spread the paper on the floor and kneeled down to study it. 'They're still going on about that daft flag business at the Eisteddfod. Would you believe it?'

Amy said nothing. Beti turned the paper over.

'Here we are,' she said. 'The Cinema Royal. All next week.

318

Norma Talmadge in *The Voice from the Minaret*. Coming shortly
. . . It's her again! *The Eternal Flame*. Oh gosh. What a name.
Norma. I wish my name was Talmadge instead of common
Hughes.'

Intent on keeping the smile on Amy's face, Beti flung her arms
about in romantic gestures copied from the cinema screen. Then
she thought of a joke and pretended to sing an operatic-like song.

'A home from home right by the Prom
Something something, pom pom pom!'

From downstairs, they heard the plaintive voice of Beti's mother.
'Beti! Your father wants you in the shop this minute!'

Beti scrambled to her feet. She winked at Amy and whispered
hoarsely.

'You hang on,' she said. 'I'll fix it in a twinkle. There's one thing
about being a sickly child. You become a world expert in getting
your own way, kid.'

'Beti!'

Beti put her fingers to her lips. 'The voice from the minaret,' she
said. 'The cake-stands are calling.'

12

ESTHER KEPT AS CLOSE AS SHE COULD TO THE SHADE OF THE TALL
hedge. In spite of her haste, she stopped from time to time to
open the large shopping bag she carried to study the condition of a
pound of butter wrapped in grease-proof paper lying in a shallow
enamelled dish. The weather was sultry and it was possible the
butter could melt faster than she could walk. She had to be careful
too, where she put her feet. A herd of black bullocks were using the
shade and blocking the path. Some had succeeded in thrusting
their heads and forequarters deep into the hedge: their tails swung

319

like partially unravelled ropes to brush off the colonies of flies that flourished around their dung and immobile hindquarters. Some lay on the ground, panting in the heat, without energy to move even when Esther made a subdued attempt to shout at them. She picked her way through the overgrown thistles and ragwort to avoid them.

The eastern side of Meifod Hall was protected by a thick plantation of firs. Their shade was more effective than the hedge. They were surrounded by a stout iron fence. Esther was able to increase her walking speed until she saw that the footpath was about to leave the edge of the wood and come out at the side of the small lodge near the main gateway to the Hall. This was not the route she chose to follow. A yard from where she stood there was a high wooden step that had been built by woodmen to make a comparatively easy crossing of the iron fence. The step suggested there was a path through the plantation. With agile ease, Esther mounted the high step, penetrated the trees, bending first one way and then the other to avoid low branches.

The wood was strangely silent. There had been a path, but the uninterrupted growth of the trees over the years and the luxurious spread of bramble where young trees had failed made it difficult to follow. More than once Esther paused and raised an arm like a compass to reassure herself she was moving closer to the Hall and in the right direction. She completely ignored the condition of the small quantity of butter in the large bag and concentrated on finding the way she wanted. A small animal peered out of a hole protected by brambles: bright eyes and a sudden glitter of teeth showed there was life in the wood in spite of the silence. Esther veered to her left where the trees were better grown and further apart. Walking became easier, although the pine needles were a slippery carpet under her feet. Once more she encountered the iron fence. Here it was much higher. Beyond it were the first shrubberies of an extensive garden. She moved along the fence until she caught a glimpse of a corner of the redbrick mansion through a mass of rhododendron bushes. She moved about, studying the fence, choosing a place to climb it. Having come so far she could not turn back.

Not far away, somewhere in the shade of the trees, a game of tennis was in progress. Very clearly, Esther could hear the sounds of the game mingling with laughter and loud young English voices. It inclined her to move quickly in the opposite direction until she saw she had reached the edge of the lawn in front of the house. A small motor car was parked in the carriageway outside the steps to the front entrance. It was a strange unfamiliar shape and Esther stared at it wonderingly until she realised that she herself could be partially visible to anyone who happened to be looking out of the numerous windows. She retreated into the shrubbery and moved back the way she had come, trying at the same time to move in parallel with a path that could take her to the rear of the house.

The game of tennis was still in progress. It was an uneven match. There were constant girlish protests from one end, with squeals and screams in the face of a fierce male service. There were noisy jokes, breathless efforts and spasms of hilarious laughter. Esther chose a path. It looked as if it led to stables or out-buildings where she could stop to take her proper bearings. The girl on the tennis court let out an elongated wailing cry. Esther looked up and saw a white ball descending. It fell on the path in front of her, bounced into a shrub and trickled meekly to rest among old leaves. While Esther was still considering whether or not to retrieve it a young man burst through the bushes. His well-built torso was naked to the waist. His grey flannels were held up by a twisted school tie. He was fair-haired and his shoulders were raw with sunburn. He carried his tennis racket in his right hand. He stared boldly at Esther.

'Where are you off to, may I ask?'

She listened intently to the loud arrogant voice as if she had to translate each word before she understood it. Reluctant to speak she pointed shyly to where the white ball lay still under a bush. The girl trilled out from the tennis court.

'Can you find it, Jack? Or is it lost for ever?'

'I see it!' He was sharp and confident. Esther shuffled out of his way. 'Got it right between my sights.'

'You clever old thing. Are you keeping the score?'

With the ball in his fist, Jack Pulford was staring authoritatively at Esther.

'Can you tell me the way to the back door, please?'

He looked at her plaited straw shopping bag.

'I don't know about any back door.' He grinned cheerfully and pointed the way with his racket. 'That's the way to the servant's entrance. Mind you don't tread on any dogs' tails.'

Esther frowned and hesitated to take the path he indicated. She had only imperfectly understood what he was saying. His manner was so frivolous he could even have been misdirecting her. The girl left on the court was getting bored.

'Jack! Come on, will you. I'll be bitten to death if I stand still. These hateful midges.'

'It's all right. Go on. They won't eat you.'

He waved Esther on with his racket before pushing his way through the bushes back to the game. Esther could hear them talking loudly as she moved hesitantly towards the house.

'Who were you talking to, Pulford?'

'One of the natives.'

'I say. You're not in India yet, you know.'

He threw the ball high in the air before he struck it with the wood of the racket.

'Blast and damn!'

The girl laughed delightedly. 'Only once again and it's a point for me. Goody-goody.' Esther passed the caged area in front of the first kennel. A brown spaniel bitch lay on clean straw sucked by five puppies. Esther stopped to admire them. Dogs in another kennel had noticed her presence. They began to bark. Esther hurried towards the house. The barking behind her increased. A woman in a long black overall with voluminous white handkerchiefs hanging out of both pockets appeared in the open doorway. Her melancholy eyes were fixed resentfully on Esther as though she already held her responsible for the disturbance.

'Could I speak with Mrs Pulford, please?'

'I am Mrs Pulford.' The barking set her teeth on edge. She waved her fist ineffectively in the direction of the kennels. 'What do you want?' She frowned and her eyes narrowed as if to show that she could not imagine what possible business such a caller could have with her.

322

'Miss Vanstrack that was.' Esther smiled apologetically for having to make such a blunt and inelegant identification.

'My daughter-in-law? She is in Scotland. Captain Pulford has gone up for the shooting. Didn't they tell you at the lodge? Who are you, by the way?'

Esther glanced ruefully at the pound of butter in her shopping bag.

'My name is Esther Parry. From Swyn-y-Mynydd. Have you any idea when Mrs Pulford will be back, please?'

'In a week or so I expect. What was it you wanted? You'd better come inside a minute. Those dogs are driving me mad.'

'It's all right.'

She had turned without hearing Esther's feeble response. Against her inclination, Esther was obliged out of politeness to follow her into the house.

Mrs Pulford's large feet were shod in loose gardening shoes. They brushed down the long dim passage in a purposeful shuffle. As she followed her, Esther's nostrils caught the succulent aroma of meat cooking in the hot kitchen. Through an open door she glimpsed a comfortable looking woman with bare plump arms, wearing a butcher's striped blue and white apron, lifting a limp sheet of pastry from a floured board.

'This way.'

Mrs Pulford had entered a small housekeeper's room. She sat down and placed her elbow on the open rolled-top desk. Her attitude was magisterial. In a large green vase by the window a mass of small red roses had begun to wither. On the wall by Esther's head was a picture of a sailing vessel dimmed by a coat of dark varnish.

'Now then. What is it?'

Dejectedly, Esther opened her deep basket. She was weary but she had not been asked to sit down. She put her hand under the enamelled dish, lifting it to show to the woman exercising authority.

'I have brought Mrs Pulford a pound of fresh butter. You'd better have it, please.'

The butter had turned into an oily liquid that trembled inside the paper ready to spill out.

323

'I'm afraid I don't really want it.'

'It is a present.'

Mrs Pulford shook her head gravely. Slowly Esther replaced the dish in the bottom of the shopping bag.

'I had better go then. I am sorry to have troubled you.'

'You had better tell me why you came here.' Mrs Pulford was not willing to release her. She sounded as stern as a magistrate.

'Our Amy.' Esther sounded tired. 'Mrs Captain Pulford was kind enough to offer to help her once.'

'Amy Parry. Your Amy you call her. What kind of help does she need?'

The question was put sternly enough, but Esther's head lifted eagerly to welcome the fresh interest taken. It seemed fleetingly benevolent.

'She's done very well,' Esther said. 'She should go to college. But we can't find the money.'

Mrs. Pulford appeared to be considering a suggestion. She sat drumming her fingers on the desk.

'Mrs Captain Pulford wanted to send her away to a public school. I was willing for Amy's sake. But my husband Lucas couldn't part with her. I'm not blaming him, but she ought to have a chance in life.'

'You want money.'

Esther shrank away from the sudden harsh verdict.

'I'm not begging,' she said. 'I wanted to ask about loans. Or make an offer to sell our little place. That kind of thing. Mrs Captain Pulford was kind enough to offer to help before. That's what I thought.'

Mrs Pulford had come to a decision. She rose to her feet to indicate that the interview had come to an end. 'I know about the girl and I'll give you some advice. Get her married, Mrs Parry, as soon as you can.'

Esther was too puzzled and disturbed to move. She could not account for the woman's open hostility. As she listened to her she stared at the bowl of roses with desperate intensity.

'I expect you don't have any idea what she gets up to. A girl on a bicycle. With that hair of hers. Fancying herself at turning boy's heads. You can tell her while you are about it to keep clear of this place. I won't have her hanging about here.'

Esther's jaw was trembling. 'Don't you talk like that about Amy. She's a good girl. She is more than good.'

Mrs Pulford gave a brief frosty smile. 'That shows how much you know. Now if you'll excuse me, I've got quite a lot to do.'

In the corridor Esther momentarily lost her bearings. Mrs Pulford stretched her arm to show her the way she should go.

'Out that way,' she said.

Esther was mumbling a phrase to herself, trying out her English before using it.

'She's better than you.' Her voice echoed in the stony passage. 'Better than you. Much better. Better than any of you.'

Mrs Pulford raised her arm again. 'Out,' she said sharply. 'Get out of this house. Evans!' She was calling a servant. Esther waved back at her angrily.

'I am going,' she said. 'How I wish I had never come. This house is too dark for me to stay in. And you are too dark and evil in my opinion.'

Her words failed her. She hurried out into the sunlight and walked away from the Hall without looking back. By the kennels she stopped to look at the spaniel bitch and her puppies. She plunged her hand into her basket and lifted out the dish of melted butter. Her head shaking with remorse, she looked at it and then tipped it through the bars of the cage.

'There you are,' she said in her own language. 'Share that with the crows.'

The empty dish slipped from her slack fingers into the basket.

13

BUNTING SUSPENDED BETWEEN THE SIDE DOMES OF THE PAVILION fluttered gaily in the sea breeze. It was still the holiday season. Chairs were set out on the concrete steps around the open-air stage ready for the Concert Party's afternoon performance. In the sunken gardens there was a steady demand for deck chairs. Miss Prydderch was having a little difficulty in reversing her car closer to the cobbled verge of the promenade. Her tongue stuck out.

'I think they've done something to it,' she said. 'I really do. The steering has never been the same since they lugged it out of the sand. And going up that awful track to Swyn-y-Mynydd didn't do it any good either. I'm sure one of the springs has broken.'

'Auntie. We must hurry. I'm so worried I can't tell you.'

'You must keep calm, darling. It's not the end of the world you know.'

'Oh but it could be. For Amy. Her whole future could turn on what you do in the next few minutes.'

'Me?'

She was satisfied at last with the car's position. She took out her handbag and turned over the flap to study the mirror mounted on the inside of it.

'Yes. You, Auntie.'

'I wish you wouldn't be quite so intense all the time. We can't all go through life dancing on the high places of the field.'

'I'm walking on thorns, if you want to know. If we're not careful it could all go wrong. I'm sure every moment counts.'

Miss Prydderch sighed fondly. Then she became confidently pragmatic. 'Well, it always does, doesn't it? To be absolutely honest I don't want to go near the place.'

'Oh but Auntie you must.'

'That horrid Councillor Cakes behaved so revoltingly towards your poor father. Intolerable creature. What a way to treat a man of genius. I shall have to ask his permission to speak to her. Can you imagine that? One of his employees. In working hours.'

'It's the only time, Auntie.' Enid frowned desperately. 'Don't you see? She's trapped in there with them. Over the shop.'

'Darling, try not to be so dramatic. Everything is such a drama with you all the time. After all, she is there of her own free will. You heard what her uncle said. It was her own decision.'

'He just wanted you to appreciate how wonderful he'd been all through the years.'

'Well he has, hasn't he? I felt very sorry for him. He seemed a very intelligent fellow.'

'I know what she's been through,' Enid said. 'I know just how she feels. She just had to get a job, Auntie. She couldn't live for another second on their charity . . . No, I don't mean that. I know they are good people. She couldn't bear being a burden on them a moment longer.'

Her eyes were large and appealing. Her aunt smiled at her affectionately.

'Why don't you just pop in by yourself, kitten, buy half a dozen nice cakes and ask Amy to pop out here for a minute. Wouldn't that be a good way of doing it?'

Enid hurriedly presented her objections to such a course of action.

'It ought to be official,' she said. 'From His Majesty's Inspector of Schools sort of thing.'

'That's what I said in the first place. A letter from the Registrar would have been perfectly simple. Dear Miss Parry: it seems that you are eligible for the Owen Thomas Bursary for Orphans. If you would care to make a formal application et cetera, et cetera . . .'

Enid interrupted crossly. 'That would put her right off,' she said. 'You've got to talk to her, Auntie. It's a very delicate moment and you will have to be at your most persuasive. Goodness knows how much of a hold those Hugheses have got over her by now. She probably feels indebted to them. You know what she's like. She's so sensitive, Amy is. And so unselfish.'

Miss Prydderch touched her niece's earnest face. 'If she doesn't want to take it up, darling. I can't force her. You must realise that. It's her decision you see. It has to be. Not mine. Not even yours.'

Enid was already out of the car. She walked around to open the driver's door. Her manner was polite and gay, but her voice was determined.

As they walked the short distance to the shop, Miss Prydderch sighed deeply to herself, moving her head about in different directions as though one part of her consciousness was still seeking an avenue of escape even while she was rehearsing the phrases she would use when she entered the shop.

'Are you coming in?' Her voice was weak. She cleared her throat and struggled to invest herself with a little more authority.

'I'll wait out here,' Enid said. 'I think that would be best.'

Miss Prydderch breathed deeply and entered the shop. Mr Hughes had already seen her. His head was set to one side ready to accept her order.

'What a delicious smell!' She gave him her most winning and gracious smile. 'Could I have some? Half a dozen of whatever they are.' She was trying to coax him into a friendly attitude. Outside in the street Enid was watching with unconcealed anxiety. She moved away when she realised her presence was unhelpful. But in a matter of moments she was back again, trying to pace about with a holiday-maker's unconcern and light-hearted lack of intention. Miss Prydderch stared appreciatively at the print on the paper bag in Mr Hughes's hand: a drawing of a bridge over a harbour with sailing boats and *Hughes Foryd Confectioners* printed as an oval frame around it.

'How pretty,' she said. 'What a nice design.' She leaned over the counter to speak in a lower tone. 'Do you think I could possibly have a brief word with Amy Parry?'

Mr Hughes looked across the shop, first to his wife and then to Beti who was standing behind the bread counter and listening intently to every word. She was recovering from a head cold and there was a red patch under her nostrils.

'Amy,' Mr Hughes said.

He was irritated by a confusion of signals that were coming from his wife and daughter. Miss Prydderch turned to shine her smile in the direction taken by his question.

'Where is she? Do you know?'

Beti was the first to answer. She sniffed as she took her handkerchief from her nose.

'She went out.'

Miss Prydderch waited for an elaboration. There was none forthcoming. Mr Hughes was holding out the bag of cakes in her direction and waiting for her to make some indication that she was about to pay for them.

'How long will she be?' Miss Prydderch asked Beti the question.

'I don't know.' Beti's manner was becoming bolder. 'She didn't say.'

Miss Prydderch glanced briefly at Mr Hughes, ready to accept any suggestion or advice he cared to give. He concentrated his gaze on the bag of cakes.

'I'll tell you what.' Miss Prydderch's manner was still unwaveringly friendly. 'I'll leave them here, shall I? And call back. And then I can kill two birds with one stone. If that's the right phrase to use.'

Mr Hughes put the bag on the counter and then moved it to one side with both hands. The gesture had the effect of anointing the bag as a thing apart.

'See you later then.'

Miss Prydderch seemed inclined to wave as she made for the door and then to think the better of it. When Enid rushed up to her in the street she walked on with her head high in the air.

'Wait until we are out of sight.'

Her lips barely moved as she muttered the command. They walked briskly to the end of the street and then stood still while Miss Prydderch wondered uneasily what to do next. A sudden breeze across the promenade made her shiver inside her dress.

'They say she's out.'

Her frown was enough to show she considered the statement suspect.

'Who said? Was it Beti?' Enid shifted restlessly around her aunt.

'Stand still, darling. I'm trying to think.'

Her concentration was broken by a man in a white overall and a white peaked cap. His arms were waving and she could hear the chink of the coins in his leather bag as he hobbled along the promenade. She smiled with a measure of relief when she realised he was chasing a small boy on a tricycle who had ridden up from the sunken garden and was threatening to break the council rules by riding in wild freedom all over the promenade. Enid clutched her aunt's arm, demanding her entire attention.

'She's a liar,' she said vehemently. 'She'd lie about anything.'

'Why don't we go for a brief drive,' Miss Prydderch said. 'And come back say in half an hour. What about that?'

Enid shook her head. 'Half an hour could be too late.'

'Darling . . .' Miss Prydderch was ready to be affectionately indulgent.

'It's a moment of crisis in her life,' Enid said. 'I'm absolutely sure of it.' She came to a decision. 'You go to the car, Auntie. I shan't be a tick.'

She gave her protesting aunt a gentle push and watched her cross the road before she turned on her heel and hurried back down the street to the broad entry alongside the confectioner's shop. The entry gave wide access to the rear of the shop and the bakery. Resolved to trespass, Enid passed boldly two baker's hand-carts parked with their shafts up in the air. Still uncertain of her approach she looked first at the back door of the premises. It seemed to be her intention to raise the latch softly and peep inside, until she heard a rasp of sound coming from the bakery out-houses. A rivulet of dirty water flowed under the door to dribble into an untidy delta between the cobbles. Enid stepped across and pushed open the door.

Amy was on her knees. She turned to face the light from the door and Enid saw the sweat glistening on her face. Flour and dough had been trodden into glutinous patches that had to be scraped from the red tiles with an old knife. In the distance, bulging sacks of white flour glimmered grey in the murky light. Amy shifted the folded sack on which she knelt, pushed her damp hair out of her eyes and lifted the long scrubbing brush, ready to resume her work. Enid was taking in every detail of her appearance. She was dressed in ill-fitting old clothes Enid had never seen before. There were holes in her stockings and in the soles of her shoes. Amy seemed to decide that she had waited long enough for the newcomer to speak and resumed the scrubbing.

'Amy!' The call was so impassioned, Amy straightened and then sat back on her heels. 'What on earth are you doing?'

Enid's words were elongated with despair and desperation. Amy shaded her eyes to look at her.

'What does it look like?' The wail in Enid's voice made her impatient and angry. 'Scrubbing a floor, of course. there's nothing wrong in scrubbing a floor, I hope.'

Enid was taken aback by so much aggressive defiance. Whatever it was she had prepared to say seemed now scattered out of reach and any fragment she could grasp totally inadequate to the situation. Amy was calmly drying her hands on her sack apron. They were red and swollen. She was stiff with kneeling on the hard floor. When she put her hand to the small of her back it was like the first sketch for the habitual gesture of a cleaning woman. She was obviously embarrassed: but it was anger in her face that made Enid shrink back until she stood with one foot outside the door.

'It's nothing to be ashamed of. So you needn't look at me as if I were a scarecrow. You can't help being in a mess when you do this kind of job.'

'I know that . . . oh I know.'

'I don't mind hard work. It's in the family anyway. I'm like my aunt. She used to scrub the school floors. Family tradition, that's what it is.'

Amy was looking down into the dark water in the bucket by her feet. She was making a joke, but Enid could not bear to hear it. 'Listen,' she said. 'Everything is going to be all right. It's going to be fine, Amy, it really is. There is a Schol for you. A good one. A bursary. Auntie Sali has been into it thoroughly. It's absolutely certain. All you will have to do is fill in a form. She's already had a word with the Registrar. And with the Director of Education. It's wonderful really . . . I . . . we . . . rushed up to Swyn-y-Mynydd to look for you. Auntie Sali got on very well with your uncle and your aunt of course . . . They said you were here . . .'

Her voice petered out as she waited anxiously for Amy to show some sign of rejoicing. Amy seemed bent on remaining polite but distant.

'Congratulations. On your report. Did you have a nice holiday?' Enid wrung her hands in a demonstration of apologetic contrition. 'I wouldn't have dreamt of going if I'd known all this was going to happen. I mean, I should have been here . . . instead of mooching about all those museums. I'm not saying I didn't enjoy it. I kept up my journal. It's full of all sorts of rubbish . . . It's sort of written to you . . .'

She stopped speaking when she saw Amy close her eyes. She came into the bakery, tiptoeing over the wet tiles to be nearer Amy.

'You've had an awful time,' she whispered. 'And I blame myself for not being here when you needed me most.'

'I don't need anybody.' The words were intended to push Enid away from her. 'I can look after myself.' She kicked the side of her shoe against a stack of baking tins sticking out from under the long table. 'I don't mind doing this. It's not as bad as it looks. I get paid and I get plenty to eat. Board and lodging.'

'Listen, Amy.' Enid spoke urgently.

'I understand exactly what you are doing. I mean I can't tell you how much I admire you for doing it.'

'Everybody works.' Amy seemed determined to remain phlegmatic. 'I'm not saying they don't. What I'm saying is that you and I have a special purpose. In this world. I'm quite sure of it. I've written it all down. I can see it so clearly. We have a whole society to change: but first we must change ourselves.'

'It's easy enough to talk.' Amy was tired. She leaned against the table. 'It's as much as most people can do to get a job. And keep it. That's what I think.'

'Oh but you can change things, Amy. You really can. It's already begun. That's what I was thinking all the time in Italy. The great change has begun!'

'Has it?' She was staring at the great kneading troughs. Enid made a fresh effort to gain her attention.

'Now then,' she said. 'You sit on the table, Amy Parry. And give me the orders. Come on. Give me the apron.'

'Not in those clothes,' Amy said.

Enid reached behind her waist for the tapes of her apron. Amy was very unwilling to be divested of her protective covering. But Enid was quicker and held on to a corner. They pulled against each other. Laughing, eager to restore the old friendly basis of their relationship, Enid tied the apron around her own waist.

'You can't,' Amy said. 'Not in those clothes.'

'There's a letter from Val.'

Amy tried to show little interest.

'He's coming here.'

'Here?' Amy sounded alarmed.

'Not *here*. To stay. Emrys is bringing him. They'll do nothing but quarrel I expect. He wants to see you.'

Amy blushed suddenly. 'Who says so?'

'I do. I'm jealous, too, I can tell you.'

'He didn't say so, did he?'

'Do you know what they did? They hired a boat and the engine broke down outside the harbour. And do you know what he did? Val. He jumped overboard and swam all the way to that rock we saw from the headland. Remember?'

Amy's face was clouded unhappily with her own thoughts.

'Now watch,' Enid said. 'You're not the only one who can scrub floors you know. You watch.'

She reached for the kneeling sack and Amy was forced to smile at her enthusiastic ineptitude.

'I'll scrub,' Enid said. 'You just watch, my girl. I'll show you how to do it.'

Black water from the scrubbing brush dripped over Enid's silk stockings. She began at a vigorous pace, determined to show how hard she could work. When Beti appeared in the open doorway, she did not notice her presence. Beti blew her nose briefly and stretched out the hand that held a small handkerchief in Enid's direction.

'What's she doing here?' Beti looked smart in her starched white overall. She seemed reluctant to step inside the bakery. There was an all-pervading smell of a perfume about her person. 'She's got no business to be here.'

Enid's continued scrubbing infuriated her. She raised her voice.

'You are trespassing, if you want to know, Enid Prydderch. So you'd better get out of here before I fetch my father.'

At last Enid stopped scrubbing. When she stood up her face was flushed and she was out of breath. Amy reached out to remove the apron around her waist.

'Are you coming for your tea, Amy?' Beti sounded calmer. She addressed Amy as though Enid was not present. 'He's letting us off early, girl. Think of that!'

She grinned confidently, pleased to give yet another example of the smiling guile that she had cultivated in a way that was peculiarly her own.

'I said, look, Dad. Amy's mad keen to hear Canon Fisher's lecture on "Old Church Bells in History and Legend". He swallowed it whole, bless his heart. And he's given us threepence each to pay to get in!'

She held out the two silver threepenny bits her father had given her, a triumphant grin on her small face.

'You never did have any difficulty in lying, did you?'

The sudden attack took Beti unawares. Her lips opened twice before she actually spoke.

'Who do you think you are talking to? You've no business to be here anyway. Haven't I just told you?'

'My aunt came into your shop less than a quarter of an hour ago. She spoke to you. She wanted Amy. You said she had gone out and you didn't know when she'd be back. That was lying, wasn't it?'

Beti decided on trying to ignore her. 'Are you coming, Amy? The tea will be getting cold.'

Enid placed her hand gently on Amy's shoulder. 'Listen,' she said. 'My aunt is in the car. Will you come and talk to her for a few minutes?'

Amy was folding up the apron as small as she could make it go. 'I can't go out into the streets like this. Not in these rags.' Enid's manner became calm and practical. 'Lend her your overall, Beti. Just for a few minutes.'

Beti grasped the lapels of her overall and brought them tightly together at her neck. Her face grew dark as she lost control of her temper.

'I'll get my father,' she said. 'He'll show you the way out . . . You and your whole breed, Enid Prydderch.'

Amy began to blush. She could not disclaim all knowledge of Councillor Hughes's family's widening hostility towards the Prydderchs: but there had to be a way in which she could clearly dissociate herself from it.

'I just want to be independent,' she said. 'A job should make you independent. That's what I thought.'

'We were having a really good time.' Beti sounded deeply grieved. 'You said so the other night. On our way back from the Royal! "We're having a good time, anyway," you said.'

'I'll get Auntie to bring the car down to the entry,' Enid said. 'I shan't be a tick.'

'We'll be off early.' The words were commonplace but Beti's head had moved towards Amy so that a rich and honeyed promise could be conveyed more powerfully through her glance and her smile.

'If we hurry and get finished.'

'I can't let her see me like this,' Amy said.

She was concentrating on her clothes and taking no notice of Beti's blandishments. A new awareness of her appearance made her self-conscious and openly confused.

'What if I go to college and fail again? I don't really know what I want to do. Except stop thinking.'

'It's just that they are in a bit of a hurry,' Enid said. 'The forms have to be signed and sent in and all that sort of thing. It's all perfectly straightforward. Auntie Sali will show you in a matter of minutes.'

Amy was biting her lip. 'I could hide most of this under a mack,' she said. 'I've got one upstairs.'

She began to walk towards the rear entrance to the house and shop. Beti stood still for a moment and then ran to overtake her. She pressed her hand against her chest, already threatened with an attack of asthma . . . 'You go with her, Amy Parry, and you needn't ever come back. That's all I'm saying.'

Amy lifted her feet to glance ruefully at the condition of her shoes. 'Don't be silly, Beti.'

Rapidly she ascended the dark stairs to the domestic premises over the shop. She left Beti gasping for breath at the bottom. Councillor Hughes emerged from the shop. He was rubbing his hands, ready for his cup of tea. His face fell when he saw Beti sinking down to sit on the bottom stair: an asthma attack was no less dreaded for being familiar. He glanced briefly at the corner of the roll-top desk which had been cleared to make a place for the battered tin tray and the teapot under its thick knitted tea-cosy. There was no way of drinking tea and summoning up all the defences that were needed to protect his youngest daughter from the old enemy. Beti had raised her arm to point up the stairs.

'Listen,' she said, wheezing with effort. 'She's in the bathroom. Stop her, Dad. Stop her.'

Mr Hughes was bewildered.

'She's leaving.'

Beti had grasped the sleeve of his white overall to shake his arm. He gazed helplessly at her thin fingers.

'That Enid Prydderch. That aunt of hers . . . Go and stop her.'

Mr Hughes peered up the stairs. If Amy was in the bathroom it would hardly be delicate for him to talk to her there. He was in any case unprepared for such an encounter. He moved to the tea tray and tried to ignore the desperate faces Beti was pulling.

'Tell me calmly,' he said. 'It's no use getting excited. You'll upset yourself. Do you want your cup now?'

Beti shook her head crossly.

'They've got her a scholarship. To go to college. Those Prydderchs. Wire-pullers, that's what they are. You've got to offer her more to stay, Dad. More.'

Mr Hughes added two spoonfuls of sugar to his tea and stirred it thoughtfully.

'It's very busy in the shop,' he said. 'We ought to open a branch really. In Victoria Road. That's a good district. Growing fast. Very nice homes.'

Beti began to recover. She held on to the banister and pulled herself to her feet. She smiled at her father and nodded encouragingly.

'Well, tell her that,' she said. 'Tell her when she comes down.'

Mr Hughes looked doubtful. The figure of his wife appeared briefly beyond the glass door that led to the rear of the shop. She held a large paper bag like a bouquet in her hand. Beyond the glass door a ghostly expression that implored for help glimmered over her face before it moved away to deal with an insistent flow of custom.

'I can't say anything definite,' Mr Hughes said carefully.

'You don't have to.' Beti stopped speaking abruptly. She restrained herself from coaching her father in some of her own secret wiles and instead awarded him with a winning, childlike smile. 'Just speak to her. She's coming now.'

On the stairs Amy paused to put a comb through her hair. Beti tried to pull her father forward so that together they would block the bottom of the stairs. He declined to move, raising the tea cup to his lips to demonstrate calmness. Beti stretched her right arm to bar Amy's way.

'Go on, Dad. Tell her.'

Mr Hughes smiled awkwardly and raised his cup in Amy's direction. 'I would like to have a word with you,' he said.

'I shan't be long, Mr Hughes. Just five minutes. That's all.'

Amy's calm excited Beti so much that she sank down gasping for breath: but she managed to do it so that her body blocked the last step on the stairs.

'Let me put it like this,' Mr Hughes said. 'Llanelw is a town with a big future. I was only saying in the council this week. In this century, Llanelw has had more royal visits than any other town on this coast.'

Amy's foot was sketching a forward movement while she nodded politely to Mr Hughes to show she was listening.

'That's enough to show the way things are going,' Mr Hughes said. 'This place has a big future and of course that can only mean that a business like this has a big future. Do you see what I mean? Now my point, as I said in the council, is, we mustn't be afraid of it. It's a kind of destiny in a way. I said it was our duty to go forward and embrace it. It's all in *The Advertiser* if you want to read it.'

Amy tried to look grateful for the reference.

'Now what I'm saying now is, where do we fit in personally, in all this? Do you follow me? Expansion. That's the way it all points. Expansion and increased prosperity for all.'

Mr Hughes paused to study the expression on Beti's face. Amy seized her opportunity to move.

'Excuse me, Mr Hughes. I won't be more than five minutes. Excuse me.'

Neatly she skipped over Beti's bent form and hurried towards the entry where Enid was waiting.

'Did you see that?' Beti shook off her father's protective hand. 'She walked over me. That's what she did. She walked right over me.'